MOMENTS CAPTURED

ROBERT J. SEIDMAN

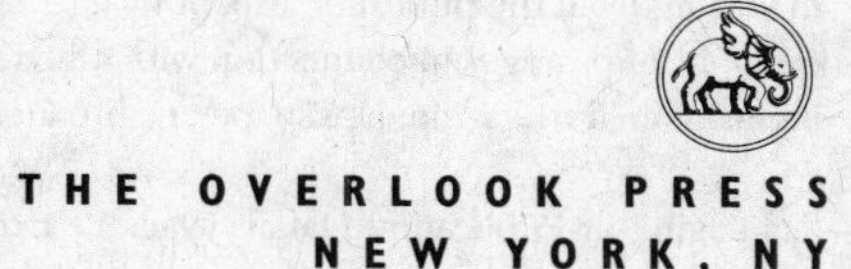
THE OVERLOOK PRESS
NEW YORK, NY

This edition first published in paperback in the United States in 2014 by
The Overlook Press, Peter Mayer Publishers, Inc.

141 Wooster Street
New York, NY 10012
www.overlookpress.com

For bulk and special sales, please contact sales@overlookny.com,
or write us at the above address.

Cataloging-in-Publication Data is available from the Library of Congress

Design and typeformatting by Bernard Schleifer
Manufactured in the United States of America
ISBN 978-1-4683-0838-9
10 9 8 7 6 5 4 3 2 1

For Patti

Author's Note

There are many ways to illuminate history. Fiction is one. *Moments Captured* is a work of fiction generously based on events in the life of Eadweard Muybridge, the pioneering nineteenth-century photographer, but it certainly does not intend to be a faithful biography. I have taken liberties with the chronology of the artist's career and have omitted and invented characters in his circle.

Chapter One

The triangulated network of the upside-down railroad trestle grew fuzzy then snapped into focus as the photographer rotated the lens. Under the black hood of his camera the stench of chemicals—alcohol, iodine, ether, silver nitrate, and the ever-touchy collodion—thickened like paste. The mixture coated his tongue and lungs just as they had recently coated the glass plate of his camera.

Muybridge stifled a sneeze and allowed himself a thin smile. It wasn't the job's danger, though, that contributed pungent urgency to the work. It wasn't even the pleasure he took from being a competent photographer. Few knew anything of the skill and dexterity it took to pour that touchy, sometimes explosive collodion over the fragile plate and, balancing the light-sensitive rectangle in his hands, jiggle the bulky glass around so it was evenly coated—not a gloppy mess or riddled with bare spots. And then, even with the most skillful manipulation, who knew what image would emerge?

Muybridge had positioned his camera on a bank of the Wallow River—now a dry slough—to shoot the railroad truss from below. It was a massive structure, at least one hundred feet long and fifty feet high. Edward could not squeeze the bridge into the frame, so equitably he sliced off both ends. The scrim of cottonwoods that lined the opposite bank lent an insubstantial green to the prairie's monochrome buff. The photographer squinted to bleed the slight color out of the frame.

Only on a Sunday morning could he photograph a deserted railroad bridge. All other mornings and every afternoon and all through the nights in the wavering light of kerosene lanterns, the iron span swarmed with men brandishing shovels, pickaxes, sledgehammers accompanied by shouted curses and the occasional bloody fight with or without the hand tools. All day and all night the graders spread and tamped layers of gravel then dirt while around them hundreds of men kept digging, lifting, hauling. But on Sunday mornings, at the beneficent order of the railroad, the workers spent two of their precious leisure hours in a non-denominational church being hectored by a stooped man in black about the everlasting virtues of patience and humility.

Moving his tripod a scant inch left, Muybridge studied the bridge, about to fix it forever—or for a decade, his photographic paper being what it was. He rechecked the inverted rectangular world. The roadbed should angle more sharply across the frame, he thought. He started to reposition the camera when, in the soothing, ripe dark, Muybridge heard what sounded like a string of distant pops. Blasting? Not likely on Sunday morning. The sounds were too light in any case, more like champagne corks than those deep air-sucking blasts of black powder booming away in timed sequence.

He pulled out from under the cloth, his eyes taking an instant to adjust. A quarter mile off, moving from left to right, a stagecoach racked and bounced over rutted ground. Behind the stage, firing rifles, five men rode in hot pursuit.

Edward rotated the tripod and ducked back under the hood. In his lens the upside down bandits gained swiftly on the lumbering coach. Swiveling the camera ahead, Muybridge saw the guard brace his Henry repeater rifle and fire. His shots kicked up dirt around the bandits' horses but did not slow them. Cloaked in billowing clouds of dust, the riders edged closer to the coach. The photographer felt exhilarated and frightened—like that time he had chased the dark funnel of a tornado across what seemed like half of the Kansas Territory to get a better photo.

The stagecoach veered left to right across Edward's field of vision until the road curved toward him and the wagon angled north in the direction of the cottonwoods—and his position. Unfortunately, the change in direction gave the pursuers a better angle on their prey. The guard took a bullet and crumpled, dropping his repeater. The driver lunged for the falling Henry, but missed. The rifle landed barrel first, bounced back onto its butt, then dizzily reversed direction, somersaulting like a reedy airborne acrobat.

Stagecoach and horsemen were sixty yards from the photographer when a bandit pulled up to the coach and leveled his six-gun right at the driver's ear. The stagecoach braked. The rider grabbed the bridle of the offside horse and jerked back hard, stopping the horse in its tracks.

The bleeding guard sprawled across the seat. A whipped-puppy moan wrenched its way out from the man's shredded guts.

"I got to look at Burt," the driver pleaded. "He's hurt real bad!"

"Payroll first, then play nursemaid!" The outlaw's voice was gravelly and commanding, yet something of an Eastern accent—Philadelphia, Baltimore, Muybridge couldn't be sure—clung to it.

Edward found himself creeping closer, using the meager line of cottonwoods for cover. As he tried to step around a dead fall, the top-heavy camera body swayed on the tripod; Muybridge steadied it. He inched toward the edge of the trees, spurred by a mindless notion of invulnerability.

This close up the bandit's face looked wiry and mean—wolflike, with a thin taut nose and a dark eyebrow that sketched a dense line across his forehead. A tricky scar raised a corner of his upper lip enough to lend one side of his face a permanent half smirk.

"Strongbox!" For further emphasis, the bandit clicked back the revolver's hammer.

Muybridge knew he could not take the picture he wanted with the larger tripod camera. He needed the speed of the smaller stereoscope, which, fortunately, hung around his neck. Yet the presence of the bulky, useless view camera comforted him.

The driver reached down and scraped the laden strongbox out from under his seat—metal shrieked on metal, the equivalent of Edward's nerves.

One outlaw's dust-shrouded horse backed uneasily. Not a sound issued from inside the coach. Empty? Muybridge wondered. A second bandit detached himself from the knot of riders and drew his mount alongside, flung open the stage door, and, pistol first, climbed half-inside.

The man's loud whistle broke the clotted, uneasy silence. He shouted over his shoulder, "We got a live one here, boys!"

A dainty revolver with a mother-of-pearl handle flew out of the window followed by a more businesslike Smith & Wesson .45. "Keep your heads inside! Or lose 'em!" the outlaw commanded. That brought a round of harsh laughter from his companions.

At least two passengers, a man and a woman, the photographer concluded.

Edward Muybridge assumed that the railroad workers' payroll was what made the strongbox so heavy. He'd just come from the Central Pacific camp, three miles up the line, where everyone—from foreman to water boy—impatiently waited for the Sabbath payday, which was ironically scheduled right after the compulsory chapel service. Already that morning he had taken five portraits, and all the laborers he had photographed—two Irish, two Chinese and one Hebrew—looked underfed.

Muybridge had come West with a purpose: to chronicle the growth of the nation. He also intended to document what Leland Stanford, former California governor and former California senator and perpetual president of the Central Pacific Railroad, had labeled, "The greatest engineering feat since Creation itself." So why was Muybridge risking his life to possibly make minuscule stereoscopic photographs of a ragtag collection of bandits? He didn't know, and yet he felt exhilaration as he tiptoed closer to danger. *Only a few seconds, that's all I have.* He thought how splendid it would be if he had a longer lens or a faster shutter. *If.*

His palms were so slick from perspiration, he had trouble focusing the double lenses. He took the shots quickly, one exposure, another and another, three pairs of the robbers recorded—if he was lucky. Edward settled the small camera back onto his chest, wiping his hands on a less-than-immaculate handkerchief.

To calm himself, Muybridge did what a photographer habitually does: He steadied the tripod. Edward thought about death for a timeless moment, put his thumb over the hole in the bulb. Just then he heard a menacing cry, "He-e-ey! What we got thar?"

Edward put his thumb over the hole in the bulb and squeezed. As the piston opened the shutter, two bullets ripped up the ground at his feet.

He shouted, "Don't shoot! No arms—I mean, I'm not armed!"

The bandits caterwauled at Mubyridge's abject humiliation, which infuriated the photographer. He wanted to charge them, tear the comical, well-armed rustics limb from limb. Meanwhile, with excruciating slowness, taking perverse delight in his victim's embarrassment, the bandit chief walked his horse away from the coach toward the photographer, who remained at rigid attention, hands pressed toward the sky. Edward wanted to shout, *You can have the stupid photo, which won't come out anyway. What's a goddamn photograph when my life's at stake?*

The outlaw was yards away from Muybridge when a woman's head thrust out of the stagecoach window—auburn hair framing a delicate yet strong oval face, with dark eyebrows set off by ivory skin. Beautiful, Muybridge thought involuntarily. Entranced by the woman, the gang stared too. Then one of the gang waved a peremptory pistol at her head, which promptly withdrew back into darkness. Muybridge thought it'd be just his luck—to glimpse her stirring image the moment before he died.

The bandit's horse crowded in, on top of the photographer now. Edward retreated a step, two. Close up, the robber's cheeks had a wind-chafed, flaky quality, like leather left in the sun too long. The eyes were slotted flatly into the cheeks, which gave his face the hooded aspect of a man hard to read at poker.

"What you think you're up to?" the bandit snarled.

Staring up into the man's scaly, skeletal face, Muybridge found it hard to lie. "Just surveying the line, sir."

From the dark interior of the coach, someone—the woman, from the sound—let out a strangled half snort, half laugh. A mounted outlaw thrust a rifle barrel into the window, and the noise was stifled.

Muybridge touched the large camera like a practiced salesman. "This is a new German surveying tool, a theodolite, the very latest development."

"Looks like a goddamn camera to me." A mirthless smile raised the live side of the robber's mouth, then a shot rang out and one leg of the tripod snapped in two. The photographer managed to catch the falling camera body before it hit the ground. As Muybridge hugged the mechanism, the robber clicked back the hammer, pointing the barrel's machine-tooled black hole directly at Edward's heart.

"You like breathing, photo man, drop it. Now." Edward Muybridge lowered his camera to the ground, nonchalantly angling the lens away from the robber.

The Colt Frontier .44-40 released three exaggerated reports, which ripped through the camera's frame. Glass shattered. Edward looked sufficiently mournful, which he was.

A bandit shouted to his cohorts, "Let's do it, quick now!"

Edward would always contend that he caught the resemblance then—the young, heavyset man who shouted had the lead robber's greedy mouth, minus the scar, the black eyes slotted almost as obliquely into the cheekbones. The younger bandit deftly shot the strongbox lock in two, the metallic ring clanging across the empty landscape like a doleful church bell. He and two others began stuffing gold coins into their saddlebags.

"Hurry up, damn it!" the boss commanded, as they hand-shoveled the glittering coins until the metal became a flowing gold arch that chunked solidly into the inflating saddlebags.

"Twenty-one, twenty-two," the photographer counted automatically. Muybridge wondered who sat beside that stunning woman inside the coach. He imagined himself swaying next to her in that worn leather seat: her smell, her soft, yielding flesh intermittently touching his arm; with the merest repositioning of his elbow he could . . . He almost laughed aloud, aware that he could be a dead man and yet, at the last instant, be thinking of a woman.

Just then he caught her slow deliberate movement. Instantly, four guns were trained on her. Still she kept gradually emerging from the coach, holding empty hands obligingly out in front where all could see. With unhurried calm, the woman turned her back on the outlaws, poised a costly calfskin boot on the iron step below the driver's seat, and started to hoist herself up.

"Where yo think yo goin', lady?" She froze, halfway up the side of the coach, holding herself with surprising ease. *Stronger than she looks,* Muybridge thought.

The lovely face pivoted toward the leader, whose pistol remained aimed at her head. "The guard is bleeding to death. Blood's pouring into the coach." Toe pointed, right knee bent, her leg drew a precise arc upward as it reached for the highest foothold. The outlaw leader kept the weapon leveled, eyes glued on her, lust vying with appreciation of her calm courage.

"Forty-two, forty-three." *The bandits can't take their eyes off her either,* he thought, and continued his silent count down. "Forty-four, forty-five."

On top now, she stripped off her kerchief and efficiently tore it lengthwise.

"Are you all right?" she asked.

"I'll . . . live." The guard's voice was barely audible.

"Not if I don't tie off this wound."

With each heartbeat, blood arched up over the guard, spraying the seat. She improvised a tourniquet, applied pressure. The guard gasped, a drawn-out, gurgling sound that made Muybridge worry that the poor man might drown on his own blood. The red arch diminished. As the woman increased pressure on his chest, the guard's knees, slowly, as though by themselves, came up to his chin. He tried to squirm free, but she bore down on the tourniquet—applying pressure until the bleeding slowed to a trickle.

Meanwhile, the man who Muybridge guessed was the leader's younger brother finished stuffing gold into the saddlebags while his comrades-in-arms rooted in the dust, scooping up random pieces. Finally, as Muybridge's silent count reached "eighty-seven"—the photographer was getting frantic about his exposure time—the gang wheeled their horses north and rode off. He was already moving toward his view camera as the clump of riders began to dip below the ridge.

"Ninety-eight, ninety-nine," he kept counting, as he scooped up the battered camera body and sprinted toward the cottonwoods that hid the Conestoga wagon.

"You all right?" the photographer shouted as he passed the stagecoach.

The guard replied through clenched teeth. "I'm gettin' tired o' yo all askin'." Then the man passed out.

"One hundred twenty-two, one hundred twenty-three," Muybridge counted as he disappeared into his wagon.

Collis Ward, junior vice president of the Central Pacific Railroad, emerged from the coach haltingly, like a man easing himself into icy water. The slender, well-tailored Ward stood six feet, two inches, with eyebrows so fair they were invisible in the bleaching light. He took his handkerchief away from his nose—the dripping blood nauseated him. "Was that Lardue's gang?" he questioned the driver.

"Yes, sir. Make a rattlesnake look friendly."

Collis Ward didn't squander a smile. The railroad had lost $12,500. The last robbery it had been $9,725; $14,300 the one before that. Ward reflectively eyed the cottonwoods, the only sign of life in the monotone, desolate landscape. On any relative scale, the debit was insignificant. Still, it wouldn't do to let these marauders go unpunished.

Travel was one part of the job he could do without: traipsing around the Sierra foothills in a dust-saturated trampoline of a coach, stomach in queasy daily rebellion, his kidneys rattling up and down his vertebrae. Ward shot his not-so-white cuffs as though to reassert his importance, then half-suppressed an unwholesome belch, flooding his mouth with bilious aftertaste. He reached inside his waistcoat for his mints, realized the case was empty. This infuriated him. Yes, he admitted he'd overreacted, been a little scared, sneaking a quick glance at the damp ring around his groin. He'd tried to cover it up with his traveling bag but the sharp-eyed Miss Hughes detected the telltale wet spot. And, as though trying to humiliate him further, she'd courted death by climbing out and facing down the desperadoes. Just as bad as that idiot photographer's trumped-up story about being a surveyor.

So here he was, in the wilderness, tremblingly aware that he could've been gunned down by the killer Lardue. One unquiet knee tapped out an erratic rhythm. Who claimed that travel broadens? Since none of the Big Four who ran the Central Pacific Railroad volunteered for fieldwork, too often the job fell to "young Ward." His current assignment was not to capture Lardue, nothing as precipitous as that. Ward was to report back to the "Associates," the "Pacific Quartet," the "Big Four"—Stanford, Hopkins, Crocker, and Huntington—about the bandit's movements and habits, the size and disposition of his gang, the amount stolen. The Associates would then devise a plan for the villain's capture and demise.

Collis Ward was not griping. Being even junior vice president had its compensations—most important, of course, appropriate remuneration. In addition, proximity to power and advisory status, if not a vote about monumental decisions, as well as access to certain expensive, well-made women. He curtly dismissed the opinionated, auburn-haired Miss Hughes as being insufficiently feminine—yes, she was powerfully attractive, but Ward could feel her contempt oozing out of every lovely pore. Beyond him. Too upper class, too rich, and much too "emancipated" for him. As they sat opposite one another in that undulating interior, every shift and rearrangement of that lush body tortured him. The nerve of her, traveling unescorted!

To calm himself, Ward reviewed the organizational chart in his mind: Leland Stanford, president of the Central Pacific, handled the bulk of the railroad operations. Charles Crocker was in charge of construction, his expertise in desperate demand in the feverish rush to push the parallel rails east, up and over the High Sierras then on to Nevada Territory and who knew how far beyond. Hollis P. Huntington spent his time—and everyone's money, the insiders' joke ran—lobbying in Washington, D.C. While the silver-tongued orator Mark Hopkins logged thousands of miles crisscrossing the Western reaches of the country to woo towns and townships and hamlets and states with the potent lure of what was assumed to be lucrative rights-of-way on America's first transcontinental railroad route.

Like any American who could read a newspaper, Collis Ward had absorbed the repeated charges of theft and pernicious arm-twisting, the shrill, envious accusations that the magnate quartet was stealing the country blind these past four years since the Pacific Railroad Act was passed. What the whiners and reformers did not know was that the Central Pacific Railroad was bankrupt, kept alive only by monthly congressional stipends and bogus stock issues and government-backed bonds and profits from the secretly related companies and the greed of citizens who believed that eventually they would reap wealth untold if the railroad could be cajoled to pass through their city or burg or insubstantial settlement.

Only intrepid, imaginative entrepreneurs could bring the Central Pacific back repeatedly from the brink of fiscal doom in order to complete an enterprise of continental magnitude. No matter how many legislators had to be bribed or how many fictional transactions debited in the account books which Ward himself controlled, no matter how many paper towns materialized out of nowhere to slip back into the uncharted voids of America's western mountains and deserts, if and when completed, the transcontinental railroad would perform an unprecedented service. For the Central Pacific—and its rival the Union Pacific, threading its way west toward that unknown meeting point yet to be spiked into America's consciousness—was tying the country together with a steel umbilical cord, bringing unity and potential prosperity and something the country had never experienced: a constancy, a reliability which one could measure with one's pocket watch and calculate weeks in advance on a calendar and which no horse could hope to achieve. Yes, Stanford, Hopkins, Crocker, Huntington, and, not immodestly, "young Ward," offered the newly re-United States the continent-stitching material embodiment of its manifest destiny—a nation bound together by their steel tracks.

Muybridge leaped down from his wagon studio and strode toward Ward, extending his hand. "Edward Muybridge, photographer."

"Collis Ward," responded the taller man with chill superiority, "Central Pacific." The words had their desired effect on the photographer, who looked impressed.

As they shook hands, Muybridge stole a glance at the woman, who remained erectly poised beside the unconscious guard. Edward silently applauded her: She didn't seem concerned about her dress, now splotched with blood.

"That was a close call." Her smile proffered a peace offering to the photographer.

Ward nodded cockily, suggesting that, above all, he had kept calm during the crisis. Knowing better, Holly directed her glance at the damp ring over his groin. Ward angled his body away from her probing eyes.

"Did you save your photograph?" Her voice was gentle and low with a hint of gravel underneath.

"Of course not." He overacted here. "You didn't help."

"I'm truly sorry, Mr. Muy-bridge"—the ripe lips fought back a smile—"But that nonsense about your theodolite, really I couldn't help . . ." She took a deep breath, her expressive mouth struggling to dam up the laughter. "My name is Holly Hughes, and I am deeply sorry. Really, I—" Holly Hughes fought to be contrite, she truly felt contrite, but the laugh welled up.

Muybridge joined in. A solitary, intrepid, armed female traveler on a stagecoach, he thought, was not a commonplace in the West.

As squeamish Ward stood conspicuously apart, Muybridge and the driver carefully lowered the guard into the stage, arranging his body across the short seat while Miss Holly Hughes deftly stuffed cushions behind to prop up his chest. Fresh seepage dyed the deer hide jacket the color of wet clay. Since the railroad camp was only three miles away, Ward ordered the driver to transport the guard to the doctor "post haste." Muybridge would bring Holly Hughes and Ward along in his wagon.

"Pity about your camera," Ward said. "Is it often the target of attacks?"

"Fortunately, this is a first." Muybridge led his guests toward the painted wagon. "But I had the camera body reenforced with steel before I left New York City. I dropped it a good forty feet at the Delaware Water Gap, yet the plate didn't have a scratch."

"Still, three bullets." Ward remained dismissive. His pinched lips seemed incapable of a full smile.

"What about your other camera?" she asked. "Will it show us the robbery?"

She was moving on the same track as he, and he liked the company. "If you'll be patient for a minute or two . . ." Edward said as they approached the wagon. He knew that the plate was useless—the glass had shattered. But he had his stereo shots.

The skins of the Conestoga wagon were painted with the legend:

THE FLYING STUDIO
EDWARD MUYBRIDGE, PHOTOGRAPHER

Collis Ward ran an inquiring hand over the wagon's covering. It was the first thing he'd done that Muybridge liked. "Buffalo?"

The photographer nodded yes. "My equipment's irreplaceable." He could have said *too costly,* or, *beyond my current means,* and explained that the bulk of it had to be imported from England and Germany, and that barely half of the gear was paid for. "I can't let it get wet. I bartered photographs with the Sioux for the skins. Interesting business, that."

"I can imagine, Mr. Muybridge," replied Ward, who could not fathom how a civilized man could deal with savages.

"The Lakota showed me how to cure the skins to make them watertight. They work well because I need light inside."

As Ward stooped to check under the wagon, Muybridge pointed to the undercarriage. "That set of springs was made to order—steel from Sheffield, England. On land the wagon's more stable." Edward hopped onto the cantilevered steel spring then leaped up and down like a twelve-year-old. Holly Hughes liked the way he moved.

As his eyes met hers, Muybridge was struck by a palpable erotic charge. An extended, embarrassed moment followed as his eyes lingered on hers. The woman did not look away but continued to interrogate him silently, a smile of complicity playing about the mouth like heat lightning. Her gaze seemed so direct, so explicit, he was tempted to look away. But he didn't.

"Any trouble in water?"

Edward turned to the questioner, partly to escape his body's turmoil. "Had a hell of a time crossing the Little Missouri." So Ward could tell that the wagon was bottom heavy. Clever, that. Still Holly Hughes's eyes did not desert Muybridge. It was as though Ward had not asked the question. Muybridge held to the point, "Almost lost my rig in the channel."

As Muybridge handed her up, he studied the swing of her skirt. Even in leather boots, the photographer recognized the calves' smooth swelling, the slender, shapely ankle. Mentally, he snapped a belated photograph: Miss Holly Hughes holding herself up by her arms, that tapering calf bare to the knee. He reviewed the length of her leg pushing against the dress, the rich slope of the thigh beyond. . . .

Inside the wagon, Holly Hughes exclaimed, "It's like alabaster—an alabaster chamber." The buffalo skins spread the light so evenly, there seemed no visible source of illumination, only a warm, diffused glow. She surveyed the banks of drawers, the glass-fronted shelves, all labeled precisely. Chemicals stood arrayed in glass apothecary jars, filling the methodical space with redolent, exotic odors. Extraordinary! A magician's hideout brimming with magic potions. *It's like a ship,* she reckoned, *with everything stowed in place*. Entranced, Holly Hughes wandered in a heady, uncomprehending daze among the rows of glass plates, ingenious-looking shutter mechanisms, snugly fitted red velvet–lined trays holding graded varieties of lenses, and, above, long-legged tripods suspended between the wagon's three arched wooden struts. In one corner stood a stall completely enclosed by thick black drapes—the photographer's darkroom.

Photographs covered every horizontal surface. Holly Hughes studied the semicircular lodges and triangular tepees of the Sioux, Arapaho, and Cheyenne; the lined, impassive face of a Modoc chieftain; the image of a looming six-hundred-foot-high granite rock face braided as elaborately as a woman's hair and sliced into two symmetrical halves by the flow of a ghost river that had dried up millions of years before. There was a shattering photograph of the wreck of a fine claw-foot dining table, once well waxed and hand rubbed, now a cherished relic tossed off an overloaded wagon and left to scorch and crack and shrivel into splinters along the Oregon Trail. Then a picture of the wagon itself and the bones of one of its human passengers, Muybridge explained, barely two miles short of the next well.

She examined a vertiginous picture of Yosemite Falls, the vertical cliff split by a frozen white scarf of water. The spray angled diagonally toward the viewer, leading, thrusting the eye out to the very edge of the paper. These were stunning, sensitive photographs, nearly as complex and rich as paintings by the finest artists she knew.

Attentive to her mood, Muybridge located two smaller photographs of the Falls, loaded a device that looked like a metal praying mantis, and placed it in her hand.

As she looked, the photographs swam, blurred, then snapped into focus, instantaneously acquiring depth. She had never seen the three-dimensional photographic effect before, and the act of gazing out into tangible space made her a little giddy. The binocular view vaguely tempted her to reach out her finger to probe the black-and-white illusion. Holly was impressed. She felt naive, suggestible, suddenly much younger than her twenty-seven years.

Meanwhile, Muybridge hefted a big, leather-bound volume onto his worktable. "Here's something I'd like you to see." He included both of them, but Holly knew he addressed her. The book's title: *Muybridge's Pictures*.

"So you think it would be in the Central Pacific's interest to invest in a photographic record of its progress, do you?"

Ward's needling smirk annoyed Muybridge, as did his restlessly tapping foot, but the question made sense—scattered around the wagon's interior lay twenty or more photos of railroad workers blasting, grading, shoring up bridge supports, laying rails. Ward was finicky, supercilious, irritating, but he was also quick, with a jackrabbit mind that bounded rapidly ahead, mapping terrain as it moved.

"Why, Mr. Ward, photography's the art of the future," Muybridge jabbed back. "Two years ago I could not have made a photograph of moving action—like our robbery." He drew a breath, plunged on. "There's a new wet plate process waiting for me in San Francisco that's said to increase speed of exposure and, if we credit the advertisement, depth of field. With that and faster exposures I might someday be able to take photos of things in motion. Photography's like progress, Mr. Ward. It constantly moves ahead, improving the basic tools, expanding its scope."

"Large claims, Muybridge."

How often, Muybridge considered, dislike is instantaneous. With Collis Ward, Edward judged his feeling was reciprocated.

Edward thumped his picture volume like a preacher. "My book records no less than the history of this continent."

The last phrase sounded pompous, rehearsed, which disappointed Holly. If this was merely a predigested sales pitch for the Central Pacific, Mr. Edward Muybridge was more grasping than she had hoped.

Edward produced a photograph entitled: WOODWARD'S GARDENS BY MOONLIGHT.

"You know the gardens, Mr. Ward?"

Ward was familiar with the Gardens and their déclassé amusements, but he didn't reply. Instead he stared at the photo, which appeared to be taken on a dark night. Which Ward knew was impossible; which Ward knew had never been done. Still the foreground revealed the broad promenade that served as entrance to WOODWARD'S PLEASURE GARDENS. To one side, as clear as in broad daylight, stood the art gallery and, facing it, the conservatory, which was fronted by a summer pavilion distinctly bearing the sign: THE ROTARY BOAT RIDE. All the other structures were there, including the cast-iron traceries of THE MENAGERIE, outlined with unnerving clarity. These familiar buildings stood out starkly against a jet-black sky.

"You're surprised? Intrigued?"

"I've never seen anything like this." For once Ward's derisive voice conveyed admiration. Holly looked on, pleased with the photographer's minor victory over this cowardly, arriviste snob.

"I guarantee you won't for quite awhile." Edward felt tempted to boast that this was his own patented process, but an instinct about the woman's earnestness stilled his huckster's tongue. Instead he picked up a complicated-looking shutter apparatus and flipped the lever. The shutter fell, but stopped when it covered only the upper half of the lens. "It's not complicated. I needed a longer exposure time for the foreground than for background."

He flipped the shutter up and let it drop down halfway. "See, the shutter moves rapidly across part of the lens but it's stopped here."

Muybridge explored her gray-green eyes. Again she did not look away. The woman's boldness was unsettling. Edward wanted to keep looking, but he had no notion where it could lead. "The lower half of the frame gives a longer exposure, which I need for the darker portion. This is my newest shutter, which I hadn't worked out when I made this picture." He pointed to the photograph of Woodward's Gardens. "For Woodward I actually used two negatives, one for land, the other for sky."

"That's cheating, isn't it?" It came out harsher than she intended. To her surprise, Holly Hughes already had an emotional stake in

Muybridge—she did not want this man to be a mere snake-oil salesman. Aside from the work, she liked his terse, compact body, the hand's authority as he pointed to a photo. She told herself to slow down. Perhaps Muybridge made inroads because Ward was so disagreeable.

"Light strikes some chemicals, an image is formed," he offered with professional aplomb. "Our eyes can't freeze time without such a mechanical aid. We can't hold on to all those discrete, split-second postures that make up even the slightest movement." She watched his fingers arch and spread as Edward slowly moved his hand toward her. "I'm a practitioner of a modern form of magic, Miss Hughes. Only a camera can create this illusion which, however, isn't exactly an illusion. It is a managed record of what's out there. Call it frozen time, a minuscule slice of life."

"Art must be about truth, about the highest forms of beauty."

Muybridge laughed, which made him look younger, Holly thought. "Art? I'm a mechanic, tinkerer, technological fiddler." Did she have no sense of humor, he wondered? Ward could have disappeared, for all Holly and Edward knew. "Obviously you feel strongly about this."

"I'm a dancer."

Her statement prompted a stern reproof in his mind: *Do not generalize from your limited experience. There are many kinds of dancers.* Still, untimely images of Edith, a skirt dancer whom Muybridge had known, incinerated the remnants of his composure. He saw Edith leaning back in a chair, her smile blatantly beckoning, eyes heavy-lidded, the pupils about to roll back into wherever they went when she reached that absorbing state. Or she would stand in the kitchen, brewing tea, say, and her fingers would wander across her abdomen, move down a thigh then circle round to her buttock, fingers luxuriating in heated unhurried contact with her own skin. The deft fingers would circle and return, straying across her belly, lower still. Pleasure lay diffused everywhere along her lean, suggestive body, and so, in such a mood, she remained avidly in touch with herself, the fingers exploring, slowly palpating a curve, a crevice, creating an ever-intensifying circuit of pleasure. Edward would watch the half-unself-conscious, half-provocative movements of her hand until, often, he put aside his work to redirect her sensual self-absorption to include them both.

"Not a vaudeville or a skirt dancer, Muybridge." Ward seemed to read the photographer's thoughts. "Miss Hughes combines ballet with innovative European techniques. She's an educator and a *feminist* lecturer as well. I learned about her profession and interests during our journey." Again that crimped half smile, as though grudging muscles refused to grant a full smile. "Miss Hughes is putting on a performance in San Francisco next month."

"You're both invited. Like your photographs, Mr. Muybridge, my style of dance is new in America."

"Then we're both pioneers."

Just then his timer rang.

"Excuse me." Edward entered the darkroom and drew the curtains around him like an outsized black cloak. He checked the floor for light leaks, lifted the virtually paired plates out of the developer, a solution of acetic acid and pyrogallol. To fix the images he dipped the first pair then the other two twinned images into thiosulfate of soda. Muybridge counted to thirty, then removed and checked the plates and ripped open the curtain theatrically.

His smile charmed her—a man delighted with what he'd achieved.

"I'm going to publish these plates. We'll introduce this photograph in a court of law, Mr. Ward. It will convict that desperado of yours."

Holly Hughes scrutinized the photographer, who looked triumphant, boyish, altogether appealing. Yes, he was interested in selling his services to the railroad magnates, but that did not inhibit her interest in the photos—or was it the photographer? Holly viewed the three sets of miniature twin images of the stagecoach holdup, saw the leader's taut, wiry face framed by out-of-focus bandits. The event itself caught forever. As Muybridge had boasted, this timorous and bold man ensnared lost history, made fleeting time itself hold its breath at his command. Her gaze shifted back to the night photograph of San Francisco, the skyline purified to looming geometric forms backlit by the stark silver glare of a full moon. Muybridge, she judged, was a man who accomplished what he set out to do.

Chapter Two

No matter how slowly Muybridge walked his unmatched pair of horses up the rising valley floor, their hooves raised a fine layer of dust. Red dust coated his and his passenger's clothes, sifted into nostrils, lined throats. The raw bleeding color insinuated itself everywhere, as inescapable as the stiff breeze running out of the southwest.

"An old trapper I knew liked to say, 'This clay's the color of hell.'"

"Then it's very beautiful there."

Such a wealth of esoterica, Holly mused pleasantly. Already Muybridge had told her about his months living with the Sioux; displayed his photographs of solitary sojourns in Panama and Guatemala; his "work" on the Pacific Coast Lighthouses, making pictures (he said "making," not "taking," photographs) of isolated lighthouses in the Oregon Territory and on the California coast. He granted her a privileged look into the heart of a volcano in his steamy photograph of "Volcan Queszaltenango, Guatemala," the rocks themselves transformed into vaporous clouds.

At fifteen he had run away from his home in Kingston-upon-Thames, England, and was shipped to New York. In New York City he "scrounged" a job as an apprentice compositor and then as a printer, working on newspapers, journals, books. Words were everywhere then: They flew from his fingers. Then images seduced him and he became a daguerreotypist—he admired the exquisite detail the process created on its laboriously polished silver plates. But the daguerreotype could create only a single fine image, he explained. They could not be reproduced. And the mercury fumes that daguerreotypists employed to etch the plates were even more destructive than the collodion he used now; they slowly chewed away at the brain rather "than blasting you post haste to your reward."

At nineteen he had met Matthew Brady, at thirty-five already a "certified genius." Working as one of Brady's handful of assistants, they documented history's most brutal and murderous war. Holly had seen not a single Civil War photograph in Edward's collection and had enough discretion not to press. She felt a foreign emotion—humility—when she compared her silver spoon upbringing with Edward Muybridge's gritty tussles with the world. His frontier exploits, his sojourns with the Indians, his mad, solo dashes into Central and South America to make photos of previously unrecorded people and places, his struggle to picture nature and this huge country—pioneer, indeed.

"Sorry for laughing during the robbery."

"Makes little difference now." He resisted granting a full pardon, which forced Holly to revise her opinion—he was not as accommodating as he first appeared. The steel was there, but it lay concealed.

"I laughed because your bluff impressed me. To try to protect your work, even at risk of your life. You behaved the way I would've liked to behave."

The woman's earnestness was suddenly almost annoying, but he responded, "You didn't do so badly with Burt, either."

"Well, blood was pouring all over me. Besides, Mr. Ward is so squeamish, I thought I ought to take the lead."

They laughed together. Muybridge distrusted beautiful women. Not because of their beauty, which he appreciated as well as the next man, but because beauty could make a woman complacent. Some remained mere projections of loveliness or sensuality or whatever the ego or husband or lover dictated, and that laziness inhibited the development of the qualities that the photographer found more compelling—character, the inner vision of herself, a combination of intellect and sensibility and sensuality which lay undiscovered or undeveloped in the most pampered women. He mocked himself silently, wondering who, indeed, was the earnest one now?

Edward studied the sheer, bloodred cliffs. Moving through this high mountain valley of the sierras was like traversing the inner lip of a scar, the earth's belly sliced open to reveal eons of geological tumult. They rolled along an open millennial book—strata of frozen time nakedly presenting upheavals of unimaginable violence occurring over inestimable eons—molten stone incinerating the bowels of the globe itself. To photograph this—its scale; to capture its tone and surpassing color. Some of Muybridge's deepest professional urges were thwarted by his singularly black-and-white world. But he didn't dwell on technical limitations, not with Miss Holly Hughes so near. He asked, "Will you meet your family in San Francisco?"

"No family. My father died two years ago. My mother's been dead since I was a child. I can hardly remember her."

"I'm sorry."

"Nothing to be sorry about," she offered. "He died at eighty-six after what one friend described as 'three or four lifetimes.'"

How pleased he was that Ward had urgent railroad business to attend to. How pleased that they had this time together—without the junior vice president's snide sniping and edgy foot-tapping. That morning when he had asked her to ride with him, he realized how lonely he would feel if she declined. This bothered Edward, solitude being such a familiar old sidekick.

They were scheduled to catch up with Ward later that evening at the next "way station," which both knew would be another squalid bunkhouse, where, among a brew of sweat, smoke, urine, whiskey, and pitch, a motley collection of snoring, drunken men would toss and shift in restive, troubled sleep, hands glued to their sidearms. The thought of her in one of those smoky, low-ceilinged sod or log rooms, her body clenched tighter than a fist as she lay awake, made Muybridge realize he too would get no sleep that night. Unless—

"Miss Hughes, I have an inspired suggestion. Why not stay in my wagon tonight? I'll sleep outside on the ground in my bedroll. I often do it in fair weather." He could point out the constellations, regale her with more tales of western and South American adventure, parade unknown worlds before her.

Her steady gray-tinted eyes weighed the proposition. She replied, "Thank you for the generous offer, but I'm afraid—"

"It would be my pleasure." The words rushed out, his cheeks flushed from embarrassment. Clearly, he breached an intimacy here. But was her objection virginal? Was he being too forward when her eyes constantly invoked opportunity? And Muybridge did hate the idea of her lying with all those dubious, dangerous men close by. If something happened, he'd have to intervene, certainly fight, perhaps even kill. Instead he imagined himself at a campfire near the Flying Studio. He saw her in silhouette, the light slowly fading as they sat together under the star-studded sky. . . .

Blankly beautiful, the red cliffs rose up. It was cooler in their shade. He heard a whippoorwill's mournful note. Crickets rasped their legs together. Unhappy with their silence, Muybridge offered, "We're all so grateful to you." Her look flashed annoyance, skepticism; Miss Hughes did not suffer the ingratiating note. "There's no doubt you saved Burt's life."

"The camp doctor did that."

Edward tried to study Holly's face professionally, but the lustrous skin, the intricately constructed shelf of cheekbones, that strong straight nose, and the generous mouth with the full, perpetually moist lower lip left him anything but detached. Even those long, supple fingers warmed him. Highlights in the auburn hair shifted in the sun, displaying a gamut of colors—red, golden-brown, ginger. The hair kept blowing across her cheeks, framing rapidly altering versions of her face—buoyant, determined, youthful, reflective, maddeningly sensual. Each look was engaging and different, and all achingly lovely.

"You look like a figure in a painting . . ." Her head whipped around. It wasn't awkward, the movement, but it was quicker and less patterned than any gesture she had made. ". . . of the American frontier." He probed, "You've been painted?"

"Yes." She replied softly, her hand traveling to her hair and gathering it behind her forehead. An older, more sophisticated Holly Hughes appeared. Remembering the nervous tic, she dropped her hand. The auburn frame fell of its own weight.

"Anyone I might have seen?"

"A French painter. . ." She would have left it there with most Americans, but Muybridge was an artist, too. "Jean-Léon Gérôme." How complex the story, how absurdly banal to utter the master's name.

"I haven't seen much of his work. In Boston, at the Fine Arts Museum, I did see a splendid canvas—huge."

She knew the painting as well as her own face. She knew the impulses from which it evolved, the preliminary sketches, the under-drawing. She knew the color buildups and overlays, the position of the light source, the erasures, the retouchings—a history of application, frustration, fury unleashed at one recalcitrant model and, finally, success, if not quite triumph.

"Something about Odysseus, I think."

"*Allegory of Odysseus.*" A shadowy smile suggested a palette of thoughts he could not survey.

"I'd like to see more of his work."

Sitting so near her, desire's fingers clenched his throat, forcing Edward's voice up into a choked, higher region. Why did this woman turn him to jelly? Because she was so beautiful and accomplished, so self-assured. Because he'd never met a woman as provocative and seemingly ready. Not used to passivity, the role reversal made him tentative. "I'd like to photograph you."

"Photograph me?" She floated up out of her reverie. "Ah, then you'll convict me of a crime, too?"

He laughed, she smiled. A bottom tooth on the left was slightly offset, not perfectly aligned. The flaw made her even more desirable. Edward became tensely aware of how close they sat—her thigh, inches away. He'd glimpsed her maddeningly attractive legs as she levered herself up on the stagecoach rail. Again, with heated particularity, Muybridge's photo-sensitive mind sketched in the smooth calf and swelling thigh—sweet fullness without excess. Her talcum scent and that tantalizing hint of lilac drifted over him like a net; he wanted to graze where those particular perfumes lay.

Muybridge scanned the valley. In front of him the horses' flanks rose and fell. Did he detect Miss Hughes breathing deeply? Or was this out-of-place self-flattery? Could he inch closer? Reach out and take her hand? Why was it so hard to be forward when she seemed to invite it? Silence congealed around them.

The mountain's slope pitched the wagon to the left, toward him, moving her closer. The body-warmed lilac washed over him, red flag to a bull. The only sounds were the creaking of the wagon and the horses' steady plodding hooves laboring up the incline. His erection pressed against the denim.

Muybridge cleared his throat, desperate to offer more than silence to his guest. "I was through here eight years ago with a couple of Astor's men." Her gray eyes prodded him for another kind of a response. But what? What? "John Jacob Astor's son wanted to buy this valley from the Ute tribe, but Running Wolf had already been cheated by a fur company agent, so he asked for a cool quarter million in cash. They came to me to negotiate. I couldn't translate because it was so funny. Truly, I laughed for half a day."

"I thought that Indians had no interest in business."

"That's what young Astor used to think."

It was her turn to smile.

"One year later they drove them all out without paying a single cent."

The valley floor pitched up steeply, and the animals began to strain. Muybridge was a firm believer in conserving his horses.

"Would you mind walking a little?"

"Not at all. It feels like I've been in that damn bouncing coach for a year. My bottom—I trust you won't mind the expression—is killing me."

A respectable woman would not utter such a word. Certainly not to a virtual stranger. Holly Hughes combined haughty, aristocratic bearing with the most lax attitude he'd ever seen in a woman. Her carriage commanded distance, the eyes, body, lips, words implied a more provocative, inviting approach.

Just then Holly Hughes stood above him, offering her hand. Half-aroused and mightily confused, Edward Muybridge touched her for the first time. Her ample breasts pressed toward him as she jumped, her weight resting on him for a split second. She pressed against his strength, her hand in his. And as her face came closer, Edward again caught the infusion of flesh-warmed lilac and talc. The dark green dress bore exotic designs, swirling peanut-shaped splashes of red and black, some Eastern motif, he guessed. A hint of a smile lifted her lips. Was she smiling at his excitement or his reserve? Muybridge didn't trust his roiling senses, though they importuned him to take her in his arms and throw caution to the warm southwest wind caressing them.

"Have you known Mr. Ward long?" he asked formally, ashamed that the dumb question would make her body temperature plummet.

"Only since the Great Salt Lake. Which seems forever." She examined him skeptically, as though disappointed with his sidestepping of the matter manifest between them.

"But you do get all too well acquainted when cooped up in the same cramped cage for four uneventful days—until the robbery, of course. Which did nothing to improve my opinion of Mr. Ward." Holly did not add that Ward had actually pissed his trousers. "He's the lead accountant and toady office lad for the self-proclaimed 'Big Four,' the 'Associates,' whatever the press so worshipfully calls them. I wouldn't let him off the hook. I insisted that the railroad is a prime corruptor of national life." She went on gaily, "Mr. Muybridge, can you guess why the Central Pacific payroll is in gold coin?"

His mind worked quickly, anxious to respond to whatever challenges she threw his way. "It's harder to keep records?"

"Excellent, Mr. Muybridge." She nodded, schoolteacher responding to an eager student. "Gold coin enables them to make their payments, as he said in a whisper, 'more discreet.'"

"They work every angle, don't they?"

"Isn't that supposed to be 'the business of business'?"

"Particularly of empire-building."

Remarks shuttled quickly back and forth, as though their discourse required a newfound urgency. "A reporter asked Governor Stanford why they employed Chinese laborers. Do you know why?"

Catechized again, he replied: "They can exploit them, starve them, and nobody cares."

"That's the actual reason. But Stanford said—I've got to hand it to him, it's clever—he said, 'They built the Great Wall, didn't they?'"

Muybridge laughed. Then he asked, "Who is this Collis Ward fellow?"

"An arriviste," she responded, realizing how snobbish she sounded. "Didn't he announce his title to you? Junior vice president, Central Pacific Railroad. He mentioned it a dozen times over the past four days. I was surprised he hadn't emblazoned it on his handkerchief."

The mention of the Central Pacific sent Muybridge to his fantasy employment as the railroad's official photographer. He desperately needed a job: He'd left New York under a storm cloud, if not a tornado, owing $572.35 to various creditors. All of which he'd unquestionably repay, Scout's honor, but not until he produced income. After Edward had turned down his mentor Matthew Brady's offer of a loan and partnership, the photographer had kicked him out, emphatically shoving the younger man west, muttering, "This city may be growing faster than any other in the bloody U.S. of A., but it still ain't big enough for the two of us, Muybridge. And I'm too creaky and sick to climb up on top of any goddamn buckboard or Conestoga wagon again."

Observing Edward's distraction, Holly asked, "You're thinking about another matter."

"Oh, New York, the past, an old friend." Muybridge shook off the past.

Jealousy unsheathed its sharp claws—Holly wondered if this "friend" was a woman. She deferred that question to ask instead about what had been bothering her since Muybridge made his improbable boast to Ward, spurred, she thought, by the junior vice president's insufferable arrogance. "You do actually believe your photograph can help capture our outlaws?"

"Theoretically, it is possible."

Holly considered, *He's twenty-seven, twenty-eight or so, a gifted photographer, perhaps too much a salesman but also the most interesting man I've met in twenty-two hundred hot and dusty miles of transcontinental travel.* Edward wasn't conventionally handsome, but he had a vivid, intelligent face—high cheekbones; a long, classical nose; intriguing hazel eyes; the full mouth, which, her body had always insisted, was the most compelling feature. "You don't waste time, do you, Mr. Muybridge?"

The hazel eyes looked at her warmly now, without hesitation. "Usually I don't find leisure so absorbing." Taking her hand, Edward indicated she could mount the wagon again. "It's level here."

Holly watched with keen attention as he snapped open each leg of the tripod, mounted and screwed the camera body into place, with spare, unhurried movements fixed the black silk hood over the instrument and checked for light leaks. Every motion was as practiced as a dancer's steps.

From higher up on the ridge they overlooked a glinting ribbon of blue water snaking across the valley floor. Rock striations ran for miles, dark horizontal lines that seemed as though they'd been inscribed on the rock faces by a giant's parallel rule. In the shadows of the cliffs, the red clay turned darker, the color of dried blood. He went to work. She was entranced by the succinct, indecipherable choreography of Edward's hands as he mixed chemicals then, with deliberate delicacy, spread and balanced and finessed the collodion evenly over the large glass plate. He studied his shot, inched the camera to the right.

"Behold."

Crouching, she took his place under the hood. He was present there, a whiff of shaving soap, some lingering tinge of not unappealing sweat. A man without a smell wasn't truly male. She smiled inwardly, imagining bottling the fragrances of her long-term lovers—Jean-Léon and Jacques. All of fashionable Paris would demand the product.

"Would you like to make the picture?"

"Yes, very much so," she replied. Silly, perhaps, but she wanted to take—"make"—that photo.

He laid the bulb in her palm, their fingertips gently grazing. "Just squeeze hard." Edward wondered how those commonplace digits could be transformed into detonators. Then Muybridge heard the familiar click of the lens, the sound that echoed through his dreams. She emerged with a broad smile, like a child pleased by what she had done.

They studied each other. He examined her riveting, changeable eyes, then Edward bent forward, prepared to kiss her. She did not turn away. At that instant Muybridge realized he held the glass plate in his hand. "I'll be back. Don't move an inch."

Holly watched him hurdle into his Flying Studio, then broke into a silent laugh. He was so shy. Why? Edward hated the idea of being rejected so much, he kept hesitating. It was quite tender, really. She wondered if he had much sexual experience—of course, she concluded.

He yelled to her through the glowing buffalo skins, "Are you enjoying yourself?"

"Hugely." She eyed the buffalo skin tent, that mobile repository of his work. Impressive, she thought again, yet . . . Holly wasn't searching for a flaw exactly, but on some level she might have been relieved to find grounds for dismissal. It was all so complicated . . . demanded time and energy . . . required tedious explanation. The task of describing her unorthodox amorous history—that required rare understanding on his part. Muybridge himself was boyishly intent and appealing, yet also thin-skinned and anxious to please. Yes, a charge had ignited as they sat thigh to thigh being jolted back and forth. This was certainly not the first time she'd felt that deep implosive tug, the ingathering of her lower body. . . . Painful experience had taught Holly Hughes that even intelligent, charming, talented men could be depressingly conventional. And then there was her distant lover, Jacques Fauconier, a huge bear of a man. . . . The hawklike face, the matted chest hair, his supple commanding fingers. . . Just thinking of Jacques moved her physically. She commanded herself: "Unfair. No comparisons."

As always when Holly had excess nervous energy, she unlimbered. She kicked her legs, gently at first, then harder, quicker, rising thrusts from the hips, backward, forward, to the side. Her neck felt ossified, her buttocks and spine nearly disjointed from days of holding that stiff upright position while being batted about like a shuttlecock and suffering excruciating boredom in the stifling, tightly sprung coach with the self-serving Mr. Ward. Holly rotated her neck then her torso, automatically counting repetitions. An image of the photographer's face broke in on her meditation with her body—thin and articulated, with sets of wiry muscles below his cheekbones. There was his prominent yet delicately formed nose, which gave the head focus, an overgenerous mouth—God, how she prized a full mouth.

She heard him counting aloud in his darkroom and matched her count to his. She flapped her arms and torso until they unlimbered, while she tossed her loosening body from one leg to the other. As her body greedily welcomed the movements, Holly became an animated rag doll. Yet her mind spoke, too: *an entire day with him, without that Ward person, not an unpleasant prospect.*

Already Edward had shown her wolf tracks and bear droppings, pointed out the effortlessly soaring pair of red-tailed hawks riding the currents up and up till they metamorphosed into pale rusty brushstrokes that diminished to twin light-beige dots until, at an indeterminate instant, they faded into airy blankness. Without his eyes she would not have seen one hundredth, one thousandth, of what passed before them that morning.

Edward burst from his covered wagon, looking elated, the print in hand. "Fine image you made, Miss Hughes." To Holly's surprise, when he handed her the photograph it was wet.

She tried to pinch it between two fingers the way he did.

"That's right, hold it at the sides, not in the middle."

Her eyes shifted back and forth from the black-and-white photo to the livid red canyon below. She spent awhile with the photograph. When Holly Hughes spoke, her voice seemed muffled, distant. "I hardly knew my mother. I can't be certain if I actually remember her face or if the daguerreotype . . ." The complexity of the matter silenced her.

The emotional intimacy registered—how fitting that a daguerreotype provided Holly with that solitary image. At the same time, studying Holly's photograph, he considered whether the next time he should add one more grain each of iodide and bromide to the developing solution to bring out more detail. The technical issue distracted him. Muybridge wasn't thinking when he spoke. "After you became a nurse, then you studied dancing?"

"Nurse?!" How could he so wildly misjudge her? Nurse indeed. Why had she been tempted to invest her interest in this buffoon?

"The way you helped Burt—"

She barked out the laugh, a seal-like noise, not remotely ladylike. Her own relief spoke volumes to Holly. "I studied medicine a little. Just part of my training."

"Training?"

"Oh, Father's idea." Her turn to be uncomfortable. "He trained me as—he liked to say—'a Renaissance prince.'"

"Princess, surely."

"No, distinctly prince. No lace or frills." She held out the sleeve of the Indian print dress. "He believed that too many women, including my mother, were debilitated by what he called 'the curse of genteel education.' Or rather, lack of a bona fide education or exposure to life. That's why they hid away in the home or took laudanum or drank excessively and were hopelessly conventional and 'less interesting than burnt toast.' My father insisted his only child be 'diversely schooled.'

"Many thought him overbearing, dictatorial. I didn't. I liked the challenges he laid out; I loved his belief that I could do what a man did." She went on, embarrassment jousting with pride. "I was taught riding, fencing . . . Competitive physical training, 'gladiatorial,' Father used to say. Not at all genteel."

Muybridge grew uneasy, intimidated by her superior sophistication. But then, he thought, maybe that's why she's so compelling.

"Once again," he said, "Don't move very far. I need a moment or two for housekeeping."

Later, after he'd stowed Holly's photo and locked down his equipment, Muybridge returned. Handing her up now felt ridiculous. She probably could have leaped up herself. Then Muybridge mounted and flicked the horses into a trot. "Please tell me more about your, I think you said 'diverse schooling.'"

"There was ballet, painting in Paris. . . ." Holly spoke rapidly, avoiding the artist's name. "It sounds ridiculous, the height of vanity, but remember, Edward, this was my father's idea, not mine. He wanted me to be . . . his ideal." She drew a rapid, light breath. "There were plusses and minuses to his approach, surely. I hope I'm not totally contaminated by his egotism about me."

Edward did not reply.

"I make him sound like an ogre. He was more interesting and subtle. He offered me a range of possibilities. 'The world's at your feet. Become what *you* like, whatever *you* choose.' His philosophy and guidance, my choice, that was the approach. In Russia, with Olga Kuznetsova, I discovered ballet. I learned more about myself in a single afternoon than I had in six years as a schoolgirl dilettante flitting from one brief obsession to the next. Two hours with her reduced me to tears. And I'm not the teary sort." Her hand traveled to her hair, absentmindedly rearranging it so it fell in rough scallops across her forehead. Now she seemed like a young girl caught in a woman's body. That imperfectly aligned tooth caught his eye. He was already devoted to that flaw.

"With Kuznetsova, I felt truly humbled, Edward, my arrogance bridled. Here was a discipline so difficult and demanding, so much larger than me . . ." She studied him, sensing he would appreciate the thought. "Ballet was an undertaking to which I could devote my life yet never complete the work. A form that would reshape me from the inside out—first the body. Time and patience, humility and discipline—ballet rewrote all my assumptions about how much effort it took to be proficient, let alone good, not to say excellent. Here was the opportunity to achieve a kind of limited perfection and, if you were devoted and fortunate enough, a moment or two of grace.

"Madame Kuznetsova never touched a dancer, yet she was like an all-powerful hand reaching down inside you, using the body to get to—what? Once that invisible hand controlled muscles and sinews and joints, it could reshape the being itself. Do you see what I'm trying to say?"

Smiling at her earnestness, he nodded assent.

"Ballet disciplines mind and character. I see it as an avenue, a possibility for us."

"Us?"

"By 'us,' I mean all women." He was lost. "Dance, gymnastics, exercise is something that women must engage in if we are not going to remain irrelevant parlor decorations."

Edward Muybridge narrowed one eye as he mentally framed the photograph. He'd call it, "Beauty Inflamed by Passionate Thought."

She continued, gauging his response, "Even if I weren't a woman I'd say this, Mr. Muybridge, 'Photo Man' extraordinaire. The current state of relations between the sexes must be improved because everyone suffers. Equality for women will make both sexes—or the contest, if that's what it is, though I hope it isn't that—not only more fair but also more engaging. That would be obvious if all of us weren't so intimidated by convention and if men—oh, you men!—weren't so terrified of change."

A sliver of fear, like a handful of snow slapped onto the spine, chilled Edward. What would it be like to be in love with someone smarter, more gifted than himself?

Her voice pitched up half an octave, stirred by emotion. "You know what I found most impressive about my father?"

Muybridge felt so close to this woman he could have been holding her.

"He was proud of what I wanted to do, my, ah, struggle. He certainly didn't agree with several of my choices, but he thought the attempt worthwhile."

"You miss him."

The gray eyes, enlarged by a mere hint of tears, grew larger and more luminous as she nodded yes.

Ahead of them loomed the way station, and on its weathered porch stood Collis Ward, cheroot in hand.

Chapter Three

In the Sierra Nevada hamlet of Beckett, population 478 at latest count, at the end of a short, double-loaded line of ramshackle wood buildings and odiferous saloons which constituted the literal Main Street, Muybridge balanced on top of a battered steamer trunk arrayed in black frock coat and vaguely matching top hat. His cravat—calculated to draw eyes—was blazing scarlet.

The buffalo skins of his Conestoga wagon had been rolled up two feet, offering a tantalizing peek at the exotic, compulsively neat interior of the Flying Studio. Curious citizens milled about, staring into the wagon or tentatively sticking their noses up to an easel-mounted photograph of Edward Muybridge, Photographer, perched on the edge of Contemplation Rock, 523 feet above the Yosemite Valley floor, staring out into what looked like a precarious future. The photographer had tacked a banner between two scrubby pin oaks:

PUT THE WORLD AT YOUR FINGERTIPS
30 Six Inch by Eight Inch PHOTOGRAPHIC VIEWS
$2
INDIVIDUAL PORTRAIT PHOTOGRAPHS
MADE ON THE SPOT
JUST HALF A BUCK
STARTLING STEREOSCOPIC VIEWS—

YOU WON'T BELIEVE YOUR EYES!
ONLY ONE DOLLAR

Muybridge noted onlookers scrutinizing Holly Hughes as they would a costly thoroughbred. Her beauty and standoffish carriage kept people at a distance. Reckoning that he had the germ of a crowd, Muybridge tipped his hat to Holly, standing alongside a disinterested Collis Ward. It was time to get the show under way.

"Folks! Step right up and see the art of the future, the new and only way to record progress *as it happens*! *As it happens*, yes folks. Step right up!"

A rawboned farm boy, about as broad across the shoulders as a young ox, edged nearer to get a better view of Muybridge perched out over Yosemite.

Edward slipped a stereoscope that held a view of the daredevil feat under the boy's eyes. "You feel if you breathe too hard you might blow me right off that ledge, don't you, son? So, please, careful. Don't exhale!"

That drew scattered laughs. The boy shrugged and very slowly shuffled one shoe back and forth in the dust, not knowing how to respond.

"Struck dumb by the magic of photography, folks."

Ward whispered to Holly, "Probably not much of a conversationalist in any case." She smiled at the line.

Muybridge went on with his barker's pitch, "Here's 'instant history' you can hold in your hand! Carry back home. Examine each and every night for as long as you and your progeny live!" Muybridge whisked away the stereoscope and handed the boy a photograph labeled, "Broadway, New York City, 1866." On the back was printed Muybridge's name. The Broadway address had been scratched out, a San Francisco location—212 Market Street—neatly handwritten in.

"Here's one gratis for you and your good folks." The farm boy's eyes reeled about restlessly, flitting birds uncertain where to land. Muybridge plunged ahead: "Pass it on to your progeny. Hand it down to your children's children. For the first time the ordinary citizen—you, me, that lovely lady over there"—he bowed to Holly—"yes, all of us can own a piece of history *forever*!"

Several in the audience of thirty or so onlookers tensed as a chunky man in a shabby gray duster shouldered his way out of the knot and up to the photographer.

"Forever, aye? Ah show you forever." The man grabbed a print of a Modoc warrior poised to shoot his rifle at an unseen target and furiously ripped the photo in two.

Holly whispered to Ward, "What is that madman doing?"

"Probably a religious fanatic," the junior vice president replied coolly. "He may object to your friend's 'graven image.' "

"Oh," Holly replied as Muybridge stepped boldly up to his challenger, reached behind the man's ear, and produced a duplicate photograph of the Modoc. "The photograph is indestructible, my friend. From a single negative I can make three, four, a dozen copies, however many prints I care to."

Muybridge fanned an array of photographs for his onlookers. Escalating the sleight of hand, Edward nonchalantly reached into the fanatic's breast pockets and produced two, three, four copies of "Woodward's Gardens by Moonlight."

"Step right up, folks," he cajoled while looping the photos through the air and settling them face up in alignment on the ground in front of the steamer trunk. "The modern magic of photography is yours for an extremely modest investment."

"Quite a showman," Holly Hughes concluded, counting heads as people queued in front of the Flying Studio while the disgruntled duster-wrapped figure, urged to vamoose, scram, and get the hell out of here by several Beckett residents, stomped off down Main Street.

"Of course he's selling an intriguing product to a bunch of yokels." Ward's voice was slightly muffled by the smudged handkerchief he held to his mouth. "The real question is, how long can this photography craze last before there's a more captivating fad?"

After those long days in the cramped coach, Holly Hughes was bone-weary of Ward's flip dismissal of those he did not have the wit or imagination to fathom, fed up with the nervous bouncing knee or leg or foot, fatigued with the rituals of the foul handkerchief constantly materializing—a discharge-spotted veil—in front of the junior vice president's squirrel-like face.

"I'd make a large bet, Mr. Ward, that photography is here to stay. Do you want to put your money where your mouth is? Or would you rather snipe at a talented artist?"

"No, thank you," returned Ward tersely, who spun and walked away.

Holly stood at the edge of the gathering watching Muybridge cajole potential clients. She heard his directing voice: "Steady now." A moment later Holly noticed a young woman with an infant on her hip standing hesitantly before Muybridge's display gazing at the photo of the Modoc chief. Holly again surveyed the rough-chiseled face, the black, insightful, uncomplaining eyes. At whatever angle you looked, the eyes followed, an effect that Gérôme himself would've approved of. "Impressive, isn't it?"

"You think so?" The young woman sounded wary.

Holly leaned down to gaze at the infant. "What a lovely child. A girl?"

"That's right." The young mother, barely sixteen, opened the shredded blanket to reveal a few more centimeters of the infant's blotched, confused face. Holly smiled at the baby and picked up the Modoc likeness. What was a mere child holding a child doing in the desolate mountains?

"You know how it is." The young mother shied, a doe about to bolt. "If you don't buy it, you'll always wish you had."

She looked at Holly Hughes as though the handsome, commanding woman had read her thoughts. "I once let a pair of silver teaspoons get away. . . ." The speaker paused so long, Holly assumed she had lost the thread of her thought. "Wish I'd got them."

Holly handed her the Modoc chief, stealing a final peek at the infant. "It's a fine piece of work." She watched the girl mother move into the short paying line, the infant balanced on one hip, photograph pinched between two fingers. She thought, *We artists have to stick together*.

As Edward's head and torso disappeared under the black hood to "shoot" a beaming couple, Holly couldn't help noticing how comfortably his thighs held the crouch. A flood of his images flickered by. Holly wondered at his power over her: It was as though this photographer had cunningly implanted a stereoscope on the inner wall of her eyelids. Even if she wished, Holly could not shut off the parade of his pictures.

"Hold it!" From under the hood, Edward's voice drifted over customers and onlookers toward her. "Steady now."

Muybridge was almost finished for the night when, suddenly, the chunky man in the shabby gray duster appeared at the edge of the crowd. He opened his long lapel and pulled out a battered Sharps rifle. He raised the venerable rifle and aimed. People stampeded, screamed; several men behind the shooter rushed toward him. He got off one shot—right through the heart of the Muybridge surrogate as he dangled above the Yosemite Valley floor on Contemplation Rock. The shooter was immediately subdued by two men, the rifle torn from his hands.

As he was led away, Muybridge turned to the scant number of citizens of Beckett who lingered. "Do we have any more lucky takers hungry for these incredible, indelible images of our world?" No one responded. "Very well, then I'm going to close my shop. Thanks for an interesting evening, my friends."

Stiff with fear, Holly waited for Muybridge to gather his gear and move toward the wagon. She only said, "You certainly know how to stir up a crowd, Mr. Muybridge."

"Usually I prefer quieter evenings. That fanatic had me worried."

"You didn't appear the least bit concerned."

"Oh, earlier I noticed the son of a bitch—excuse the expression—was nearsighted. I thought he might miss the photo and hit the original."

Holly said good night. He insisted on helping her get settled. An hour later, having assured himself that Holly Hughes was relatively safe and comfortably bedded down in a separate, half-curtained alcove off the main room of the General Store, with Collis Ward mummified in a serape only a few yards distant, Muybridge sat alone in his wagon in front of stacks of coins and wrinkled bills, the evening's meager take. His account book lay open. The photographer owed his Eastern and European creditors $527.16—the unchanged, daunting figure emblazoned in red ink at the bottom of the debit column.

As he finger-pondered his way down through the scanty pile of currency, Muybridge felt as though he had spent the journey west peering over his own shoulder. He had crossed a huge continent, photographed a changing world and documented what remained of a rapidly vanishing one, and met a magnificent woman, yet he was chained to his burdensome past. Before deserting New York, Muybridge had scrupulously written each creditor, explaining that he had "prospects" in San Francisco and that repayment would follow once he was "established." Brady had offered a loan, muttering that it was "a reasonable way to consolidate his accounts." Edith had wept and offered him half of her modest savings. Edward had refused both, grimly answering that he'd rather have his creditors suffer than his friends.

"Fifteen, sixteen, seventeen . . ." Six months earlier, Muybridge had conceived yet another grand plan for fiscal salvation—to create a pictorial history of the Westward expansion: "An invaluable record," he'd labeled it in his imagined advertisement. Also, "An irreplaceable resource for schools and universities," "A gift that everyone in the family—young and old—will cherish and enjoy." How many times had he repeated the same canned phrases to himself? How long could good faith tolerate the insistence that, any day now, every solvent American would own at least one volume of Muybridge's *Vast Expanses of America*? Despair geysered up.

"Seventeen fifty." He was almost out of coins. "Sixty." Irony of ironies, Holly imagined him as being precisely what he was not: the fastest-talking photo entrepreneur roaming the Wild West. She'd gazed up at him with her unsettling gray eyes, weighing his overstated gabble and shabby legerdemain. In fact, he was a mediocre salesman. Occasionally, when Edward could whip up enough enthusiasm to regale the crowd as he had done this evening, he could sell a slim fistful of photographs. But he could work up to that pitch only occasionally. Something failed when prodding himself to repeat the act often—as though being obliged to hawk the wares compromised his belief in their value. If only he were offered the heralded bargain with the devil, any deal at all to escape the pressure tightening down on his skull like a huge clamp as he tallied the diminishing pile of coins and schemed and fretted about where the next quarter or dime or nickel would issue from—only he had no notion of where to locate a devil to bargain with. The pitiful stack before him kept shrinking. "Seventy, eighty, ninety, ninety-five, thirty-four dollars. Eighteen oh-five, ten, fifteen." Ten nickels later he was reduced to pennies. "Sixty-six, sixty-seven, sixty-eight, sixty-nine, seventy, seventy-one . . . That'll buy half of one lens, not the tripod. Plus . . . " Redundantly he glanced at the debit column. "I owe five hundred and twenty-seven dollars and sixteen cents." Edward slammed his fist into the pile of dimes, shouting, "Goddamn son of a bitch!"

The coins hopped up and scattered, like startled sparrows. A few trickled between the floorboards, but Muybridge was too angry and frustrated and exhausted to crawl under his wagon to pursue those precious metal disks that night.

Chapter Four

Next morning, a half mile from the way station in the half light of a multicolored dawn, Muybridge pulled hard at his single oar, hearing it creak and complain in the oarlock he'd forged and tethered with a metal spring to the tailgate of the Conestoga wagon. Edward rowed shirtless, but he wore a straw skimmer in homage to his sculling days on the moody, tidal Charles River. Because of this morning ritual, the photographer was in passable physical condition. The skimmer slid forward, blinding him, but he felt lubricated now and wouldn't reach up and break his rhythm. The worn straw scraped his brow; he smelled the familiar conjunction of pastoral field and accumulated sweat. Streams of sweat soaked the white twill trousers, salt drops scoured his eyes, but he kept pulling. Muybridge imagined that if there were a hand large enough, it could squeeze him out like a sponge.

His mind drifted to Brady sweating—his body temperature ran hot, the old man liked to grouse. For the disease that threatened to take him off—cardiac fever—occasioned not only profuse, sporadic sweats but also "a pain of the heart." An image assaulted Muybridge: "Confederate Unburied Where They Fell on Battle Field of Antietam. No. 551." Sweat-drenched Brady, as they wrestled those corpses into a semicircle of nineteen—count them. The gray-uniformed soldiers framed by two scrubby background oaks as the curve of death led the viewer's eye toward that innocent, distant hedgerow to the far right.

Their camera could not capture even the slightest movement. Thus "our great subject," those soon-to-putrefy bodies that lay absolutely still, all movement stopped forever. Serried images flashed before him in recall: Photos of crudely stacked bodies—or rather, not stacked but piled and thrown and flopped on each other because death-rigid limbs resisted orderly arrangement. Then there were the down-at-heels, sweat-rotted boots. . . .

Edward stroked until his shoulders ached and grudging abdominal muscles demanded he slacken the pace. A gravity-defying wave of nausea fought its way up from his belly until it scorched the back of his throat, but he choked back the bile, finding it hard to believe that a healthy body could produce such a foul taste. Muybridge pulled a few more strong strokes, adding a final grudging pair. As a cramp clenched his right triceps, he collapsed over the oar wrung out, exhausted.

He heard a distinctly feminine cough, spun his head around, and saw Holly Hughes emerge from behind a cottonwood. She walked toward the wagon, overtly assessing Muybridge's body.

"Glorious, isn't it?" She paused, eyes locked on his torso for an unhurried moment, then she slowly looked skyward. Her mocking eyes returned to Muybridge's stomach and chest as she asked, "Mind if I study your stroke?"

"To . . . morrow . . . may . . . be." It was hard to catch his breath.

"Just a few more pulls. Please."

Against his better judgment, Edward took a perfunctory pull at the oar.

"Stronger," she commanded, leaning down over him.

His mouth tasted like a sewer; muscles felt shredded. Throbbing tissue twitched and shivered in places where he didn't know muscle existed.

He pulled once, twice, a shuddering third time as she observed. She did not comment that his back was too curled to achieve maximum reach and power, that his feet were more than the optimal three inches apart and, worse, not truly parallel. With his feet positioned like that, his knees would never "open up" correctly and give his stroke the power he sought. Bemused, she thought, *Perhaps there'll be time for refinements another day.*

The fourth time Muybridge leaned into his pull, she reached out and placed a hand on his bare stomach. Under cool fingers, the muscles contracted. He stopped, stared up into her all-absorbing eyes. Her parted lips waited only inches away.

"Of course it's a contraction exercise." The lilting voice sounded professional, his volunteer sculling coach. "I generally suggest stretching as a complement, especially for a man of your age and, uh, physique."

"*'Physique'?*" Muybridge prided himself on taking care of his body.

A smiling Holly Hughes quickly stripped off her navy skirt and emerged in scarlet bloomers. Astonished, he examined the baggy trousers, which were tightly gathered around her ankles. Edward recoiled slightly—he hated seeing this gorgeous woman dressed in those ungainly, hideous bloomers.

"Let me demonstrate."

She pointed her feet in opposite directions, then Holly Hughes somehow managed to firmly flatten both heels on the ground. While this first position looked difficult, the next appeared physiologically impossible. Her spine undulated itself into a rippling *S* wave, each vertebra as graceful and flexible as those of a swan's neck. Miss Holly Hughes appeared more fluidly hinged than other human beings. "The idea is to generate tensile strength."

Not knowing what to say, Muybridge laughed mirthlessly. "'Tensile'?"

"I guarantee you it will create real strength."

"I'm strong enough." He dismounted from the wagon. If he shook himself like a dog, he could've sprayed her with sweat.

"You say you're strong enough?" she taunted him. "Would you care to wrestle?" The eyes, that face, the moist parted lips, everything seemed to send another message.

"I'd love to, Miss Hughes, but we've only just met."

"I am serious."

"And I'm not accustomed to wrestling with a woman."

"Afraid? Oh my, my, you're terrified of me." Her gray-green eyes blazed in mocking challenge. Muybridge realized that he'd seen the same vicious spark in a boxer's eyes. Yet there she stood, a feminine ideal misshapen by those masculine trousers. Muybridge determined to end this nonsense. "But suppose I . . ."

Defiantly she thrust out her formidable jaw.

"Uh . . . I injure you? That's possible, you know." He continued, "How can a self-respecting man wrestle with a woman? Where would I grab, uh, hold, where can I put—lay my hands, say? What happens if—" Before Muybridge finished, Holly Hughes took two running steps and dove. The photographer found himself on his back. She moved above him and, snatching an arm and levering it behind him, flipped Edward onto his stomach.

Struggling to slip free, Muybridge swore not to hurt Holly. Yet he had to strain and push and shove to wedge his body away from hers. It took exhausting, then almost frightening, effort before her hands slid apart, and he broke clear.

"Miss Hughes, Holly, please, can't we discu—"

Standing now, Muybridge managed to keep her at arm's length until she dropped to one knee, scuttled around behind, slid up his back, and caught him in a full nelson. He broke the grip by fiercely jerking his arms down, spun back to face her. Muybridge realized with dismay that this was a contest in earnest, a fight he couldn't win without hurting her—if he could actually win. He felt honor bound to restrain himself even while embarrassment and frustration gnawed at him, uncertain why the hell they were wrestling in the first place.

Holly feinted to her right, which made Muybridge lean that way, then, like a practiced barroom fighter, she butted her head hard into his chest. It hurt like hell and sent him down again. She flopped alongside the photographer, slipped a leg under him, wrapped the other over his chest, and locked his torso in a powerful scissors hold.

Muybridge lay gathering strength for a long moment, not knowing if he should laugh or pound her with his fists. She had all these moves and strategies while he thrashed, a defenseless idiot, at air. The woman's thighs were wrapped around his chest, a position he felt both ludicrous and seductive. In Muybridge's universe, things did not proceed this way.

He was struck by a terrible thought: Maybe she was insane. As his labored breath mingled with her lilac scent, he remembered Holly Hughes climbing out of the stagecoach, virtually daring the notorious bandit to gun her down; he heard her laughing madly at his own feeble attempt to protect the camera. Panic seized him: *Out here in the middle of nowhere, wrestling with a demented Amazon—I'm a dead man.*

Desperately summoning every ounce of strength, he wedged Holly's legs apart, his face half-buried in her tantalizing breasts. On top now, Muybridge worked to pin her, but she squirmed and flopped and wriggled like a wet fish. Flat on her back, she flipped him, and they rolled over and over in the dust. Muybridge struggled to regain his dignity but he felt cornered, with no notion of what to do next except to hold on for as long as he could. Then she cradled his face in her hands and kissed him on the lips, hard. She whispered hoarsely, "Edward, I adore wrestling with you."

He barely managed to return her dusty, sweaty kiss.

Maybe because the foreplay that did not seem like play lubricated his body, maybe because his muscles had been measured by hers or because both were covered with layers of hard-won, unromantic dirt, he escaped the self-consciousness of the first time. His mind did not oversee his movements. Their bodies, familiar with the other's contours, found the satisfying touch, the responsive spot. Her mouth, her tongue discovered shifting pleasures in his. No mind-orchestrated delays, no counting backwards or riveting his attention elsewhere to slow himself down to hold off the end. It was blessedly easy. In the fast-changing early morning light, their bodies provided prodigies of feeling, volumes of pleasure.

Afterward, Muybridge sat up on an elbow and examined her, his eyes recording every centimeter for future delectation. "Your exercises didn't make this." Holly's breasts kept their shape even while lying on her back. He caressed her prominent, dust-coated nipple. "Or this."

"Nature had a hand in it." Satisfied, she lay at ease under his roving appreciative gaze.

As he ran curled fingertips lightly up her thigh, Holly shivered involuntarily. Edward kissed her and leaned back as contentedly as a sultan, viewing a huge, cloudless blue sky. She sat up and those taut nipples tilted toward him, still registering her pleasure. Half-joking, Muybridge asked, "Does this mean we're engaged?"

"Not to be harsh, but that's so conventional, dear Edward."

"Tell me, what *does it* mean?"

"It means that we enjoy each other immensely, that we're new dear friends, that—"

"Rather close friends," he responded, his tongue insinuating itself down her belly toward her vagina. He wanted to revive the sex to sidestep the awkward barrier he'd thrown up between them, but she shifted away to avoid his eager, questing tongue.

"You're a fine lover, even now, only our first time. You're an incomparable tour guide and traveling companion, an artist with a fascinating mind. But lovemaking doesn't necessarily mean a long-term commitment. Please understand that." The crude, rehearsed words—a speech—her rhetoric pummeled his heart.

She didn't like being so direct either, but Holly's position on lovemaking, and what lovemaking implied, needed serious and immediate clarification. Better to tell him now than let assumptions accrete then have to unearth her bedrock beliefs.

Holly closed his lips with her fingers; he wanted to rip her hand away. "Let us ripen slowly."

As off-balance and humiliated as he felt, Edward couldn't tear his eyes from her. The sun brushed Holly's skin golden brown, tinting the eyes honey-gray. Her pupils acquired more depth, whether from pleasure or consideration of what he'd said he couldn't tell. "Perhaps we're strangers, as you suggest. . . ."

"Oh please, Edward, don't overstate it," she replied softly, not wanting to spoil this or hurt him.

"For strangers I think this is an excellent beginning."

"So do I, so do I." She stroked his face sincerely, her fingers trying to tell him how much, already, he meant to her. Several arguments urged her to be silent, but candor spurred her to speak: "But . . . ," she hesitated, "love should be given freely, taken freely."

"Free of what?"

That night, she rubbed herself against him like a cat, gently turned him over then covered his body with hers, sliding up and down then humping him from behind. They tried new positions: sidesaddle, then Holly above. She wet her finger and slowly inveigled it into his buttocks.

He came quickly that time. Later, after she had climaxed, Holly greedily implored, "I think I want another." Together, they obliged her.

After lovemaking, Muybridge lay in his camp bed beside a sleeping Holly Hughes. Looking down, he admired the weight and sweep of the multihued auburn hair that contrasted so strikingly with her dark eyebrows. The long lashes, which once in a while rapidly fluttered as she slept, momentarily brought Holly's flushed, still face to life. His eyes traveled over her firm full breasts to the pubis, the shock of dense auburn hair. Every limb, every curve was ample without excess, this warm pleasure-giving, pleasure-taking vessel filled to the brim. Such a rare combination—unlike many women he'd known, here was beauty of movement, not confined to static poses. Moreover, she offered teasing glimpses of sexual intensity and intellectual reserves that he had never encountered before. Her splayed legs, her body's sheen, the lustrous skin, made him hot again.

Theoretically, he'd always believed that a woman could be a peer. He'd even fantasized about finding a peer, the ideal partner. But, until now, Edward had never met her. And now this woman offered—take it or leave it—an unapologetic, vertigo-inducing notion of who she was and what she deemed inalienable to her. Such a vivid definition seemed a revelation to Muybridge, who had always felt slightly protective toward his women. Ah, the protection had its flattering moments, but the position offered less than full mingling, total immersion. He admitted that his perceived superiority involved condescension as well as affection, the sort of indulgence one feels toward someone younger. Why? Because women were protected. Because society's design excluded privileged females from life's rough and tumble. In Muybridge's world the question of whether women could or could not do what men could do was moot. It was simply that because of certain inflexible conventions, not a single female undertook what males did. Until Holly Hughes.

Now, as this long-limbed, complex creature lay breathing beside him, Edward looked down not on simply his equal but, quite possibly, someone more talented, venturesome, and committed than he was. She expanded him, disoriented him, stretched him on what he'd experienced so far as an extremely pleasurable rack. And so candid: "There!," "Lick me," ". . . coming"—as in "I'm coming, Edward!" Her spoken words were wild aphrodisiacs.

Muybridge silently thanked Collis Ward for this time with Holly. Ward had been called away because of another railroad emergency—a keg of blasting powder had exploded and killed one worker. The tragedy left Holly and Edward moving west together, without the junior vice president. Muybridge guessed that Miss Holly Hughes was capable of flouting any convention she wished. Still, it was simpler this way: no public condemnation, no snide glances, no excuses or apologies, especially to or from Ward.

His studio, the wagon itself, seemed transformed. Lenses, cameras, shutters, the outsized apothecary jars, surfaces layered with prints, even the buffalo hides were enhanced by her presence. Enhanced because now these were not simply his work tools; but because each item served as capsulated narrative, a way of sharing his history. Which he had done nonstop with Holly for the past two days. Odd, that for all the rapture of this novel experience of sharing his working life, there was also a kind of dispossession. Muybridge found it strange to feel such transport, such communion in his mobile monastic cell.

When she woke, Holly laid her head on his chest. In the lamplight, her eyes searched his, as though probing for access to the depths of his being. He would have given anything to let her in, but he wasn't sure how. "That two people can make up their own rules . . . That you can touch me anywhere I like, anywhere, that you can eat me with those naked eyes . . . No one else dictates what's possible or proper." She offered this deliciously, lasciviously, promising still other satiating delights. "It's a little miracle, isn't it?" He agreed wholeheartedly, hoping she would not turn too philosophical. "Maybe love is truly revolutionary, Edward. Or we can make it so."

"Holly. . ." Her earnestness leaned over them, a weighted curtain poised to drop down. He had to make her laugh. "I can't imagine any public forum where the question could be debated."

She didn't crack a smile but raised her head and studied him fiercely. The jaw thrust forward pugnaciously, like the gage thrown down before wrestling. "From what I've been told, few married women experience sexual satisfaction. You know how destructive that is to relationships? To a woman's sense of herself? To *life*? Imagine my sisters gritting their teeth, lying rigidly, and thinking of the ceiling or dinner preparations or simply about getting it over with." She took a deep breath. He realized this wasn't easy for her. "Women must demand sexual gratification. It should be our birthright, as it is for men."

He wanted to bask in the fleeting instants of indwelling pleasure, to absorb the moments when the body's languor obliterated the mind's implacable clamor. "Holly, I couldn't agree more." Complicity was intended as a way to free her from graveness.

But she was launched. "Believe it or not, one of the reasons for the women's gymnasium movement—you're the first male in entire North America to know this—is to encourage women to know and appreciate their bodies." Two fingers molded and stirred her nipple. Holly trapped his hand and moved it down to her belly's more neutral terrain.

"My Boston colleague, Amanda Craft, told me about her aunt, mother of three, standing over the crib of Amanda's infant boy. The aunt, in a dither, kept gaping at the child's tiny penis." The word sounded anatomical, not at all like the warm, flexible tube of flesh resting on his thigh. "Finally the aunt said, 'So that's what it looks like.'"

"Wait. I don't understand. I thought you said the aunt had given birth to three children."

"I did." She brought her face closer. "They were all girls." Muybridge realized how ignorant he was of women's experience. "Edward, you have to imagine total, unlimited ignorance. They made love—though I doubt that's the correct term for what transpired—beneath bedclothes under the cover of darkness. This grandmother had never seen a man's cock in the light of day." She touched him fleetingly. The movement was matter-of-fact, not erotic. "Never. Amanda and I tried to laugh about it, but we both wept."

"Men have to be instructed, too," he said, hoping to prise Holly away from her earnestness. "How to create pleasure for women."

"Are you the man for that job?" Tension constricted her throat as she moved above Edward, mounting him.

Chapter Five

Edward and Holly drove the Flying Studio west through the towering sierras toward San Francisco, visiting the scattered minuscule settlements that had sprung up along the proposed Central Pacific right-of-way. In those raw, fledgling hamlets, their existence predicated on the transcontinental railroad's anticipated boom, Edward would set up his "show" and display his photographs and offer to take photos "instantaneously and on the spot" for anyone interested. After initial reluctance, Holly would function as shill, cajoler, model (the stack of photographs of her grew taller), and, when his hoarse voice gave out, his barker.

She saw, from the inside, how he went about his work—just where to center or "off-center" the shot, the importance of angles in a frame, how light could be manipulated. In spite of Edward's insistence, quoting Matthew Brady, that photography was 70 percent technology, 20 percent commerce, 9 percent chance, and maybe, if lucky, 1 percent "art, which really means craft," Holly steadfastly maintained that he was an artist. But Edward declined the label, unwilling, as he said affably, "to take myself so seriously."

Muybridge never admitted to Holly how much he owed his creditors, nor how anxious he was to set up a studio in San Francisco and start earning what he hoped would be a decent amount of money. But he did speak to her about Brady's offer of the money and partnership.

Muybridge had refused, knowing that Brady had too long cultivated the habit of command, and that he himself had actually outgrown being junior partner. To assuage what felt suspiciously like guilt at deserting his mentor, Muybridge told Holly, "After being out in the world on my own making photos, after the suffocating realities of the Civil War, I hated the lies of the studio—the insipid painted backdrops in front of which 'clients' stiffly pose while I try to coax something like a realistic expression—forget a smile—out of them." Lying on her side, loosely wrapped against the mountain chill in a worn buffalo robe, Holly was not posed stiffly. "All I could see was an endless sequence of brides and babies, babies and brides. You'd think all that New York City had to do was to make babies and get married."

"In that order?" she replied. "By the way," she continued, "I've taken care of that issue. I have the latest diaphragm from my doctor in New York. So don't you worry your handsome head. Tell me more about the past."

Instead of sitting in a studio, Muybridge had wanted to crisscross the country, move north, south, east, and west as impulse or insight moved him in order to capture the United States in its entirety, the vast, multifaceted, harsh, magnificent, overscaled land, a nation tentatively ready to come together after the lethal wrenching apart. Brady had once responded to his plan, "You seen one mountain, you seen them all. You seen one battle, you seen all you'll ever need. Ain't that right, Sport?"

To her it seemed like they stood still while the Sierra Nevada rolled by. Stirred by frequent pleasure and the wonder of their thoughts and bodies working in concert, she sat astride their horse-drawn float, observing a series of gradually changing tableaux, and talked, argued, agreed, discussed, talked some more. Time was their ally then. Edward told her about his early days photographing the then seemingly timeless, now moribund, world of the Plains Indians; his travels in Central America, threading up and down on vertiginous mule tracks over mountain passes among natives who had never seen a white man—how he had to wait shivering in a Guatemalan lean-to for two days for the foggy drizzle to lift from a peak so that he could make a panoramic shot of the mountain range, which he showed her; how he had hauled his equipment on his back for ten miles over treacherous trails after his packers refused to cross into an enemy tribe's territory; how he had persuaded three Indians to lower him in a woven rush basket over the edge of a cliff. She questioned why they did not drop the basket and make off with everything he had. Muybridge replied, "They liked having their photos. Never seen themselves before. Besides, I only paid them half up front. The rest of the gold was under guard back at base camp."

Compared to those early excursions, the West now seemed almost tame: an occasional raid by a ragged band of demoralized Cheyenne or Sioux playing out the hopeless endgame; a sneering, leather-faced bandit or two cropping up once in a blue moon. And even then, everyone knew the outlaw's first name, surname, and middle initial and had certified bank audits as to the full amount that he had stolen over the months. And how many murders he had notched on his gun belt. Wilson L. Lardue had four, to be exact. Edward's attitude astonished Holly since—after Europe, after Paris—America seemed so anarchic and wild, so limitless and thus beyond the understanding of those domesticated, long-established worlds.

Slowly, ineluctably, his experiences in the Civil War began to seep out. He couldn't muster the strength to relate how savage their salvage operation was, how they repositioned the corpses to make a more gruesome shot, how they dragged in the dead rebels and even an occasional civilian or two to swell the numbers, how they tried to fend off the stench by cigar smoke and swathing their faces in bandannas but nothing kept it out. It painted the body, clung to the clothes, infiltrated taste buds. Even now, Edward thought he could still smell it on damp days.

"Too much honor got killed here," Brady had intoned to his querulous assistants when they resisted the melodramatic staging. "It's shit simple, boys. The North must prevail or our national morality's defunct." He pointed to the stack of corpses. "We gotta win at any price." Thus the horrors of war—wood-block cuts incised into the nation's consciousness from Brady's team photos—appeared in *Harper's*, *Frank Leslie's Illustrated,* and sympathetic daily newspapers. So far, Edward couldn't bring himself to unveil the photos themselves.

* * *

On the road, he talked to everyone they met—drovers and carters, a traveling salesman hawking a miracle tonic for every ailment from baldness to barrenness, a dubious circuit judge whose appointment came through a business associate of Leland Stanford's, an undertaker who blithely remarked, "Just remember, every bad is good for business." Muybridge's mind sponged up facts—the location of a new telegraph line; the details of a copper mining operation; where to ford a creek; the settlements' growth rates; the number of colts and foals (4) born that spring on a struggling, hardscrabble ranch; a revived silver deposit wrested from a played-out claim; a superior brand of axle grease. He talked of bridles and bits and hobbles, of grass and timber, of water—often of water. (The last winter's light snowfall in the High Sierras worried the locals about next year's well levels.) Unusually for Holly, she listened much of the time. She enjoyed seeing him cast the net and pull in whatever he might catch. He was a lucky hunter.

One afternoon near Dutch Flat they overtook a couple's wagon, the wife as thin and worn as the bleached translucent bones scattered along the trail. Muybridge whipped up a bountiful lunch of fresh-killed turkey and wild mushrooms that they'd picked in a lush meadow the afternoon before. The husband stuffed himself greedily while offering up a symphonic potpourri of slurps, belches, and odious farts. Head tilted to one side, the rail-thin wife pecked at her portion, watching her husband's gluttony as though imbibing vicarious nourishment from every bite. Holly and Edward exchanged perhaps ten words with the couple in an hour then parted without a thank-you from their guests.

Later they overtook a dilapidated wagon with four kids and three dogs, all walking alongside the outsized wheels. "Permanent outriders," he'd called them, betting Holly that the kids and dogs had skipped or walked or trotted over the last two thousand miles. Later he talked about how bad it must be back where they came from to hurl them westward on their precarious trek. What lay ahead, none of them knew. Holly pressed money on the mother, much to the woman's chagrin and relief.

The worst moment came when they gave almost all of their freshly killed game—a brace of quail and a rabbit—to a dust-begrimed, exhausted-looking couple with a tethered scrawny goat and a puny, putty-colored infant. Edward was particularly tender with the baby, cradling and petting him, feeding him goat's milk from a bottle. Driving away from their campsite, Edward said the obvious: "That poor kid won't last a week."

Along the trail Holly Hughes had the unfamiliar sense of being protected. She was not comfortable with the feeling, but accepted it as somehow necessary in America's extravagantly Wild West.

Edward photographed everything that called to him—a glade where tall, soft grass still embraced the curving form of a sleeping doe; towering peaks and distant valleys; a gnarled oak and one towering, stately Dutch elm that, twenty feet above its roots, branched as gracefully as a dancer's upraised arms. He scaled rocks and climbed eighty feet above her to make a photograph. She tracked his every step as he clambered up and up lugging heavy camera and slender tripod to a mossy, treacherous ledge carved out by a sheer waterfall. The shot caught the spray describing an eternal semicircle.

She danced for him, intimate communications that he treasured beyond price. Happy and, at times, unaware of the fact, Holly sang or hummed—tunes that welled up out of her satisfaction. Enthroned in self-regard, he thought proudly, *This woman's body hums for me.*

Lying back late one night, Edward sent a blind hand over her thigh. Holly shifted, letting those fingers play. She moved again, closer. His hand traveled down and worked on her, hard. A stroke, another, and she pressed up against his fingers.

"Edward, Edward."

Urgent insistence, part demand, part supplication. He added a second finger and rolled his knuckles down to increase contact. Her breath came sharply. Her fingers slipped down beside his, which at first surprised him, and together they worked on her. To Edward it seemed like elegant composition—her fingers wildly working at the core of her pleasure while at the edges he played accompaniment. Her head traced slow arabesques on the bedroll pillow, auburn tendrils trailing. He watched her teeth lock, jaw distort, mouth twist open greedily. Light beads of sweat lay strung along her upper lip and clavicle—his erotic pearls. Her eyes rolled back into her head, the whites revealing the candid ugly beauty of climax. She came, her hand implanting their intertwined fingers deep within her. Later, in the middle of the night, she woke him, whispering those inspiring hot words, "I want another."

Next morning he didn't hitch up the horses but instead challenged her to a horserace. Holly looked surprised, since he was ultracautious with his precious team. They tore along the ridges, through the woods, ducking limbs, leaping deadfalls. Holly was a fine rider, but the rugged terrain had her grasping the pommel for dear life, which amused Edward. Then, at full gallop at the last instant, he grabbed her horse's bridle and swerved the animal away from a stretch of ground pocked with prairie dog tunnels. They let their lathered horses rest by an oval mountain lake, its dark bottom shaded by evergreens. They swam naked to cool themselves, then made love by the shore. Afterward, as he tented in her long hair, she thought, *The man's such an unique combination of reason and wildness.* His unpredictability, his passionate interest in everything reshaped settled assumptions. *He,* she thought, *is a gift.* Which is precisely what he thought of her.

He showed her the photographs he had been withholding: the shattered bodies and, worse, the scattered body parts; a brutal shot of a dead horse—the impossible angle of its forelegs, the flaring hairs of the nostrils, terrified incomprehension lingering in its single open eye; the mountain of worn boots and broken-heeled shoes that living Union soldiers picked over in the evening after an engagement or battle. Neither spoke during the viewing.

They couldn't have been farther from Paris. Three nights before they were to reach San Francisco, Holly lay naked on the buffalo robe. Edward had built a fire for warmth and to deter the wolves. Eerie fire-thrown shadows roamed in and out among the rocks, obverse extensions of the tongues of flame licking ineffectually at the dark.

"I want to tell you this, but it's not easy for me to describe the Paris I entered as a child of seventeen." Muybridge felt fearful of her past, but he also coveted each scrap of information about his love, the tip of an iceberg he longed to explore. He didn't want to dig out the heart of her mystery, but his devotion asked for a more fleshed-out history, firmer outlines.

"Jean-Léon Gérôme." The agile trill of that French "r" impressed the photographer, lent the name weight. "I first visited the studio with my father and a family friend." She did not mention Jacques Fauconier's name. Yet. As she spoke, Holly remembered entering the anteroom with her father and greeting Gérôme and Jacques, remembered the painter's quarters as it had looked that first morning, north light, as it showered down from the skylight, spotlighting the three men so central to her life. As clearly as she saw the firelit spruces and pines, Holly visualized the twenty-foot-high wall that ran the studio's length and on which many of the artist's celebrated paintings were first displayed. She saw herself peering into the small bedroom beyond the public space, the bed poised at the vanishing point as though in a Renaissance painting. Later, Gérôme had called the forced perspective "my funnel." All funneled down to the bed. She had accepted the painter's formulation of the primacy of sex, committing herself to both enjoying and tending his masculinity—as ardently, scrupulously, devotedly as he tended his brushes and hand-ground pigments. She glimpsed Gérôme's ageless, cunning face, her first lover—and next to him, at the master's ear, her second. She saw Fauconier's prominent forehead, the meaty slab of cheekbones and savage, hawklike nose that contrasted with his stylish clothing and impeccable, prematurely gray hair and unlikely sky-blue eyes. Two men. How many nights had she seen those two faces as intimately as she saw Edward's this evening? How many nights had she lain with Gérôme and, later, with Fauconier?

She went on, "Father had known Gérôme's teacher, Ricard, when he studied in Paris."

"My friend Bierstadt studied with Ricard."

Her face lit up. "Albert Bierstadt was Gérôme's favorite German painter."

"We worked together with the Modocs. The U.S. War Department officially labeled us 'The Artistic Team.' He drew, I photographed, and we battled over which was better." Adding a German accent: "'The expressiveness of drawing and painting,' says he." Back to American again: " 'The clarity and objectivity of the photograph,' says I."

Alternately shadowed and illumined by fire, her gray eyes smoldered and gathered such depth that he longed to stop talking and make love. "Such a distinctive vision, my friend 'Beer-City.' That's my name for him. Have you seen his painting of Sioux warriors on the Plains?"

"No."

Muybridge continued, "It's set outside Fort Laramie. The 'hostiles,' who look anything but hostile, are standing in a crescent, looking out of frame. His half-moon forces the eye to circle back left to right to the first and most arresting figure, an Indian scout—not ennobled but substantial, large, brooding yet distant, clearly a man to reckon with. A terse painting without sentiment."

She saw Gérôme standing before the canvas of *Quest*, a paint-flecked finger moving scant centimeters above the color-saturated surface, tracking the "eye's odyssey," explaining to her how he led the viewer's eye around the picture plane "like a dog on a leash, frisky yet willing."

"There's a tone to the grass—dull, late-winter brown," Muybridge was saying. "It's like staring at a corpse. But underneath, Bierstadt insinuated a faint trace of green. Hardly visible, the merest suggestion . . . If you know the Plains, the painting takes hold of the lapels and drags you there. It's so precise, I could date the moment when the long grass picks up that special tint. There are maybe three or four days in late April or early May depending on the amount of snowfall and spring melt when that half-tone appears, and he's captured it—the only time that hue appears, like an actor entering on cue. You feel you're looking at *pure potential.* That crusty old bastard Beer-City throws off these gems of perception no one has caught before."

"Not even a gifted and brilliant photographer?"

"Not even him," he admitted. "Your friend Gérôme would agree with Beer-City. In spite of our running argument, we're so limited. No color. Not yet a whiff of movement. Even our widest frame is cramped compared to a big canvas. The stereoscope can create the illusion of depth, but only after you shove an unwieldy device before your eyes." He breathed in as though his nasal passages were blocked. "I fear we'll never achieve the same expressiveness or realism as paint. But you know all this."

She did.

"When I get back to San Francisco, I'll give you one of Bierstadt's sketches for that painting." He gestured toward the wagon. "I know it's in there somewhere."

Imprecision about the photographs was hardly his mode. Holly assumed that Edward knew where the drawing lay, in what drawer, under which set of sketches or prints. But as they approached their destination, as the end of their idyll loomed literally beyond the horizon, both found it harder to be candid. She would go ahead, find rooms for herself, settle in. He was to travel to Sacramento to do official work for the State of California and also be introduced to Leland Stanford. One or two days later he would reach San Francisco. There, in the unfamiliar city, they would meet again. Both understood they were about to enter uncontrollable terrain. Both feared that life together would never again be this intense, so pure and untroubled.

But Holly needed to tell him more about herself. Even if it was painful, he had to know. "The first day I visited the studio, in the presence of my father, Gérôme asked if I'd pose for him."

"How presumptuous."

"I had just turned sixteen. My father was livid. He said, 'She's a child.' I know he was being protective, but father's condescension struck me as a provocation—I was a petulant child myself, too big for my britches—in retrospect, my relationship with Gérôme seemed preordained."

The emotional jolt stung like a thump to his sternum, an area adjacent to his heart. Of course he'd surmised that she and Gerome had been lovers. But why did Holly insist on making him confront her erotic past? To rub his nose in the parade of prior lovers? No, that wasn't it. Instead, these recitations were manifestos, and he was under unspoken orders that demanded him to try and absorb and understand. Edward chafed under the conscienceless ease with which she force-fed him her past. "Holly, I understand your impulse to relate this to me, but it's not necessary."

"I have to tell you about my past. It wouldn't be fair if I didn't."

"I'll listen, but under protest. I have the feeling that you're more concerned about issuing a credo than relating your life story."

She considered arguing the point but held off. He was partly correct, but there was so much to relate. Holly wanted Edward to understand, otherwise she would be misrepresenting herself, denying him access to her beliefs. "Father left Paris shortly afterward. I stayed at home, with the housekeeper as ineffectual chaperone. . . ." She paused. "When I first posed for Gérôme I was painfully shy." Holly rose naked on the Sioux buffalo robe—her face lost definition and grew rounder, the erect shoulders slumped, the ample bosom caved in till her chest appeared much flatter. Before his eyes this mature, confident woman became a shy, uncertain child. He imagined Holly, seven or eight years younger, as she first stood naked before the painter—the supple, long-muscled body with those delicious twin sinews where her thighs joined the torso, even they appeared less developed. Her hands wagged and crossed skittishly across her breasts then thighs, trying to shield herself from view. There was no way to cover all.

Mental pictures of his own models—Edith, Clare, Sandra, and Walking Deer, the Pawnee beauty—streamed past. Was the parade his mind's retaliation, a feeble stab at sexual competition? Each had posed for hours before his lens, and with Edith, Clare, and Walking Deer it often ended—or began, maybe—in lovemaking.

Holly interrupted his reverie. "He was beastly about posing. Gérôme knew precisely what he required and would manipulate my body with infuriating detachment then leave me frozen in disgusting, stricken postures. I hated that." Her body struck an array of poses—arm flung back awkwardly; crouched like a cowering child; torso twisted so it pretzeled back over itself, forehead abjectly touching the earth; a leg stretched behind, knee bent at an improbable angle. Certain postures looked grotesque, yet ungainliness did not diminish erotic impact.

"Le Mâit—" She groped for words, "Gérôme kept exploring—always exploring, as though searching for an unknown joint or muscle group or hinge, an overlooked anatomical posture. 'Try this.' I would strike the pose. 'No, not that, this.'" Rapidly she assumed different poses. They flashed like photos before his eyes, like one of his flip-books—motion out of stillness. "As much as I resented being used, he was Le Mâitre. The Master," she translated. Even Muybridge knew the meaning of the term. "And this laying on of hands was"—Holly stared at the fire—"stimulating."

He writhed inwardly. She read that in the way he angled his head and torso away from her as though trying to escape a blow. Yet without this background, how could he understand or truly love her? She could not pretend to be a woman she was not.

"The shyness passed. One day he pronounced me ready to model for his class. After the first or second day, the men's eyes began to stir me."

So graphic, he inwardly objected, why so damned graphic?

"There were moments of transcendent boredom. I would spend the morning in ballet classes at the Opera, then rigidly hold a pose the entire afternoon. Diametrically opposed exercises, really. My legs would go numb; my feet ache. The rounds of the arch—I can still feel that exact pain, here." She extended one graceful, articulated foot and fingered the locus of the pain. "My calves throbbed and cramped. When he allowed me to rest, I had to elevate my legs on an ottoman. I kept a gown over the Chinese screen, so I could slip into it when I couldn't stand any longer.

"But the work was as addictive as opium. I enjoyed displaying my body. I liked exciting them. Power. You virtuoso lovers know all about power."

Flattery and complicity, Muybridge weighed the aptness of her appeal. Yet how to beat back those vicious, growling fangs of jealousy? Jealousy of time long past? Absurd, yet . . .

"Edward, I was their visual whore."

He'd had enough. "Don't exaggerate. Modeling is a centuries' old tradition. Your painter wasn't alone in this. I employ models, too. Lovely young women."

"Of course, of course, I've seen. I admire your nudes. They're delectable." Though she offered this concession to his talent, Holly refused to be diverted, not with her compulsion to tell him all. "But it was never more than visual display. Outside the studio few students so much as looked at me, spoke to me. Not a single one ever approached me."

"They were so frightened of *Le Mâitre*?" His accent was atrocious, but Edward intended to mangle the honorific. She missed the irony.

"Frightened, in awe . . . He was a hard man, testy, difficult. I was clearly his woman, and as such unapproachable—as others had been before. I was young, Edward, and in many ways proud to be the master's pet."

"So unlike you now."

That hit home. "I was a child," she confessed again. "Gérôme was thirty-one years older than me."

Old enough to be her father, he thought.

She seemed to read his mind. "Edward, don't say it." She plunged on: "He was a whirlwind, debonair, charismatic, a genius pampered by all of Paris." The dancing, variable firelight seemed to thrust her closer then whisk her away—erratic light attuned to his emotional tumult.

"You know, many of his paintings are huge, entire worlds to themselves. And there were frenzied drawings of women—for one year, actually eleven months and sixteen days—principally me, but others, too. Women obsessed him. He often said women were the only subject of interest to him. He claimed he would've preferred to live in a matriarchy." She drew a breath, her eyes gauging Edward's emotional temperature. "For a girl, it was flattering to be a part of that world."

"Were you jealous of the others?"

Ah, she thought, the question he's been waiting to ask, the question within the larger question. She softened for a moment. "At times, certainly." Then, "But the enterprise was so ambitious, devoted to art, to beauty."

"Ah, those pompous, larger-than-life abstractions again. They offer blanket excuses for cruelty and self-indulgence, give cover to emotional dishonesty. It's horseshit. We artists are such superior beings, we can have the entire cake and eat it, too."

"Oh, God, maybe you're right, maybe it was self-serving, an elaborate house of cards designed to bolster the Master's ego. But it didn't feel that way then. Too much exceptional work was done. That was his life—painting, studying nature, and the particulars of light and shadow and mastering the appropriate brush strokes and making love, all fueling the mix. He needed to feel loved, potent, powerful." Her eyes asked: *Edward Muybridge, what man doesn't?*

And what, he questioned himself, *is the reply to that? Me and only me, an exclusive contract with this one woman forever? Will I, like a priest, demand daily repetitions of faith? Weekly renewal of eternal vows? And even with verbiage, how to flush insecurity out of a tremulous heart?*

"It was as simple—and maybe as profound—as that. You learned that the rules of monogamy or domesticity were social conveniences, altogether arbitrary."

"One can certainly think of other ways of arranging these matters. They may evolve strangely. But they're not 'altogether arbitrary.'"

Her head shook ever so slightly, a barely discernible tremor. How passionately she spoke about the old painter. Would he ever generate such lasting significance in her emotional universe?

"There was a quality of commitment in the work for which traditional rules didn't apply. Gérôme was inventing a new way of seeing, a new form of painting. You, of all people, should understand this."

"I agree about it to this point. . . ." She flushed and brightened, anticipating agreement. "There's an unalterable selfishness about artists."

"We're the most selfish people in the world."

"Don't romanticize the goddamn self-absorption," he responded sharply. "Are we so damned privileged and important that no one or nothing else matters?"

"But jealousy is conventional, too, a habit."

"Is that what Gérôme believed?"

She ducked the question: "There was such fervor, such moving concentration." Transfigured by memory, she was aflame, back there again, in Paris.

"Gérôme would stand for hours, reflecting, visualizing, sketching the painting's figuration or studying his brush strokes. Circling, surveying—like those hawks you pointed out—waiting to pounce on the slightest misstep in his own work! I went out one afternoon after breakfast and returned at seven that evening, and he was locked in the same spot, analyzing, criticizing, attacking the weaknesses, appreciating the painting's strengths.

"I sometimes wondered if he could actually step into the picture, wrestle with the foreground, insert himself into the background to explore and tame the remotest corners. All this without moving. We used to joke that the spiders spun webs on him. The maid was ordered to feather-dust the Master when he was working on his revisions."

They'd reached a dead end. He wanted to shout, *Rhetoric! Lies! Convenient self-delusions!* Quietly he offered, "Bombast, my love." Meanwhile, he wondered how good was "Le Mâitre's" work? Was that the real issue? Whose work would endure—his or "Le Maître's"? Who took on—and achieved—the greater results? How could he be an artist, plying a trade that was not considered art? And, of course, no one could win a competition with a dead lover.

Holly felt her emotions ice over: that last painting of her, her fury at Gérôme . . . Why was she defending the old reprobate now? For a nonnegotiable principle, that was why.

"Retouching was passionate movement. Once he decided, Gérôme worked rapidly. The closest to ballet I've ever seen." She laid her fire-warmed hand on Edward's forearm.

"All right, if you want to distract me, go on, distract me," he teased. He couldn't stomach another syllable.

"Sometimes there was no talk, only the brush." She could hear the bristles making feathery scratching, inscribing colorful trails across the canvas. "Or the pencil." Again, in her mind, she heard the sounds—a quick stroke, another, then light, rapid movement over the paper, like the scrabbling of fingernails on a hard surface, sounds without apparent form or discernible direction, like an orchestra tuning up. "The pencil was most enthralling because he drew so quickly and surely." Her body clenched, remembering. "I often thought I could feel his hands on my thighs, my breasts."

Muybridge pulled her to him, his reservations swept away by her words.

Later, she asked, "Do I ever intimidate you?"

"No," he lied as calmly as he could. She made him angry, jealous, fearful, impatient, not emotions to be proud of. Yes, he thought, there were times when she overpowered him, made him feel weak and, worse, sneaky, underhanded. How could he capture her completely when she was still moored to her past?

On their last day together they stayed in bed, in a rough-hewn inn east of Stockton.

"I thought that posing was behind me. Then I realized I do the same thing on stage."

"It's not the same at all." Edward caught a hint of condescension in Holly's eyes, which, after last night's blather, infuriated him. He responded with strained civility, "Dance is a precise, formal discipline—'Art,' as you like to call it."

They disagreed enough to make things interesting, she thought. "I choreograph the seduction of an audience using *what* as my instrument? My arms, my face, my legs and thighs, my breasts—all part of the lure, Edward. Because the movement has procedure, and tradition doesn't persuade me it isn't about sex."

"It's about much else, too. Discipline, years of training, music, the practiced gesture that creates an exquisite line. It's about fantasy, too—an idealized form of beauty."

She watched Edward's divining rod twitch and sway. It pointed toward her, the lubricious muse. "Okay," he said, glancing down with a smile. "I have to admit, your dance is the stuff that certain erotic dreams are built on. But, intellectually . . ."

Holly's laugh told Edward she appreciated his ability to deflect her earnestness.

"Did Gérôme like his women?" The French syllables sounded impoverished in his distinctly American mouth. He could not roll the "r" with her trilling richness.

Her mouth gaped open to accommodate a rush of feeling. "Does a tornado like the earth? It rips it up, flings around trees. *Liking* was hardly the issue."

They kept postponing their parting. He intended to leave Holly at Stockton, but they drove on to Antioch, then Pittsburg, and finally Edward put her on the ferry at Richmond across the Bay from her destination. He was scheduled to meet Leland Stanford in Sacramento and also to photograph the California State Capital building. In three or four days they were to reunite in San Francisco.

They said good-bye with restraint, the ferry being public. As the boat pulled away from the wharf, she reflected: How fine the journey West had been, an erotic idyll of unhurried talk, thoughtful accords, and spirited disagreements, warmth, and affection. Each drew deepening pleasures from the other, as from a continually augmented well. Lately she had noticed dark clouds passing over his brow—clearly he, like she, was uneasy about the new world they were about to enter.

Ex-Governor Leland Stanford possessed the true politician's head—oversized, with voluminous, inky black eyebrows and undersized, penetrating dark eyes which broadcast confidence and authority. Stanford's massive head was matted with thick brown hair, and his face covered with a dense, sculpted beard that ended in a devilish point. His velvet frock coat was cut full to emphasize the governor's scale—he stood six feet, two inches and topped two hundred fifty pounds. From his fob pocket hung a hefty gold chain that weighed two pounds. Next to Leland Stanford, Collis Ward, with his skeletal face, absent eyebrows, and loose limbs, looked like an insubstantial footnote.

Framed photographs of Governor Stanford with President Ulysses S. Grant as well as presidents Lincoln and Hayes, and senators Seward and Chase—along with Queen Victoria and crowds of German royalty Muybridge did not recognize—decorated the library walls. Prominent, too, was a framed advertisement from the front page of the San Francisco *Clarion* trumpeting the start of the Central Pacific Railroad's race east across the continent. Dated January 7, 1865, it read:

WANTED 5000 LABORERS FOR CONSTANT
AND PERMANENT WORK

Newspapers, books, stacks of official-looking papers cluttered all horizontal surfaces, which lent the formal space substance. The principal furnishings—Stanford's huge rolltop desk, his overstuffed chair, the eight-foot-long, double-wide chaise longue—were scaled to the governor's girth and height. His celebrated cane, tipped with the bulging gold nugget that Stanford claimed to have lifted out of the Sacramento River and was rumored to be the start of his fortune, stood at the ready in an ornate solid-silver umbrella stand.

"Governor, Edward Muybridge." Collis Ward introduced the photographer to Leland Stanford.

The ex-governor's handshake was as formidable as his presence. Edward returned the pressure. They tightened their grips. An awkward moment ensued, with neither man willing to back off or let go. Facial expressions ran a quick gamut—smile, tension, discomfort, frowning impatience, annoyance. But they clung to each other, neither submitting.

Still hand in hand, the big man said, "I was impressed with a number of your photographs of our railroad, Mr. Muybridge." Though he didn't speak loudly, Leland Stanford seemed to be addressing a crowd. He slipped his free hand onto the photographer's forearm and forcefully extricated his right. Stanford gazed at the liberated hand, then shook it as though summoning it back to life. "Ward tells me you're the best available with this camera device."

"There are a handful of talented professionals, Governor. Brady's as good as they come. So is Carleton Watkins, W. H. Jackson, myself. As to 'best,' it's difficult for me to toot my own horn loudly."

"Mr. Ward says you'd like a favor from me," the governor said. Ward's smile looked boxed in, as though his mouth had been pegged down at the corners.

Muybridge summoned a hearty laugh. Something about the governor and this setup made the younger man hostile. Not too hostile though, for Muybridge needed Stanford and his nascent cross-country railroad. "Actually, no favor, Governor. I'd like to provide you with a service." His throat muscles seized up; he realized how much rode on this pitch. He went on, "You'd no doubt like the stolen payroll recovered?"

"You mean the entire twelve thousand and five hundred dollars?" It was the first time Edward had heard the sum. Ward, hovering near the massive governor, silently tapped one foot as though in rhythm to their exchange.

"The sooner we begin, the more we'll recover. You know that I made stereoscopic photographs of the robbery?"

"So Ward told me, Mr. Muybridge." Leland Stanford listened, twirling his thick gold chain. "And you think your photo can convict our robber in a court of law?" The question ended skeptically.

"I'm going to try to print the photograph on ordinary newsprint."

Now Stanford's gold chain whipped aggressively through the air, cutting mesmerizing, gilded arcs. "I'm told it cannot be done."

"That simply means it hasn't been done—yet." Edward Muybridge had an excellent idea of the source of the governor's information—his former colleague and old rival from the Brady days, Theodore Lochlin, the photographer whose uneven work hung on the wall. "However, if I can't work out the transfer to newsprint, I'll ask my friend Homer Winston—you all know Homer's work." The governor and Ward exchanged glances at the name of California's premier lithographer/draughtsman. "If I have to, I'll ask Homer to prepare an etching from my photo. We'll print a couple of thousand sheets featuring the bandit's face."

Stanford avidly followed the photographer. "And what will you do with these sheets?"

Edward asked, "Governor Stanford, how many people does the railroad employ?"

"What is it, Collis? Ten, eleven thousand?"

Ward replied crisply, biting off each syllable, "As of last week, 11,386." Like a parent egging on a precocious child, Stanford accepted the figure with a pleased nod.

"I'd like you—I mean the railroad—to offer a five-hundred-dollar reward—in *gold coin*."

Stanford's glowing smile dimmed a notch, shaded by a passing mental cloud. Collis Ward looked caught out; the uncontrollable knee bounced rapidly up and down. Muybridge had slipped the governor a clue to Ward's indiscretion: The Central Pacific paid its workers in gold coin, a fact that Holly had learned from the junior vice president. Cash made it more difficult for government auditors to track the millions in bond revenue and loans that Congress had shelled out to the Central Pacific.

"Gold coin?" Stanford's eyes burrowed into Ward, who averted his look.

"Your couriers, foremen, engineers, clerks will distribute circulars galore up and down the right of way in every settlement, hamlet, and backwater from here to the California border." Muybridge ordered himself to stop overplaying his hand. "Five hundred dollars in coin and enough circulars and I'll guarantee we catch this murdering lowlife within a month."

The gold chain swung closer to Muybridge. "How much will it cost me, apart from the exorbitant reward?" Stanford deftly caught the watch and studied the dial.

"Two hundred dollars should cover my operating costs."

As an obscure, backwoods dry goods merchant, Leland Stanford had grubbed and scraped and bargained for every penny of profit for fifteen long years. As an empire builder the habit endured, only the stakes had grown colossal. "Make it one hundred and seventy-five dollars; you got yourself a deal."

"I do not negotiate about costs, Governor. Profits maybe, but never my costs."

That wrung a wry smile from Leland Stanford, though not from Collis Ward. The younger man eyed the notebook in his hand as though he needed to jot down a note.

"I must have a thorough accounting."

"Naturally, Governor." Edward's voice turned buttery, accepting this minor victory.

"As I mentioned, Ward painted glowing pictures of your work. I'd enjoy seeing these 'vast expanses of America' sometime soon."

"Whenever you wish, sir. But I must explain it's not the entire country yet. Still, I can show you the most comprehensive portrait of the U.S. ever assembled. You might consider the possibility of having someone—and, Governor, under the right conditions, I'll happily be the paid volunteer—document the progress of your inspiring transcontinental railroad."

If the governor desired, he could hire Muybridge as official photographer of the Central Pacific's portion of the transcontinental road. The prospect overwhelmed, it captivated Muybridge, for there was no more epic way to complete his documentation of the United States. The job could provide steady income, relieving the money pressures that buzzed like a ripsaw through his consciousness. Edward smiled internally, realizing how far his harried mind had developed this fantasy for no sound reason. Meanwhile, the unleashed, fat, gold pocket watch again coursed through the air mere inches from his face. "I propose to photograph the work daily, to follow the particulars of this exceedingly complex process, to document work and workers along with your spectacular breakthroughs."

Ward's forehead furrowed, as he said, "Mr. Muybridge is an exceedingly talented—and ambitious—young man."

"We need more like him," Stanford exclaimed. "America fuels

appetite, Mr. Muybridge. The bigger, the better. Fortunately, we're blessed with unlimited resources: Forests with numberless board feet of timber, lakes bigger than European seas, coal seams so deep our geologist thinks they may run all the way to China." He smiled at his limp joke, a wide, platelike smile marooned in the midst of the large head. "And, to date, we've also been blessed with a political system with sufficient foresight not to inhibit individual initiative. You know"—Stanford seemed to inflate, to grow massive enough to embody the expansiveness of the North American continent itself—"not since Creation itself has so much energy been loosed upon the world as that unleashed by our noble American experiment."

"You're forgetting the Flood, Governor."

Stanford's paunch jiggled, a smile brightened the dark heavy features, yet he made no sound. The governor reminded the photographer of the wily old buffalo he'd once photographed, the leader of the herd who had survived countless winters and innumerable battles, and had the scars and the cowed followers to prove it.

Leland Stanford gestured toward the far wall. "Do you know Ted Lochlin's work?"

Muybridge walked over to the wall where, up close, he scrutinized the official portrait of Stanford as governor of California, then examined a second photo which caught the governor leaning out of a Central Pacific locomotive, his head covered by an unlikely looking engineer's cap. The poses were clichés; the second print was marred by several specks of dirt.

"I see two of his prints on the wall."

"What's your opinion of his work? Be candid, man."

"He's not in Brady's class."

The governor hesitated a long moment, his coal eyes tunneling into Edward's. Not a muscle of Collis Ward's face moved. Then Stanford burst out with a full belly laugh. On cue, Ward joined in, tenor to the governor's resonant basso. Leland Stanford, president of the Central Pacific Railroad, magnanimously flung open the towering mahogany door of his private office as though declaring that all the world lay before the young photographer.

"I want to confer with my partners. Come see us next Tuesday in San

Francisco, Muybridge, at Crocker's bank. By then you'll have our decision on your, uh, intriguing proposal for the Central Pacific." The large congenial voice boomed across the leather-walled study while the face remained shuttered and unrevealing.

Chapter Six

Hunched over and straining, two bullet-headed, thickly muscled men jockeyed the cherry hutch across the oak floor. Two armchairs and several crates clustered in a corner of Muybridge's bare living room. Framed and unframed photographs lay strewn in stacks on the windowsills, the floor, the tops of crates, a sea of overlapping images which Holly longed to shuffle and redeal each time she surveyed them.

"Where you want?" grunted one breathless laborer, eyeing a stunning photograph of Holly Hughes arrayed in a long white gown.

She pointed at the far end of the room. "Against that wall, please." The sweating pair hunched down and, crablike, made mincing progress, the slender hutch swaying precariously. At the far wall they eased the top-heavy piece down. Holly eyed the hutch's position with displeasure.

"A little to the left."

Not a word was spoken. Holly saw no sign given by the movers. Yet they knew from the other's breathing or the flex of the knees or tightening of biceps the instant to heave together. A kind of choreography, she thought, wondering if she could incorporate such movements into a new dance.

"I'm sorry, a little more."

Again the gleaming surface, a supersaturated blood color, heaved up. The antique tottered forward, then ascended vertically as one jackknifed mover scurried backward and, just in time, managed to steady the shifting load.

Muybridge slipped two folded dollar bills into the hand of one sweating man, then the pair exited.

"Your rooms will be lovely, Edward."

He tried to sound casual, but anxiety, like an untipped foil, edged his voice. "I'd like them to be our rooms."

"I appreciate the offer, I do, but I need my own apartment. I need space for practice." She laid a gentle hand on his wrist. Muybridge gently disengaged that cool, condescending hand. "And there's the piano." She rattled on. "It's possible I may have a dance student or two."

All this consoling palaver to pacify what he experienced as a gut-rending rejection. In the twenty-two days that Muybridge had known Holly Hughes, she could not have been more responsive or passionate, inclined to his thoughts, and in tune with his body's interests and demands. Yet, for the three days since he'd returned from Sacramento, she had been edging away. Now Edward felt he was chasing a fleeting shadow, hunting her up stairs, down hallways, trailing ever so slightly behind but never getting close enough to behold Holly as she moved ahead of him just out of sight from room to room.

His rooms. Her rooms. Why was he so concerned about her keeping an apartment? In fact, rationally he could have argued the opposite—that rooms for Holly were essential for appearance's sake. They had discussed the propriety issue, and Edward told his love that, quite honestly, he would be happy to become engaged to her or marry her, for that matter—if she wished to avoid public comment about their "arrangement." She thanked him and, graciously this time, did not deliver her canned "I'll never marry" oration.

So why this tedious discussion which went nowhere? Because Edward knew that having her own rooms meant potential escape for this apostle of "free love." Which to him translated not into the theoretical but into the concrete, though as yet unknown, form of another lover. Or lovers. And on this single question he possessed no standing whatsoever, for her life and "philosophy" predated him. So what did it matter that Gérôme was dead while other males—whom or how many?—remained poised exhaling torrid breaths on the far side of the Atlantic?

He slogged on, "I'll take larger quarters. Hire a hall. Buy a piano." The stab at humor did not disguise his distress.

"I have to be able to jump out of bed in the middle of the night. Make noise. Jump. Run. Sing. Yell." *This clinging wasn't worthy of him,* she thought. "Do my calisthenics at any time, day or night."

"I adore your calisthenics."

Holly considered: *Edward does believe that, but he is besotted, too much in love.* Yet she was too, as much as he, Holly protested vehemently to herself. She wanted to yell, *Stop doing this to me, to us*. Uncertainty made him finger affection's delicate fabric roughly, making her afraid that the fragile, elusive gift might tear. *Don't turn love into an idiotic child's game*: *He loves her more than she loves him.*

Years before, because of the mess with Gérôme and Jacques, that cursed painting and the even more disastrous aftermath, she had pledged herself to independence even from the most adored lover. "The thought of not having my own rooms is intolerable, Edward. I won't, I can't do it. Not even for you. As much as I care."

Muybridge heard her, outwardly calm. His eyes skittered over to the cherry hutch she had given him, peered into its polished depths as though the explanation of her resistance was locked inside.

By late afternoon, Holly had returned to her hotel and Muybridge was focused on a matter almost as resistant as his problem with Holly. All week he had combed the scientific literature about attempts to print photographs on newsprint or ordinary paper. He studied the process of etching daguerreotypes and extensively researched the new "swelled gelatin" process, hoping to find a key in the technical literature for a method to print Lardue's photo. Edward spent days working out one process, then another, but no technique would reproduce a photographic image even on the most costly stock. He fiddled with Fox Talbot's gauze netting in the attempt to break up the solid tones of the tiny image of the notorious robber. Without that print, Wilson Lardue wouldn't be caught and jailed by his own image, as Muybridge had so casually boasted to the governor.

After a week of unflagging effort, mounting expense, and too little time with Holly, Edward had contacted his colleague Homer Winston, who at times had worked cheek by jowl with Muybridge and Brady during the war. Back then Winston had sketched with rapid acuity scenes of bloody action that the photographers' pathetically slow lenses could not capture. Muybridge and Brady took turns saying, "We'll take the dead ones, Homer. You draw the quick." Winston's reporting was applauded throughout the Union states.

Now Muybridge peered over Winston's shoulder as the artist sketched from a stereoscopic shot of the bandit. Muybridge corrected his friend's drawing, insisting that the bandit's upper lip lift asymmetrically on the left to give him the proper sneer as it turned down on the right. Muybridge urged Winston to reshape the dark shadow under the eyes until the visage turned wolflike, to sheer a bit off the cheekbones and hone that pointed nose. At last, reasonably satisfied with the likeness, Muybridge watched Homer Winston painstakingly incise an etching onto a metal plate. From that plate they printed 239 sheets, though by the two hundredth the eyes and cheekbones were losing definition. Winston etched a second plate, then another and so on until the engraver had produced eleven etchings. By the end of a week they had printed twenty-five hundred handouts.

Suddenly circulars bearing the likeness of Wilson Lardue materialized everywhere—pasted on the fronts of buildings and curled around hitching posts, stacked on the counters of banks and post offices and general stores and stables and saloons. Coaxed by winds, the handouts fluttered and dived and settled and rose again all over San Francisco, papering the hills and gullies, scudding through the sky or sinking into the Bay, draping themselves against walls and over posts and on board sidewalks as well as the steep, ubiquitous, rickety wooden stairs used by citizens around the city. Pedestrians slipped on them, kicked at them, folded then discarded them, or swatted them away like a mutant breed of flat white flies. Then, aided by the Central Pacific employees, the circulars traveled east, working their way up into the sierras, over the railroad right of way until every town and hamlet was plastered with the bandit's hard-bitten, scaly visage; until virtually every man, woman, and child knew that thin eccentric scar which seesawed half the mouth up, the other half down.

Like tumbleweed, the flyers relentlessly moved east. Horses shied from the sudden white fluttering; riders cursed the ghostlike sheets that rose, like startled quail, from out of nowhere and left their mounts skittish.

Still no one cursed the presence of Muybridge's flyers as intensely as their subject—Wilson Lardue himself. In a minuscule settlement in the sierra foothills, Lardue ordered his gang to hunt down the errant sheets of paper as they had formerly hunted down Union soldiers and corralled Central Pacific payroll shipments. Six-gun in hand, Wilson Lardue dashed around picking them up off the streets, in the saloons, out in the hills and the ravines. Lardue alone ripped up and scattered at least two hundred of the incriminating documents. But chasing his printed image was dispiriting work. And the photographer and his patron, Leland Stanford, devised their own response: They printed another fifteen hundred sheets. Lardue felt increasingly haunted by the countless, ineradicable likenesses, the ugly, distorted, yet increasingly familiar effigies of his fervid black eyes, sunken cheeks, and that half-smiling, half-bitter antiphonal mouth.

As soon as they got their cut of the railroad payroll, two of Lardue's gang ran off, scared away by their leader's visibility. Lardue chased away at gunpoint two others that he suspected might be dreaming about turning him in for the five-hundred-dollar gold coin, which left only the one called Johny. Finally, Lardue himself implored Johny to get the hell out. This was painful for both men and Johny, the younger brother, resisted. But Lardue insisted that, if the worst came to pass, they needed one survivor in order to "cut down the bastard Photo Man" who started this manhunt in effigy. Johny vowed vengeance and rode off.

A haggard Wilson Lardue sat in a saloon at a round table, his chair drawn up in the corner, back levered against the wall. The bandit fanned five greasy cards in his left hand, leaving the right hand poised at his hip. In front of him, a small pile of bills and coins and a half-empty whiskey bottle. Arrayed around Lardue at the oval poker table was a beefy florid man who wheezed erratically in shuddering draughts; a swarthy dude of a gambler who, each time he shot his cuffs, drew the undivided attention of the other four men at the table; a round, white-haired, grandfatherly figure with the largest stack of bills and a sly, demented expression; and the kid, a brash sliver of nascent manhood whose six-guns dwarfed his undernourished pubescent body.

Lardue won eight dollars on a straight, then lost twelve after he bumped on a pair of jacks. As the kid raked in his take, the florid-faced gentleman drunkenly lurched to his feet. Lardue made a lightning move for his Frontier Colt, clearing it from the tooled leather holster. The entire saloon went deathly still, all sound instantly sucked out of its layered, shifting smoky air.

"Takin' a trip to the can," the man slurred drunkenly, raising a peaceful pair of open palms in Lardue's direction. "The can, man. That's where I'm goin'."

The drunk leaned his weight on the back of a chair, lurched forward a half step, rocked back toward the bar, careened two steps away from Wilson Lardue. The bandit was resettling his pistol into the worn holster when the big drunk lurched left, toward the outlaw. The man tottered there, as though uncertain where to locate the back door.

Meanwhile, at the table, all eyes hung on the kid's fleet, dexterous hands as he shuffled a blur and slipped the sticky deck to his right.

"Cut!" he demanded in a scratchy, adenoidal voice.

Lardue reached for the deck with his left hand as the drunk slopped back toward the bandit. Suddenly the big man took three fast, mincing steps and banged hard into Lardue's chair. Wilson Lardue grabbed for his Colt, but the drunk jackknifed his weight onto the bandit's right arm, which responded with a sickening crunch. The kid smashed a pistol butt into Lardue's gun hand while the grandfatherly gentleman slammed Wilson Lardue in his Adam's apple, which sent the bandit leader to the floor, gasping for air.

Instantaneously, Sheriff William Bartell and eight deputized citizens stormed into the saloon. Guns drawn, all stared down at the body writhing on the sawdust-covered floor.

Lardue spit out most of an incisor yet managed to exclaim, "How about we split . . . the take . . . Remember"—he wiped a flood of blood from his mouth with a sleeve—"I could do . . . lot better than five hundred dollars . . ."

The Sheriff's rifle butt cleared out more of the bandit's teeth before Lardue had a chance to sputter, "for you boys."

* * *

Despite heavily booked social calendars, most of fashionable San Francisco managed to attend at least one day of the trial of the notorious bandit. Governor Leland Stanford was conspicuously present along with Horatio Dirk, the editor of the San Francisco *Clarion*, the city's most influential newspaper and the "megaphone," as Stanford privately quipped, of the Central Pacific's governing clique. Hollis Huntington, Central Pacific's lobbyist, put in an appearance. Dirk, never one to miss an opportunity to pump up circulation, assigned Luke Ransom, the *Clarion*'s star muckraker, to cover the event.

Holly Hughes, Edward Muybridge, Collis Ward, the stage driver Frank Newton, and the now recovered guard Burt Bingham each identified Wilson Lardue as the gang's leader. To the delight of Leland Stanford and the other railroad magnates, five thousand dollars in gold coin and roughly thirty-five hundred dollars in currency was recovered from the desperado's remote sierra hideout. The Central Pacific claimed most of that money since, over the past two years, Lardue had stolen an estimated $28,567 from the Big Four. The presiding judge, Alfred P. Burling, was an ex–state senator and a Stanford judicial appointee. So it took minimal prescience to foretell that the railroad would receive at least a fair share of the recovered loot when the court got around to divvying up the money among Lardue's several victims.

When Muybridge took the stand, he tried, as much as possible, to avoid looking at Wilson Lardue. But each time Muybridge inadvertently glanced that way, Lardue's unwavering eyes locked him in his sights. Eerie, thought Muybridge, staring down the barrel of the bandit's homicidal rage.

Toward the end of the trial, the prosecution laid out the six virtually identical paired photographs of the robbery and offered the jurors a stereoscopic device to view them. By the time the photographs were introduced, Holly and others had testified that Wilson Lardue was indeed the robber, so there was a certain redundancy to the act. Still, the San Francisco *Clarion* chronicled the event with the banner headline:

MILESTONE

ETCHING COPIED FROM PHOTOGRAPHS ADMITTED FOR THE FIRST TIME AS EVIDENCE IN THE GOLDEN STATE COURT.

On the final day, before the jury announced its verdict, Wilson Lardue leaped up and shouted, "Stinking goddamn little photographs! What kind of shit-ass evidence is that?"

A red-faced Judge Burling hammered his gavel and shouted for order. "Another outburst, Mr. Lardue, and I'll cite you for contempt."

"You're right there, Judge. I got contempt for the whole proceeding here."

"That'll be two contempt citations," said Burling.

Wilson Lardue retorted, "What you gonna do, string me up twice?"

The jury brought a verdict in eight minutes, which occasioned Luke Ransom's loudly whispered quip, "They barely had time to say hello to each other." Wilson Lardue was found guilty of armed assault, attempted murder, and three lesser charges. He would be sentenced to fifteen years in the California State Penitentiary.

As Edward took Holly's arm and led her toward the back of the courtroom, Wilson Lardue managed to shuck off two guards and lunge at the photographer. "You're dead, Photo Man! Dead as dirt!" Lardue's wire-thin lips were chalk white while the rest of his scaly face, inches away, flamed with rage. Four guards converged, subdued the shackled man, and dragged him backward toward the door, boot heels scraping, eyes still riveted on Muybridge.

Edward felt like he'd been branded. He found it difficult to shake off those demented eyes. For days afterward, Muybridge had the terrifying apprehension that such demonic hatred would somehow invent a way to pursue him. Muybridge, who had not carried a handgun since his photographic tour of the Central American highlands, bought himself a mint Colt Walker—six rounds of protection in the form of a nine-inch .44-caliber revolver. He kept the heavy weapon on him at all times, to Holly's consternation. She commented only once, "There are two kinds of men, those who carry guns and those who do not. Why did you have to be one of the gun-toters?"

Muybridge replied, "This is the Wild West, Holly, not the boulevards of Paris. Lardue is a cold-blooded killer."

"Yes, and he's in prison."

That ended the discussion. And soon the threat of Lardue himself ended. In a subsequent trial for the murders of a Central Pacific engineer and his coalman, Wilson Lardue was found guilty. He was hanged one week later, on April 16, 1868.

Only death sometimes is not as simple as we expect. In fact, the State of California had to legally murder the murderer twice. On the first try, the trap didn't open completely, and Lardue swung by his sinewy neck for over two minutes, gasping for air and wheezing expressive, if indecipherable, curses at his executioners. The second time was successful, if that is the fitting expression.

Chapter Seven

Late afternoon light spilled over Muybridge's photographs, smearing the gold of the opulent sun onto the jumble of black-and-white images. On the wall hung two shots by Matthew Brady, one of a staunch, sun-bronzed Union lieutenant, his blood staining the gray uniform, the life fading away from unstoppable seepage. In the other photo, Brady's assistant Minter had caught the misty Gettysburg hills moments before the cannons erupted. In the foreground, Brady and Muybridge stood up to their waists in clover, of all things, and there was a ripe cornfield in the middle distance. The framing hills looked sleepy and pastoral, not hinting at the unprecedented butchery to come. For here ten thousand young men would be slaughtered in seventy-two hours—the largest mass murder in human history. Muybridge averted his gaze from the landscape, unable to shut out the importuning throngs of dead men in his mind's eye.

Later, peering into a magnifying glass, slowly, one by one, Edward scrutinized his stereo shots of the robbery. Instead of examining Wilson Lardue's feral, knifelike face, the photographer concentrated on a blurred background figure. "Johny," Edward muttered aloud. "Damn it, Johny, come into bloody damn focus!" For a fleeting instant the younger bandit's nose and forehead snapped into discernible outline then, an instant later, the image blurred, turned indistinct. Muybridge blinked rapidly, closed his eyes, shook his head hard. The limits of his technology snapped shut, like bars of a cage, and, frustrated, he hurled the magnifying glass at a wall. Luckily, the glass did not shatter.

Muybridge took three steps backward, spun on his heel, and punched at the row of hanging prints of the stagecoach robbery. The photos hung from a clothesline strung across the room, and the photographer moved lightly on his toes down the line, ducking his head as though from an opponent's blows and delivering straight, rapid jabs. The door opened as he shot a crisp left hook at the sixth and final photograph.

He smiled absentmindedly as Holly shucked off her gray cloak. She crossed to the row of photos, greeting Edward with a passing kiss. The act was familiar yet intense, sensual enough to suggest that they had not yet settled into domestic routine. She briefly clung to him, trying to interpose herself between Muybridge and his obsession. He felt literally suspended between the problem presented by the half-dozen miniature, dangling images and Holly's enticing lips.

"Hard at work?" she asked, breathing warmly into his ear, her face inches away.

Holly's rich, invasive fragrance struck its usual distracting blow. He sidestepped the stirrings, pointing to his prints. "Holly, tell me, does this fellow here"—his finger stopped at the background figure of the bandit he called Johny—"look like Lardue?"

Holly examined the first photograph, then moved down the line, recognizing now that each of the paired stereoscopic prints was slightly more exposed. "I understand what you'd like me to say, but I cannot see the resemblance. The stereo isn't big enough to give you sufficient detail. Plus, he, whoever he is, moved. No, I can't make out his face."

Half-amused, half-annoyed he listened to his own words parroted back. How much she enjoyed making the occasional photo. And that first time in his new darkroom, her wonder as the image of San Francisco Bay floated up out of the developing bath touched him. He studied the last print—the one that gave him a glimmer of hope for a positive identification—while she crossed the room behind him.

He heard a door open. Edward did not think of Holly again until, in his peripheral vision, he picked up a white flash. He saw the dress settle on the beige-and-red-striped loveseat, a costly house-gift from Holly for his rooms. He accepted the ironically named loveseat—too small, too fragile for any true act of love—because he was tired of fending off her generosity. In her petticoats Holly looked more elegant than the pair of long-legged storks that decorated the lacquer Chinese screen. Another expensive present. His rooms, her rooms—how pleased he was that she was almost always here.

"So Stanford approached you after the trial." A third petticoat draped itself on the loveseat's arm, her warm body's smells misting over the furniture. "Did he offer the gifted photographer a proposition?"

She left her clothing scattered around the room, half-covering chairs, draped over a settee, casually collapsed on the floor. *Slovenly*, he thought again. But the criticism was obliterated as he watched Holly raise her long arms to discard another petticoat. How could mere arms be so compelling? Was it that they led to her shoulders, neck, and face, then farther down through a blazon of her indisputable charms?

"He thanked me. Ward chimed in and asked if I always win my bets." Edward paused. "Technically, I don't feel like I had won."

She laughed, baring the comical out-of-line tooth. "You didn't tell them that, did you?"

"Of course not." As usual, the implied critique annoyed him.

Having spent so much time abroad, Holly believed he was her America, her newfound land. Like the country itself, enthusiasm and curiosity and expertise combined with a reality-denying naïveté. Did Edward believe his talent insulated him from Stanford's Machiavellian machinations? Did the photographer actually think that Stanford would be a beneficent patron?

"Oh, and the governor invited me to dine."

" 'The governor,' the governor is it?" The tone was light, but to Holly the honorific clanked like a counterfeit coin against a till. Stanford's detractors nicknamed him "the Counter Jumper," a hardware store owner who had staked countless miners to their food and Ames shovels and Ames picks and a plethora of panning and mining gear while gouging them with such exorbitant interest rates that he ended up holding princely quantities of the gold they broke their backs for—those scant few who struck it rich. "When are you dining with your 'governor?' "

"Thursday next."

"Not a single penny's reward for all the thousands you recovered for him?"

The photographer shooed the question away: "That wasn't our arrangement."

"Please help me understand: You need money, you won't accept it from me. What about Stanford?'"

"I already explained this to you, Holly," he replied with mounting impatience, "I have a strategy."

"He's not trustworthy. He'll have his own agenda."

"Of course he'll have his own agenda. That's not the question."

A dazzling petticoat wrapped itself around the loveseat. In her undergarments she was all straps and intriguing silk, intricate overlapping intimacies. Just under the layers her body awaited, lean, strong, remarkably smooth and shapely with those lithely muscled legs. Even across the room he could conjure up her moist, fleshy smell, somehow akin to the slippery opulence of oysters, only finer still. He reshouldered the argument as though lifting a weighty stone. "Stanford offers me what no one else in the country can, surely you see that."

"Admitted. Only you have no way of predicting how devious he'll be."

"He wants my professional competence. That's simple enough."

She plunged on. "You believe you're in the driver's seat, that you can establish the rules of the game. It will not work that way, Edward dear." She wanted to nudge him away from Stanford's practiced ruthlessness. She knew these men, her father's colleagues. She wanted to surround and insulate Edward, to offer her own uncompromised largesse so that he could do what he did best, his work. Why did he resist her aid?

"Suppose they crown me official photographer of 'the greatest human undertaking ever mounted?'"

"Suppose indeed . . ." But she was on dubious turf here, since Edward was uniquely qualified for the job.

To date, their lives had been relatively solitary. Their intense reunion in San Francisco, setting up his rooms and studio, furnishing her rooms—even the running debate about his and hers—all of that had been an extension of the honeymoon, with the two of them virtually alone together in the raucous, polyglot, teeming city. Now she felt outside forces—beyond her control—closing in, hemming up their idyll.

* * *

As she dressed, Holly watched him working—the familiar half-quizzical, half-expectant expression trenched temporary furrows in his smooth brow. How well his mind matched his body. Mind and body were restless counterpunchers—tense, darting, rarely at rest. Not systematic but swarming, reacting, able to encompass complex issues not by mental organization or a grand unitary theory but by bouncing off a problem's surfaces, correcting, compensating, figuring yet one more angle of attack. He was visceral, with a gyroscope's dizzying yet unconfoundable sense of balance. (He'd shown her the magical instrument in a recent copy of his *Scientific American* magazine.) Movement was his element—like hers, she thought again. Pleasurable idea. Only after their lovemaking did he relax and drift, and that was the closest he came to repose. Even in sleep he remained restless, entwining his body in the sheets, the quilt, her thighs, calves, arms, breasts.

She emerged from behind the Chinese screen in an ankle-length off-white gown. Her dense auburn hair was pulled back, which set off the cheekbones, the haunting hollows of her cheeks. Muybridge, who looked up from his prints to escape the blurred, almost identical, images, saw still another face—the severe, ascetic Holly Hughes. He knew that Gérôme—had she stayed in Paris, had the old man not offended her, had he not died—could have gone on painting Holly forever.

She fastened the other pointe shoe. Her weight rested on one tensed calf while the free leg was bent at the knee, foot extended, each toe joint articulated. Oval face angled down, neck arched, back curved, to Muybridge's eye she was all roundings, firm taperings, graceful swellings, no straight lines.

She pushed off her left leg and began to wheel around the room, making long-limbed ballet lines. He studied her with particular attention, filing away distinct, fleeting images, while at the same time uneasily aware that each of these pictures would fade, that his leaky memory would not retain the spectrum of changing expressions. Muybridge's deep desire was to stop time and fix each particular instant forever. He cursed the arbitrary limits of what his eye or mind or memory could retain. It was like being chained in place in a magnificent picture gallery. He stood immobile as one image was placed before him and immediately whisked away, then another and yet another equally compelling thrust in its place. On and on until beauty itself devolved into a titillating blur, too fleeting to be held and embraced and fully appreciated.

Her mood changed. She elevated onto her toes and slowly began to turn. The broad expanse of forehead glistened as Holly twirled faster, faster. She spun on and on, her eyes flashing at him like a lighthouse beam at each full circuit, her smile ever so slightly distended by the rotation. Holly slowed, then, without pausing, extended her long right leg forward, left leg back and languorously lowered herself to the floor, completing the split. Fully extended, she swirled her torso in measured, elegant circles, then—how she did it he would never know—brought her legs back together as effortlessly as a pair of scissors closing. She rose from the floor as though lifted up by an invisible hook above. Instantly, she executed a flying cartwheel, a deft backflip, and climaxed with a leaping forward kick, raising her leg in front of her until it grazed her forehead. Watching Holly left him wrung out.

"Darling, that was wonderful—airborne poetry."

"Which did you enjoy more?" She patted her face with a towel. "The dance or the dancer?"

"Impossible to separate. I *have* to photograph you dancing. It's been haunting me since we met. I have to catch you in motion."

"But even I know that isn't possible. You've spent the last two months explaining that your equipment isn't able to. Even if I move slowly, the image blurs, yes?"

"Precisely the point—it's my challenge, my Grail. Imagine, you in motion! You *and* motion!"

"You're a dreamer and a fanatic."

"The worst kind." He took her in his arms and began to waltz Holly around the room. She supplied accompaniment, humming softly.

As they danced, she slid forward against his body, so that Muybridge took more of her weight. Edward and Holly danced on and on. His parlor wheeled by in a controlled spin, the six almost identical photographs of the robbery and Brady's Civil War battle prints blurring together as they circled. Still holding her, Edward halted by a table where, with his free hand, he flipped open the latest album—Holly enveloped in a flowing cape, hair piled up on her head like a haughty Russian tsarina. The page turned to reveal a girlish Holly Hughes emerging from the bath, damp ringlets framing her face, her body turned toward the camera—and him.

"When you're in front of me, I can hold your smile. . . ." The next shot caught Holly in profile, which emphasized her strong nose and full, expressive mouth, the substantial jaw which anchored those delicate bones and lent her face power. "Or that particular profile." He turned another page. Here Holly's pupils were luminous, liquid, so large they seemed magnified. "I can catch a certain expression in your eyes." Muybridge flipped forward again. She wondered how her face could assume so many shadings and expressions. Did it indicate uncertainty, weakness of character?

"The frustrating thing . . ." Muybridge continued intently. She adored this mood. "What drives me to distraction is, I can never hold all of your expressions together in my mind." More Hollys, all beautiful, quickly riffled past as he rummaged forward then flipped back in his photo album. "I cannot keep you complete"—Muybridge cradled her face in his hands—"until you're actually here." He paused to look at her. "When you're in front of me, all the expressions flow together. They become one, the being herself, you." He kissed her. "When you're here, all the pieces fuse together with a little explosive charge."

"A *'little'* charge?"

"Oh," he replied, smiling, "sometimes it's more, uh, potent." They turned to each other hungrily.

The aroma percolated down into her sleep, so she smelled coffee before she woke. A cup and a hard roll sat on a tray on her side of Muybridge's big bed. The cup pinned down a note.

> Memorable evening. Love to linger but the Governor's gardens call. Tonight at 8.
>
> Yr. devoted photographer

Luxuriating, she sank back into the down pillows. She felt a rich, teasing exhilaration return as her body recalled their lovemaking. How satisfied and full she had felt. Yet, in the buttery morning light, how easily she could begin once more. Her fingers moved languidly downward, coming temptingly near. . . . He had said, "Your breast my pillow, your thigh my feather bed." She found him interesting, charming, adorable, amusing, loving. She launched a chain of many words to encircle this man.

The smile started between her legs. She quietly laughed, yet the heat kept rising. *Strumpet,* she thought to herself complacently. *Why not more satisfaction?* He woke her in the dark, then fingered and tongued her until she came; a little later he'd bellowed as he climaxed. Afterward, he said, "It's fortunate my downstairs neighbors are in Oregon."

"Imagine what Mrs. Smythe would say."

"Do I have to?"

Imitating Mrs. Smythe's faux Oxbridge accent, Holly continued, "My deah-h-h, did you hear those dreadful cats wail-ing for hours? Ghast-ly, really. Kept me up the en-tie-her night."

His head shook on her belly—sex and laughter, laughter and sex.

Since her arrival, Holly had been scouring San Francisco's barely extant feminist circles for a potential ally or two. To date, only a few candidates had emerged. Did her halfhearted pursuit of the local feminists have anything to do, she asked herself, with her spending more and more time in his rooms? Her clothes were scattered everywhere. *Strumpet* and *sloven,* she mused complacently. And, for the present, her own rooms were alien, an arm's-length fiction—she'd barely moved in; really, she lived here, with him. So why did she behave so hurtfully with all the posturing about the sacred issue of her own rooms? Why not just give them up?

A quarter of an hour later, after intense stretching, Holly stood on one leg and twirled. With each revolution her head whipped around and focused on the same spot on his wall, the heavy braid lashing at her throat.

A loud knock interrupted her routine. Holly threw on a long robe, opened the door. Before her stood an oval-faced, balding middle-aged man with a carbuncular, alcohol-ravaged nose, droopy lips, and rubbery clownlike features.

"Edward May-bitch live here?" The spongy cheeks trembled, the speaker's mouth yawed open, revealing an uneven aggregation of rotting teeth. His tone hovered between unctuous and belligerent as though, not knowing which tack to pursue, he was trying both.

The man peered over her shoulder into the apartment. Holly closed the door a bit and slid into his sight line. The man reached into the pocket of a threadbare gray waistcoat and produced a slim, official-looking document. "I got me a notice here . . ." He shook the notice at her like a flaccid stick, rested a dirt-spotted, asymmetrical pince-nez unsteadily on his nose and began to read: "To repossess two cameras, four Zeiss lenses, a develo—".

Her mind at full tilt, she cut him off, "How much does Mr. Muybridge owe your client?"

The bailiff eye's reeled to the bottom of the page, dragged up the figure. "Uh, two hundred fifty-seven dollars and forty-three cents."

"Hand me the document!" He inched to the left, and she glided back to block his line of sight. The absurd spying and blocking game continued—when the bailiff moved one way, she slipped over to intercept his view. Finally, he stood still.

A brief glance at the notice sufficed. She thought: *So that's why he left New York. Not because of Brady and the offer of partnership*.

As soon as Holly's brow furrowed with concern, the bailiff assumed he had the upper hand. "I don't want to make threats of a physical kind. . . ."

He took a shambling half pace forward. Holly strode to her left so adamantly he staggered back a step. She clenched her right fist professionally, thrust out her assertive jaw. "Under no circumstances will you enter this room! Is that clear?"

The bailiff's head retreated a few inches.

"Wait here!" she commanded. His rubbery face stretched and dished, subsiding into an uneasy smirk. She shut and chained the door. Inside, a less belligerent, smiling Holly Hughes sat down at Edward's antique cherry desk, removed a slim leather portfolio from the bottom drawer, and with a firm hand and soaring heart wrote a bank draft on her account for $257.43. She thought about waving her walking stick at the man to see terror further scramble his unsettled features. But she passed on that and marched back. At the door, she handed the draft to the bailiff.

"The debt is paid. *In full.* I never want to see you here again. Do you understand?"

His skulking eyes avoided her glare. He accepted the slip of paper, silently mouthed the written sum as he read, checked the bank's address, officiously folded the draft in two, and slipped it inside the elongated subpoena. Blindly, he probed for the opening in the vest pocket of his greasy waistcoat.

She closed the door and leaned back against it, a beatific smile illuminating her features. Someday soon, she would settle the matter with him. Edward would be enraged, indignant, "humiliated." Yes, his absurd male pride would demand a reckoning. But meanwhile, if the photographer needed a patron, she could not imagine him finding a more loving or generous one.

Chapter Eight

In the middle distance, the picturesque fields of Leland Stanford's Palo Alto estate were dotted with low-bellied, suede-colored beeves and lustrous, long-stemmed horses. Closer to the governor and his rotund guest, a three-board white fence circled the mile and a quarter racetrack, inscribing parallel white lines across the manicured grass. The larger of the concentric tracks was alive with thoroughbreds moving counter-clockwise at different paces through their workouts. In the inner circle, sulkies and drivers circled clockwise around the dirt oval. Standing at the railings, trainers and a slew of Stanford's equestrian personnel observed the horses' gaits and clocked the racers' times, transcribing each workout into the proper columns on precisely ruled charts.

Leland Stanford leaned back in his steel-reinforced portable field chair while his guest, Abbot Berkeley, stood tensely, infrequently puffing on a much-chewed blunt cigar. Berkeley was five feet, five inches, as round as he was tall. At forty-eight, Berkeley, the West Coast's leading shipping magnate, seemed miraculously youthful, with baby-smooth skin. Privately, Collis Ward insisted it wasn't a miracle at all: "The man's preserved in blubber."

As a horse and sulky approached the two millionaires, Stanford raised his field glasses. Both men concentrated on the high-stepping gait of the governor's celebrated trotter, Occident. The animal thudded closer, hooves shedding an unbroken spray of dirt.

"There!" he shouted. "Right there!" The governor pointed at Occident as Harry Harnett, his sulky driver and chief trainer, wheeled by their positions at the rail.

"You're mad!" Berkeley declared curtly as he chomped down on the cigar butt.

"You're blind!" Stanford retorted. "I swear I saw all four hooves off the ground at the same instant!"

Abbot Berkeley emitted a deprecatory laugh. "Not even your charlatan's eye is quick enough to see what isn't there, Leland. Every single horseman and driver I spoke to, even your exercise boys—"

"They know nothing!"

"Frankly, Stanford, this argument is tedious, pointless, a yawn producer. Of course if you care to back up this harebrained conjecture of yours with a wager, *Governor*. . . ."

Stanford knew he was correct. After all, he had just observed all four of Occident's hooves simultaneously off the ground. And he'd observed the phenomenon dozens of times before. But Stanford could not prove the fact. "What would you say to fifteen thousand dollars' worth of conjecture? Would that alleviate your boredom a little?"

Abbot Berkeley lit up again. Taking an appreciative pull at the stumpy cigar, his ferret eyes followed the strapping trotter into the far turn. "You've got yourself an extremely pricey bet."

Muybridge waited in front of the baroque-frame building that bore the generic label: OPERA HOUSE. He surveyed the crowd and, quantitatively and qualitatively, reckoned that Holly was doing very well indeed. Carriages and gigs, four-in-hands and coaches, an elegant brown leather barouche, a high-slung phaeton, a one-horse brougham, and a square landau transported fashionable San Francisco to this unique evening of transplanted European culture. Three of the Central Pacific's Big Four—Chester Crocker, Mark Hopkins, and Hollis Huntington—had already filed in, accompanied by their bedecked, bejeweled wives. Each had acknowledged Muybridge's presence by a word or hearty handshake. Horatio Dirk, *Clarion* editor, and his star reporter, Luke Ransom, had chatted amiably with the photographer about the much-awaited, much-discussed debut of Miss Hughes.

Edward glanced up at the large, hideous poster of Holly. Below the garish rendering of this surrogate Holly on toe in a white tutu ran the legend:

MISS HOLLY HUGHES

RENOWNED EUROPEAN DANCER

AND LECTURER ON MOVEMENT

IN PERFORMANCE

ONE WEEK ONLY

JUNE 11-17

Citing venerated theatrical superstition, Holly had barred him from a backstage visit prior to the performance. In fact, she clung to her privacy. She needed to stretch and unlimber and gradually negotiate her way into the elusive and mysterious tempos of her body so that, when she stepped onto the stage, she would be primed to move. No distractions, no nervous chatter, not even heartfelt wishes would do.

Standing outside the theater, the photographer reckoned he was more nervous than Holly herself. She was about to fling herself on stage and whirl about for one hour and ten minutes, while all he could do is lounge stiffly in his formal clothes with his heart wedged halfway up his esophagus and hope that everything went, well, brilliantly.

A stunning blonde alighted from a gig and made her sportive way through the crowd, drawing dozens of approving male and critically appraising female eyes in her wake. She had piquant, lively features, a saucy upturned nose, palpably soft, round cheeks, and a shower of golden ringlets down to her shoulders. She boasted a pretty bow-shaped mouth, with a smile that intimated rare delights. As she approached Muybridge, her smoldering eyes caught his—the effect was dazzling. Muybridge marveled that he should feel such a potent charge from another woman on the night of Holly's premiere. Yet his eyes followed as she sashayed forward, her golden aura diffusing through the crowd—ducats scattered to the masses by a beneficent, if suspect, queen.

* * *

Backstage, Holly rose to her toes in the minuscule dressing room. She had shoved a rickety table and a chair into one crowded corner, but still could not swing her arms freely, for fear of hitting a projecting shelf. As she eased into a constricted version of her warm-up, Holly tried to chase away the butterflies rising and wheeling and diving about in her stomach. The fluttering impulses worked both as enemies and as goads, byproducts of anxiety and the surfeit of energy that always percolated up before a performance.

San Francisco's Opera House was a scaled-down replica of the Vienna Opera, a steep, intimate theater seating only 324. Red plush covered the walls and every seat. From the ceiling dangled baroque crystal chandeliers, and all that glittering glass reflected the glories of outlandish plaster ornamentation held hostage by ranks of cavorting pink putti and pudgy sexless cupids. A three-story red velvet curtain—now drawn—screened the audience from the stage. Luke Ransom contended that the Opera House sported the decor of a whorehouse without a whiff of its utility.

When Mr. and Mrs. Leland Stanford swept in, trailed by Collis Ward, Muybridge fretfully occupied a post at the back of the Opera. The ex-governor marched up and offered Muybridge his usual crushing handshake. "We're looking forward to the performance."

Muybridge responded, "It will be a revelation. But I feel as nervous as a bridegroom."

The remark drew a subdued chuckle from Leland Stanford. Mrs. Stanford, a quiet woman who looked rather heavier than the last time Edward saw her, smiled with distracted politeness. They moved off to their seats.

In the front row, dressed in a modish waistcoat and high-cut, tightly fitted trousers, lounged a tall stranger, displaying more stocking than virtually all of San Francisco's gentlemen combined. He was handsome in a brutal way—stony slablike forehead, hawkish nose that picked up the forehead's thrust, and dominant jaw. His most striking feature was his brilliant blue eyes, cold and bright and, like diamonds, able to suggest great shifting depths. The stranger stared fixedly at the spot where the two vertical halves of the curtain joined, as though trying to peer backstage through the curtain's most vulnerable juncture.

The gaslights dimmed; the crowd hushed. The five-piece orchestra, hired at Holly's expense—she had paid for the entire undertaking—struck up a popular romantic waltz. The curtain parted and, on a bare stage, Holly Hughes appeared in a light green, almost transparent tunic gathered underneath her breasts and at her hips. Below, an ankle-length culotte was slit up the front to allow her legs unrestricted movement. Looking at her, the men and women in the audience responded restively—this was a daring costume. She stood there unabashed, her body offering a classical anatomy lesson—that full, mature body with its long-limbed strength and feminine litheness.

Hard to believe, Muybridge considered, *she was once a pudgy child.* Now he felt uneasy seeing those shapely legs and her swelling chest—formerly his exclusive domain—on public display. Was he prudish? Jealous? Not exactly; he was proud of her beauty. It was her boldness, the courting of prurient, sanctioned public lust that unsettled him. Desire and censoriousness vied, crackling the Opera House air. He could already hear the livid tongue-wagging about her provocative display. Yet why not? Didn't she insist that the body was to be celebrated? Meanwhile, the assembled sets of eyes traveled up and down and over the full curves; eyes swarmed and tarried to admire or deplore her ample breasts, those sensually curving legs, full thighs, proud face.

Holly remained absolutely still, letting the audience absorb her form. She drew deep breaths, to calm herself and also to impose her rhythm on the audience. Taking her cue from the harpist's rapid, ascending arpeggio, suddenly she exploded into action—leaped high into the air. From rest to movement without apparent transition—the audience sucked in its breath. Then she appeared to be everywhere at once, twirling and gliding over the bare stage, rising and dipping and spinning to the very edge of the apron until she threatened to sail out over the audience.

Her movements imparted grace to the columned backdrop, lowly floorboards, and formerly neutral stage. Like an unearthly, silvery, gravity-defying bird, Holly soared and wheeled and spun in midair. Her hands and fingers descended and flowed and swept and ascended, her feet and arms and long legs, which she could somehow extend even in midleap, drew expressive serpentines or rendered swift, potent outlines which modulated, without apparent transition, into soft willowy gestures.

Shaping and changing and infusing the air with pleasure or poignancy or unutterable loveliness, her fingers and limbs and the many faces of Holly Hughes told exotic tales, imparted flowing fantasies to the rapt onlookers.

The music accompanying the ballet changed into the sprightly popular tune "Uncle Ned." Without warning, Holly did a backflip, then a gliding leap which led to a front somersault and a slick forward roll, followed by a series of smart tucks and rolls, and then, incredibly, she stood erect, the body immobile as a statue, on one unbending toe. The collective gasp was like a shout. And Muybridge, seated in the second row, exulted.

As he inwardly hoorayed and applauded for this remarkable woman, Holly's eyes brushed and caught Edward's. Always she found his eyes there, supporting, encouraging, buoying her.

Now Holly executed a blur of cartwheels, a sequence of flashy backbends and jackknife twists, spin rolls and standing flips that carried her back and forth and down and up the stage. She was in the middle of her dangerous one-legged leap when her heel caught and she almost lost her balance. A pained voice blurted, "No!" Not a single individual in the theater wanted the flawless execution marred. Somehow Holly regained her footing and continued through daring acrobatic feats, climaxing with an agonizingly slow split punctuated by a haughty toss of her head and a corkscrew flourish of her hand.

She could feel the crowd imperceptibly swaying in their seats, in her orbit. From now on she could "dance" the audience; seated, they would move along with her. As her eyes randomly surveyed beyond the gaslights, suddenly Holly spotted Jacques Fauconier.

He shook his substantial head approvingly, smiled an insinuating smile. This smile insisted: There would always be a place for him within her. The absurd irony struck her, that Jacques Fauconier, whom she hadn't seen in almost a year, had arrived at precisely the wrong moment—the very richest, sweetest moment of her life with Edward. Perverse master of timing, she thought, as though, six thousand miles away, Fauconier had sniffed out her happiness and came bolting over the sea to plague and harass her or, at the very least, contest the issue of primacy. *Jacques, here,* she thought dumbly.

Stunned, Holly worked automatically now, drawing on a reservoir of years of practice and performance, a mine shaft that tunneled into the core of her being and would've enabled her to dance in her sleep.

She made a quick offstage change into thick wooden clogs then, to "Oh, Susanna," a song she detested, beat out a resounding tattoo with her cloddish footgear. She glanced from Edward to Fauconier. There each sat, unaware of the other, yet in such terrible, almost comic, proximity—Edward could've reached out and touched Jacques's shoulder.

The clamorous ringing of her shoes insulated Holly from the two lovers below. She tapped faster, faster until the wooden boards resounded under the staccato attack, and the eardrums of onlookers in those first rows ached from the hammer rhythms. At the height of this barrage, her torso moving easily, her legs striking like freewheeling, expressive pistons, Holly's mind moved ahead to her next costume change. She thumped offstage left, leaving her audience's ears still ringing. She slipped off the thick clogs and began the change into soft leather shoes and a floor-length skirt as the musicians broke from frenzy into Stephen Foster's syrupy "Swanee River."

Holly was so distracted by her lovers' proximity that the costume change took longer than she'd calculated, and she had to signal the violinist to play the first five measures of the theme again. The repetition caused an awkward entrance. Meanwhile, she bemoaned the Frenchman's startling, jack-in-the-box appearance. Holly cast a tortured peek—Edward's eyes met hers, with Fauconier's a split second behind—only one row and two seats apart. An instantaneous thought: Had she been perfidiously waiting for Jacques all along? *No,* she concluded. But there was the hotly contested issue of her rooms. Her body stiffened, Holly's breathing locked. She hesitated yet another unconscionable moment as the music again reached her cue, then Holly Hughes forced herself back on stage to ringing applause.

A patch of pure white sand had just been smoothed across the apron, which brought Holly closer to the pit—and her two suitors. The applause continued until a voice shouted, "Silence!" And the house grew reverently still.

The change from clanging wooden clogs to the smooth, sibilant hiss of the sand dance soothed everyone but the performer. All eyes stayed riveted on her as, under her feet, the sand whispered in hushed, brushlike strokes, a lilting lullaby. Her feet cunningly raked the sand into complex, shifting patterns, evoking a sonorous hum—like a mother quieting an infant—as she moved toward the side of the stage and deftly attached a string to her skirt. As she danced, lulling her audience with somnolent rhythms, Holly struck the first pose of her "transformation dance"—the country maid.

She strolled and sashayed and postured innocently until she worked her way back to stage right. The violinist pulled on the barely visible cord, and the first layer of costume was whisked from her body. The audience audibly inhaled its surprise while, before their eyes, Holly Hughes became a Mexican senorita. She danced a tarantella, her feet a moving blur, her body angled back so steeply it seemed that she would topple over. Then the string anchored to her costumes peeled away another layer and instantly she turned into a flamenco dancer, her boneless torso skewed and raked back, head haughtily upright, eyes hooded, and heels loudly flashing. She rhythmically stomped her way through three minutes of the dance, the full skirt whipping and rising and trailing in erotic arabesques around her exposed thighs, the skirt seemingly as animated as the fan she brandished thrillingly above her head. Eros pulsed from her as she pursued an imaginary partner, moving with heated strides around, near, around, closer to the phantom male. Her passionate abandon, Holly's rigorous virtuosity . . . Muybridge could almost see the air trembling in her wake. The violinist jerked the string again: The formfitting flamenco costume peeled away, the fan fluttered off stage, and Holly leaped high in a spotless white tutu. Transformed into an aristocratic Russian ballerina, Holly Hughes soared across the stage. Her body, her arms drew charmed spirals, delicate ellipses, entrancing lines. Utterly at home in ballet, her authority and grace dazzled, it overwhelmed her audience.

Of course Muybridge had seen her rehearse many times. Yet he had seen only separate parts of a routine or, sometimes, an extended series of movements that she'd interrupt to alter footwork or accentuate a gesture. He'd never witnessed a complete run-through in full costume and makeup. Edward watched this woman of changing faces and moods as she reconstituted herself, as she flaunted a disorienting range of character and movement. She amazed and astounded the dazzled photographer, who, until this night, thought he knew her almost as well as he knew himself.

Meanwhile, Holly twirled and glissaded, spun and leaped. She dipped and turned and effortlessly soared. Floating above the stage, her body seemed held aloft by the air itself—as her arms drew poignant curves and shapely arabesques through yielding, supportive space.

She finished her finale and bowed, triumphant and exhausted. She bowed again, bowed once more to Edward himself, trying to evade Fauconier's riveting eyes that were perched so close to her lover, then Holly retreated behind the towering scarlet curtain.

The audience, led by Edward Muybridge and the tall, thickset, elegant Frenchman, erupted. They cheered and they clapped. They yelled and stomped and demanded more. "Encore! Encore!" filled the air. The audience roared their appreciation until the crystal chandeliers tinkled in sympathetic accord. "Bravo!" Edward shouted at the top of his lungs. Muybridge believed he had never been happier, he felt so overjoyed and profoundly moved by her—and for her. "Bravissima! Bravissima!" cried the insistent, brutishly handsome stranger to the left, one row in front of him.

As the applause continued, Holly parted the curtain and stepped onto the apron, sending a shower of fine grains of sand into the pit. Smiling, ebullient, relaxed, she bowed with auspicious grace to the wildly applauding crowd. Leland Stanford caught the photographer's eye and nodded his approval. At that moment, Muybridge believed that the entire world was in tune.

Finally, Holly held up her hands to quiet the audience. The ovation swelled for fully another two minutes, but eventually individual shouts became audible, then scattered cheers, thumps, and claps. Muybridge and Jacques Fauconier were still pounding their aching palms together when Holly began to speak.

"Thank you, thank you with all my heart. I'm deeply pleased that you appreciate my work."

Stiff, a little stiff, Muybridge thought, as hoarse, frenzied voices rose again and chants of "Encore! Encore!" shook the hall. Holly waited patiently, until hands were too sore to clap, throats too rasped to cheer. Her eyes shifted between the two men—talent, innocence, and energy the one; cynicism, charm, and expertise the other. It struck her that such comparisons were demeaning to all three of them. She raised her palms again asking for quiet.

"Thank you. Thank you very much. I want you to understand that my performance tonight would not have been possible for most women in the audience." The assembled quieted gradually, cast adrift by this statement. "Not because of the training I've been fortunate to have, not because of any talent I might possess."

Muybridge's mind plunged ahead, but he could not read Holly's direction here, which made him supremely nervous.

"Tonight, in lieu of an encore, my friends, I would like to say a few words about dress reform for women."

Holly Hughes had transported the audience and, for the moment, the sense memory of her artful loveliness shielded her. Holly parted the curtain and dragged a slate easel onto the apron. On it, Muybridge—and 323 other spectators—recognized a large drawing of a corset. His impulse was to laugh and cry at the same time.

"As I said, a word about dress reform—and the cor-set." Muybridge detected a slight tremor in her voice as she chopped the word in two. Meaning, he guessed, that she, too, was nervous about what would follow.

At the sight of the drawing the audience had quieted. At the word *cor-set,* onlookers hushed. Few of the fashionable women or men in the Opera House had ever uttered the word in public. In San Francisco in 1868, such a pronouncement was an insolent vulgarity, though each woman seated in the theater was tautly encircled by the selfsame garment; and earlier that evening each had voluntarily gone through the tedious process of self-encasement, stuffing their torsos into an intricate array of buckles and ties and hoops of bone and steel.

"Nature consecrated the shrines of our bodies, but in our time, fashion is destroying them. Cor-sets"—once again she sliced the word into two cringe-evoking syllables—"literally cripple and even murder women, for these devices deprive us of the natural muscle tone necessary for life, indispensable for childbearing."

"This is an outrage!" Muybridge did not have to turn to recognize Leland Stanford's shout.

The governor was livid. He felt deeply insulted. He grasped his wife's hand, and, if he could have, he would have stopped up her ears. He judged Miss Hughes's outspokenness a threat to decency, a challenge to the rules by which he and the community abided. If only she had been content to remain quiet, to woo with her beauty and talent. Muybridge watched in impotent anguish, his eyes locked on his love. At the same time, the photographer suspected that the governor's eyes were fixed on him. Edward thought: *In other eras, Holly would have self-righteously gone to the stake for her vision—along with other so-called witches.*

On stage, Holly Hughes pointed to the white chalk drawing on the slate as confidently as a schoolteacher instructing pupils about the times table. "This is a typical corset, which I daresay most, if not all, of the women seated here tonight are wearing on their persons."

In front of Holly, over three hundred men and women sat in pained silence, as yet unwilling to destroy the multistranded, fragile web of beauty she had woven for them.

Her pointer traced the hourglass shape of the undergarment, moving inexorably down toward the upper thighs. "As all women know—" A sibilant hiss, startlingly loud in the silence, erupted. A swelling wave of discontent swept through the house as people grumbled and murmured and shifted in their seats.

"The cor-set has its own tight waist." The pointer limned the layers of the midriff. "Underneath, we pile on what are prudishly referred to as the 'lower garments.' Each of these has its own perverse binding."

Someone roared, "Stop this!" Another plaintively gasped out, "Please!"

From isolated spots around the hall, booing and hissing erupted. Muybridge tensely gripped the arms of his seat, as though trying to hold back the rising flood of indignation. "Disgusting!" The first voice again, ordering her, "You must stop this! Now!"

The large man in the first row leaped up, turned, and addressed the entire house: "Kindly allow Miss Hughes to finish!" The opulent French accent filled the hall. Stunned by his outburst, the Opera House stilled. Muybridge examined the foreigner, who insouciantly sank back down into his seat and stretched his long legs into the aisle.

On stage, Holly took advantage of Fauconier's temerity, understanding that she had only a brief interlude. "Usually *twelve* to *sixteen* layers of cloth gird the abdominal muscles—our God-given muscles, those muscles indispensable to breathing, to walking upright, to the sacred act of giving birth. . . ." In the gaslight, Holly's face assumed an aura, not unlike the illumination surrounding the head of a New Testament saint. Holly was fulfilling her destiny—and sealing her fate in provincial San Francisco.

"Scandalous!" "Filth!" "Obscene!" Derisive shouts showered down, like an artillery barrage landing closer and closer to its target. Muybridge spun around to identify her accusers, but voices were everywhere. Meanwhile, Holly stood defiantly on the apron, a strained smile cramping her generous mouth. A rain of programs hit the stage—a half dozen of those wretched effigies of Holly Hughes scattered at her feet.

People were up and moving now. Couples indignantly stalked up the sloping aisle toward the rear. Well-dressed women streamed toward the exits accompanied by their sheltering, outraged male companions. The theater surged away, trying to escape contamination. She stood at the edge of the stage and yelled at retreating backs, "You find it repulsive to listen to what I say? It is too shocking for your ears?"

A big, agonized voice pleaded, "Enough! Enough!"

"Women are forced to wear them working in the fields, in factories, on the streets. They break ribs. They contribute to weakness and fainting because women cannot breathe properly."

"Shameless!" "Hussy!" "Disgusting!" From all sides voices were hurled like spears at her. Shouting escalated; shoving at the exits grew epidemic.

"Do you, who refuse to listen, who call me shameless, understand how these garments have stunted our growth and damaged our health, how they've bruised and misshapen our internal organs? In the past two decades infant mortality in America has soared! More mothers die in childbirth *here* than in any 'civilized' country on earth! We have incontrovertible medical evidence why. Yet you turn your polite, offended backs and stomp away unwilling to listen to reason because of outmoded propriety."

Edward sat in the second row, seat two, yet it was difficult to hear Holly's voice over the tumult. "This suffering and pain and death is . . . the result of an arbitrary and insane male notion of beauty. The hand-span waist. . . ." She actually measured her own wasp waist with her hands.

"The full bottom—these are harmful, unnecessary, destructive fantasies."

A ripe tomato hit Holly's shoulder, spattering across her spotless tutu. She scornfully picked bits of red pulp from her chest and flicked them to the floor. At the same time she could not help asking herself: *Did someone come to my performance with dinner jammed into a pocket? Did he anticipate being outraged?*

Stanford returned to the orchestra section, detoured down to the second row in order to catch Muybridge's eye. His wife was not in sight. The ex-governor glared at the photographer as if to say, More about this later. Then he spun round and stalked up the aisle. The governor's second departure supplied the official close to the evening—as when a minister reaches the back of his church—and most of the remaining onlookers fled.

Only a remnant of the audience stayed, including the striking blonde woman Muybridge had glimpsed outside the theater. In the front row lounged the bold, elegantly attired Frenchman, while a few seats away from him, Luke Ransom of the *Clarion* scribbled feverishly.

She addressed the near-empty theater, determined to finish her speech. "You are literally killing us, breaking our bodies and spirits, yet you claim to be the offended ones. Even women, my sisters, who suffer every day from this cursed, unnecessary device, won't listen to me—even though their bodies constantly tell them that every word I speak is true."

The house was virtually deserted, so Holly addressed a scattering of retreating backs. "Mark my words, the cor-set is doomed, a temporary aberration of dress. Though no one, not even the Deity herself, knows how long the process will take." Holly shivered as though from cold, crossed her bare arms and chafed them with her palms. Muybridge wanted to take her in his arms. Instead, he leaped to his feet and applauded. Jacques Fauconier clapped and cheered as loudly. The blonde beauty and a handful of others stood and quietly joined in. As Luke Ransom scribbled away, the partisans' enthusiasm ascended thinly toward the ceiling of the towering empty space.

The blonde, who was seated halfway back in the orchestra, meandered out. There followed an awkward moment as both men waited for the other to move. Edward Muybridge held his ground. Jacques

Fauconier studied the photographer, taking his measure. Then, recognizing he was on the American's turf, Fauconier inclined his head slightly, turned, and walked up the aisle.

Backstage, Edward found Holly seated on the floor, trying to work a muscle spasm out of her calf. Sweat-drenched hair clung to her forehead, a snug scalloped cap framing her face. She looked bruised, vulnerable.

Edward dropped to one knee and began to knead the tissue around the knotted muscle as she had instructed him. He worked gently at first, probing the cramp's dimensions, which felt as hard as an oak bole. He felt his way into the wounded flesh, gradually advancing deeper inside her body. Degrees of pain and discomfort swept across Holly's face like cloud shadows trailing over a hillside. He could calibrate the pressure she wanted by the set of her teeth. As his fingers probed the grudgingly loosening muscle, he realized how much pain she had to endure in order to dance so well.

If she'd been in a different mood, he would have suggested how strange it felt administering pain in order to provide relief. He would've joked, *Here's a little poison, dear, to help you recover.*

"When I almost fell . . ." She so wanted to be brave. "Audiences are hostile when you slip or make a mistake they notice. But there are always a dozen small missteps they don't detect. An audience is psychologically conservative: They want to cling to the good work; and they desperately want to return to the moment before you slipped."

His fingers probed and stretched and tried to remold the node in her calf. Now her muscles softened, becoming pliable. He had to be very gentle now.

"They don't come to the theater to watch failure. They pay hard-earned money, they dress up and take an evening off to be transported out of daily life. When the artifice crumbles, they're pitched back on the performer's—and their own—shortcomings. They're not sitting in the theater to see a damned dress rehearsal."

"But you didn't fall, dear."

"I didn't have to fall, don't you see?" she asked impatiently. "If you slip, if you almost fall—like me tonight, out there—you threaten the enchantment. Couldn't you taste their fear and anger? After a slip, they teeter on the edges of their seats outside the self-contained bubble; they're waiting, judging. They don't want you to fail but, for the moment, they know it's possible. If you puncture the illusion, they sit thinking, or rather vaguely feeling, that you're unworthy since you threatened the fantasy that you try to create and they come to experience. Puncture the illusion and you put them on the qui vive.

"Once, in Paris at the Opera, I thought about incorporating a slip into a dance—just to provoke and manipulate the reaction. But I never had the courage to do it."

"You have enough courage, maybe an excess of it."

Her impulse was to slap him, spit at him. Instead, she glared over his shoulder at the spotted wall mirror.

Muybridge rested his tired wrists on her leg while considering this thought: *She can make defeat interesting*. "How can you be so calm about Stanford, about the craven cowardice of your adoring audience? I'd like to take the entire ignorant lot and horsewhip them."

"You don't see what I'm trying to tell you. You don't understand what happened between me and them tonight, do you?"

How bitter she felt, so profoundly bitter that part of her misery was channeled at Edward's lack of understanding, not at the scorn-deserving mob. As though his inability to understand her theory of "The Fall" unmasked a deeper betrayal than the boos and execrations, as though his incomprehension was cousin to the tomato spattering on her abbreviated, formerly spotless white costume.

"It's not just ignorance. A few women and I fight against a closed system, one so ingrained and well-wrought that most Americans, even a man as sensitive and intelligent as you, do not recognize it."

"Closed system?" What the hell was she ranting about now? he asked himself, impatience rising.

"This society deliberately denigrates us. It fails to educate us, insists upon keeping us in the dark. This is not whimsical historical accident. Men—the rulers—are so terrified of women's potential that you—the male—will do anything—regardless of how base or foul—to prevent *us* from realizing ourselves. Aware of it or not, every single person collaborates with this design. For God's sake, Edward, we fought a bloody war—a war you photographed—to free slaves. Women are still slaves. We'll remain slaves until there is a fundamental change."

"I don't like to see you suffer. I hate when these smug fools attack you."

"Of course what happened tonight hurts me. But my pain is what you'll always consider first and, though I appreciate that personally, my pain isn't actually the point." The gray-green eyes softened yet Holly's voice abraded, as though intentionally scouring away Edward's concern for her.

"Theoretically, I thought I was well-positioned to help American women in the struggle. Tonight I feel like a foreigner. Not only rejected and ineffectual . . . Come on, we both know I courted trouble here. I was pushing these provincial bastards hard! What's most difficult is that now I feel utterly useless."

She brushed damp hair off her forehead, revealing a curving brow still flushed with exertion. There was not an inch of her that Edward did not adore—brow, feet, calves, the hairs on her wrist, the soft down on her flushed cheeks.

"Women have to throw away, burn, eliminate those absurd, murderous garments. We have to walk and run and learn gymnastics and swim and ride and dance. And wrestle." Finally, she threw him a smile. "We need to build physical strength in order to liberate our inner strengths. Did you know that today, in 1868, there isn't a single gymnasium in the United States that will allow a woman inside? Not a single cursed one."

He recognized her performance and the impassioned, deliberately provocative lecture as Holly's finest hour. She stood alone, clothed in the transfiguring aura of her beliefs, declaiming truths she knew her public fanatically denied. She had at least half-anticipated the outraged response. What else could she expect? She was right, but why court disaster? Why glory in rubbing San Francisco's upraised, thoroughly provincial noses in her beliefs?

He realized that the Frenchman had applauded as long and as loudly and as sincerely as he. His heart knotting his throat, Edward asked, "And who was the enthusiastic Frenchman?"

How tactful, she thought. "Jacques Fauconier is an old friend. From Paris."

His face fragmented: The full mouth crumpled, a cheek sagged, his right eye glazed over. She had never seen him reveal such uncertainty. Holly almost laughed at herself. Her creed—her precious sexual freedom—was about to be tested. Edward, a skilled emotional sleuth, would now understand the real reason for her own rooms. The subterfuge and special pleading, her selfishness . . . Holly convicted herself, yet . . .

"Would you like to spend time together with . . ." He could not finish the phrase. What could he say? *Your friend?* A badly pronounced rendering of *Fauconier?* Or: *Your old lover?* He was furious, hurt, but he would not plead with her.

"I have to speak with him . . . only for a minute." She resisted the impulse to pledge anything more concrete to Muybridge. After all, this was who she was, is, must be. Yet something made her add, "Edward, I'll go home alone." In spite of her bedrock principle, this time Holly offered Edward a smidgeon of the relief he sought.

Muybridge was at the door when she said, "Women booed me. Women shouted 'Shameless,' 'Hussy.' They're so accustomed to being considered inferior, they cling to second-class status. Men tell them how to think, how to feel, how to live. It's like a drowning person grabbing a waterlogged board. It can't keep her afloat, but that's all there is."

Edward moved back across the room.

"They don't even know their own best interest, my sisters." Tears that weren't really of weakness filled her changeable eyes. "They think I'm the enemy. Imagine."

He kissed Holly tenderly and tenderly said good night.

As the door closed behind him, her imagination supplied Holly with this: Fauconier standing outside the theater leaning on his cane, nonchalantly puffing a thin cigar. She saw Edward rigidly approach Jacques Fauconier, remove a quartered handkerchief from his breast pocket and lightly flick the ironed, snowy linen across Fauconier's face. Barely any impact at all, an insult without weight or injury. The image of that white square drifting across Fauconier's skin replayed again. Again. The next image placed Edward and Fauconier forty paces apart, facing one another under damp trees that seemed to weep on them. Then both silhouettes simultaneously turned and raised their weapons. . . .

Holly sat trapped before the smudged mirror. She reached down to massage what remained of the hurtful knot in her calf, thought of Edward's hands probing her body, shook off the feeling. Holly began to remove her false eyelashes, hoping she'd be able to think more clearly when confronted by her everyday face. She sent an exploring hand into her hair. *What miserable timing, Jacques,* she moaned internally, *How could you do this to me? Why now? Please, not now!*

She heard his resolute strides coming down the bare hall. He knocked, she said "Enter," and Jacques Fauconier forged back into her life as though he had been absent for only a few days. She felt conspired against, as though an unacknowledged niche in her being lay perpetually open for him.

Fauconier assumed that Holly and he were lovers, that they would always be lovers. Though Holly categorically wanted to deny it, the assumption was justified. After the incident with Gérôme's offensive painting *The Slave Market,* she'd advocated free love loudly and publicly. Even now she felt desire stir, betraying her from within. Only six months ago the sound of his voice uttering certain invocations was enough to make her wet.

He leaned gloved hands on the familiar silver-tipped cane, drinking in her face, her figure. Fauconier's own face had the bluntness of a hatchet, a bludgeoning, unrepentantly masculine face, centered around a wide chiseled mouth. His blue eyes narrowed contemptuously. "What insolence! Such unrivaled provinciality!" He squared wide shoulders as though shrugging off the audience's disapproval. "Don't they know what Paris says of you?"

"Unfortunately, they don't understand French."

The smile approved her remark.

Trying to remain as neutral as possible—and aware of the absurdity of the pose—Holly asked, "Jacques, what in the world are you doing here?"

He remained fixed on the other side of the cramped, third-rate dressing room, his eyes surveying Holly's body, his eyes caressing her breasts and thighs like a starving man in a fine restaurant. He seemed bemused by her insistence on maintaining distance, trying to tease out what titillating sport she contemplated for them.

"I was on my way to Alaska. I thought I would drop by for your opening."

Holly paid him back with a wavering half smile. "Of course I'm delighted to see you. I appreciate your coming." The coolness was intended to cordon him off from her, to improvise and secure new ground rules that would maintain their distance. "I must tell you. I'm in love."

He crossed the room in a stride, lifted Holly, and kissed her hard. She did not respond. Surprised, he gently lowered her to the floor.

"You didn't listen, Jacques." She took a step backward, feeling like the protesting virgin in a banal melodrama. "I'm in love."

Fauconier rejected the notion that Holly's being in love with another man made any difference whatsoever to their relationship.

"I noticed the lucky devil." Jacques Fauconier's eyebrows lifted into thick circumflexes as he continued. "Holly, my dear, at certain moments the world becomes unbearably dispiriting to me. It's embarrassing when so many people behave like asses and fail to appreciate talent and beauty—genius. You gave a magnificent performance. You also offered some perfectly sensible remarks on dress reform. Then all that backwoods *Sturm und Drang* erupted."

Even as he spoke, Fauconier's eyes worked to move her, his eyes probing, drinking her in. She could feel the charge being mounted, as clearly as if buglers had sounded the attack. "My darling, I came halfway around the world to see you."

"I appreciate the exaggeration, Jacques. But it's six thousand miles, and you explained you have business here."

He smiled. "Actually, it's up north, near the Arctic Circle. Mining interests in Alaska, Secretary Seward's last and greatest folly, they say. I'm betting with the secretary against conventional wisdom."

"As usual."

He had anticipated making love to her all the way from Paris, over the isthmus of Guatemala, through countless, circuitous miles of watery waste and steamy jungle and hordes of buzzing malarial mosquitoes. He helped himself to her hands. "I'm overjoyed to see you." His fingers rested on the pulses of her left and right wrists. He listened, counting the heartbeats.

"Overjoyed." By reading her pulses, Fauconier was trying to gauge the precise degree of her body's response to his proposal.

His smile proclaimed: *I read you like a gambler reads his marked deck.* Yet, somehow, this no longer seemed true. Without informing him, Holly had altered the rules—rules she had invented, rules that allowed for two lovers. He had journeyed around the globe to be refused for reasons he could not fathom. Still, the sexual charge was there, he could see it in Holly's luminous eyes, feel it in her pulses and the wary tension in her forearms, as though now his presence was a blow to be warded off.

Fauconier would have pressed, attacked, harried any other woman into submission. Or, if sufficiently provoked, he would've taken another woman by force. Holly was different. Ultimately, it had to be her decision because he would not, for the world, offend her. How she had introduced this conventional ethic into their unconventional existence he could not explain, yet, by some inexplicable crook or hook, it loomed between them.

Holly offered no encouragement. Still, after such intimacy it was absurd to pretend indifference. Internally, she mocked herself: *Love should be freely given, freely taken.* She said, "I'm extremely happy, Jacques." His fingers tightened on her wrists until they almost hurt. "We will not make love," she added, then freed herself.

"I'll accept this for now because you insist it must be. But I believe you've betrayed not just us but also your own principles."

"Jacques, I'm in love." No pleading, stating a fact.

His eyes never left her face. "I have business in Anchorage on the southern coast, my dear. Then I trek inland. I can still get in before the snows, and there's a mound, if not a mountain, of gold allegedly lurking there. I'll be up there for a month or two. But I'll return."

"I will look forward to it." Firm politeness was intended to mask her agitation.

They chatted sociably, if tensely, about Paris and mutual friends: what Hilaire Haas's recent paintings attempted, what they achieved and didn't. He told her what was on at the theaters, about the latest exhibitions, how Madame Thiebaut was misbehaving herself and with whom. Holly inquired as to the health of Philippe Lavoix, Fauconier's partner. A journalist friend had exposed the political corruption of the mayor of Lyons, a writer they knew had scandalized Paris with his new novel about social advancement and sexual hypocrisy. Or was it, she asked, sexual advancement and social hypocrisy? Prince Rudofsky's lover, Andre, had committed suicide as he vowed he would on his fortieth birthday. During the conversation, neither mentioned the name of their mutual friend, the dead painter. Finally, Fauconier said, "I trust quite soon this affectation will pass and we'll resume our intimacy. But I beg you not to wait too long. I don't know how much pleasure we will be able to take when I'm old and crippled."

"And me?"

"You'll never be old or crippled."

Smiling, Holly thought about her aching knee, the bruised right instep, that implacable knot in her calf. Recently she seemed a collection of pains and aches, shredded muscles and fraying tendons. She offered him first one cheek, then the other. Jacques Fauconier kissed each hot, porcelainlike surface, then slipped his arms around Holly. He pulled her to him roughly, wanting to feel her breasts and pelvis and thighs against his body. He needed her to remember their former pleasures. While he held her, Fauconier slowly trailed his fingertips up and down her bare shoulders. His tentativeness touched her beyond reason. His hesitation made her want to reach out to comfort him, to comfort them. Jacques Fauconier looked into her eyes as though searching for the Holly Hughes he knew. Then he turned and stalked out of the dressing room.

In bed, Holly tossed and turned, plagued by images of her men. Edward and Jacques insinuated themselves into her mind's crawl space. Back and forth her emotions flew. She saw two distinctly different hands—Fauconier's spatulate and massive, Edward's veined and long-fingered and adept. Then her lovers' fingers got mixed up, as though both had been reconstituted into a single monstrous, hybrid hand.

Holly rolled onto her back, pulled the blanket to her chin. She lay in the half light, her eyes tracing the intricate, raised plaster curlicues that twisted and turned on the ceiling like her unsettled feelings. Holly's gaze doubled around and back and over the design, trying to thread through the maze, parse out meaning. In fact, she had expected seismic erotic eruptions when Jacques surged into her dressing room. Yet, when he touched her, the sensual charge had been surprisingly tame. He had not attacked—this time. Fauconier's tactics, she guessed, involved reintroducing his presence, which he assumed would work on her like a delayed fuse.

She tossed and turned for another hour on the sweat-drenched bed. She argued to herself that it would be imposing on him, then Holly hurriedly dressed and left the apartment. Minutes later, she climbed the stairs to Edward's rooms, where she quietly let herself in with her key. Naked, she slipped into his bed and kissed him hard, wanting to wake him. Sleepy, he turned away. "Make love to me," she whispered urgently. "Make love to me."

Afterward, Holly cradled Edward's head in her hands, kissing his eyes and face with rapid, greedy kisses until her lips seemed to flutter over his skin like a hummingbird's torrid racing wings. She kissed him passionately, appreciatively, lovingly, leaving him breathless. "Please understand. He's an old friend and lover." The last word cut a gaping hole through Muybridge's being. "But I'm in love with you." It was the first time she had uttered the words.

Later, watching her sleep, Edward fought the base impulse to sniff her skin to see if he could detect the other male presence. In the end he did not. Still, Edward was astonished by the intensity of his demeaning jealousy, startled by the confusion and fear that trailed in the wake of his love like a wheeling flock of seabirds.

Chapter Nine

"Listen to this." Holly rattled the printed sheets of the *Clarion* until they crackled. " 'Dancer Outrages San Francisco's Elite.' Byline by your bosom buddy Luke Ransom." Muybridge, who had read Ransom's front page article three times already that morning, let her leaden sarcasm drop.

"'In a blatant display of uncivilized effrontery, as offensive as her ballet dances'—*ballet* dances? What a dolt!—'as offensive as her ballet dances were beautiful, Miss Holly Hughes, the Parisian artiste, managed to first charm then morally offend the glittering social world of the City of St. Francis.'" The paper took flight, newsprint pages peeling apart. Two sheets fluttered toward the fireplace while another planed and banked, draping itself over the brown-and-white-striped chaise where, as usual, her clothes were heaped.

Holly's dark eyebrows drew together. "The scurvy bastard," she snarled. "Edward, I understand what you believe Stanford will do for your beloved book and career. I can list the incentives he may use to tempt you. But I would be eternally grateful if you refuse his offer."

"He hasn't offered anything yet."

"But you have already begun." She waved her hand. Images of horses were everywhere—drawings and etchings and woodcuts of horses trotting and cantering and galloping, illustrated volumes opened to prints of charging stallions, high-stepping trotters and carriage horses, every imaginable breed, size, shape, and color of equine quadruped depicted in every conceivable state of motion. "I keep wondering when it'll start smelling like a stable in here. Stanford wants you to be his pet photographer. He'll ask you to sit up and beg scraps from him like his other spineless lapdogs. Imagine, having to spend your days with Collis Ward and 'the Governor.'"

"That's enough, Holly!" They glared at each other like enemies. His hostility was fueled by Holly's superior tone and the validity of her statement—Stanford's employees were flunkies. But, if not Stanford . . . Edward saw a dismal professional life stretching away forever—a picture of himself grubbing for coins in the dirt under his wagon, a universe of babies and brides, brides and babies. Stanford offered a problem of consequence, one that would call forth great effort. The millionaires' whimsical wager about the trotting horse's stride, that bet was the gossip of San Francisco, and that would translate into public exposure for the photographer. If Edward succeeded, he would be applauded more loudly and widely—and possibly more profitably—than when his woodblock convicted the thief/murderer.

"Our relationship will be purely professional—assuming I'm offered the position and I take the job. Stanford's vulnerable, Holly. There's a substantial amount of money involved. He desperately needs a photographer to transform him from laughing stock into prophet overnight. I am the only qualified candidate. This business could not be more straightforward."

"That's my point: Nothing is straightforward with Stanford! Even if you demonstrate that all four legs or hooves leave the ground at the same instant—something that not a single sighted person in the world believes possible except for Stanford—even if you win this bet for him, he will invent a way to torture you." She paused. "Why?"

Muybridge was studying depictions of horses, trying to screen out her question.

"Because you are my dear, dear friend. And I have violated Stanford's Neanderthal notions of what's morally acceptable. I've kicked over San Francisco's Lares, their obese, local household god. Or is it the Penates? You will be asked to pay for my offense with blood or flesh—or both."

Her eyes resembled an exotic crystal, with shifting, scintillating highlights suspended in their depths.

"Photographing the horse is only the first step. It's not simply about finishing my epic." He patted his incomplete photographic history of the United States. "If I'm able to work out the mechanisms, I will be able to capture moving objects. I'll be able to photograph *you dancing*. You see, it's the timely, subsidized solution to my new life's work."

She paced the room, her eyes scanning and measuring the images of horseflesh he'd collected. To state it correctly without insult or hurt, to block this job with Stanford yet not to condescend to Edward—it proved an impossible assignment. *So good intentions and even love,* she reflected, *sometimes are not sufficient.*

Muybridge pulled out the calfskin wallet that she'd given him and coolly doled out fifty dollars in gold coin. He neatly stacked the gold in five rows on the lustrous cherry sideboard. "I appreciate your generosity. Thank you for paying the bailiff the other day." She looked like she'd been caught in flagrante. "I'll fork over further payment on Friday, when Chester Crocker hands me the check for the photos of his house and garden."

"I, I—"

"Holly, I said I'm grateful for your generosity but, please understand, I can't have you bailing me out when I'm behind on my bills." Until this moment, Edward had not mentioned a word about Holly's covering his debt, and she'd nearly forgotten about it. Edward had discreetly waited until he had enough funds to pay a part of the sum to her. *Lovely, honorable man,* she thought, happy to be outmaneuvered by her lover.

"I know you meant well, but the situation's demeaning to me. And also to you. If a man can't earn a living . . ."

How pleased Holly would have been to underwrite his research. What better match could there have been—his talent, her munificence? Then Stanford had dropped the challenge into Edward's lap of capturing the action of his damned trotter. Inadvertently, Stanford had hit upon the perfect bait for this inspired, hardheaded man.

Holly was in her own rooms, a place she rarely visited, when she heard a sharp knock. She opened the door and before her stood a strikingly beautiful blonde, who introduced herself as Denise Faveraux. Denise flounced in wearing a flamboyant green dress with a plunging neckline, draped herself on the arm of a comfortable armchair, and began, "Miss Hughes, your performance was top-notch. Of course the local yokels are too stuffy to buy your corset talk, and of course you were being provocative."

Holly offered a chilly, "You are presumptuous, Miss Faveraux."

"Hey, you enjoy shocking people. So do I. Or I used to. I'm reformed." She laughed a throaty laugh that dispelled any notion of reform. "You like showing off your legs; so do I." She lifted her dress above her knees, displaying slender, shapely legs and the hint of thighs beyond. "My billing says I'm a dancer and singer, but I'm not a real dancer like you. No, I couldn't pick up your toe shoes." Holly felt unsettled, wondering what this gorgeous, unpredictable demimondaine wanted from her. The dress remained suspended like a question mark above her knees.

"Miss Hughes, I need your help. You may be the only woman in the city who has the guts to throw in with soiled old me." Denise Faveraux dispensed a dazzling smile. "What needs to be done has to be done by us, by women. You are most obviously a woman, and you're no pushover. That's why I tracked you down."

Holly remembered seeing Denise among the few remaining enthusiasts in the Opera House.

"I need us to pair up to work on a dangerous assignment." Dropping the dress, she rubbed her hands for emphasis. "It involves, uh, poking around in Chinatown. It could mean danger—oh, I said that. I'd do this solo if I could, because I adore the idea of freeing a slave. Like our Union soldiers did in the Civil War. But this is a two-woman operation. I need a beautiful, cunning partner to distract that pig of a bodyguard. A decoy. You're the right—well, really, the only—candidate.

"I rehearsed what I have to say to you so that I'd keep it straight—I guess I feel stage fright before such a, such an artist." Again, the brilliant smile which modulated, spectrumlike, from notoriety to candor.

"Before I go on, let me tell you a little of my story because I see you're not cozy with the idea of me yet. Though I am cozy, if I do say so myself." Her nostrils flared as she crossed her legs. Holly—the opponent of corsets—wondered if this woman was wearing any undergarments at all. Denise breezed on, "I used to earn my living on my back—at least most of the time on my back since most men—poor dummies—are so unimaginative. That apparatus of theirs, you know, it's so easy to deflate, make it a harmless, curled up little worm. They invest such puffed up pride in that dangler."

Holly felt punch-drunk. "After retirement from the front lines I became a madame with my own small but profitable enterprise—a whorehouse to the so-called elite of San Francisco—references needed, private customers only; no walk-in trade. Mostly men, but a few well-heeled ladies, too." Her eyes appreciatively traveled up and down Holly's body. "I sold out for a good price, and for the last three years I've been an actress. I can't sing. I can barely hoof it. But the clucks seem to enjoy paying to look at me." Denise spun off the chair arm and whirled for her hostess. Holly nervously wondered if this woman would proceed to disrobe. "Oh, please, Miss Hughes, don't look so damn judgmental." Denise angled her nose higher, miming Holly Hughes's superior air.

"But my past isn't the point. It's the Chinese prostitutes." Miss Faveraux inhaled deeply, suddenly emotional, sitting back down on the armrest. The switch was stunning: a real person peeked through. "You see, these women are *slaves.* They're only babies—sixteen or seventeen, very tender when they land here—after they're shipped all the way from China. Under contract. Some big Chinese outfit handles it, and the contracts' terms are unbreakable forever.

"These girls have to service countless men. They live in filth, they're fed hogs' swill, they're underpaid even by our streetwalkers' standards. Twenty-four hours a day, seven days a week, they are kept in the house. Twice a week they 'air' them—let them out one at a time—but always chaperoned by a goon. Because they're too valuable to the whoremongers to let even one single girl-child go."

"Miss Faveraux, the plight of these young women is unfortunate, even moving, but I don't understand. . . . Why speak to me about this?" The statement was formal, offering no opening to Denise.

"You have guts." Denise struggled to be polite. "You stand up to them, and not enough of *us* do. I could press a male friend into service, but somehow using a man . . . there's no poetry there."

"What is your proposal?" Still, the frosty distance, as though Denise were a supplicant.

With a toss of her head Denise tossed Holly the bait. "Rescue one of them!"

"Rescue a Chinese prostitute?" It wasn't a question, rather a way to buy time.

"Yes. A friend, the woman who cleans for me, she works in a Chinese house. She's had contact—sign language—with a few girls. The place would make a pig vomit. There's such despair and fatigue and terror in their faces. A suicide last month. No hope—lines of men around the clock. Miss Hughes, I've been on that particular rack myself. So I want to give one of them a life. If you help me, we can do it, rescue one, then another girl. Then another." She paused. "I want all of those young women to have a ray of hope."

The emotion was so genuine that Holly's heart tensed.

"Also," Denise continued, her voice harder now. "It will scare the jism out of the scum-sucking boyos who profit from our slavery. Like our own underground railroad. 'Ladies Only,' see?"

Holly frowned, trying to tamp down the excitement creeping up her spine, threatening to inundate her reason. The madness of crawling so far out on a wobbly, unstable limb . . . She took a venturesome step forward. "We'd need a plausible excuse to be seen together."

Denise Faveraux shot off the chair's armrest like her seat was scalding. "If you're too embarrassed to work with me, Miss Hughes, there's no point—"

"No, not at all. Please sit down." Denise kept moving toward the door. The silhouetting light behind testified that, clearly, Denise wore no undergarments.

"I came here for your courage, Miss Hughes, not for your condescension. Good day, Miss Hughes."

"Call me Holly, please. And, Ms. Faveraux, don't overplay your hand."

Denise hesitated as Holly went on, her mind priming itself. "If the issue comes up, we'll say you're studying dance with me. And I've become fascinated by, say, Oriental movement. I'm developing choreography for a dance that will incorporate these Oriental types of gestures." Holly demonstrated: She angled her head and smiled as her fingers paired and unpaired themselves in precise, stylized movements. Holly took a few mincing steps as though enshrouded in a tight kimono. Denise reluctantly smiled at the mime.

"All right, good," Denise conceded, uncertain the subterfuge was necessary for the joint caper but willing to indulge her prospective conspirator. She turned serious: "But remember, this could be dangerous."

"What's next, partner?"

Denise outlined her plan, concluding, "When the time's right, I'll be in touch. Next week, I think. I have to be sure the girl I've picked out—her name is Sung Wan—has the guts to make the jail break."

"In the meantime, is there anything I can do?"

Denise Faveraux shook her ringlets no. "Not until I contact you."

They grasped hands. Holly moved up onto her toes, as though ready to begin a new dance. For the first time since her concert she felt alive. The prospect of wrestling with the messy, fallen world beckoned Holly Hughes like a long-lost friend.

Chapter Ten

Harry Harnett, Stanford's chief trainer and nonpareil sulky driver, hosted Muybridge on what he called his "six bit tour" of the Palo Alto stock farm, pointing out in his flavorful Cockney the latest conveniences, including running water in each spacious, well-appointed horse stall. Harnett, rumor had it, was Stanford's prize in a wager with an English Duke who was willing to bet his top horseman on the outcome of a race with Stanford's champion thoroughbred, Mahomet. The Duke lost, and Harnett crossed the Atlantic to work in Palo Alto.

Muybridge could not help being impressed with the seamless precision and scale of the operation. Everything was spotless and functioned flawlessly; everything had its place—tack, water, feed, men, suave quadrupeds. And every conceivable item, the Englishman had repeated emphatically, was engineered "to assure the emotional and physical well-being of these noble animals."

They spent time looking over Occident, "saying hello to him and letting him sniff your acquaintance and make friends—if he cares to," as Harnett glossed. Impressed by the trotter's stall, Muybridge quipped, "Finer accommodation here than the Regency Hotel."

"Costs more, too."

Harnett and Muybridge immediately took to each other. Edward liked the Englishman's military directness and authority, his honed, assured movements. "All these innovations in stock-breeding and our stable's record racing speeds are the work of the guv himself. Did you know that, Mr. Muybridge?"

"I did not."

Curiously, Edward considered, the grounds of the vast stock farm—248 horses, 312 employees—seemed staffed mostly by undersized people. There were young apprentices and exercise boys and scaled-down stable hands along with miniature, seemingly fleshless men (the ectomorphic jockeys and sulky drivers), all of whom, in their daily work, conformed to patterns as inflexible as the diminutive figures hourly circling the clock on the village church tower. After their workouts, horses were walked for precisely timed intervals by light-boned exercise boys on the cooling-off track. The colt barn adjoined the "kindergarten," where the one-year-old colts and foals were trained. Horseshoeing went on next to the well-ventilated brick building that housed the blacksmith's forge and Tim White, the giant blacksmith (a notable exception to the diminutive rule). Harnett noted that the forge was centrally located in the great court, equidistant from the grandiose stallion stable, the smaller brood mare stables and the indoor training stable, the latter used for workouts in inclement weather. The feed mill, south of the court, ran constantly all year round, Harnett explained as its chimney belched drafts of odiferous smoke from the mammoth copper vats below. These vats perpetually boiled up a high-protein mixture of oats and barley along with an undisclosed number of secret ingredients (the principle one of which smelled like molasses) from a recipe concocted "by the gov himself." Distribution of the feed was handled by a half dozen cooks, a raft of underlings, and scores of stable boys who doled out each horse's measured portion like alchemists turning base fodder into nutritional gold.

Not a single errant scrap of paper or lump of manure lay about the paddocks for more than ninety seconds before a slight male form darted out to spear it or sweep it up. Maybe, Edward mused, Stanford believed that cleanliness would assure proximity to the deity.

Having completed the tour, Harry Harnett led Muybridge across the expanse of lawn that stretched for a mile in all directions. Skirting those two concentric dirt tracks—dark brown ovals in a sea of green—they halted at the three-tiered white rail. On the inner track, trotters moved clockwise; on the outer one, glossy, long-limbed thoroughbreds sprinted in the opposite direction. The two great circles turning in opposed directions approximated a clock mechanism—wheels within wheels. *An appropriate metaphor,* he thought, when about to go to work for a man as exacting as the governor.

"The outer track measures one mile," Harnett explained, "the inner, six furlongs. The training system, it's called 'Stanford's Rules.' With it, we've revolutionized racing." He pointed to a handsome gray gelding cantering effortlessly around the bigger track, his scaled-down rider straining to hold the huge animal back. "Mahomet," Harnett proclaimed reverently.

His eyes never ceased tracking the gray, studying his legs' extension, the churning hooves, the sleek coordinated strands of Mahomet's chest muscles gathering then releasing, then gathering again. "The idea is to take a colt and train him for endurance, track sense, competitiveness. All that can be taught—if he's fast. Speed is inborn, Muybridge. Hard as we try, we can't inject speed. But we can make inroads in endurance, which maybe translates into speed in that last furlong.

"See that pole?" Harry Harnett pointed to an upright white pole bearing a large, white "6." "Right there, Terence'll give him his head."

As the horse came up on the numeral 6, the exercise boy slid forward in the saddle, slackening the reins. One moment Mahomet was moving at an easy canter; the next instant, the horse hit a flat-out gallop—so quickly that Muybridge's eyes found themselves half a head behind the animal. Watching the strapping horse cover the final two furlongs, Muybridge felt tense and exhilarated, as though he himself were up and riding.

As Mahomet flashed across the finish line, Harry Harnett waved a clenched fist in the air. "That, Mr. Muybridge, was the sustained burst of speed we sweat and slave and train for. Mahomet here, and Sallie Gardner, and your horse, they got it, mate."

By "your horse" the trainer meant Occident, the fabled trotter; a powerful, coal black, ex–cart horse that Stanford had spotted fifteen months earlier doing his best to swallow the bit while furiously backing against the traces at the corner of Sacramento and Fulton. The governor had approached the unsuspecting milkman, completed a thorough hands-on inspection of the horse, and on the spot handed the gasping owner two hundred fifty dollars. Then Stanford pulled the animal out of harness and led him away, stranding the milk wagon in the middle of the busy intersection. Three months later, Occident broke the world's trotting record for seven furlongs. The stud fees, Harnett intimated, already exceeded the former world record, held by Abe Edgington, another of Stanford's celebrated pacers.

Muybridge was contemplating the scale of the three main barns (the stallion barn alone had sixty-two stalls) when suddenly, behind him, came an anguished snort. He spun around and saw a slender, barely pubescent boy struggling to hold onto the bridle of a rearing roan mare. The panicked horse tossed its head once and then again, jerking the boy a few inches off the ground.

"You son of a bitch-bastard!" the boy screamed. "I learn you!" He yanked on the bridle with all his weight, ripping the mare's head down, then wrenched the bit sideways, ravaging the roan's mouth. The horse keened a strangled whinny and reared, its eyes rolling up, leaving only the panicked whites. The boy clutched the bridle as the animal whipped its head side to side. Muybridge watched the frail lad being flung about until the mare abruptly stopped. The jolt threw the child to the ground. Mouth dripping blood, the animal pawed the earth.

Then Harry Harnett somehow had the mare in hand, stroking its muzzle. "Easy, Fritzi, easy now." As he gentled the animal, he studied the boy and continued in the same quiet tone, "Clear out your gear, Jerrold. Get gone in ten minutes. There'll be no such treatment here."

"But Harry—" The thirteen-year-old was close to tears.

A crowd of jockeys and handlers along with a rotund aproned cook and the looming Negro blacksmith gathered around. Jerrold desperately searched each face for relief, for sympathy, for hope. A diminutive white-haired stable hand spat into the dirt beside the offender. Another youngster about the groom's age slammed a fist into his palm as though prepping to pummel the miscreant. To everyone at the stock farm, Jerrold (last name unknown) had ceased to exist.

"You know the guv's orders."

"Harry," the boy pleaded, "I need the job. My ma—"

"You'll have to look elsewhere." The small, wiry man, light as smoke on his feet, was unmovable. There was no appeal beyond Harry Harnett. "Now go."

A moment before, he had been one of the acolytes in this paradise for horses and bantam beings; suddenly, as he walked away bowed and weeping, Jerrold was banished from animal Eden.

After Harnett ordered the mare led back to the barn "to be tended to" by one of the half dozen vets, the chief trainer slipped over to Edward. "The second and first commandments of the guv's rules—never a foul word, and not a hand lifted against the animals," he spoke reverently. "Here we train with kindness."

The sanctimoniousness pricked Edward. "The governor has a heavier hand with his railroad workers." Harry Harnett winced; his head shimmied disapprovingly from side to side as though trying to slough off Muybridge's transgression. The trainer excused himself, "Time to take Occident out for a spin. Maybe I'll see you later." He was gone before Muybridge could respond.

Edward wandered around the paddock, berating himself for his aggression yet pausing to nod or exchange abbreviated pleasantries with Stanford's employees. He thought of Holly's outburst—beholden to no one, she could outrage whomever she wanted at will; desperate for work, he had to bite his tongue.

Strolling past the gorgeous, glossy horses returning from the track and meticulously curried animals prancing over to their workouts, steeped in the smells and sounds of the horse farm, Muybridge abandoned the larger question—How in the world does one accomplish this insane, never-before-tried feat?—with its plethora of subquestions—What cameras? Lenses? Shutter speeds? How to time multiple shutters?—for the less ambitious yet significant problem of the best location for his photographic set up. After all, the contract called for him to begin on Friday, in two days. And with the commencement came his hotly awaited first check.

Edward would have liked to position his cameras on the long straightaway on the outer track. But the outside track was reserved for flat racing, so he settled on a straight section of the inner circle near the sixth furlong pole. As he weighed the pressing professional matters, Edward fretted over Holly's coolness, since he'd felt a drop in temperature dating from the contract signing with Stanford. Had Stanford's huge, censorious frame interposed a barrier between them?

Muybridge didn't see or hear the governor until the darkly bearded, beetle-browed force was on top of him.

"Are you studying the problem or wool gathering, Muybridge?" Though the irony came sugarcoated, a challenge was tucked into the question. The governor assumed that labor was the natural state of grace, and every other condition constituted a not insignificant reenactment of The Fall.

Stanford was draped in a tent-sized, spotless, ingeniously tailored frock coat, cut to emphasize the barrel chest and long, powerful arms and minimize his bulging belly. The carefully trimmed beard and devilish goatee centered his square, fleshy features; the bulbous nose seemed a monument, not a defect. Large, glistening diamond studs decorated his white shirtfront under the usual black string tie. The gold watch chain ranged catenary-like from lapel to his fob pocket.

In spite of Holly's concern, negotiations about the "the Trotting Project" had gone smoothly. After token resistance, Stanford had acceded to Muybridge's demand that the governor cover all of the experiment's costs. The photographer was to be paid a substantial weekly allowance. All rights to the photos—to publication, and copyrights to all inventions and the revenues derived therefrom—would be shared, with Stanford, the investor, taking a 60 percent share. Any apparatus subsequently manufactured "as a direct result of the experiments" would become joint property—according to a complex division-of-spoils formula. Muybridge could purchase any equipment he desired from the Trotting Project at reduced cost, the price of the apparatus to be determined by a detailed depreciation schedule. Nothing in the single-spaced, twenty-two-page agreement seemed objectionable to Muybridge or to the lawyer he had hired from a streetcar ad to review the agreement.

Stanford leaned heavily on his gold-tipped cane. "You know I have no intention of losing the amount I've wagered. But don't construe my motives too narrowly." Whenever Stanford moved his arms, the black frock coat rippled with shifting, glistening highlights, making the velvet come alive, like the fur of a rangy leopard.

"I'd like your studies to correct all erroneous notions about how these magnificent creatures move. Secondly, and most important for us at the Farm, the result will serve horsemen around the world as the underpinnings for a truly scientific theory of animal training."

"The idea being"—Muybridge translated his employer's soaring ambitions—"that once we have a detailed understanding of how horses actually move, you'll be able to train them more efficiently."

"Efficiently, intelligently, scientifically." He uttered the final word as a benediction, then gave Muybridge his first full-blown smile, which was surprisingly winning.

"You witnessed the dismissal of an errant exercise boy," Leland Stanford said as he scanned his teeming private domain—flat racers sprinting or cantering or walking, the light spokes of sulkies spinning around the inner track. "The rules here are simple yet inflexible. We have a procedural philosophy, which means that there is always more at stake than a single individual's assertion of prerogative or opinion." The inflated rhetoric dug at Muybridge like a saw blade. "Anyone who disregards social conventions, as your friend Miss Hughes did blatantly the other night, does so at her or his own peril."

Muybridge would always like the fact about himself that he did not hesitate. "In fact, Miss Hughes is correct, Mr. Stanford, in spite of society's dictums about what is properly uttered, or not uttered, aloud. The corset damages women's health by destroying muscle tone, which is essential to every living being. I've read the medical research. In England, where it is possible to openly discuss these matters, the Society of Surgeons concluded that an inordinate number of complications in childbirth—for both mother and infant—are the direct result of the corset's destruction of female musculature. The corset can crush and misshape the unborn child, too. Miss Hughes . . . Holly"—He asserted their relationship now—"has been accused of barbarism. But the true barbarism is to inflict grievous injuries on mothers and babes. True barbarism is the false gentility that allows us to turn away from lethal consequences."

"If these are matters of science," Leland Stanford responded, "the Opera House, in front of a *mixed* audience, is hardly the appropriate forum for the discussion."

"We're talking about saving lives."

Stanford drew himself up to full height, about to respond. Then Muybridge felt the wave of anger break, washing away self-serving concern for his new job. Anger rescued him from a future of endlessly second-guessing his own hedged second-guesses. "I will not discuss the matter further, Mr. Stanford. I've made my views clear, I trust as clear as Miss Hughes's. Please don't allude to my personal life again ever, sir, or I will quit."

Stanford's mind moved quickly: he'd already spent twenty-two hundred dollars on cameras and lenses. His head carpenter had purchased the surfeit of materials that Muybridge had ordered for his "camera shed." The day after signing, Edward had deposited his first monthly one-hundred-dollar expense check for incidental photographic supplies. More significantly, San Francisco and the Bay area waited for the photographic experiments to begin, the *Clarion* having announced the undertaking three days earlier. Currently, San Francisco odds makers were offering eight to one in favor of Abbot Berkeley.

Stanford turned from Muybridge to survey his animal kingdom. Muybridge joined him in following a sleek black mare moving easily down the homestretch. The governor quickly jotted a note in a slim leather notebook. "Sallie Gardner . . ." Stanford nodded toward the mare. "That new exercise boy's not pushing her enough through the last three furlongs." Eyes glued on the mare, Stanford scribbled another notation, a simple plus sign followed by the numerals 3 and 4, then a question mark. "And she needs to carry a bit more weight." He indicated the question mark on the page. "I want to build her strength because she's so fast, she'll be heavily handicapped when she races." Muybridge observed that the notebook's facing page was filled with similar hieroglyphs. "Such marvelous animals, so responsive, Edward."

So now they were on a first name basis. Thus ever among colleagues.

Stanford's blunt hand clamped down on Muybridge's shoulder, as subtle as an eight-pound sledgehammer. "You know one of their greatest virtues?" Edward looked up into those undersized, pitch-black, hard-scrabble eyes. "They don't quit on you."

As Muybridge strode across the paddock, past the elegant, high-clearance horses, he pondered the fact that he had spoken forthrightly and not been fired. Now he could continue to pay down his debts (a check for $150 was on its way to Biggs and he'd send off another $100 to Russell and Clark that evening, leaving only $185 outstanding for the Dallmeyer lenses). He could even buy a new pair of boots, though the double-breasted charcoal gray English suit he'd eyed longingly in Austen's on Union Square would have to wait.

Fiscal relief was attended by thoughts of Holly. After the ordeal at the Opera House, she had thrown herself into work with the local women's organizations. Holly had joined a Suffragette Committee, addressed tea gatherings and social clubs, and one night had lectured on dress reform to a scant audience in a drafty, ill-lit hall. (Muybridge and the porter were the only males in attendance.) Her life had been busy, agitated, and public. Still, Muybridge understood that, though women's causes were of great consequence to her, Holly was in mourning. Only a trickle of people had attended the remainder of her concerts. She'd need to build up an audience before scheduling any future dance performances. In the meantime, she seemed enervated and distracted.

Muybridge whistled aggressively as he passed through the imposing entry hall of Stanford's rambling Palo Alto mansion on the way to "the Chancery." (Another bothersome minor aspect of his employment—every building and room he entered had a title.) The photographer felt more complacent than usual, for he had taken control of certain aspects of his life—first by confronting Stanford; and now on his way to pick up his fortnightly check. In honor of Holly, he whistled "Uncle Ned," a tune she'd danced to at her triumphal/disastrous concert.

Edward found Meachum Steward, Stanford's head clerk, on his feet before an upright desk, a pen clutched in his spectral fingers. Muybridge observed the clerk at his fussy ritual—dipping the pen into the inkwell, tediously writing, precisely blotting the ink, blowing the sheet dry, then starting over by dipping into the dark well again. As the clerk stood upright, hand moving, he produced an odd, light scratching sound—like a mouse scrabbling industriously behind a porous wall. Muybridge, who considered this copying process hopelessly inefficient, wondered if there might be a more deft way to do Meachum's work: perhaps a way to eliminate that dipping, say a pen that held ink? A gravity-fed tube or canister of some kind? He ordered himself to make a mental note.

"The Chancery" was furnished with floor-to-ceiling bookshelves, all lined with ranks of dated ledgers; except for the narrow aisles, the floor was crammed with row after row of wooden filing cabinets.

Muybridge couldn't resist the gibe. "You were standing in that position when I left two weeks ago."

Steward glanced up, his dim eyes captive behind the curved surfaces of his gold, wire-rim spectacles. He spoke without irony, "We're extremely busy this time of year."

"Ah." Edward reckoned that Stanford's head clerk was perpetually busy. The photographer glanced at the papers. Three identical pieces of stationery bearing the Governor's letterhead lay side by side on the slanted desktop. All bore the same date and heading, the same salutation. The text of the left-hand letter was being copied verbatim onto the two right-hand sheets. Halfway down that page, the letter broke off—Steward was working on this line, scratching perpetually onward left to right.

"Forgive my curiosity. I hope this isn't a state secret," Muybridge asked, "but why three identical letters?"

Meachum Steward's eyes moved sluggishly laterally, fishtailing about in their reflective dungeons. "The governor requires three fair copies—one is mailed to the interested party, another is kept in the attorney's office, the third I deposit in the files." Meachum nodded at the serried ranks of cabinets lining the space. The photographer thought of the contract he had recently signed—twenty-two pages for Meachum or a sub-clerk to write out in longhand then laboriously recopy, letter by letter, line by mind-numbing line, and then a third time. Around them, thousands of duplicate pages were stuffed into the cabinets and left to molder: his contract, the Central Pacific archives (which Holly would have given anything to dive into to pry loose any tidbit concerning the railroad's malfeasance), countless agreements with contractors, clandestine deals with state legislators and local politicians, the crucial land surveys that had levered tens of millions of dollars and untold tracts of land out of the U.S. Treasury—Stanford was a stickler for procedure, Muybridge surmised, in the event that even a single detail was ever in dispute. This last thought made Edward's stomach queasy.

Chapter Eleven

The measured drawing nailed to the side of the stable drew all of Harry Harnett's attention: "Beloved Jesus, the man's right." Harnett's expression was equal parts embarrassment and displeasure. "The wall's off, lads." The lads he addressed were Stanford's stable hands, Ned Quick, a tall, dark, lean eighteen-year-old, and Willy Jackson, a blond, burly young man of twenty.

"The plan doesn't lie." The clock was ticking for Muybridge—he had no time to waste, so he couldn't encourage mistakes. "Don't ever overrule me on whim, lads. Follow the drawing. If you have a question, *ask*!"

Ned, the feistier and less conventional of the pair, was tempted to explain that he'd argued against a dark green wall for a good ten minutes before Willy had persuaded him that Muybridge couldn't have wanted white.

Harry Harnett's impulse was to keep the peace. After all, except for that early slip about the guv, which was a deucedly stupid thing to say to him of all people, Muybridge seemed a decent enough sort, and the photographer even had a feeling for horses. A big plus in Harry's book. Also, the four of them would be working together for two or three months, at least as long as the governor's commitment to the undertaking lasted. "The good Lord built the world in seven days," Harnett said, "but it'll take us a fortnight before we get your wall right, that blasted thing standing on its own and the concatenation of your fancy gear in place."

"The good Lord did his own carpentry." Muybridge saw no point in being too rough on the boys. "Only first He had to teach Himself how to read plans."

That drew relieved smiles from Ned and Willy. Together the two men—with the boys peering over their shoulders—went back to scrutinizing the drawings. Muybridge had located his shed-to-be on the track's north side, directly opposite furlong pole 6. The angle of the wall's backward tilt—60 degrees—was written in undeniable figures on the sheet. ."

Harry asked the question the other two had been wondering about. "But why the sixty-degree angle?"

The photographer replied, "I need to brace it from behind, not in front."

Ned: "Why?"

"Because I don't want any of your animals running into struts."

Watching the work, Muybridge was reminded of a Honduran family he'd photographed rebuilding their thatch hut after a devastating tornado. "Harry, you ever visited Central America?" Edward could picture the tall peaks jutting up behind the tiny village, the startlingly green vegetation with a twenty-foot-wide swathe of destruction erratically zigzagging up the slope, leaving in its wake shredded, mangled leaves, tortuously twisted branches and splintered tree trunks. Arriving two days after the storm, the photographer had never forgotten the random wantonness of unleashed nature carving that path.

"No, but you have." The boys, who were hammering along with the two carpenters, paused to gather yet another tale of adventurous lives as yet beyond their ken. Harry gestured them back to work.

"You saw my photographs?"

"No, the guv gave me what he calls 'a briefing.' I feel like I know just about every hellhole scrape you passed through in the last decade—the full bloody itinerary. The boss is always thorough."

The idea of Stanford riffling through his past, scrutinizing his life's labyrinthian byways, perhaps prying into his occasional indiscretions had worrisome features. So Holly was right about this, too: Stanford's resources were vast, his reach seemingly limitless, his examinations microscopic. *What a strange way to spend time,* the photographer reflected. But when time equaled power, investment of that sort could be productive.

That afternoon, as the hammers gouged into the farm's pastoral peace, the two boys and two carpenters raised a grid of beams to brace the wall's first ten-foot section. The hammering and sawing continued as sleek, handsome trotters whirled past, the sulkies' wheels creating the illusion, at times, that they were spinning backward.

By five o'clock three days later, the thirty-by-eight-foot wall stood in place.

Now Harry Harnett dutifully followed Muybridge's finger as it inched along the drawing. "The camera shed will face the wall right there." On the sheet the shed appeared as a low building; according to the one-half inch equaling one foot scale, it would measure thirty feet. Running almost its full length, forty-two inches from the ground, a two-foot-high rectangular slit had been cut into the shed's face. The cameras themselves were to be positioned inside at twenty-one-inch intervals. Directly across the track, on the drawing of "the Great Wall," as the boys dubbed it, a series of numerals appeared from 1 to 20, each number spaced twenty-one inches apart.

Muybridge's index finger tracked from wall to shed and back. "First we'll position the cameras twenty-one inches apart. Theoretically, that should give us enough time for the shutters to work." Edward's hands approximated the distance. "We'll want a vertical line marked right on the wall, at each of these spots." The finger ticked off the measurements. "Each camera will be placed directly opposite. If you're right, Harry, and Occident moves at thirty, thirty-five feet a second—"

"He's right," Willy blurted out the alleged fact, then reddened, his pale skin as scarlet as a rooster's comb.

"Then the twelve-camera arrangement might work. If necessary, I can always add a camera or two."

Ned chimed in brightly, "All we'd have to do is build a bigger shed."

Harnett groaned at the thought.

Willy played the realist: "As long as the governor—praised be his name—dispenses his blessings."

Muybridge added, "But that's not our supreme problem." They waited expectantly. "Occident moves too fast for even the best shutters, so I'll have to somehow improvise a quicker device, which ain't a piece of cake, gents. Otherwise I could shoot for weeks and only get a blur. Then there's the further problem of how to create a timing mechanism that will work." He paused, seeing he'd lost his audience. "How can I explain this? Well, how do you time a dozen shutters on a dozen cameras to go off in sequence at the exact instant our steed whizzes by at *thirty-five feet per second*? I've got a vague idea about how to proceed, but I don't know if it will work." Six eyes were glued to him, mutely asking if the undertaking had the remotest chance of success. "I'll tell you, friends, there are dozens of problems ahead of us no sane man has ever attempted."

Ned laughed. "So we got to be loco to do this?"

"Loco, beserk, crazy. But, theoretically, it can be done."

"Theoretically" became their refrain: Whenever they confronted what seemed an insoluble problem—and there were numerous exhausting, unproductive dead ends; whenever Ned or Willy miscalculated or fudged a detail; whenever Muybridge was frustrated and fumed or sulked or yelled at them, one would chime in, "Theoretically, it can be done." For a time the phrase buoyed them.

Six days later the two boys stood in the dimness of the completed shed. Muybridge crouched by the first camera, his eyes scanning the limited area of the track framed by his single lens. He shouted, "All right, Harry."

The boys watched the sulky glide down the dirt track, Harry Harnett cantilevered out behind the sleek, high-stepping black trotter as horse and driver raced toward the cameras—Occident's great, rippling body poised on four points of hoof and muscle and bone. Ned, functioning as the photographer's eyes, reported, "He's rolling down, fifty yards away." A pause. "Forty yards, thirty now." A quicker beat. "Twenty . . . ten!"

Off to the left Muybridge heard hooves and the whirr of the sulky before he saw the trotter. Ned touched Muybridge's forearm, Edward hesitated a final split second, waiting for the action to materialize at the far left edge of the camera's field of vision, and squeezed the bulb.

Under the hood Muybridge heard the sulky racing off to his right, the light wheels whirring away like an outsized Singer sewing machine run amok. In his black silk cave, Muybridge knew, immediately and incontrovertibly, that the photograph was useless. He wasn't to blame. It wasn't even the equipment's fault.

"It didn't work," he announced sternly as he withdrew his head and faced them.

For a moment the boys were too crushed to respond. Then Willy mustered, "Are you sure? How do you know?"

Veins on Muybridge's forehead erupted, a string of taut, subcutaneous blue wires. Still he spoke quietly, "Am I sure? How do *I* know? I know when I make a photograph and when I do not." He exploded, "I've been doing it for goddamn ever!"

Without another word, Muybridge retreated into the darkroom at the back of the camera shed. He realized, as he should have realized weeks earlier that, even if he could locate or improvise a sufficiently rapid lens and then calculate how to work out the intractable business of the timing of a single camera, let alone a bloody dozen, he did not have sufficient contrast to record an image of the coal black horse moving that fast.

The lads tiptoed around outside, preserving a churchlike quiet, the silence intended not to offend but which conveyed Muybridge's initial failure more loudly than if they had cursed and execrated him.

Harry and his young coworkers watched grimly when Muybridge carried the wet photograph out of the darkroom and held up the shot. There were two technical failures: the slow lens, which created the smear, and the problem of contrast. These were caused, in part, by the dark background wall. He berated himself, *Black horse on dark wall!* Edward spun, thrust his chin below Ned's jaw and ordered, "Whitewash it!"

"What?" Ned's quick eyes darted uncertainly from Muybridge to Harry Harnett back to Muybridge.

"The goddamn wall!" Muybridge, more amused than he let on, pointed to the tilted surface of his thirty-foot wall. "Every inch of it. Two coats! I want it whiter than white!"

Later, as Ned Quick and Willy Jackson slapped whitewash on the boards, Ned calculated that there were 34,560 square inches of the back-tilted monstrosity. Willy asked, "What did he mean—'whiter than white'?"

Only it wasn't as simple as two coats of whitewash. "Theoretically," the white wall was supposed to provide sufficient contrast to make the photograph. That afternoon Ned again touched Edward's forearm as the horse flashed by the stark white background and Muybridge released the shutter slide. This time, when he developed the photo, he found his hand too slow: Both the front and back hooves ran together into unintelligible smears. Again and again that long afternoon Edward tried until, by six o'clock, he concluded the camera could not be manipulated manually. Occasionally he would get a shot, but a single photo was insufficient. Besides, the hand-triggering would never work for two cameras, let alone the madly ambitious dozen needed to document the horse's stride. He needed to devise a faster shutter—though if he could produce such a device, he did not know.

To accurately measure the height of the trotter's hooves, Edward sketched a series of horizontal lines running along the length of the whitewashed wall, spaced two, four, and six inches from the ground. If he ever actually made the photo sequence, the markings would precisely gauge the distance of Occident's hooves above the ground—if indeed all four of the horse's hooves left the ground simultaneously.

At his apartment that evening, a restless Muybridge straddled a leg of his dining table, a blank sheet of drawing paper before him. His problem: to design the fastest shutter ever. At ten o'clock he caught glimmerings of an idea. "Maybe a kind of double shutter," he muttered, unable to complete the thought. But he droned on, and after more hours he realized that doubling the travel speed of the lens was impossible. The alternative involved cutting down the distance that the shutter must travel—not unlike the double lens he created for Woodward's Gardens. If he could halve that distance between the shutters, "Eureka! It just might work."

"What did you say, dear?" Holly glanced up from the writing table, where she was making notes for a pamphlet on women's suffrage. She wore those shapeless navy blue bloomers that Muybridge found so antierotic, her hair bunched up in a straggly bun. He had never seen her look so unattractive. Once more, his rooms were draped in the wake of her wardrobe. Such carelessness, indication of . . .

"Nothing. Shop talk." He sketched painstakingly, trying to visualize a two-part shutter that would slide in horizontally from both sides. Or, instead, perhaps, a drop shutter which would work top down and bottom up.

Half-joking Holly offered, "Obviously you had a wretched day. Would you like to hear about mine?"

He wasn't paying attention, yet something in her voice urged him to look up. She smiled, a full, warm smile drawn up from the deep well of her being. Her face expressed the pure pleasure of being with him.

Looking at Holly now, resentment slipped away. Edward pondered her smoky eyes, relieved of things extraneous. In spite of the problems with his work; the strain of Stanford and the governor's implacably nosy enforcer, Ward; the boys' infuriating twin expectations of a major breakthrough any instant; in spite of his and her abrasions and the decidedly male specter or two from her past life, Holly visited him as a form of grace.

He smiled back at her. "Thank you, dear. Thank you very much."

"For what?"

"Just thank you." He turned back to work.

At one a.m. the floor was ankle-deep with discarded plans, his total usable output meager scratching on multiple sheets and jumbled, cryptic half-digested notes. The photographer knew he risked an explosion, but he barged ahead. "I'm certainly glad we didn't throw away your money on this wretched enterprise. I don't want you wasting precious capital on a doomed proposition."

He was begging Holly to approve his arrangement with Stanford, a gift she could never offer. Yet some reserve held her acid tongue, something deterred Holly from telling Edward that he shouldn't fashion a backdoor contrivance to enlist her support. Both were so bruised when only a few hours before they had been so close. Holly elected to dwell in the comforting shade of that prior concord. Also, she was nursing her own seed of bad faith—a growing concern for her old friend Fauconier, from whom she hadn't heard in over a month. After all, Alaska was more dangerous than Paris. Holly also worried about the pressures Fauconier would generate when he stormed back into her life. How deviously she behaved when, like the soppy heroine of a puerile dime novel, she tried to will Jacques Fauconier back to France without his scheduled stop in

San Francisco. Holly had always considered herself forthright, not self-deceiving. Tonight she found herself dividing her life into compact compartments, like the dull, utilitarian gray platter on which French soldiers took their rations—meat and gravy behind the raised groove that separated the plate into thirds, potatoes carefully segregated in another sector, vegetable quarantined in the last. Was there any way to keep Fauconier and Edward apart? Had she, like those battered tin plates that tinged every bite with metallic overtones, neatly segregated her life between first Gérôme, then Fauconier, and now Edward? If so, what about her vaunted "free love"? Was love "free" when the modus operandi was serial, one at a time? Indeed, as Edward had asked, what in the world *did* the term *free* mean?

"You made the decision to settle the absurd bet between rich reprobates. You and I, we both believe that someday, eventually, you, 'Photo Man' himself, will cobble out a solution."

Later when he wanted to make love, she objected that she was too tired. They had not made love in three days. He rolled around in bed long after Holly slept, tantalized by a rising and falling erection. He considered relieving himself but, finally, just after three o'clock, Edward drifted off. At four a.m., fast asleep, Muybridge heard the frantic scratching of a pen. In his dream he saw Stanford's clerk, Meachum Steward, at his upright desk. Steward dipped into the inkwell, pushed the pen across in that left-to-right, black-and-white parade of characters, blotted with exaggerated prissiness, dipped again. The scratching noise faded. Weighted by fatigue, Meachum's hand moved ever more slowly, as though he had been copying without cease for weeks on end. His fingers started a slow awkward dance in the attempt to shake off their fatigue. Muybridge wondered, as one sometimes does in a dream, why in the world he was having this bizarre vision. The photographer awoke with a start, half-expecting to find himself beside Meachum's desk in the Palo Alto office. He looked at Holly, whose full mouth just hinted at a smile. Edward kissed her gently, rolled over, and instantly fell back to sleep.

Chapter Twelve

As Holly Hughes and Denise Faveraux passed along Stockton Street through imposing iron gates into San Francisco's Chinatown, the thoroughfare was thronged with people, goods, and scores of unintelligible Chinese signs—ideograms pinned to shop walls or draped from guy wires or hung in windows. The highly visible pair strolled by crammed, minuscule, tunnel-like shops selling vivid silks and aromatic teas, stacks of fragile porcelain teacups and bowls and mounds of shiny lacquered ware. The caged chickens and bloated quacking ducks that lined the sidewalk gave way in the next stall to glass tanks of entwined eels and rainbow-colored carp and crabs and oversized tortoises. There were sprays of graceful greens and massive cabbagelike growths and strange bulbous gourds of all shapes and colors. A jumble of smells confounded their senses—fish and joss sticks and sandalwood and, somewhere, the unmistakable overripe, gummy essence of opium. Around them a range of alien sounds—hyperactive syllables of ever-changing pitch—hurled back and forth like singsong metal quoits as men in full blouses, their hair in tight braids dangling down their backs, hawked their wares amid the indecipherable din. Chinese men wore what looked like inverted soup plates for head coverings, while their wide pantaloons billowed and flapped in time with every step. Several women displayed chalk white faces with plucked, precisely arched eyebrows above dark almond eyes, which made them appear like rigid-faced, porcelain-skinned dolls. The women moved with short, mincing steps, a walk, Holly suggested to Denise Faveraux, that emphasized their vulnerability. To which Denise replied, "Yes, men like it when we're easy to topple over."

To rally her, Denise offered, "Don't forget the ironclad contract." Holly had indeed seen the contract, smuggled out of court by a lawyer friend of Denise's.

> For the consideration of $800 agreed upon, paid into my hands this day, I, Li Ng, will prostitute my body for the term of eight years. If, in that time, I am sick one day, two weeks shall be added to my time; and if more than one day, my term of prostitution shall go on an additional month for each day of sickness. If I run away or escape from the custody of my keeper, then I am to be held at the place of my keeper for the rest of my natural life.

A hugely obese Chinese man loomed ahead of Denise and Holly, calling, "Lookee two bits, feelee four bits, dooee six bits." Beside him stood two frail, scantily clad Chinese women, girls really, who leered lasciviously at both male and female passersby while the barker-pimp piped his refrain in front of a seedy-looking house. Denise glowered at the threesome. Holly, who was all eyes, felt like an innocent child.

Denise indicated a horse-drawn streetcar slowly pulling a load of bug-eyed tourists through this exotic landscape. "The tour people and travel agents compete to show Occidentals the wonders of Chinatown. I'm surprised they don't offer a scheduled stop at an opium den. 'Step right up, lie down, and have a pipe. . . .'"

Her companion replied dryly, "Maybe next year."

A little farther on the opium smell thickened. Below her, through a filthy basement window Holly glimpsed a room where dim outlines of multiple bodies reclined on a couch, their heads, limbs, almost touching. Or perhaps these images were self-supplied, as she remembered one of those lethargically blissful afternoons in Paris when the unctuous, grinning Chinese proprietor kept refilling her pipe as she lolled beside Jacques Fauconier and felt her entire being steeped in the drug's languid, murky essence.

She remembered a Ming Dynasty etching of an orgy that they'd examined at length as they lay there, huge penises embedded in enlarged labia, a never-ending chain of penises leading from one to another orifice, to a vagina, breasts, a mouth, a hand, an ass, with fingers, too, helping the human sex chain make yet another transition to yet another body. She'd never forgetten the expression of one impaled woman—head thrown back, mouth open ecstatically, one nipple distended, throbbing red. . . . The scene in the filthy basement window allowed Holly's mind to run riot. In the midst of the teeming street she suddenly felt hot, wet. She wanted to stretch her body, touch herself.

Holly's eyes sought the neutrality of the sand hills that towered above Stockton Street, carrying her vision up to the higher slope, barren and gullied by San Francisco's hard rains. Nob and Telegraph Hills passed before her gaze. Swinging back to the Bay, she recognized a half dozen thousand-ton clipper ships, a host of barkentines, and a pair of paddle-wheeling riverboats. The sailing vessels seemed alive, their flying white canvas breathing, snapping, and yawing while throwing off throbbing flashes of light as their masts tilted in and out of vertical. Scattered here and there throughout the Bay were the rotting hulls of abandoned ships slowly descending into the mud, carrion picked clean by thieves and tides.

Denise touched Holly's arm in front of a restaurant at the intersection of Stockton and Pacific. "In the midst of this squalor, there are a few decent restaurants. And here"—she pointed to a sign—"our future friend and her bodyguard-jailer punctually appear at one p.m. every Tuesday afternoon." Following Denise into the dimly lit vestibule, Holly recalled the Chinese curse, "May your child be a girl." Girls were routinely sold by parents to rid themselves of yet another mouth to feed and to save on the dowry price. The hundreds of pubescent females who were shipped by merchants to America arrived terrified, bewildered, without a syllable of the language. Each girl, according to her perceived physical charms, was auctioned to the highest bidder, then entombed in a whorehouse. All this reminded Holly of *The Slave Market,* the painting that had caused the split with Gérôme. How abused she'd felt when he finally allowed her to look at the canvas—the model was nude, the Arab buyer's hand was forcing open her mouth, as though inspecting a horse's teeth.

The two women sat down in the redolent restaurant, looking like leisured Occidental women without a care in the world. Denise ordered wonton soup, steamed dumplings, lobster Cantonese, and egg foo yung. (Denise explained, "This restaurant serves a mild cuisine from the southern province of Canton.") Holly ordered only the soup and ate very little, but Denise threw herself into the meal, eating and sipping with gusto and brandishing chopsticks like febrile pincers.

To calm her friend and pass the time, Denise Faveraux reeled off tidbits of her personal history. "Before I took to the 'legitimate' stage"—the notion of legitimacy apparently amused her—"I started, as we all start, as a non-professional." Her blue eyes seemed to beam light off the walls of the dark interior. "My mom abandoned the farm and my father and moved with me to Cincinnati. I was very young—actually a choir girl—when the inevitable happened: seduced by an older man." Denise offered an ascending light laugh while her eyes calmly searched the entranceway for the anticipated arrivals. "Our minister. Lutheran, very strict." Again that glittering up-the-scale laugh. "From the first I enjoyed it. I don't mean *really* enjoyed it. No, that took much longer. Even now, usually, it's nothing. Or a fluttering pleasure." She doled out silvery notes. "But I had power, that was clear from the first. Power *is* pleasure then?

"I went to work at sixteen. It didn't take long before I had to make a scheme for myself, a way to gain control, any kind. The job, the craft, was a business opportunity. A girl—no education, no background, no status—with breasts and legs could make a living." There was irony, bitterness, and comprehension in Denise's statement. Holly felt, oddly enough, the way she sometimes felt with Edward—her privileged background was, here, a deficit that couldn't be erased.

"It didn't take long before I knew the problem with my work, apart from men's stupidity and brutality, which was all too common. No, the worst problem was disease. In the house were three infected girls, one younger than me." With her chopstick she lifted a pale cushion of folded dough, which she'd identified as, "Shu mai. A steamed dumpling to you, dear." She continued earnestly, "Two older women were literally falling apart—a finger missing the top joint, and pathetic, teary Elaine with her nose half-eaten away. Another next door went insane from syphilis. We heard her screaming until the Madame put her out of her misery. Shot her."

"But these women, they had customers? No man in his right mind would . . ."

"Ah, dear, they're so rarely in their right minds. That's a joke. These poor creatures were 'retired.' They did housework, changed our sheets, drew baths, emptied chamber pots. Madame Bisquet had a half a heart. I may overstate. Maybe a quarter.

"Imagine the horror for me, a novice. For weeks I had the same nightmare: I looked into a clouded mirror and couldn't make out my face. I lit a candle and moved closer, and saw . . . where my nose should be . . . a gaping hole."

"A hole?"

"Raw bone." She hurried on. "The next day I hired my own doctor, who inspected me thoroughly. And, fortunately, blessedly"—she crossed herself then knocked on the wood table three times—"found nothing amiss. He was young, not bad looking, and he explained that, in my profession, it was odds-on that beginner's luck would not hold out." The dumpling hovered unattended in her chopsticks.

"I quit, ran away. I swore off men—no fucking for three weeks. Back then that was a strange experience. But no fucking meant the money dried up. With my last twenty-five bucks, I went back to the handsome doctor and laid the cash on his desk. I asked him, 'Is there a way to tell when a man is infected?' The young doctor was very obliging."

"How?"

"He handed me a condom made out of sheep gut and told me to insist that every single one of my clients use it."

"And they followed orders?"

"They did—or they didn't get any. Even the governor." Denise divulged this startling news with a twinkle.

"And the governor?" Holly tried to mask her avid interest.

"Ah, Leland." Denise smiled a complicated smile. "Yes, even the governor. In the bad old days I was known to make the application of the tender little sheep tip a stirring event." Holly took Denise at her word.

"Since you brought up Leland, I wanted to tell you I'm not exactly his mistress."

Holly was surprised.

"You could say he reserves a lot of my time, but it's more like I'm on retainer. He's a reliable income source. And I have my stage act, which brings enough. But, even if I didn't act, I would not want one man—especially Leland—to run my show."

This is a clever beauty, Holly considered. She prompted Denise, "Tell me more about your doctor friend."

"He taught me to recognize the canker, and subtler symptoms, too. I became the on-the-job expert. Enough to protect myself. No disease ever." Again she rapped on the wood.

"I'd teach other girls, too, but only the ones who'd listen. Over the years I dispensed one hell of a lot of sheep gut. The company ought to have offered me a discount."

Beautiful and seductive and deucedly clever and crystal clear about how to survive. Holly thought, *If we can pull this off, how much Edward would enjoy hearing about our adventure.*

"So you insisted on inspecting your male . . . ah. . . . your clients?" Why, in spite of herself, did she feel—and convey in those words—an irreducible grain of condescension? Odd, because she admired and respected this dazzling woman.

Denise thought about the slight for an instant, then replied, "Yes, I was—and still am—very careful about my men. One has to be. Don't you think?"

Holly thought, *How graciously she handled my affront.* "But back then, economically, could you reject . . . ?"

Denise scanned the restaurant. She, too, was getting anxious. "The day I rejected my first client . . . What a moment, my pet. I felt like—what?—an admiral standing on the prow of his ship after a battle. No, a dancer on the stage apron after a superb performance. What a feeling. Being choosy didn't hurt business. Do you know what I did after the first month or so?"

"No." Holly could barely concentrate, she was so nervous about the event to come.

"I upped my rates." She laughed. "Holly, men are stupid when led by their cocks. But even with stiff dicks they're not suicidal. They don't want to be infected any more than I do. Being my own doc gave me control over my life for the first time."

At that instant a slight, doe-eyed young woman entered the restaurant. Sung Wan was chaperoned by a burly Chinese man in a lavish brocade cape. He was as wide as he was tall, with a dished face, protruding ears, and a forehead that looked muscle-bound. Everything about the man bristled—ears, hair, eyebrows, muscles. With Sung Wan leading, they strolled to a nearby table. Denise appeared nonchalant, but was giddy from the stress. She nodded in the direction of the table and softly remarked, "This is it, Holly Hughes. We're about to go on."

Sung Wan's features were unexceptional, except for a broad, arching forehead and dark, absorbing eyes. Her face had been painted that blank and eerie white favored by Chinatown's professionals.

Before Sung Wan and her guard appeared, the drama seemed unreal to Holly, arm's-length playacting. Now, with the young woman sitting stiffly in her cushioned banquette, the dancer's stomach churned in what felt like contrary directions. Her heart pounded. Holly automatically brought the spoon to her mouth, but she no longer tasted the lush broth. She sipped the steaming black tea unaware of its acrid bite.

Denise continued as though unperturbed as Holly's heart thundered against her ribcage: "I managed to put away a serious amount of cash. I've thought about giving up 'the stage,' running off to New York or Rome or Paris—That's where you lived, yes?—and living off the interest. But what would I do to kill time? I don't have hobbies; I'm not exactly a reader." With raised eyebrows she scanned her companion. "You really are magnificent, dear." She reached for Holly's hand, stroked it.

Holly blushed scarlet as the drama began: Sung Wan stood, bowed respectfully to her beefy male shadow, and moved toward the "Ladys Lounge," an adjoining room with a bucket toilet and the predictably fly-specked three-quarter-length mirror that gave back clouded images of those struggling to freshen up. Denise waited through a few more deep breaths, rose, and followed Sung Wan into the toilet.

On cue Holly opened her purse. This caught the attention of the pug-faced, wide-bodied guard, who scrutinized the white woman suspiciously. Holly fished out a prerolled cigarette then rummaged in her purse but found no matches in the capacious depths. She cleared her throat, turned toward the burly escort, and said, "Pardon me, do you happen to have a match?"

He looked vacant, as though he did not understand a word she said.

"A Lucifer, fire, *match,*" Holly pleaded as she struck an imaginary match in the air while holding the cigarette toward him.

The man stood, moved to Holly's side, and gallantly lit her cigarette. Meanwhile, his gaze flitted uneasily back and forth from Holly's enchanting gray-green eyes to the Ladys Lounge.

Inside the bathroom, Denise Faveraux spoke rapidly in phonetic Chinese. "Escape. Must come. Freedom." Four well-rehearsed words, the limit of her hard-won Cantonese. The terrified Sung Wan looked blankly at her would-be rescuer. Denise pointed to the jimmied window and indicated the carriage waiting outside. "Escape, freedom," she repeated, recycling half of her Chinese vocabulary.

Seizing the young woman's hand, Denise mimed the procedure needed to climb over the windowsill. Sung Wan remained paralyzed—behind her, familiar, abject slavery; ahead, if she dared, the terrifying unknown. And all the while a beautiful white stranger with golden hair kept urging her to step through the window. Denise repeated: "Must come. Freedom." The young woman in the clinging yellow silk sheathe hesitated, her white face passive, immobile, helpless. Her eyes offered not a flicker of interest or recognition. Denise stepped closer and gently placed her forehead against the young woman's. They stood awkwardly together with their foreheads touching, Denise stroking Sung Wan's hair while uttering soothing guttural sounds, like a mother calming her child.

Sung Wan gave herself over to the blond stranger. Taking Denise Faveraux's hand, she placed a delicate, slippered foot on the windowsill and stepped through the frame. In full sunlight she seemed a slender apparition, as delicate and fleeting as a crystal teardrop. Denise retreated long enough to shove a solid wood chair under the doorknob. Then, a few steps behind Sung Wan, Denise Faveraux crawled through the window into the expectant day.

* * *

Back at her table, Holly asked in English, "Is your family still in China?"

He glanced uncertainly at the Ladys Lounge, replying with a thick accent, "Yes."

"And what province are you from?"

"Canton," he said slowly, drawing out the rhythmic off-rhyme.

"Ah, the cuisine of emperors." Buying time for Denise and Sung Wan, Holly felt danger's exhilaration beating over her like a huge bird's wings. "Would you like a cigarette?"

As Holly offered her cigarette case, she watched the thug trying to think: his mind moving heavily like a coach mired in sand. She thought he thought: *Why is the white woman talking to me?* Such strangeness had never occurred before. Still, he did not possess the necessary links. *Ah, the joys of translation,* Holly inwardly joked, thinking how much Edward would appreciate that notion. Requiring this lug to think in English slowed him down. Meanwhile, Holly felt cleaved in two—half of her seated in the restaurant's main lounge, lit cigarette in hand; half outside, frantically hoping that her partner and the young woman were climbing into the waiting coach. She strained to hear hoofbeats in the back alley.

"Do you have sisters, brothers?" The mindlessness of the question amused and insulated Holly. But would she be deft enough to steal sufficient time for her coconspirators?

Sung Wan's guard awoke from Holly Hughes's spell. He bowed coolly to the ravishing woman, spun on his heel with impressive delicacy for such a big man, and, up on his toes like a prizefighter, bolted toward the lounge door. He didn't bother to knock or shout a warning. He hit the door with his shoulder, but it barely budged. The man hit the door again, throwing his sizable bulk into the assault. The door shivered, held. The restaurant came alive. Waiters yelling in Chinese scurried to turn aside the madman's frenzied attack on the innocent door; customers scrambled for the exit or ducked behind tables. Shouting escalated, a woman screamed; another screamed louder. Meanwhile, the man kept hurling his body at the door marked "Ladys Lounge," crying out with a lover's urgency, "Sung Wan! Sung Wan!"

Holly stood, dropped three dollars on the table, more than enough to cover their meal, and started for the exit.

The Chinese man turned her way as she moved, his agonized expression stating his dilemma: Should he bash away at the door or pursue the white woman? He hurled his frame at the solid oak. Now it creaked and threatened to break but once again held. Waiters' hands groped to stop him, but Sung Wan's jailer threatened his countrymen with a series of stylized gestures that immediately made them retreat.

The man wailed again, "Sung Wan!" The cry reached Holly's heart—all of love's twisted anguish and hopeless failure embedded in two syllables.

Holly Hughes heard his body hit the door, heard the oak splinter, then the furious cry came again as more hands fought to subdue this maniac. She was at the restaurant's door, moving rapidly while briefly exchanging pleasantries with the owner. She saw the Chinese tough spin lightly and charge after her.

Heart churning, she was outside, moving up Pacific Street away from the restaurant. A few steps and she whispered, "Safe." Holly thought she was in the clear, insulated by the crush of pedestrians, the welter of foreign faces, smells, sounds. But an instant later, the burly guard strode beside her, nostrils flaring, face contorted by fury and confusion. It took all of Holly's considerable fortitude not to sprint away.

"Where she?" the man grunted, his breath coming in shuddering gasps.

"How dare you accost me!" She broadcast her indignation loudly, as though speaking from a stage to her audience. Strollers looked astonished, appalled. People in passing carriages strained to see what the problem was. Then an unprecedented incident occurred. The Chinese man reached out and dared to seize the arm of a fashionable Caucasian woman. Movement along the street ceased. Horses seemed to halt midstride. Delivery boys hustling along with their wicker baskets froze. For an extended moment, silence blanketed the bustling intersection. Then voices, Caucasian all, shouted, "Stop!" "Unhand that woman!" "How dare you!" "Arrest 'im!" From a horse-drawn, double-decker tourist tram a woman shrieked, "String the yellow bastard up!"

Men converged on Holly and the bodyguard while the street resounded with shouts, blaring whistles, running feet. Four uniformed policemen materialized out of nowhere. The burly Chinese man, surrounded on all sides, did not, as Holly assumed, fight or try to break away. He physically crumpled, seemed to deflate before her eyes, as though the muscles that buoyed up the barrel chest had been surgically excised by the white threat.

"Do you know this man?" a rotund, baby-faced policeman asked Holly Hughes.

"I never saw this *person* in my life." The man began to protest, but powerlessness subdued him.

"Was he trying to rob you?"

"I really can't say. For some unknown reason he actually grabbed my arm." She raised her left forearm as though it were a foreign appendage.

The Chinese man didn't bother to look at the perfidious woman who entrapped him, betrayed him. Like the women he had enslaved, he stood passive, a dumb creature being led to slaughter. Holly had little time or inclination to study him, for the policeman politely said she was excused and then he and his colleagues half-led, half-dragged the man away.

Earlier, Denise had explained that "after Sung Wan's liberation" there was to be no contact among the trio, possibly for a week or two, since contact might implicate them in the "good kidnapping" and, possibly, jeopardize their ward's hiding place. Fortunately for Holly's nerves, Denise Faveraux's note arrived the next morning. Holly opened the thin, blue envelope with uncertain fingers.

> So far all's well. Our private underground railroad rolls on. So many thanks for your courage and being the decoy for that slob. Keep the vow of silence and lie low until we meet again.
>
> Denise.
>
> P.S. We did good, didn't we?

The plan was to hide Sung Wan temporarily at the home of the formidable Miss Augusta Hannibal, one of the most vocal suffragists in the Bay Area. The decision about Sung Wan's future would be made by other unidentified women in "the cabal," though Denise was privileged to consult with them about options for their ward.

Chapter Thirteen

Fortunately for Muybridge's photographic experiment, during much of the fall of 1867, Stanford was away on pressing and secretive railroad business. Rumors of pending financial doom along with construction delays in the Sierra Nevada Mountains raced around the stock farm like unbroken colts. In November, the earliest snow in three decades hit the sierras, abruptly halting progress on the easternmost construction of the Central Pacific Railroad. Meanwhile, the rival Union Pacific kept rolling steadily west from its starting point in Omaha across the flat, unresisting Plains. The rumor mill had it that the rival railroad was bounding forward at the unprecedented, juggernaut pace of eight miles per day.

Back in Palo Alto, the photographer's battle to devise a fast, functional shutter torturously dragged on. The clock kept ticking; costs escalated. The statistical harpy Collis Ward made daily visits to the sixth furlong pole to check on progress. Twice a day each day for an hour or more, Ward observed, the unquiet leg bouncing or tapping as he scratched out voluminous notes on Muybridge's every action. Ward's presence did not improve the photographer's disposition or his staff's confidence.

The camera shed now held twelve cameras, all aimed across the track at the back-angled, whitewashed eight-foot-high wall. Late one afternoon, standing in the shady shed, a rattled, exhausted Edward Muybridge decided to confront the burgeoning crisis of confidence head-on. "This work has been underway for almost two months now. You may all wish to be doing something more entertaining—training horses"—he nodded at Harry Harnett—"or riding hell-bent around the track." He fixed his gaze on Ned and Willy. He had their eyes now.

"Up till now, each of you has been receptive and helpful. It hasn't been a waltz, and it's not going to get easier." He paused. "But stick with me, and we will conquer our problems, we will achieve great things." Muybridge wasn't certain that he'd succeed, but, sure as hell, he wasn't about to admit the possibility of failure to his sagging associates.

Every day at the forge Muybridge worked alongside Tim White, the towering blacksmith, who heated and pounded, bent and tempered rods and thin steel cylinders. Muybridge handled a range of calipers from minute to microscopic, compulsively checking the ratchet device and each element of hardware—its screws and nuts and slender bolts—for the wooden shutter mechanism until they met his exacting specifications. The paired vertical slides—one moved up, the other down—were held open by two powerful, hand-forged steel springs connected to the armature in the side of the camera. Finally, at last, Muybridge held what he hoped was the world's fastest shutter in his hands: a miniature guillotine designed to slice optical reality into the briefest fragments ever beheld.

With Muybridge carrying the camera and shutter like the Host itself, together the colleagues moved to the shed, younger acolytes in the lead. Behind them strode Tim White, who stood six feet, five inches, and weighed over 250 pounds, and next to the blacksmith came the diminutive Harry Harnett, less than half his weight and needing one and a half quick steps for every one of Tim's.

Though he believed his shutter was viable, Muybridge could not be certain. To catch the fleeting trotter, he calculated, the mechanism would have to work in one two-hundredth of a second, faster than the human eye can blink.

Ned whispered under his breath, "Fastest camera in the West." His hand dove for an imagined six-gun, cleared his thigh, and aimed straight at Willy, who doubled over—as though shot—and started laughing.

Though he wasn't in a laughing mood, Muybridge smiled—he'd been surly too often recently.

Fifty yards up the track, Occident stood between the traces, his bridle gripped by a tense groom. A light film of sweat covered the animal's chest and back, making him look like an artist's glossy dream of horseflesh, all sleek black lines and pulsing, flowing muscle. Occident backed impatiently, shaking his head up and down as though nodding an emphatic *yes* to a pressing question.

Harnett sprang into the sulky, pointed the horse and rig up the track, cautiously moving against traffic. Beyond the far turn, the trainer swung the sulky around. Then Harry Harnett whistled sharply, imitating the crack of a whip. The horse leaped forward. It took only a few strides before the light sulky raised dust streams, delicate curling lines that clung to the back edges of the rolling wheels. Muybridge watched the twin squibs being thrown off, light brown trails drawn uninterruptedly through the air. Someday, Muybridge vowed, he would photograph it all—the horse, the sulky, the taut smile on Harry's bony face, even those barely visible outriders of dust. Occident raced nearer. *Now!* he thought, and Muybridge squeezed the bulb of his camera and heard the shutter's telltale click.

Moments later he almost had what he wanted. The dust had clouded the silhouetted image of Occident's legs, obscuring the positions of the rear hooves. But the form was there, the outlines just about readable. The next step was to tamp down the dust. Moments later, Edward held up the photograph for Ned and Willy and shouted at the top of his lungs to Harry, "We're on our way!"

"So you're going to settle the guv's bet?" Ned asked, breathing his relief into the question.

"Or die trying."

That evening, for once, they left each other heartened and at ease.

He burst into the flat, rushed to Holly, took her in his arms. "Holly, my love, to the untrained eye it looks like a wretched, miserable blurry silhouette, but I think I've done it!" He whipped out the photo. "It was late in the day—"

"I'll say." It was past nine p.m.

"And dusty. You see, the shot's blurred, but only by the dust! If we water the track—to keep the damn dust down—and spread enough white around to give the contrast I so desperately need, I think—I actually believe—I will get my photo." He added, "Which is only the barest start, since I need a lot more than a single miserable shot of the demon trotter. But at least we have a beginning."

Ordinarily, she adored him in such moods. This evening, however, her mind was split in two: deeply pleased for Edward, and also worried about Fauconier. Holly had heard nothing from him in two months, and it was already late fall. She had imagined him lying on the frozen tundra; she saw him eviscerated by bear, skewered on the antlers of moose; or, more realistically, knocked senseless and keelhauled by a clutch of thugs in a dingy, sordid bar. Yet these imagined catastrophes paled compared to her fear that, one day soon, Fauconier would descend upon San Francisco, and she would be forced to confront her old and new loves.

"I still have to work out the hardest question: how to take a dozen photos in sequence while a horse trots by at thirty-six feet per second."

Holly had been busy. She lectured and organized and pamphleteered and attempted to arrange a ballet class for San Francisco's women. The executive director of the Young Men's Christian Association kept repeating that all "appropriate rooms" were already booked months, if not years, in advance. She was buoyed by the delicious secret of Sung Wan's bold rescue, though it felt odd not to share the triumph with Edward. Denise had sworn her to secrecy, insisting that the Syndicate that imported the Chinese women had been known to kill those who interfered in its business operations. So secrecy it was. Most of all, Holly missed performing. The fact that San Francisco would never again applaud for her, that all her dedicated work meant nothing here, was galling.

Later that night Muybridge drafted a letter to the United States Patent Office. It read in part:

> My intention is to take photographic views of animals moving rapidly under speed, in order to determine the posture, position and relation of their limbs in different portions of their step or stride. . . .

> My invention relates to a double-acting slide shutter, with the means for operating the same, which is graduated so as to gauge the position of the horse and the posture of its limbs.

A half hour later, Muybridge asked Holly if he should address the salutation to "Dear Sir" or "To Whom It May Concern."

"'Dear Sir.' It's less impersonal. I doubt there are many women occupying executive positions at the U.S. Patent Office."

Muybridge started his second letter after eleven. It was addressed to *The Philadelphia Photographer*, the prestigious journal. In its pages, photographers exchanged ideas and information and guardedly reported innovations—after first mailing a letter to the Patent Office. He wrote easily this time, pleased to be informing his colleagues about the new device. As Muybridge finished the description of the mechanism, an image of Stanford's clerk standing at the upright desk in front of a stack of letters popped into his mind. Meachum Steward's hand, as always, was scratching forward left to right—an image that floated through his mind these days.

The next morning an invitation on the governor's flowery stationery lay on Edward's worktable in the Palo Alto shed. "Excellent work," the text read. "Please come to tea on Friday afternoon. I urge you to invite Miss Hughes. R.S.V.P." It was signed in Leland Stanford's outsized hand.

He handed her the invitation that night, in bed. Holly adamantly refused. "I can't imagine what I could say to him—other than he's a bastard guttersnipe. I see no positive outcome there, Edward."

"So I'll refuse for you."

"Yes. You understand, don't you?"

"I understand."

They had made love infrequently since the night of Holly's performance. Muybridge tentatively eased his hand under her nightgown and onto her belly. The skin felt warm and smooth, a yielding silky tension. Muybridge nuzzled her belly and let his lips wander over her flesh. Her stomach muscles gathered ever so slightly, and he pursued that tension, following the contracting muscles, hoping they'd become a wave and sweep over her body. Heat rose from Holly; her pearly smell engulfed him. Gently, lightly, as though only suggesting the possibility of lovemaking, his tongue grazed and skimmed her belly. The tongue circled, doubled-back, moved lower. She shifted and he moved on, closer to her center.

"Edward?" Her voice held a question. He sat up on his elbow. When Holly was eager for sex, her eyes would melt. There would be a moment when, suddenly, the gray-green irises would liquefy and passion would pool there, absorbing her, inviting him. Now her eyes suggested warmth, but they had not melted.

They lay side by side, Holly staring up at the ceiling, trying to escape the mood she had been trapped in for weeks now.

"Since that night . . ." She asked him to read her mind, to understand the bitterness of her public spurning. Forcing out the words was like hefting a boulder uphill. Speech was too clumsy to describe the outrage. All her exacting training and long-term patience seemed useless, fruitless.

Stroking her auburn crown, appreciatively studying the multitude of reds and rich browns held captive in her hair, he said, "I know, I know."

Only he didn't really know, Holly reflected. Watching his erection droop, she considered relieving him, but she felt too empty and distant to dispense even that pleasure.

How long they lay there, Holly did not know. She invoked reason and persuasion to stir herself as she lay indifferent beside her lover, her nightgown provocatively drawn above her thighs. She told herself that she needed it and that, certainly, he did too. She argued that she owed it to him, though guilt did not impassion Holly. Meanwhile, she remained unmoved, she who rarely needed encouragement, who delighted in sex, loved lovemaking. She might have remained as she was all night—dead below her waist, tortured above her neck—listening to his strained breathing, if she had not detected his smell. Edward bathed frequently. He scrubbed his body and especially his armpits yet, even immediately after his bath, a combination of sweat and effort and something that to Holly evoked sex clung faintly to him. She moved her nose a fraction closer to his armpit and guardedly inhaled. *Erotic smelling salts,* she thought. Holly breathed him in now, letting his male smell work on her. She laid her head onto Edward's chest and nuzzled there. Her fingers slipped over his stomach until they reached his groin. Until they began, she did not know how frustrated and empty her body felt.

He brushed her breast with his lips, tongued then sucked her nipple. His tongue became her sensual conductor, probing, awakening, alert to the nipple's response, its aroused, independent life. He marveled that that bit of flesh could concentrate such delights.

Holly responded by moving over him, then sank down on his semihard penis. He arched up, struggling to stay inside. Her pelvis hungrily slid and sank onto his half-hard cock until Edward grasped Holly's hips to channel her movements. He had to fight to stay with her. He arched up higher; he moved with her as his mind worked frantically to call up erotic images—Holly's tongue flickering in heated dance over her lips, her mouth gaping wide in lovely-ugly pleasure, the flush of those priceless sweat gems on her face and chest, the luminous heat in her eyes after she came. He saw her fingers inch down.

"Christ, I love this," Holly moaned. "I've been so—what is it?—knotted up inside. . . . I go a little crazy . . . when we don't make love."

"I know the feeling." He slipped his tongue into her mouth, hoping to further arouse himself.

She kissed him and leaned forward, a nipple grazing his chest. The light brush of that rigid nipple . . . Suddenly he was there. Her belly and chest, her thighs and breasts turned liquid, a fluid skin that flowed and rippled and gyrated around his erection. They rushed along in a boat, swiftly moving toward a falls and, beyond, thrilling rapids. She plunged ahead, belly tilting wildly as her body's need gained on her. Holly turned intent—thrusting herself up and down on him, their bellies slapping together, her thighs closing and opening almost too wide. She rose up, sounded again, the thigh and lower body muscles working in needy, opulent unison. He worried her fierce thrusts would eject him, feared he would not stay inside. On his back below her, he stretched and planed and dug his heels into the mattress and arched his torso up on his shoulders and somehow, just somehow, managed to cling to Holly as she exploded into her need. At the climax, she offered mysterious, heavenly labial gutturals. He came quickly after her.

"You're a miracle," he said when they lay resting. "You don't dole out pleasure. You're like—what?—a natural phenomenon, a . . . geyser. Holly Yellowstone." The overstatement charmed her.

She realized how much she adored Edward and, simultaneously, how much she enjoyed men—their smells, tastes, all the varieties, and subtle and not so subtle differences. She compared Denise's vast experience with her own limited, if adroit, trio. Holly laughed and he asked what was so funny.

"Life. You. The two of us. At times it's glorious, isn't it?" No lecture this night.

Toward morning he awoke with an erection and reached out to caress a sleepy but receptive Holly. This time he rode up high against her pubic bone. Edward loved that contact, the hard reality of her and that luscious internal wetness, the fabulous contradiction of solid and liquid, hard-soft wet heat. He played with her sensitized clitoris, bringing them both off almost together.

"Do unto others, I say." Her hard gasping breaths, the pleasure-won smile, her mad, lambent, pooling eyes made him feel like a triumphant sultan.

She settled against his thighbone, her thighs sticking to him. A little later she started to rub her pussy against that thigh. Lust overtook them again. This time she squeezed her breasts together: taut nipples scored his chest. The pointed, hard-flesh nubs drove him wild. As she came, the dew covering her cheeks and forehead and chest was manna, a gift of a shimmering, sensual heaven.

He licked her crooked tooth, then licked individual sweat beads off her chest until, smiling, she told him to stop. "You deny me, woman?"

"Enough for now, stud. Enough."

In his sleep an exasperated Edward found himself watching that clerk copy a letter. *Why,* he asked himself, *am I stranded in this ridiculous dream again?* Meachum's hand sloped on, transcribing character after character. Finally, the impatient dreamer peered over the clerk's shoulder in order to read the message—only to find the handwriting illegible.

In the morning he turned to Holly and sleepily muttered, "That idiotic dream I've been having." Auburn strands strayed loosely over her shoulders; her sated body, thighs open, legs splayed, retained vestiges of the night's visitation.

"Stanford's scrivener again?" Edward nodded yes. "You weren't too worn out to dream?"

He kissed her and sent exploratory fingers over her chest.

"I want to know how much it costs to copy those letters."

"Why in the world do you care?"

"Imagine all over the country, thousands of overworked, crimp-clawed clerks—in the long run it may be cheaper to photograph the papers." Holly looked puzzled. "I'm thinking like an entrepreneur. Maybe that's my next employment opportunity. Stanford could show me the mansion door at any moment. Ward's jotting notes like he's got shares in the pencil-making factory. The experiment's taking for bloody ever, burning up his cash like firewood in January."

Kissing her forehead again and again, Edward's lips registered different temperatures, the range of her brow's climates. His fingers negotiated their way down toward her pussy.

She trapped his hand, too sore to let the fingers rove. "So you want to economize for your employer, is that the idea?"

"Not charity. I need an insurance policy, dear, in the all-too-likely event that the ex-governor looks for a less expensive obsession than the one he's currently bankrolling."

Edward's new realism pleased her so that, for the first time since the performance, she sprang out of bed and danced for him. She twirled and stopped, twirled and froze.

"Once more!" he insisted.

Holly leaped and froze, twirled then stopped.

"Again!" he demanded, sitting up. She repeated her movement. "Darling, don't you see? It's that simple."

"What is 'that simple'?"

"The stop and start, start and stop." She watched the cheek muscles gathering, releasing as this new idea played like a refrain across his slender face.

"The eye is not quick enough to actually *see* you move. Suppose all that is involved in seeing motion—or, more truly, in the perception of motion—is a series of still photos. If the stills move rapidly one after another then it—the object, in this case the world's most intelligent and irresistible dancer—appears to be in motion. Like a flip book." He got up, held her arms apart, moved them above her head and stopped. "Gradations of the movement, that's the magic key. Maybe the eye *reads* movement in the transition from position A to B." He lifted her right arm to the side, parallel to the floor. "From here"—he moved the arm down—"to here. Your dancing is a sequence of individual frames. But our eyes can't separate each frame because you move too quickly for them to capture the sequence."

She was interested, to be sure, but . . .

"Freeze!" he commanded. "Don't move a bloody inch, Holly."

Naked, Muybridge sped to the cluttered worktable and picked up a flip book. He opened it, revealing a series of Albert Bierstadt's drawings of a roan horse. Edward turned to the first page and began to thumb slowly through, front to back. Holly watched: on each page the position of the horse's hooves altered ever so slightly—a little higher, then higher still, and so on till they reached the top of their arc and started down toward the ground. He threaded back to the first page and flipped through more rapidly until the horse looked like it was walking. When he flipped still more rapidly, this time, the horse appeared to trot.

"God, it's so simple, Holly. It's been staring me in the face for years. Right here. A simple child's toy." He waved the flip book. "The mind or eye or both must continue the motion. See?" He flipped through. "All it is, really, is a series of photographs, one after another. Moving the photos in sequence will do it!"

"It's finally happened, dear. You've gone stark-raving mad."

Ten minutes later, as Muybridge buttoned his frock coat, ready to ride south to the Palo Alto estate, Holly confessed, "I've been thinking about Stanford's invitation to tea. No matter how much I loathe the miserable counter-jumper, it feels cowardly to tuck my tail between my legs and run away. After all, refusing would send such an arrogant message."

"I don't know, Holly . . ." Internally, Edward questioned what could go wrong in such a meeting. Conclusion: everything. While looking in the mirror, Muybridge knotted then fluffed out the flowing silk cravat she had given him. He didn't feel like himself so dandified, but Holly liked him to wear it. "Maybe you should avoid—"

"Why in the world did he invite me? Does it make any sense?"

Perplexity knit her eyebrows until they threatened to temporarily unite. "I'm tempted to find out."

"Then accept, dear." Muybridge kissed her and put on his Stetson. "If you'd like to."

"I may. I very well may."

As they embraced she squeezed herself against him, kissed him fervently, then spun and danced off.

Holly danced because she felt better than she'd felt in two months. She kept moving around the room in this flood of high spirits then, after he shut the door, she slowed. Hearing him ride off, she stopped. Holly wanted to run and call Edward back. A now daily panic assailed her: how to goad or bribe or seduce herself into practicing, to return to the discipline she loved beyond measure or words? She calmed herself by saying aloud, "Start, it will be fine. Just begin." The clock rudely ticked on; she remained immobile. Finally, imitating Kuznetsova, she ordered, *"Commencer!"* Holly did not move. Her father's reproving face appeared. He used to say, "Self-pity is the worst sin because it's the most crippling." Once when she objected that it wasn't a sin because no second party was injured, he replied, "To throw away talent is to create inexcusable waste. There's not world enough and time as it is."

Her father's voice goading her, Holly grudgingly stretched and bent and reached for the ceiling, opposing muscle to muscle until she felt a sharp twinge in the left calf. Even now when she moved quickly the pulled muscle bothered her, though over the months the pain had retreated down into the tissue. The pain submerged within her leg flooded Holly's mind with unbidden images of the performance. Yes, she had danced well that evening, with the city at her feet and the pair who loved and hounded her seated below.

She kept pushing her body, tentatively working around that aching muscle until she warmed up. Still favoring the left side, Holly gingerly launched into her workout. The knotted muscle began to unlimber. She danced for one hour by the clock, remembering Kuznetsova's adage: "You miss one day of work, you know it. Two days, everybody in the troupe knows it."

It was nine-thirty when she heard the postman's crisp step moving up the walk. Holly spun automatically toward the door, like the compass needle pointing north.

Jacques Fauconier's bold, potent hand appeared on the front of the envelope. Anxiously she ripped it open and read the French:

> My Dear,
>
> Though I behaved like a thorough gentleman at our last meeting, do not believe that I felt remotely like one. I burned for you. I stood before you like an uninitiated boy, not knowing how to advance. At the same time, sense memory tasted your lips, your tongue, your pussy, your indelible flesh. Keeping us apart seemed artificial and perverse and oddly provocative, too. I simply wanted to take—no, *regain*—what was ours. I assumed that you felt as I, that you and I were eternally beloved friends and passionate, understanding lovers, that neither time nor space could alter the agreement that constitutes our being. From out of nowhere, a strange, impenetrable barricade was thrown up—a barrier that you could, at will, with ease, tear down; a barrier raised only by you without the courtesy of consulting me. Understand, it is impossible for a man to change his body's feelings about a woman he adores. I will never understand how women find it possible to turn on and turn off their sex like a kitchen tap. I know you well enough to believe that you are not playing the tempestuous tease. You have never dissembled about any issue of consequence. You tell me you are in love with this Muybridge. Fine. But you must accommodate another love who watched you emerge from girlhood's shadows into unrivalled womanhood, a lover who has stood and will stand beside you through all pleasures and difficulties, who appreciates your character and beauty, and even adores your few mostly minor flaws. Are you not the same woman who argued that love may not, cannot, be measured or quantified? "Love is infinite," you gloriously declaimed before Jean-Léon Gérôme himself! "Love grows on love." "Love has no preexisting rules."
>
> I miss, I expect, I beg and demand your love.

A "J" covered the bottom third of the page.

Chapter Fourteen

Up in the Sierra Nevadas, where the Central Pacific Railroad kept inching its way east, four feet of snow had already accumulated, and it was only early December. Two hundred miles west and six thousand feet lower, in Palo Alto, Edward Muybridge stood in full sunlight with Ned Quick and Willy Jackson.

Inspecting the camera shed, the whitewashed wall, and the lime-covered track, Edward measured his progress. Twelve cameras were now in place, twelve mechanical eyes poised to record the movements of Occident or another fleet-footed trotter—if his experiment worked. As Muybridge surveyed his tiny, intricate fiefdom, Holly drove her gig into his field of vision. Edward watched her competently thread her way through the paddock, swing the gig around the cooling-off track, then snap the reins lightly, urging the pair into a smart trot.

Edward handed her down, aware that she needed no assistance. Introductions were brief. Even ebullient Ned Quick turned skittish, and shy Willy seemed about to bolt. Holly's notoriety had preceded her.

"Edward's told me so much about you, Ned." Her smile could have melted a glacier. She turned toward Willy. "You as well, Willy." He seemed to blush down to his muck-stained boots. "I want to thank you both for being so generous and helpful. Edward tells me he could not have made such progress without you two."

The boys murmured their replies, not knowing how to respond to Holly's largesse.

Ned led Holly around the shed, reserve contending with pride as he pointed out Edward's innovations—the stop-time shutter device; the speedy lenses arrayed in order one through twelve.

"Impressive," she said. Knowledgeably, she manipulated the shutter. All heard the familiar click. "For months I've been looking at drawings of the camera shed and that angled wall." Holly smiled as she pointed across the track toward the white wall as a trotter wheeled by. "It's exciting to finally see the layout itself."

Muybridge felt disappointed though not surprised that Harry Harnett did not walk the two hundred yards from the paddock to greet Holly. Muybridge understood where Harnett's loyalties lodged. Though both boys were charmed, they literally kept their distance, as though afraid that whatever she had was contagious. Waving good-bye to Ned and Willy, Muybridge and Holly started the mile drive across the lawn to the mansion, with Holly at the reins.

Muybridge hugged her. "Thanks for coming, my friend."

"You begged and implored me, didn't you?" She was in a foul mood.

Impatiently, Muybridge blew a pocket of air out of his mouth. "As I recall, you volunteered."

Holly's head whipped around, ready for warfare.

His eyes said: *Either we're in this together, or . . .* She looked away, taking in the tasteful estate—the track within a track, the tall barns with their symmetrical double rows of windows, high and low ranks of panes glinting in the sun.

Holly took his hand. "Somehow, Edward, we'll weather this."

As Muybridge snuck a kiss, she made the little throaty, cooing sound that flattered him. His face inched closer to hers. "You have a talent for making people feel good about themselves—when you care to." He nodded back toward the camera shed, where Ned and Willy were conscientiously spreading a new lime layer on the track.

Her mouth tensed grimly as she stared ahead at the governor's rambling, irresolute stone pile of a mansion. "Why didn't your Mr. Harnett put in an appearance? I would've enjoyed meeting him."

"I suppose he was busy."

She hated sugarcoating. "Edward," Holly said, rolling her large eyes.

"Well, he is Stanford's employee."

"So are you, dear."

The mansion loomed closer. Edward burrowed his nose in Holly's hair, then wondered if Stanford's thousand eyes were watching them even now.

Then there was Denise, standing beside Stanford: Muybridge remembered the unabashed appreciative look she directed at him the night of Holly's performance, as though he had been singled out for the promise of exquisite pleasures. Edward smiled internally, wondering what had happened to his oft-expressed suspicion of beautiful women? This year, in San Francisco, he was madly in love with one beauty while, on the flawless croquet pitch, he basked in the uninhibited warmth of another.

The foursome of Holly Hughes and Edward Muybridge, Denise Faveraux and Leland Stanford stood just beyond the mansion's shadow on the groomed lawn. To the uninitiated eye, the thick turf appeared to have sprouted strange, white metal excrescences. A series of eight hoops (designated "wickets") outlined a rectangular playing field that measured the official twenty-eight by thirty-five yards. At a spot near the middle of the grassy rectangle, a pale peg of beech wood stood directly behind a pair of hoops. This, Stanford pointed out, was the final wicket. According to Stanford, a player had to pass a wooden ball through two of the metal wickets and hit the last peg "to be crowned the victor."

In her demure dove gray dress with gathered sleeves, Holly looked statuesque and aloof, a latter-day Diana. Her mallet swung freely in her hand as she moved among the croquet wickets, nonchalantly studying the layout of the pitch. During the tour of the house and at tea, Holly had said little. Stanford, on the other hand, was voluble, expansive, wooing Muybridge by offering to set up a studio on the estate to photograph the movement of dogs and cats, elephants and seals, ostrich and camel, creation's menagerie studied in all its multitudinous forms of motion. What an incalculable boon to human knowledge such photographs would be, he crowed. Biology and anatomy, medicine and art, the sciences as well as the humanities would benefit from such pioneering, comprehensive research. When Muybridge suggested they study human locomotion as well, Stanford had looked at Holly Hughes. "Human beings are the universe's most fascinating—and recalcitrant—subjects."

Holly had responded with a restrained but heartfelt, "I couldn't agree more." A half-relieved smile fought its way onto Edward's tensed lips. Yet he remained on his guard, anticipating trouble.

Muybridge watched Stanford lean down and speak quietly to Denise Faveraux. The ex-governor of California, putative paragon of domestic virtue, protector of women's ears in public, stood on the tailored croquet pitch steps away from his mistress. Mrs. Stanford was away in Sacramento visiting her mother. Or so Harry Harnett had told Muybridge. So was this tea party/croquet joust a calculated affront to both Holly and himself? Not to speak of Denise Faveraux? Or did the invitation assume a certain companionable worldliness on the part of each of the players? Edward had already recognized that Holly was especially friendly to Denise Faveraux, which surprised him a bit. Her befriending a woman of less-than-impeccable morality seemed a departure. Indoors, at tea, the two had spent time in animated conversation, as though they knew each other which, to Edward, seemed unlikely. But the thought slipped away into the golden afternoon. Side by side, the two were stunning—Denise gay and carefree, Holly elegant and severe.

Observing them, Muybridge commented, "What a pity I didn't bring my cameras."

"We're here for blood sport," Denise offered. "Not to stand for hours and pose for you." She struck a stiff pose, arm raised, head tilted back.

Stanford chuckled, his large, curiously high belly moved up toward his throat. Muybridge thought, *Oh god, does he wear a corset, too? Maybe that's why . . .*

"Suppose Miss Faveraux and I pair up against you and Muybridge?"

"Perfectly acceptable," Holly answered stiffly.

Stanford responded pleasantly. "You and Edward can take the blue and black, Miss Hughes."

"I'd prefer the red and yellow, if you please."

Leland Stanford warily eyed Holly Hughes, a seasoned gambler weighing whether he faced a fellow professional or yet another tinhorn.

"You'll begin, Miss Hughes?" Stanford sounded a courtly note.

She approached the red ball and studied the shot. The wicket stood twenty-five yards away, at the end of the first leg of the rectangular playing field. Choosing the shorter of the two mallets, Holly spread her legs and flexed her knees slightly. She took a practice stroke, inhaled, held her breath. As she drew back the mallet in the approved "center style," Holly wished that she had the presence of mind to wear bloomers and not a full skirt. Of course Edward despised bloomers. A minor flaw, she mused; in spite of the tension, she almost smiled. Then she swung.

Thwack! The crisp sound of wood on wood reverberated across the lawn. The ball shot off and rolled toward the first wicket. The quartet watched as the red sphere sped on until it touched the white wicket's front edge and stopped, well aligned.

Stanford approved. "Splendid, Miss Hughes."

Muybridge considered, *Perhaps Holly had perfected her game with an English lord on plush Oxfordshire turf—or beside a moneyed French count in the Auvergne. Or with the towering Falconier, or whatever his cursed unpronounceable name was. Perhaps her father's dream about creating an accomplished Renaissance prince wasn't so farfetched.*

Trying to imitate Holly Hughes, Denise Faveraux drew the mallet back between her legs. But her long skirt got tangled up in the instrument's head. She flexed her elbows spastically, lunged forward, and missed the ball.

"Oh Christ."

Stanford took the shorter mallet from her hands and replaced it with a longer one. "You don't have to hit the ball center style."

"Leland, I can't hit the damn thing any style."

Stanford demonstrated an approved procedure. Addressing the ball from the side, he swung the mallet like a golf club. He wrapped his massive arms around Denise and guided her practice stroke.

"Can I take a practice swing?"

The other three responded too eagerly. "Of course." "Certainly." "As many as you want." Denise eyed the others skeptically. "I may not know the game, but I'm not a moron." Holly guffawed, a sharp braying sound; Muybridge hadn't heard that laugh since he'd made his stupid remark about her being "a nurse."

Denise pivoted and lunged again. The mallet skimmed the top of the wood sphere, which dribbled feebly off to the left. "Pure folly," Denise grumbled as she followed her ball.

Muybridge made solid contact—a sharp, dry click as his mallet hit the wood—but he hooked the ball. It shot off to the right and rolled across the boundary into the rose bed he'd photographed some weeks before. He, too, trudged off after his ball.

Soon Denise was hacking at the blue while Muybridge attempted to drive the yellow in a straight line toward the elusive wickets. Both wandered errantly back and forth across the pitch, trying to guide their balls through the unyielding order of the wickets, which remained shut like a portcullis to their sallies. Meanwhile, Holly Hughes and Leland Stanford proceeded apace through the white metal hoops, three, then four, soon five wickets ahead of the awkward neophytes.

The two men momentarily moored alongside each other at the northeast corner of the pitch. Muybridge was again trying to line up his approach to the impenetrable third wicket while Stanford positioned himself for the "fourth back," only four wickets from the game's conclusion.

Muybridge topped his ball, which rolled weakly to the left and snuggled an inch shy of Stanford's black ball.

"Governor, let me ask you a question."

"Anything." The expansive, courtly manner prevailed.

"I've been thinking about your clerk Steward." Stanford peered at Muybridge as though responding, *Whatever for? I never think of him.* "Do you have any idea how much you spend a year just copying letters and documents?"

"Not the slightest. Why in heaven's name do you ask?"

Muybridge paused uncertainly. A day earlier he had decided not to ask Steward about the cost of copying Leland's documents, certain that the clerk would report the inquiry to "the governor." Muybridge did not want Stanford to suspect that the photographer was casting about for other potential employment—his insurance policy if the trotting horse experiment went bust.

"You see, I'm wondering what the cost—" Edward broke off to move out of Holly's way as she positioned herself for the next shot, a stroke behind Stanford at three back. "I wanted to know your costs because it might be cheaper to photograph them—make photographic copies."

Edward didn't expect an immediate positive reaction, but he expected a response. Instead, Sanford remained impassive.

Stanford eyed Holly's ball avidly, but it lay out of his own ball's path, screened by the wicket. Muybridge's blue ball lay temptingly near. The ex-governor expertly tapped his ball into Muybridge's. This gave Stanford one free shot. He placed a foot on top of his black ball and took a lazy practice swing. "I very much doubt that photos will be cheaper."

Muybridge leaped at the bait. "Why?"

"Not at the rate you're throwing money away on our photographic project." Stanford slammed the mallet's head into his own ball, which he had clamped tightly under his glossy handmade boot, sending Muybridge's ball arcing past the first wicket off the pitch while his own ball remained unmoved, locked securely in place.

Stalled in front of the third wicket, Denise, whose interest in the game was in full retreat, missed a dead-on shot. "Mr. Muybridge." She gestured toward the array of wickets. "Doesn't it look like a lunatic planted a row of bucket handles?"

"Perhaps it's the governor's new cash crop?"

In sunshine now, her hair captured and concentrated so much ambient light that she appeared ringed by a halo. Only this was no angel's halo, not with Denise Faveraux's candid playful eyes, wet lips, and come-hither smile.

Neither Holly Hughes nor Leland Stanford smiled as they approached the penultimate wicket in a virtual dead heat. Meanwhile, Denise and Edward struggled to pass through the fourth wicket, which left the mixed pairs at opposite corners of the field, forty yards apart.

Leland Stanford spoke softly to Holly Hughes. "You are a gifted, uncommonly attractive, and accomplished woman. If I hadn't observed that from your dancing, your croquet would convince me." Holly nodded stiffly, noting the compliment without ceding ground.

"Tell me, Miss Hughes, what perversity makes you solicit trouble?" In his hands the mallet resembled a matchstick. "Most women accept, if not enjoy, their position. After all, women needn't go out to earn money or fight wars or engage in the sordid or trivial realities that make or break men. Women attend to what's truly important—children and the home, the center of all American values."

For Edward's sake, Holly mentally restrained herself. She ticked off several stunning retorts, but aloud said, "Let's imagine that many women do enjoy their lot, though you shouldn't underestimate economics as a motivating force in their apparent docility."

Yards away, Muybridge swung wildly and topped the ball, sending it skittering a few feet. Denise swung and missed entirely. She laughed so hard she sank to the ground. *Stunning,* Muybridge thought again as he eyed her tapered ankles, the flare of her calves. He extended his hand. Denise shifted slightly, revealing more leg. She took his hand but made no effort to rise.

"I feel so inept."

"That makes two of us, Miss Faveraux—"

"Denise," she cooed. "Please, Mr. My-My, Muy—"

"Edward. It's easier."

"Edward, I have a secret feeling we aren't going to win this contest." She laughed, still clutching his hand. He helped her to her feet. "I refuse to take this game seriously anymore," she declared, this woman who did not appear to take anything seriously. She released his hand, barely glanced at her ball, and whacked it with all her might.

He followed suit, and they both watched his ball skitter away in vaguely the same direction as hers. Side by side they headed off in pursuit.

Meanwhile, Stanford dropped to one knee to study his approach to the wicket. He rose, reexamined the shot, speaking quietly to Holly, "Your speech was an affront to decency."

"Not decency, *convention*. I'm surprised you don't recognize the difference." Anger would diminish her reasoning powers, she instructed herself, and she wanted to argue well with her nemesis.

"Your performance was magnificent. You had the audience spellbound until you went out of your way to show contempt for your admirers."

"I'm not only an entertainer, I'm an educator. The concept is to meld performance and education." Her fury building, she tended it now, bringing righteous outrage to a controlled boil.

Thirty yards away, Muybridge glanced at the other couple. "Leland didn't have to knock my ball that far." He spoke facetiously. "After all, it's only a game."

Denise replied with greater intensity than he imagined she possessed. "Leland takes everything seriously." She lowered her voice. "To tell you the truth, Leland is altogether as bad as he seems."

Muybridge laughed. He stroked the ball with surprising accuracy in the direction of the wicket.

"He enjoys having a good time." Her perpetually wet lower lip turned the phrase lascivious. Denise's blue eyes pressed a sensual dare upon him, as blatant as her full, uplifted breasts, inviting Edward to—*What?* he wondered. Stanford was her employer, paramour, and Holly was Edward's love. . . . But Denise Faveraux seemed to dispel all sexual certitude.

Holly Hughes measured the distance to Stanford's ball, bent down to eye the lie of the grass. *Blood match,* she thought, a minor but not unpleasant way to repay him for her Stanford-engineered ostracism. She smacked her ball smartly. The red careened forward and struck Stanford's black, forcing it to roll behind, though not through, the penultimate wicket. It would cost Stanford at least one stroke to realign and a second stroke to knock the black ball through. By then, the game would be over. Leland Stanford, president of the Central Pacific Railroad and ex-governor of the State of California, chewed his lip as he surveyed the lie of his ball.

Holly said, "Don't lecture me about morality, Mr. Stanford. You corrupt the American political process, bribe and bully and blackmail senators and congressmen and state legislators, mistreat and starve your railroad workers. I need no lecture from you." Her mind's eye supplied Edward's photograph of three emaciated, exhausted Chinese men huddled together above the rock-strewn ground on a precarious, half-finished trestle bridge in the High Sierras. She saw the charred body of a worker, his innards splayed in discrete globs over the landscape, the man having been blasted into eternity by a few too many grains of blasting powder.

Stanford turned oracular, "We sold the nation a dream of its potential,

Miss Hughes, the monumental vision of being united from coast to coast. They bought it beyond our wildest expectations. All Americans know the transcontinental railroad will be a lasting, monumental achievement."

Holly replied: "Mr. Stanford, your survey contains deliberate inaccuracies, including the fact that you 'moved' the Sierra Nevada mountains *ten miles closer* to Sacramento in order to receive additional government funds—"

He shot back, "What you and your bleeding heart reformer friends can't comprehend is that our railroad is in step with our country's needs and desires. Fortunately, citizens are willing to reward us for our intrepid undertaking. We face untold dangers and costly problems. We grapple with natural and political obstacles. We are willing to take such an epic gamble in order to turn the abstract dream of national unity into reality. You smear the enterprise with labels of paltry personal greed without understanding the railroad's purpose."

"How much money and land will you drain from the Treasury and siphon into your own pockets?"

"After the Great War between the States that so divided us, how can one put a price on national unity?"

Unperturbed, Holly Hughes smacked her ball, which rolled through the wicket and knocked up against Stanford's black one. He stared at his ball mock Medusa-like, as though trying to transform it into a boulder.

"After that evening in the theater, I did some research on the phenomenon of Miss Holly Hughes." She waited. "You were born in New York City in 1840. Your mother died of congestive heart failure when you were eight." Stanford might have been reading from a printed page. "Let's see, your father, brilliant financier and stock market innovator, died four years ago, in 1864." Holly's fingers clutched the mallet tighter. "Your father's contacts were legendary—from artists and politicians to kings and emperors. I would've enjoyed his company. I like to believe he would have enjoyed mine. I know your father was a good friend and occasional business partner of Senator Emerson Spalding of Massachusetts. Undoubtedly you'll ask Spalding to look into our negotiations with the U.S. Congress. You'll find everything absolutely aboveboard." Holly said nothing, but remembered with pleasure her godfather Spalding's horsey, kind, square-jawed face.

"But I digress." His lips curled. "You were raised by your father to be independent. You were tutored in a variety of skills, including, let's see, chess, cooking—you're an excellent chef—weaving, painting, dressage, fencing, marksmanship, wrestling, Tae Kwon Do."

She dropped the mallet head to the ground, leaned on it, trying to fathom how this man had gleaned such an explicit anatomy of her existence. She spun the mallet to and fro as he continued, "What have I forgotten? Ah, ballet. You were a bit too old to become a great ballerina, though obviously you are an extraordinary dancer." The mallet kept revolving in her hands, mashing down the grass. "You were a student of the legendary Kut-nes—"

The mispronunciation scraped on Holly's finely tuned nerves, like a cello hitting the wrong note.

"Kuznetsova," she corrected, realizing that, to Stanford, information meant power—power to read her life's roadmap, which in his lexicon translated into power to intimidate, coerce, or blackmail. She spun the mallet, aware of what an excellent weapon it would make.

"There is more, a good deal more. But today's lesson concerns your amorous history. I'm not sure about the current status of your French lover Jacques. . . ."

Holly Hughes kept the mallet handy as she paced off those three steps between them, wound up, and smacked Leland Stanford resoundingly on the cheek. As large as the governor was, he staggered back and almost lost his balance.

A dozen yards across the lawn, Muybridge and Denise Faveraux heard the sharp report of flesh on flesh. Edward sprinted toward Holly and Stanford, mallet clenched in his hand. He heard Holly shout, ". . . not because I have anything to be ashamed of, but because you are intolerably rude! Rude and insolent to a guest on your own farm!"

She spun, put her boot down to trap her red ball, and slammed into it with the mallet. Stanford's black sphere skittered across the lawn and under a privet hedge teased into the shape of a dove.

"What is it?" asked Muybridge, viewing the glowing, throbbing outline of Holly's handprint, all four bloodred fingers etched across the governor's cheek.

Leland Stanford wanted to lift a comforting hand to his fiery face, but he refused to grant Holly that satisfaction.

"You enjoy crushing people, bending them to your will, even when it requires strategies as demeaning and coarse as this." Holly spun to face Edward. "Mr. Stanford was about to recount sotto voce his carefully researched history of my love life. He has a mind too impoverished and soiled to fathom that there might be candor between a man and a woman. You know about my past, Edward." She paused, anticipating her lover's agreement. For a long moment, Muybridge stood frozen, unable to assent. After what seemed like a betraying pause to both Holly and Edward, he answered, "Yes, I do."

"You see, Mr. Stanford wanted to be certain there were no lovers omitted from the list. If you wish, I'll fill in the names."

Edward moved to Holly, took her arm, and steered her a few feet away from the governor, then took up a position between them. "That's unnecessary."

Leland Stanford, who had drawn himself up to full height, said, "You're not curious, Muybridge?"

Edward's arm went rigid, his fist clenched automatically. He stepped up to the governor, thrust his jaw into the beefy, oversized face. "I'll remind you, this is entirely our own business."

Denise, who had just joined them, felt as though she had stumbled into a family quarrel. "Calm down," she said ineffectually. "Everybody, please calm down."

Stanford smiled bleakly. "Blessed are the peacemakers."

Muybridge exploded, "You are constitutionally incapable of imagining a relationship built on trust and tolerance, on . . ." He couldn't come up with the word. Edward's fist remained clenched. Holly saw this, as did Denise Faveraux—voluminous Goliath looming over diminutive, embattled David.

"Did you invite us here to deliberately provoke this incident?" As Muybridge spoke, he understood that all of his work was wasted, that fantasies of photographing the trotting horse, let alone of later capturing Holly as she danced, were finished, for Stanford would fire him on the spot. He saw the fiscal abyss gape open as he almost shouted, "I quit, you bullying bastard!" A blindingly dull sequence of young brides and squalling, fidgety, snot-nosed toddlers paraded before his eyes henceforth and forever more. The vision forced Muybridge to revise what was to be his ultimatum: "I will quit on the spot unless you apologize to Miss Hughes."

Stanford's internal struggle was as complex as Muybridge's. On the one hand, it had been years since anyone had spoken to him with such insolence. On the other, and more costly, hand, he had fifteen thousand dollars on the line. Plus the $8,986 he had spent to date. Plus the humiliation he would suffer publicly if he lost the bet. Plus he knew he was right about the animal's gait. Not only had this photographer started down the costly track toward proof; no other photographer in the country could do what this big-mouthed lackey had already accomplished. And even if there were another candidate for the job, a new photographer would mean practically starting from scratch. More expense, more time. Stanford knew this because he'd ordered Ward to look into recruiting a backup candidate or two, including California's official photographer, Theodore Lochlin. But no one measured up.

Stanford's frown broke into a broad, ironic grin. He bowed with mock courtliness toward Holly and uttered this: "Miss Hughes, I apologize." Internally, the former governor of California vowed to make the ex-dancer and the cocky jay of a photographer pay for those words more than either one could ever imagine or afford.

Holly did not acknowledge his apology but spun and strode across the manicured turf.

Muybridge followed. He understood her well enough to know that she would never again speak to Stanford, that if, by some odd miracle, Stanford did not fire him, his working for "the governor" would be an increasingly nettlesome burr between them.

Edward caught up and took Holly's arm. She pulled away angrily. When they reached the carriage, he offered his hand to help her mount, but she leaped up herself. They were starting down the formal, half-mile-long drive of towering eucalyptus and sycamore when Stanford's voice fell over them like a noose. "Be here at eight sharp tomorrow morning, Muybridge! You and I have work to do."

Chapter Fifteen

Ignoring Stanford's command, early the next morning Muybridge drove his gig south to the incipient city of San Jose. In a twenty-minute powwow with Russell Caldwell, mayor of the nascent urb, Edward laid out a plan for photographing the city's records. The photographer demonstrated his novel approach by creating, on the spot in four minutes, exact replicas of three laboriously hand-copied documents. He then offered to copy twenty-five ledgers, roughly fifteen thousand pages, for the modest cost of thirty-five cents per page. The total expense to the city would be twenty-two hundred dollars, unless a second copy was desired, which Muybridge would supply for "a mere fifteen cents per page." After haggling, Muybridge agreed to supply the paper. The photographer was certain that, at his price, he could turn a handsome profit and save San Jose at least twelve hundred dollars per year in clerks' and copyists' salaries. Mayor Caldwell opined that savings of twelve hundred or so per year in a budget of twelve thousand dollars would provide ringing campaign oratory when he ran for reelection in another six months.

The San Francisco parlor was overstuffed and too hot, strewn with a surfeit of chaises, bric-a-brac, and wealthy dowagers. Holly introduced Denise Faveraux to Augusta Hannibal, who looked her up and down from behind her lorgnette as though examining an Oriental sideboard of questionable provenance. Denise had on a daringly cut green baize dress, which revealed more flesh than all of the other women in the room combined. Holly realized that, once again, Denise did not wear—perhaps didn't possess—a single undergarment.

"How do you do?" Miss Hannibal asked stiffly.

"I'm quite well, thank you. So lovely to be here, in such a *lovely* home."

Denise looked defiantly uncomfortable under the scrutiny of this snooty, wizened old lady, an ally of Holly's allies in the feminist struggle.

Isabel Crawford, a concave-chested, unimaginative heiress, joined the tense circle. "What sort of work do you do, Miss Faveraux?"

"I'm an actress. But formerly I was a *madame* of a brothel." An edgy smile pasted on her face, she spoke louder than necessary. Stunned silence modulated into writhing discomfort. No one in the room knew what to do or say—not Denise, not Holly, certainly none of Holly's feminist colleagues.

After the ungainly pause, Samantha Holiday, a round-faced fortyish spinster with lusterless, dun-colored skin, bustled over. "You were a madame, you say?" She stood, all ears. (Kindhearted Samantha had oversized, protruding ears. They were further emphasized by the tight bun into which she stuffed her moplike, sumac-colored hair.) "I can't imagine more difficult, more dangerous work than prostitution."

"To be honest, it was mostly boring."

"How could it, uh, be *boring*?"

The group splintered into two camps—the appalled and the fascinated. Denise went on, "Like most work, the profession's predictable."

Quizzical or hostile eyes scrutinized Denise Faveraux as though she were a lab specimen. Then Samantha innocently turned to the others, "Amazing, my dears, what one can learn if you ask the right questions. How long were you, ah, in the profession?"

"Twelve years."

"Was it lucrative?"

"For me and some others it's lucrative—if you're careful. You have to know the ropes, the *ins* and the *outs*."

"'Ins and the outs,' get it, ladies?" Samantha breathed out a girlish giggle, then asked earnestly, "Uh, what was the most frightening, uh, problem you ever had to deal with?"

The question piqued Denise's curiosity. She hadn't expected the insulated crones to have the vaguest insight into her ex-world. She'd come to this superheated hothouse because Holly had pleaded with her. Denise considered it payback for their Chinatown adventure. "To be honest, I was really frightened only once."

That surprised her audience. An overweight forty-year-old volunteered, "Why? Tell us what happened?"

Was this what it felt like to teach kindergarten? "I couldn't figure out what the bast . . . the man wanted."

Commercial transaction or not, sex is about power, Holly reflected. The big question: To whom is one willing to give up power—or from whom to grasp it? Or both, she inwardly smiled, imagining the reciprocated joys shuttling back and forth.

"What did the man want?" Samantha tried to sound calm but a bubble of air—a loud burp—escaped, to her embarrassment and the others' amusement.

"It wasn't about sex. Or what I think of as sex. He wanted to smack me around." This was shocking—Samantha winced; faces twisted; a mouth gaped open; eyes fled, lost their bearings, did not know where to land. "He wanted to hurt me, beat me."

"Why would anybody . . . ?" Consternation fluttered around the room, distorting their self-satisfied faces.

"What did you do?" Again Samantha asked the sensible question.

"I yelled for the bodyguard we kept on call for bad times. The bully was out on the street before he could unbuckle his belt."

Why did she lie to them? Meanwhile, she saw a moving image of that wide leather belt smacking down across her shoulder. He'd struck her once and she'd screamed and cowered behind the bedstead. The second blow caught her other shoulder. He had the belt starting up again, its metal buckle aimed at her head when the guard crashed in and grabbed the bully's arm. On damp days she could occasionally feel a bitter pinching—like a sting—in her left shoulder. The scar wasn't large, but it would mark her as long as she lived.

The women swamped her with questions—about the outfits she

wore, about men's weirdest desires, about her most interesting regular customers ("Few and far between," she answered); about whether she "derived pleasure" from her encounters. She answered fairly candidly—Yes, she was known for the occasional outrageous costume—bare nipples and bare crotch for instance. Denise continued to a hushed audience: Men were pigs and worse, though fortunately not every last single one of them; on occasion she actually had sexual feeling and when she did, well, she quipped, "I rode it as far as possible." That brought the house down.

Samantha looked abashed, yet she managed to stutter out a question, "This is awkward, Miss Faveraux. . . . You have more knowledge than I do. Penises, they come in shapes, don't they?"

"All shapes and sizes, dear, with prominent veins or little-bitty twigs with hardly any veins at all. You have big ones, thick and crooked and curved ones, proud upstanding darlings, and dumpy little droopies that are no use to anyone at all, male or female." Her graceful hands outlined a variety of shapes as laughter became general. She could have been illustrating them on paper, her fingers' gestures were so graphic and informed.

A woman choked out, "But even the big ones don't stay big for long."

"Not often enough," came Denise's reply.

A smile playing around her full mouth like heat lightning roiling a summer sky, Denise studied Holly shamelessly. "If you're asking me about satisfaction, about that superb moment, often that *came* from my sisters."

The room tensed, like a cable pulled taut; Holly could feel the tremors traveling down the cable in that moment right before it snapped. "After the boys withered and slunk away . . . starting and not finishing, that's evil for your temper. Frustrating, very. Sometimes we took solace from each other—that's what these *sisters* did for me and each other." As her eyes surveyed Holly's full form, Denise parted her legs. Backlit, Holly could follow every curve, could sense blatant bare skin under her dress.

The hostess had had enough: "Ah, we all find this fascinating, truly fascinating, but we do have business to cover. Can we look at today's agenda?" She weakly pointed at a wall chart as though it might erase Denise Faveraux's testimony. "Samantha has prepared a speech on the voting question, and I must be at the lawyer's with the petitions for the

Berkeley suffrage initiative by five. I hate to interrupt Miss Faveraux's captivating, not to say unusual, narrative, but we must convene now."

Samantha moved to the front of the room, centering herself under a dour, sexless portrait of Augusta Hannibal. Samantha began: "I have never met a man who was such a traitor to these United States that he did not believe but that our government rests upon the consent of the governed. The motto of our first Revolution was 'No taxation without representation.' We are supposed to live under a system created 'by and of and for the people.' Yet the Constitution, the sacred law of the land, denies that we women are people, with the full rights of citizens.

"Men claim that women do not want the vote. Yet opponents of female suffrage forget that the ballot is not a compulsory exercise: Given a choice, those who wish to sit amid the ashes of outdated notions of womanhood while the risen Phoenix wings her way toward a brighter dawn will have the right to remain at home and knit or nap or sip sherry or whatever pastime they wish to pursue. We will not drag our retrograde sisters to the polls forcefully, but we do want this sacred right for ourselves."

Polite claps sounded. Denise yelled out, "Tell it, sister."

"Some argue we do not have time to vote: This objection is all too often advanced by women who have all the leisure in the world to have their hair curled and tinted and primped and ironed and their gowns fitted and all twenty of their nails buffed. Our opponents pretend that we delicate creatures have no interest in the vote: Does anyone now believe that a woman would hesitate to slip her ballot into the box to support a measure protecting her home or her children, to stop an unjust war, or to help poor laborers or bring comfort to the lower orders?"

Denise interrupted, "Take that 'lower orders' out. It's condescending as hell."

Samantha colored, white to red. She struck out the phrase on the spot, mumbled, "I'm sorry. I wasn't thinking." She seemed to lose her place.

Denise softened, "Go on, go on, dear."

"We have a vision, a vision of a time when a woman's home will be the wide world; her children, all those whose feet are bare; her sisters, those who need a helping hand. We have an openhearted, generous vision of a new knighthood, a reborn chivalry, when men will fight not only for women, but for *the rights of women.*"

Applause. Augusta commented that the speech felt a little long. Isabel responded that it was perfect as it was. Holly remarked that one objection to women's suffrage was the fear that they would respond more liberally than men about certain social issues. Which indeed Holly hoped and expected would be the case.

Suggestions piled up, which Samantha recorded in hastily scribbled notes. She promised to deliver a revised draft of the speech by next Saturday, so that each could comment. The talk was to be delivered publicly in ten days.

Denise had rehearsal, and as she and Holly rose, Samantha came over and clutched Denise's hand. "Thank you so very much for coming and talking with us. I learned so much. We—I think I speak for all of us—would greatly enjoy your coming back."

Yes, yes, many seemed to agree. But others, including Augusta, had retreated to the opposite end of the room in quiet outrage.

"Thank you. I'll try to schedule a date." Without shouting out her disdain for these privileged women, Denise made it clear that she had no desire to go through this charade again. Samantha looked crushed. Meanwhile, Holly chastised herself for trying to meld two antipathetic female universes.

"Well?" Holly asked when she and Denise stood outside.

"I like Samantha."

"I like her too. She doesn't bury her head in the sand. But that wasn't my question."

Denise shook her ringlets without triumph or pleasure. "Dear, there's nothing here for me or my sort. They're insulated do-gooders. I don't know anybody like them. They're not *real* women—poor women, street walkers, waitresses, hookers, charwomen, those who clean and scrub and take shit from everybody. Until they can look me and ladies of the night and factory workers and the rest of the 'lower orders' in the eye and see us as 'sisters,' as women of value, your whole goddamn female claque won't amount to a hill of squirrel dung."

"Denise, you have to start somewhere."

"Not with the rich."

"I believe that we can lead all women."

Denise offered a compromise. "I'll make one suggestion, but only because *you're* involved with these biddies. Have them visit a whorehouse—I can give you several addresses and an introduction. You ask these insulated biddies to do that one night of 'fieldwork,' then we'll talk turkey, my love."

Thirty yards from the six furlong pole, a trained eye would have detected a series of twenty-four parallel strings stretched across the trotting track, each eight inches off the ground. A skittish, exhausted Muybridge thrust his head out of the camera shed yet again and shouted, "All right, Harry."

Muybridge heard Ned's thinly disguised groan answer his command.

Fifty yards up the track a hot, dusty, discouraged Harry Harnett quietly muttered, "Goddamn waste of time. Feel like a horse's ass." Occident was in training for an upcoming race. Today's replacement was a trotter named Abe Edgington. Each time Harnett steered Abe Edgington past the camera shed, it took at least twenty minutes to reattach the strings to the twenty-four springs that moved the shutters, to smooth out the hoof prints, and give the boys time to rake yet another layer of white lime onto the track "for contrast." The photo plate refused to catch the fleet animal. As usual, Muybridge fumed and fretted and went back to work. Harry felt he should've been working out the horses. Plus he needed to prepare Occident for the California Stakes. Though he wanted the governor to win the damned bet, Harnett wasn't sure how long he could keep driving Occident or Abe or another trotter past the cursed shed. Over the past ten days, they had repeated the same sequence a thousand times, so often that Harry thought he would swoop down off the sulky and throttle the photographer if he had to hear that phrase, "All right, Harry!" one more time.

Fifty yards away, inside the shed, Muybridge again imagined the glossy animal hurtling toward the camera shed, hooves vibrating in that four-part, ground-shaking drumbeat rhythm until, at the last moment,

Occident broke stride. Or swerved. Or tried to wheel around. After each deflating failure, the photographer cajoled or wheedled or demanded, "Just one more time." "I need to readjust the number three lens." "Tighten up on those first four, no the first six strings, Willy." "Sorry, we have a problem with . . ." That problem corrected, inevitably he shouted the detested trigger phrase, "All right, Harry!"

Grudgingly, Harnett clicked his tongue at Abe. The horse jumped forward. In three strides Harnett, tough whittled plug of a man, was cantilevered out behind the trotter, swaying with the roll of the sulky.

Muybridge watched the horse approach yet again. He could see the hooves stretch and lift then extend in that oddly circular pawing motion, imagining the articulation of each joint in the animal's legs and cloud of dirt clods spurting up behind. He could smell the sweat and faint, rich sweetness of manure, hear the groan and creak and stretch of resilient tack leather. Harry, Abe Edington, and the sulky hurtled toward the camera shed: The sequence was embedded in the photographer's mind, even in his dreams, as indelibly as dripping water scoring a rock.

By now, the stock farm had become, emotionally, an armed camp. Harry Harnett, once lively and forthcoming, volunteered nothing. Willy Jackson had withdrawn into a monosyllabic shell; even Ned Quick turned tentative and touchy, as though afraid to be too helpful to the increasingly suspect photographer. Muybridge felt he was about to be shoved off a cliff by the entire staff, who, he sensed, unanimously agreed that he had outlived his welcome. Yet they were closing in on this—the cameras were now fast enough. Now he only needed to trigger the shutters in a more reliable sequence.

Edward watched with tentative hope as the high-stepping horse struck the first string and tripped the lead camera lens. The horse broke a second and a third string, then the big trotter shied. Harry pulled on the bit, trying to keep the animal in line, but Abe Edgington lunged left, bolting out of his pace.

As Muybridge sprinted onto the track, he heard the camera shutters going off one after another all down the line. Which meant he had to throw away another dozen ruined plates. More expense, more lost time, increased surveillance from Ward, who, Muybridge could feel, was sharpening his talons for the kill: death to the project, a blistering farewell to one struggling photographer. Muybridge shouted at the retreating sulky, "Damn it! Damn it, animal, you can't swerve!"

Starting back to the shed, he spotted Collis Ward at the rail, noting his every move. Muybrdige had an inspiration born of fear. He shouted to Ned and Willy, "Bury the strings, boys! We'll have to bury every goddamn one of the goddamn strings!"

The photographer recognized that Collis Ward held the dreaded account book. "The governor budgeted, ah, eighteen thousand dollars for the Trotting Project," Collis Ward read aloud. "You're $3,467 over . . ." He let the figure sink in. "Already."

Muybridge responded by grabbing a gleaming Ames shovel and starting to dig.

Ward spoke again, his eyebrows eradicated by the sun's glare. The curious blankness of the face contrasted with the pronouncement: "The governor contacted Samuel Montague. . . ."

Collis Ward waited for a reply. Muybridge kept digging.

"He's the chief engineer of the railroad."

"I know who he is."

"The governor thought Montague might be able to assist you. . . ." He didn't voice it, but the unstated message was clear enough: *before the guillotine falls on this project.*

The photographer completed a shallow trench roughly six inches wide and six inches deep. His trench stretched along the first camera's sightline across the track to the wall. Edward deliberately tied two new strings to the shutters of the paired lenses of camera one, then played out the strings, laying them in the trench.

"How wide is the sulky?"

Ned Quick estimated the width with his hands. Muybridge barked impatiently, "Four feet? About four feet?"

"Just about," answered Ned.

He passed Ned his shovel. "A trench this depth and width will do. Like mine."

Playing out more string, Muybridge stalked away from the camera shed. Holding the spool, he laid the string in the trench, covered the string with the earth he'd dug up, and tamped down the dirt over the string so that it rested two inches below the track's surface. Edward played out an additional twelve feet of string and repeated the process, tamping down dirt until the two parallel strings were covered. Then, standing at the far edge of the track near the slanted, whitewashed wall, Muybridge pulled the last five or six feet of string out of the ground. Willy and Ned watched the photographer as he worked. Harry Harnett leaned back in the sulky seat, resting Occident and smoking a cheroot.

Muybridge explained, "If we can line up the sulky's inner wheel so that it passes over the strings, it'll work, goddamn damn it to hell!"

Ned alertly asked, "Why?"

"Because if Abe can't see them, he isn't going to break stride or shy away from the strings." Harry, wearing a quizzical expression, slowly shook his head, which made it seem like his neck needed oiling. Muybridge's three coworkers had experienced his congenital optimism too often.

Ned asked, "Do you get it, Willy?"

Willy Jackson drew himself up to his full height, six-foot-two. "I ain't stupid, you know."

Muybridge flicked a hand signal at Harnett, adding the words, "All right, Harry."

The sulky driver's head jerked back in silent disgust. His mouth twisted, as though he'd swallowed a sour cherry.

This time, with the strings buried and Collis Ward unblinkingly looking on, Occident did not shy. The cameras all fired in sequence. But when Muybridge developed the plates, not a single photograph was clear enough to read. In spite of the others' disappointment, he felt guarded elation. He knew he had an adequate trigger mechanism. And that allowed him to focus on the final problem, the most insoluble of all.

In his apartment Edward sketched rapidly, blunt strokes that threw off fat, authoritative lines. Soon the outline of the rectangular shutter mechanism emerged. Holly, who felt she could draw the device from memory, turned up the gas lamp to provide more light.

"I don't need that," he groused.

"But today was a breakthrough, isn't that what you said?"

"Burying the strings was a start, but I should kick myself for not figuring it out sooner. I still can't catch that animal on my plates. All that money, the wasted weeks of effort. Not to say my colleagues' goodwill. Harry can't look me in the eye. I'm living on borrowed time."

"Why are you concerned about their opinion, Photo Man? It isn't a popularity contest, is it?"

"I have to work with them every day. They're integral to the process." Holly's noblesse oblige briskness annoyed him. Only the independently wealthy could be wholly free of others' opinions.

She ceased massaging her knotted calf. "Lean forward." He complied. As she rubbed his neck, Holly felt relieved to escape her own distress and at the same time annoyed that Edward was not more attuned to her emotional tumult. Paradoxically, she would not have him too attuned. Complex demand, she recognized stolidly. That morning a second letter from Fauconier arrived. He was about to conclude his business and believed that, if all went as planned, he'd be in San Francisco in two or three weeks. Holly felt uneasy withholding this news, which made her uncomfortable with herself. But what could she tell Edward? That her former lover was about to materialize? That the unspoken question they'd been wrestling with since Fauconier's untimely appearance was about to shoulder its way to center stage? She kissed Edward, partly for love, partly as compensation.

His thoughts were not with her. "My life is measured out in dozens, Holly. Twelve exposed plates; twelve coating solutions—you know how expensive the materials and the chemicals are?"

"But isn't that why you went to work for that bloated toad, the patron of unlimited resources?" she said, but managed to hold back the petty, provoking, *I told you so.* "Stanford's not going to fire you. I know his sort—he won't give up on the bet. Too much is at stake—reputation, money. That's where he lives."

"I'm way over budget, Holly. The project's approved week to week now. They're peering over my shoulder every moment."

Holly had always assumed that Edward would make his photographs, even if Stanford misunderstood how and where a horse's legs went and lost his bet. Now the stench of failure hovered around Edward. Failure would send his professional status plummeting. Not to say his confidence. Fragile thing, confidence—she had never felt so unsure of herself as now.

"Have you talked to the gentlemen in San Jose? What did you call that idea about photographing their documents—your 'insurance policy'?"

"The mayor seemed enthusiastic. I'm feeling hopeful."

"Don't count the money yet, my love." Not for the first time, she wondered how someone so intelligent could misinterpret the most obvious things. "You're the classic idealist, Edward. You believe that talent and dedication can restructure everything as it ought to be—or, I should say, as you would prefer it. Unfortunately, the world's not that pliable or benign." He hated that superior, *I understand the realities while you, dolt, are naive, a babe in the woods*. "All those times your chemicals aren't mixed in exactly the right proportion or the collodion doesn't flare or the frame isn't in focus—"

"I never missed focus in my life."

"That's not my point. Things don't always work out the way one would prefer. After all, you're asking a municipal government to do something reasonable."

"In the first year alone I'd save the city twelve hundred dollars."

"We know that, but stop being willfully naive, Edward. You're asking *politicians*, of all people, to be reasonable and reform a system they're tied to. Compared to that your twelve hundred dollars is pin money."

He sucked on that word *naive* as though it were a bitter pill she'd shoved down his throat. But, in fact, Muybridge had no idea if the city of San Jose would accept his offer to photograph their archives. He knew only that they should.

Chapter Sixteen

The next morning Muybridge arrived at the stock farm late. Approaching his camera shed, he saw a stranger inside. Edward found himself sprinting along the dirt racetrack. As he ran, he realized he was tired of life's complexities. An ironic smile overtook him—Edward Muybridge, whose greatest enemy had always been boredom, who had always courted complication as a way of enlivening, or possibly justifying, experience, had enough on his plate to last him a mighty long time.

He shouted at the stranger, "What the hell are you doing in there? This is strictly private, sir!" The man kept his back to Edward. He did not flinch or flee but calmly continued to study a camera.

Muybridge had almost reached the entry to his little wooden cave. He yelled again, "Those are valuable lenses!" Neither Ned nor Willy was in sight.

The man craned down over camera number two, so Muybridge reckoned that he would have to somehow shove or guide the intruder past camera number one to get him outside. Internal alarms rang: *Cameras at risk*—the safety of his fragile instruments and their state-of-the-art Dallmeyer lenses was his first priority. Edward primed himself for the fight, right fist clenched, palms sweaty, mouth desert dry. *Minimize shoving inside the shed,* he commanded himself, *or months of work could be destroyed*.

The intruder turned toward Muybridge. "Samuel Montague," he

announced, extending a hand. Muybridge looked once, blinked, then stared at Samuel Montague's face: The right eye was conventionally centered but the left eye, as Edward watched it, wandered off into a corner. Both eyes were the color of anthracite, coal black.

"Edward Muybridge," the photographer said. So this tall, robust man with the wandering left eye was Montague, legendary chief engineer of the Central Pacific. "Mr. Montague, I would appreciate it if you would keep out of my—"

"Mr. Muybridge, I'm standing here because the Central Pacific Railroad has been my employer for the past four years and also because I have great respect for you as a professional." His smile seemed to wipe years from his face. "I have no desire to steal anybody's thunder, least of all yours. I was especially taken with the mountain views of Honduras and Panama. Those shots after the hurricane—extraordinary. The track of destruction . . . And how in the world did you get that panorama of the high ravine? Did you hitch a ride on a condor?" Montague chuckled at his little joke.

Muybridge felt disarmed.

"I haven't been stone deaf to the fierce rumblings coming out of the stock farm rumor mills," Montague continued, "but I have enough sense"—he tapped his head—"not to credit what I hear. Particularly since I read about the trotting horse experiment in the upcoming issue of *The Philadelphia Photographer*."

"But it's not published yet."

"Browning, the editor, knew I'd be interested and sent me the proofs."

"You know Browning?"

"For years. We were at university together. Please, if I am going to be of use to you, I need a full briefing."

As they examined the photographer's innovative shutter, Muybridge made a gut decision to be candid. "I'm running out of time, I'm way over budget. And Collis Ward is hovering."

Montague's left eye errantly wandered in the direction of the mansion. "Leland Stanford is not the easiest gent to work for. But one of his select virtues is that he demands the best, which is why you are here and I am here." For once the two eyes moved in accord and fixed on

Edward. "He lays a table unstintingly, as long as a project retains his interest."

Muybridge accommodated Montague with a history of the project, ending with his last, insoluble problem: the failed attempts to make the dozen shutters click on and off in timed sequence as the trotter wheeled by. "I've got the shutters triggered by springs that pull as the sulky wheels roll over them. But the animal is going so quickly it's either out of the frame or almost out of the frame each time. Or else the string pulls the camera so far out of alignment the shot is useless. I'll need at least ten, or possibly a dozen, images to prove the point beyond question. If there is a point."

"Coordinating the cameras by hand won't work." Montague thought aloud. "Too imprecise, too many cameras."

Samuel Montague bent over and scrutinized the spring mechanism. A moment passed, then he offered, "First of all, Mr. Muybridge, string is too thick for your purpose. Thin wires would work better. Galvanized, I know just the material." The engineer added, "What you've accomplished so far is impressive. Splendid work. The final question is, as you say, this matter of the trigger mechanism." A sulky flashed by. "Muybridge, don't despair." Montague's left eye continued to track the sulky. "You're coming down the homestretch."

Once again the engineer appreciated his own joke. Muybridge was less amused, "Well, I'd better hit the finish line soon. Or else."

"Patience, Edward. I may call you Edward?"

How difficult, Muybridge considered, it had been to work without a colleague—being left to bounce solitary thoughts off the inescapable confines of his own mind. At last Muybridge sensed a thin glimmer, a ray of sunlight infiltrating a leaden late afternoon sky. Then fear grabbed him. Perhaps Montague was Stanford's spy, installed to undermine the project.

Montague posited a riddle for the photographer: "What's predictable and reliable yet also breathtakingly faster than any other earthly force?"

"I haven't the foggiest notion."

"Mr. Muybridge, Edward, sir, did you ever consider electricity?"

"As a matter of fact I did. But I don't know how to regulate it effectively."

"You have paper at hand?"

Muybridge produced a roll of drawing paper.

Glancing back and forth from camera two's shutter mechanism, the engineer sketched steadily, throwing out a web of spidery lines. "Speed and predictability, twin virtues—how to trigger the mechanism more quickly and reliably than any human has done to date anywhere in the world."

The engineer whipped off a schematic sketch of the existing shutter. He then drew a thin line leading into the shutter and another coming out of it. Edward heard Samuel Montague murmur to himself, "Electromagnets." He cackled, as he said, "Pandora's box." Montague aimed his good eye at the photographer. "When badly deployed electricity is as unpredictable as the Homeric gods . . . How to release that power under restraint? How to harness its blinding speed and bend it to do our will? How's that for an Olympian quest?"

For hours the two sat in the cramped shed or strolled about the paddock, trying to determine if and how they could devise a functional shutter mechanism.

"An electromagnet could magnetize your shutters. If we arrest the current, both shutters will be released like that." He snapped his thumb and his third finger. "The way you've constructed it, one shutter will fall, the other move up. In this drawing"—Montague pointed to his latest diagram, which he placed on top of a stack of precisely aligned sheets—"we'll expose a smidgeon, say, an eighth of an inch." He smoothed out a new sheet of paper on which he rapidly scribbled calculations. "One thousandth of a second, will that do it? Fast enough?"

"I think we can work with that." Muybridge almost felt a smile issuing from within.

As night fell, Muybridge wrote a brief note to Holly. Regretfully, he explained, he would not be home until much later, if at all. He and his new colleague Samuel Montage, chief engineer of the Central Pacific, were toiling away at a promising scheme for the recalcitrant shutters. Edward preferred not to break their momentum. Dispatching Ned Quick, he told the boy to emphasize that Montague's approach looked promising. For a month Holly had heard no encouraging words about the project.

Hours later, they had worked out the following on paper. Using thin galvanized wires, Muybridge and Montague would attach the springs on the upper and lower shutters to a magnetic latch. Montague designed his proposed electromagnet as a coil of copper wire wound eighteen times around an iron core, which would function as a battery. "Theoretically," the electrically charged magnet would release the latch and trip the springs holding the shutters. Muybridge's original shutter was contrived to allow two boards to slip past one another so that a small opening in each board aligned with the other shutter for what Montague calculated would be that minuscule fraction of a second. The lenses would be exposed precisely long enough (they hoped) for the image of the passing trotter to be fixed on the light-sensitized plate. The electromagnet itself would be charged as the sulky wheel rolled over the other end of the wire, pressing it onto a metal plate to complete the electric circuit. All this would happen "instantaneously."

It was almost 3:00 a.m. when Montague, sipping a snifter of the governor's fine brandy, said, "Muybridge, this may be your current travail, but it feels like a vacation to me." Edward asked why. "Don't tell Stanford, but I'm not sorry to escape the sierras for a few days."

"We've heard it's a bad winter."

Samuel Montague emitted a testy laugh. "The *worst* winter since they began measuring snowfall. Twenty-eight men dead already and counting. I don't want to calculate the number of fingers and toes bitten off by frost. Or the sick bay casualties. Appalling, absolutely appalling." His voice grew huskier. "Already there's over *seven feet* of snow. We spend all our time shoveling, almost none laying track."

"Twenty-eight dead?" Muybridge felt shaken. The figure the *Clarion* had printed was six.

"The Chinese may have built the Great Wall, but they're dying in droves building the transcontinental railroad. I've tried to reason with Stanford, but it's no use."

"You spoke with him about the deaths?"

"And the casualties. You know, simple, inexpensive precautions would help—protective clothing, better grub, campfires strategically placed along the right of way to warm the extremities, frequent rest breaks, a more competent doctor, and several more of him. 'The Associates' claim my demands are too costly. Out of the other side of their collective mouth they goad workers to bust their backs at top speed. Slavery in a new form."

They turned back to work, and after another half hour of technical details accompanied by a half dozen sketches, Montague spoke as he manipulated his pen. "Your dilemma isn't unlike mine, you know."

"In what way?"

"We're obliged to tunnel through a mountain. Going over the summit would cost a fortune and take more time than we've got, so tunnel we must. From my calculations, the longest tunnel—the one we're working on now—is over *four hundred yards*, a bloody quarter mile through solid granite, toughest rock on the planet." Montague rapped the table as Muybridge whistled in appreciation of the difficulty. "And I, Herr Chief Engineer, have never designed nor constructed a tunnel even half that length. For that matter, no one else in the world has either.

"Okay, to make it trickier, the black powder we used to use for blasting, its charge is difficult to control. There's a promising new explosive called nitro—nitroglycerin. It's cheap and five times more potent than the powder. But it's touchier than a hibernating bear and a hundred times more potent than the fiery gun cotton and ether—your collodion." He pointed to Muybridge's graceful apothecary jars.

"I read about nitro in *Scientific American*."

"It'll work for us—with proper handling. The blasters need intensive training how not to blow themselves to kingdom come. Who knows how many more will self-destruct? Meanwhile, the tunnels won't wait. I've surveyed for *fifteen* tunnels, Edward. Fifteen! And that doesn't count all the trestles, the cuts, and fill.

"We need eight hundred, a thousand more workers. We'll have to rush them up to site without training, assuming we can exhume that many vertical bodies. Meanwhile, we're bogged down in infernal snow, and there's more snow forecast. I'm asked to work miracles up there." The engineer pointed upward, to what the faithful might have mistaken for heaven; Edward knew Montague meant the High Sierras. "Perhaps you'll come and visit the big show?" The good eye and its errant partner almost converged on the photographer.

"I'd very much like to—after *we* solve our *shutter* problem!"

At dawn the next morning the unwashed, unshaven, bleary-eyed pair staggered out of the camera shed into a blazing sunrise. Edward's mouth was foul. He felt light-headed, as though he'd had too much booze. Everything about Samuel Montague looked wrinkled and limp. The older man caught their reflection in a window.

"We make quite a distinguished pair, Muybridge."

Too tired to laugh, Edward managed to elevate his eyebrows slightly.

"I can have five or six electromagnets ready Thursday. Suppose we try them on your state-of-the-art cameras? That'll give us a notion of whether they'll work with the trip wires."

"What about six? A nice, even half dozen."

"Why not?" Samuel Montague paused. "I like the idea of galvanized, my lad. At least the wires won't rust."

"Here's hoping they won't snap," Muybridge said dolefully, still not certain they were out of the woods.

Holly read a small article buried in the back of the *San Francisco Clarion* for January 9, 1868, with equal parts indignation and curiosity; indignation for obvious reasons, curiosity because she could not fathom why Leland Stanford's pet paper continued to find her newsworthy. Maybe she ought to be flattered that they took her so seriously?

DANCER AGITATES FOR "NEW" WOMEN OF AMERICA

Miss Holly Hughes, the dancer who only a few months ago scandalized a Bay Area audience with her brazen discourse on women's undergarments, is back on the attack. Yesterday, in front of a scant female gathering, she urged that all local women organize for the right to vote. Miss Hughes demanded that her so-called "sisters" join a march on an unspecified date in January to protest the lack of franchise for the gentler sex. This march is to be coordinated with similar demonstrations in a few widely scattered American cities—New York, Boston, Chicago and Philadelphia, to list the most prominent. The fiery female demagogue asked the assembled for a record turnout for the event.

Miss Hughes, who, it must be noted, has lived most of her adult life in Paris, France, offered critical—several eyewitnesses said "insulting" and "shocking"—remarks about "the passivity of San Francisco's female population." She stridently demanded that women "take control of their own lives," asserting their independence from "domineering husbands and demanding families and all those who would deny us equal rights and equal status."

She continued, "To date, no woman in the world has ever spoken her whole heart and her whole mind. The mistrust and disapproval of the vast bulk of society throttles us, as with two massive hands pressing at our throats. We mumble a few pathetic words, leaving a thousand better formulations unsaid. It is my belief that when my sex achieves its rights, there will be ten eloquent women where there is now one eloquent man."

Near the end of her rambling and subversive discourse, Miss Hughes urged her erstwhile allies to disobey San Francisco ordinance (#324-577-5), which prohibits public protests of more than ten persons without a City-approved parade permit. Miss Hughes asserted that the permit had been applied for three times so far but the applications were rejected "for no sensible reason other than the desire to silence the City's core of progressive women."

She concluded with pointed hostility, "Why should we suffer the denial of citizenship? Why are we willing to face jail for our beliefs? To accept multiple insults and indignities without tears or complaint? Because we enter this contest knowing that the rules are rigged in favor of complacency, indifference and baleful ignorance. But, I promise you, dear colleagues in the struggle, they will not remain so for long."

Seeing her own words in print, Holly realized that a spy had infiltrated the lecture hall—a woman who had surreptitiously scribbled enough notes to give Luke Ransom the bare bones of his report.

Holly clipped the article and placed it in a folder labeled H. HUGHES, ATTACKS. She riffled through newspaper clippings and stopped at an article near the top of the pile—byline Luke Ransom.

RADICAL PLAN FOR WOMEN

> The dancer Holly Hughes announced last night an attempt to erect a building in San Francisco to provide "a clubhouse" for women's activities, including an all-female GYMNASIUM and a SWIMMING POOL. Miss Hughes appealed for donations and claimed that she herself would match any monies received on a dollar-for-dollar basis.
>
> To date, no San Francisco property owner has been willing to sell or rent property to the importunate Miss Hughes.

Holly placed the latest clipping on top of the stack and closed the file. Blocked everywhere, she felt as though she were seated simultaneously on both ends of a seesaw, suspended in midair. In the past two months, Holly had visited a dozen large spaces in and around San Francisco. No one would sell her a building; no one would rent her a hall. How could she remain here, unable to do what character and training had decreed for her? For several weeks Holly had considered returning to Paris. But escape seemed cowardice, and Edward was here.

She began pacing around his apartment. She thought of her father—he would've taken off his meticulously ironed white gloves and fought bare-knuckled against Stanford and conventional morality. Holly vowed that, somehow, she would perform here: that she would create a gymnasium for women. After all, what was her money for?

She selected a file labeled RAILROAD, CENTRAL PACIFIC. Holly skimmed several thick government reports, thumbed through a stack of correspondence and newspaper clippings. In answer to one query, a New York newspaper reporter named Adam Bedite wrote that the Associates had borrowed heavily—to the tune of eight million dollars—from the Central Pacific Contract and Finance Company in order to finance the Central Pacific Building Company. Bedite wrote to her: "In October of 1867, someone—still unknown—conveniently destroyed fifteen volumes of the Finance Company's account books."

Holly herself had discovered that, when Stanford was governor, he'd signed seven acts directly benefiting the railroad. She also put on top of the file a clipping from the *New York Herald* reporting on a congressional loan of $100 million to the Central Pacific Railroad. "One hell of lot of zeroes, Leland," Holly muttered, then jotted a note to Emerson Spalding, the

Massachusetts senator and her father's old friend. Spalding, a sometime Stanford ally, was chairman of the Interstate Commerce Committee, which regulated (to the extent that anyone regulated) the nation's railroads. In the letter, Holly explained her fascination with the ongoing attempt to construct the transcontinental road. She explained that she was planning a book and would welcome whatever information was available about government cooperation with the Central Pacific and the Union Pacific, including a comprehensive schedule of Federal loans and land grants and portions of any relevant congressional testimony. She was particularly interested in what the senator could tell her about the nature of Hollis Huntington's lobbying efforts in the nation's capitol and around the country. She signed off offering her best wishes to Spalding, his wife, and their three sons.

At Holly's invitation, Denise came to her rooms for tea. They sat in front of the fire as Holly poured.

"You were right," Holly said. "I feel embarrassed about dragging you to the meeting. I didn't understand how limited they—we—all are."

"Holly, I just shoved sex and a little taste of the lowlife down their privileged gullets. I enjoy scandalizing them. They're not awful, just ignorant." Denise stretched catlike. Holly wondered if she purred. "Tell me, how many of your proper lady friends would've dared help Sung Wan? Who, by the way, sends her best to my partner. She's in Monterey living with an elderly Chinese couple a friend of mine knows."

"That's good news." Holly went on, "It was thoughtless, though, exhibiting you like that."

Denise patted her friend's hand. "Not at all. I sort of enjoyed terrorizing the hen coop. Just learn from this." Denise did not let go of her hand.

"Learn what?" Holly stood up, extricating her hand as she rose.

"What you can't do." She paused to let the thought sink in, then restarted: "I'm about to try to rescue another girl. Will let you know when I've figured out who. And where we'll dine afterward." A sly smile now enveloped her face. "By the bye, I'm dead serious about the comforts of women." Again she stretched languorously, her breasts rising toward Holly as though on command.

"I'm quite satisfied as it is."

"Don't get huffy, darling. And don't blame a bloody whore for trying. You are so beautiful." Denise's eyes were like hands, roaming all over Holly. "And I love the picture of us together. I find it so very stimulating."

Denise reached for Holly's hand again, but Holly pulled it away. "Will you please stop this?"

"If you really want me to stop, yes." Denise offered a taunting smile. "But don't think the offer's permanently withdrawn."

Holly said quietly, "I'm flattered."

"Hey, what are friends for?" Denise gestured at the teapot, speaking with a throaty quality. "Is that thing empty or can I get a goddamn refill?"

Holly lifted the elegant China pot and poured.

In 1868, San Jose was a provincial city of fifty-six hundred souls. The San Jose city fathers had exhaustively discussed the merits of Edward's intriguing, novel idea. They had argued and debated, objected and counterobjected. They had judiciously weighed the pros. However, each council member had also judiciously enumerated the cons of Muybridge's proposal, concluding that fewer clerks meant less patronage, which translated into reduced political heft.

Not privy to the internal reasoning of the city fathers, Edward Muybridge viewed his offer as a cheap, fast, and effective means of copying San Jose's irreducible mountains of documents. The photographer also assumed that, at thirteen miles removed, San Jose lay beyond Leland Stanford's reach. But the ex-governor, who had eyes and ears all over the state, had been tipped off to Muybridge's proposal by the Honorable Mayor Russell Caldwell himself. The mayor's communication confirmed Stanford's original hunch—that the photographer's question about the cost of Meachum Steward's copying was not generated by innocent curiosity. Leland Stanford knew that a dependent employee was a loyal employee, especially when that employee had a tendency to run up debts. Thus the ex-governor silently prevailed in a contest unknown to the photographer. By a vote of seven to two, the San Jose City Council rejected Mr. Edward Muybridge's "intriguing but insufficiently developed proposal to photographically reproduce" the city's records.

Chapter Seventeen

All morning the carriages rolled up the mile-long, tree-lined drive to the stock farm. High-stepping brown thoroughbreds, statuesque dappled grays, sleek mounts with rippling variegated coats pranced or trotted or paced briskly under towering oaks and symmetrical, fountain-shaped elms toward the stallion stable. The carriages pulled by these exquisite animals collectively carried thirty or so well-heeled gentlemen on that crisp winter morning to witness Stanford's triumph or defeat, the long-awaited, much-publicized attempt to photograph a horse in the act of trotting. Everyone present shared a passionate interest in horseflesh, and a select handful came, too, out of scientific interest. But whatever else excited their attention, each wanted to see whether or not Leland Stanford had sacrificed four months and a rumored twenty to thirty thousand dollars to a bout of self-inflicted hubris. Many deferential apparent allies in attendance silently prayed for his comeuppance.

All morning the odds remained essentially the same, though around 11:45 a.m. there was a slight tilt in Stanford's favor. Nevertheless, as the gentlemen arrayed themselves at the three-tiered railing minutes before the midday starting time, the worthies insisted that, at eight to three, Abbott Berkeley—and centuries of conventional wisdom about the horse's gait—would prevail. Horatio Dirk, the *Clarion* editor, managed to get down a last-minute bet, unearthing a lumber tycoon willing to wager five hundred dollars against Stanford.

San Francisco's male leisured class, with their whiskered faces, encased in tailored waistcoats and high leather boots, impatiently waited for the drama to commence. Less elegantly attired, and relegated to the crowd's periphery, stood a clutch of reporters armed with notebooks and a scattering of their colleagues, the quick-sketch artists, who stood poised over drawing pads.

Berkeley, in a dove gray morning coat, puffed too often on his ripe panatela. He wore a matching gray top hat and a conspicuous scarlet ascot. Sweat made his pudgy face gleam so brightly that Collis Ward remarked sotto voce, "When I came too close to him, I literally had to turn away. The glare was blinding."

"He does look a trifle moist," Dirk replied.

Ward held his upper body rigid while his foot moved up and down at a characteristic tempo. "Don't you know, the cigar's his cologne." The remark wrested smiles from Luke Ransom and Horatio Dirk.

Inside the tiny camera shed Edward could barely breathe. He tried to banish self-doubt, but the specter of failure would not let his mind stop its jittery, incessant flight. A few feet away, Montague unhurriedly rewrapped the copper wire around the electromagnet that encircled camera three. Willy Jackson compulsively raked the twenty-yard stretch of track in front of the shed while Ned Quick, two steps ahead of him, threw down gusting fistfuls of white quicklime. Hardly anything remained to be done, which made it still more nerve-wracking for the photographer.

Stanford approached on Crusader, his massive bay riding horse—"The only animal in California strong enough to carry the governor," as some quipped. Beside him, on what looked like a Shetland pony, rode Denise Faveraux sidesaddle. The closer she came, the brighter she appeared.

Muybridge attended her progress, hoping this rising sun was an omen. "She's the only thing on the estate more beautiful than the horses."

Montague glanced up from his tightly wound skein of copper. "Don't let Harry hear you say that."

Driving the light-wheeled sulky, Harry Harnett approached the shed. Muybridge walked out and patted Occident's neck. "We've been through a lot together. Do it for us, old sport."

Until this moment, a slight coolness had lingered between Harry and Edward. "Thanks, Harry. . . ." Muybridge looked up into the wind-lined, sun-creased face. "For everything." Harry cocked his head, shook the photographer's hand.

"Save the thanks for afterward, Muybridge." The voice was gruff, but their agreement had been reforged. Harry headed the sulky up the track.

Samuel Montague tapped the newly wrapped electromagnet to check the connection then hooked up the wires that ran to camera three's shutter. All twelve devices were now ready.

Edward hand-signaled Ned Quick, who raised his megaphone. "Gentlemen, lady"—Denise Faveraux nodded in recognition of the little joke—"post time!" Men's eyes drifted first to Denise then down the track to the tense driver and his magnificent steed.

Ned Quick put his hands together in attitude of prayer and stage-whispered, "Just this once, Edward, please. For your boys, for dear Willy and me." Willy Jackson, privy to what was about to be requested, studied Muybridge anxiously, as though waiting for the predictable explosion to follow.

"What in the world do you want now?!" Muybridge tried to sound calm, but months of tension, all that accumulated frustration and nervous anxiety, flooded in.

"Please don't yell, 'All right, Harry!' Avoid that cursed phrase. Give him that gift this once."

"Boys," Muybridge pledged, almost smiling, "as long as I breathe, the phrase will never again pass my lips."

Moments later Muybridge leaned out of the camera shed. He understood, retrospectively, how grating, how intolerable the utterance had become. Yet, against his will, those words wedged themselves into the space behind his tongue, threatening to leap out. Unable to trust himself to speak, Muybridge simply waved his hand and nodded to Harry Harnett, to the delight of the boys.

Stretched along the rail were San Francisco's most powerful individuals: Chester Crocker, Mark Hopkins, Hollis Huntington—three of the Central Pacific's Big Four. There was Stacey Bowker, the head of the California National Bank; Preston Newhall, scion of the Newhall mining fortune and the city's most successful real estate magnate. They and others had come to see Leland Stanford's public humiliation or triumph. Not a man in the crowd had even passing interest in a recently solvent photographer named Edward Muybridge. Edward wryly realized that, with one large bet on himself at eight to three against, he could assure his fiscal future. But he had concluded that such behavior wouldn't be sporting—in spite of his nerves and the melodrama surrounding the event, he believed he knew the outcome.

All eyes were on Occident, restlessly pawing the dirt. At the rail Luke Ransom quipped, "If there's one horse in the world whose four hooves don't touch the ground, it's that stud."

Collis Ward responded, "You've forgotten Pegasus."

"Leland didn't own Pegasus."

"If he wins, he'll make a bid for him."

"Or get Harry to graft on the wings."

Sixty yards up the track, Muybridge heard Harry Harnett whistle. Edward no longer needed to watch Occident. He could visualize the animal's powerful, ground-consuming stride, the swift, articulated beauty of its gait; he could feel the hooves' rhythmic tremors as they hit the earth and lifted, hit and lifted in a smooth yet powerful four-part syncopation more subtle and involving than the most sweeping waltz tune. The sound clopped nearer, Muybridge felt cool and calm. He was ready.

Occident's enveloping rhythm encircled him like sweet wood smoke. Edward looked straight ahead—now he saw the flash of hooves before his eyes, each sequential movement isolated and discrete. At that instant, the photographer would later swear, he distinctly witnessed all four hooves suspended in air. Suddenly, in the infinite circling of the globe around the sun, in the immeasurable spinning of our planet, Muybridge stopped and froze time, reined it in, tamed it, held it still. (He himself had done this only twice before "in practice," with inspired technical assistance from his friend the engineer Montague.) He heard his twelve shutters click open then sequentially snap closed, a rapid-fire succession of barely audible yet, to Photo Man, infinitely resounding clicks, sounds which not a single one of the absorbed gentlemen heard at all. Muybridge thanked his eyes and his mind, his acumen and his discipline for that singular moment. He also thanked Montague for leashing the electric genie.

In the darkroom, he didn't sweat; his hands were adept, rock steady.

These twelve photographs would make his reputation, perhaps his fortune. Muybridge knew this, but tried to brush the thoughts aside as, one by one, the images emerged from the bath. In the first photograph, Occident was silhouetted, front left leg cocked and raised up above the track's white lime, the front right and back right hooves still anchored to the ground. In the second photo, the animal's left front leg was higher than before, the right front and right hind leg pushing backward and now starting to hint at their imminent lift. In frame three, the left front leg, bent at a right angle, was clear of the ground while the right hind thrust back, nearing take off. The right rear leg was poised, too, and the left foreleg bent under the animal's belly as it cleared the track. Muybridge paused, knowing the next exposure was what he and Stanford and the assembled crowd had been waiting for. So he played out the time like a trout on his line, savoring the expectation of the evidence he was about to unveil—it was like gathering all feeling into one great ball, stoking pleasure while building toward release, like holding off gratification to impart pleasure first. Now, finally, it was his turn.

"Here it is!" Muybridge shouted at the top of his lungs. He clutched the irrefutable evidence—the single photograph for which he had absented himself from his beloved, around which he had concentrated more energy than seemed possible or necessary or even sane. . . . The fourth photo of the twelve-frame sequence revealed each of Occident's legs clear of the earth, suspended in air. The shot caught the right front leg in the act of starting downward. But the tilted wall's horizontal marking stripes—which ran along the bottom of this image at measured distances of six, four, and two inches above the ground—plainly revealed the hoof at the lowest black stripe. Two saving, brilliant, colossal inches above the track! The left front leg was bent up under the horse's chest while the right front leg kicked backward toward the ever-pursuing sulky. Occident's left hind hoof almost touched the ground. Almost. But, again, as clearly evidenced by the horizontal black markings, that hoof, too, was in flight, airborne precisely two gravity-defying inches.

Behind him, he heard Stanford's gasping, expectant breathing. Muybridge turned and ceremoniously exited the dark room. The photographer held up the fourth shot and remarked conclusively to the former governor, "Here it is, Leland! Behold!"

Leland Stanford stared at the fourth shot. As though myopic, he moved the image closer to his eyes, back again, closer, then the big man spun toward Edward with triumphant appreciation. Muybridge had detested Stanford's preemptory arrogance; certainly, he'd always hate the way his boss had behaved toward Holly. Yet at that moment Edward felt pleased for his patron.

Meanwhile, Abbott Berkeley seemed on the point of liquefying, he was sweating so profusely. Flushed, furious, drenched, and flustered, he bellied his way through the crowd huddled around Muybridge and Stanford.

"Let me see! Let me look!" he ordered in a petulant, cracking adenoidal voice. Stanford formally laid the wet photograph into Berkeley's glistening palm. Abbott Berkeley examined the dark, silhouetted figures of the horse and the sulky and its driver. He could make out the outlines of Harry Harnett's beard and flat-brimmed cap, the angle of the whip descending through yielding air. Berkeley's head jiggled up and down, like the uncontrolled spasm of a puppet undone by a broken string. He screamed with shrill defiance, "Fake! Deliberate fake!" The wattle-laden triple chin cascaded and rolled and seemed to tumble inward, as though his face were imploding into raw fat itself. "This is outrageous, Stanford! Fraud! Cheat!"

"As you know, Berkeley, this is not a fake. It is a still damp photograph of Occident trotting. The first of its kind and also the fourth of twelve sequential photos. You can examine each of the revelatory dozen at your leisure. We have *all* seen Mr. Muybridge take the photographs. We have *all* seen him remove the plates. No one stood beside him in the darkroom itself"—Berkeley seemed to light up as he grasped at that final straw—"but the darkroom was inspected by you and your man only seconds beforehand. Two men stood guard outside when Muybridge entered, the same two were still standing outside when Mr. Muybridge emerged a moment ago. There has not been the slightest opportunity for fakery or chicanery, which I would not countenance in any event. All of the *gentlemen* standing here"—he indicated the eager auditors—"know this to be fact." Stanford's black, pebble-hard eyes narrowed, as though drilling into Berkeley's face. "You, sir, have no recourse but to behave *as a gentleman* should. . . ." He growled the final three words, "And settle up." The crowd grunted or nodded its concurrence.

"I want you to recall, Mr. Abbot Berkeley, that you had the gall to actually laugh aloud when here at this spot I told you I saw all four hooves of my horse off the ground. Reflect on that costly laugh as frequently as possible. I await your check in the full amount."

Surveying his guests, Leland Stanford's voice inflated, "I want all of you to attend a celebration at my home this evening. Abbot, you are invited—if you care to come." He nodded with benign largesse to the vanquished. "Thank you all for being with us on this memorable, this historic, this remarkably fulfilling day."

Stanford pumped Edward's hand. Others crowded around until the group parted and a beaming Denise Faveraux advanced toward the two men as though scattering pleasure ahead of her. Denise kissed the photographer, a clinging, surprisingly intimate kiss for so public an occasion.

She came wrapped in a rich, flesh-warmed musk that left Muybridge giddy and vaguely aroused. Smiling, she whispered enigmatically, "To the victor . . ." She moved to Stanford, whom she also kissed. Most eyes remained locked on Denise Faveraux as she retreated toward her carriage.

Edward muscled his way over to Samuel Montague.

"Thank you." Edward extended his hand. "I never could have climbed the mountain without you."

"I simply applied the icing, son. Just smeared a tasty and colorful icing on your excellent pastry." Montague laughed. "Hate to say it, but I must get back to the snowy heights."

Muybridge caught a last glimpse of Denise Faveraux's shining crown as she drove off toward the mansion. Montague said his farewell. "Come and see us in our wintry home, Edward. I guarantee you a fascinating visit, a crash course in modern technology and related disasters."

"I'll see what I can do."

Edward saw that his other three associates stood patiently waiting at the camera shed, aligned as though at a formal reception—Harry in front, Ned next, Willy in the rear. How satisfying to play host on Stanford's turf. "All right, Harry." In response, Harry barked out a conclusive laugh. "We had one hell of a stretch of uphill sledding. Thanks for your patience, tact, and genius."

"I'm glad it it's over. I'm glad we did it for the guv. . . ." Harnett's loyalty elevated Stanford in the photographer's eyes. The fierce, slender whiplash of a man paused, then added, "And for you."

Affectionately, Edward pumped the hands of Ned and Willy, saying, "You two were staunch and tireless. You stuck with me even when you lost faith. No one could ask for more."

The good-byes exhausted him. All he wanted was rest—to see Holly and share his victory with her. But that would have to wait until much later that evening, after Stanford's victory party.

As Muybridge approached Stanford's rambling, eclectic mansion, he professionally quizzed himself on how to best photograph the exterior. (He had already finished reshooting the principal interior rooms.) Outside he'd need a series of shots. Why? The asymmetrical pile had an aleatory air—it was self-contradictory not only in scale but in style: center section colonial, east wing in oversized neo-Gothic, west wing reminiscent of a porticoed Southern mansion. How to compose a photo—impose order—on a jumble? He could break it in three, but that wouldn't serve the whole. Ah, another puzzle.

Inside, he passed through the entrance hall, surmounted by a mosaic of the zodiac—an archer and a goat, ram and bull, crab and lion and a tempestuous virgin all stretched across the glittering interior sky. He moved on to the rotunda, a soaring two-story room crowned with a massive, light-tinting amber skylight. Looming over the photographer's head, twenty feet above on the mezzanine, were semicircular mosaics of America, Asia, Africa, and Europe—Stanford's imperialist desires concretized. The same well-dressed men who attended the trotting horse demonstration milled about on the ringing marble floor, and at their sides lounged women in shimmering, changeable silks and luminous, slippery-looking brocades. The crowd seemed to be sipping champagne and speaking all at once.

Muybridge nodded to Chester Crocker, the banker and treasurer of the Central Pacific, who had buttonholed a young importer and was cataloguing the difficulties inherent in the slow, costly sea routes around Cape Horn and the malaria- and bandit-ridden take-your-life-in-your-hands portage over the Guatemalan isthmus, which provided the only way to transport the tons of supplies required for construction of the western part of the transcontinental railroad—other than sailing around the Horn.

The photographer peered into the billiard room where, under the heads of rhinoceros and lion, moose and a tawny lion, two guests cued their balls and circled back and forth around the flawless green rectangle while onlookers wagered on each shot.

He nodded to several acquaintances in the Pompeian room as he studied the space, considering again tactical approaches to his ongoing photographic assignment in and outside the mansion. The walls and ceilings were painted in that red-clay wash that made the Pompeian murals so haunting. Heroic Roman marble statuary—or were they copies?—anchored the corners of the room. A magnificent Ottoman rug dominated one wall, its entwined flowers mingling with complex, abstract motifs on a creamy white background. Delicate Roman figures crowned the apses above—a sibyl gazing up to the heavens for augury, a half-nude sylph surprised by a hairy, importunate suitor in her improbably luxurious sylvan bath, a chesty nymph staring into a clear pond, bewitched by her own loveliness. The entire set throbbed with the warm output of a hundred gas lamps.

On a large ormolu—or was it gold?—table in the middle of the room were arrayed, in double ranks, a half dozen aligned newspapers and journals, freshly printed for the next morning's newsstands. On the right, the pro-Stanford column was headed by the *Clarion*'s banner headline:

TIME FROZEN IN ANOTHER STANFORD FIRST:
PHOTOGRAPHS TAKEN OF A TROTTING HORSE!

The copy began, "Ex-Governor Leland Stanford announced . . ." Edward's eyes skimmed the column for his own name, which did not appear until the fifth and penultimate paragraph on the jump page. His eyes skipped to the newspapers in the left rank. The Oakland *Bee* fumed, "FRAUD IN PALO ALTO. DOCTORED PHOTOGRAPHS CREATE FURORE." The Richmond *Call* announced, "FAKED PHOTOS STIR EQUINE DEBATE." The *Call* began, "Edward Muybridge, a self-proclaimed 'professional photographer' in the employ of ex-Governor Leland Stanford, today tried to perpetuate a heinous hoax by pretending that . . ."

Muybridge felt as though he were plunked down at the wrong end of a telescope. Fake or genuine, the photos were not the issue. In this war of newsprint only political allegiance mattered—who backed Stanford, who opposed him. Throughout the months of experimentation Edward had persisted in the assumption that the work, if it could be accomplished, would speak for itself clearly and loudly. When, at long last, he was able to hold up to the world an undistorted mirror of reality, Edward had naively believed that the act itself would be sufficient. A proof would be proof. Instead, his photographs became yet another partisan counter, a meaty tidbit to be chewed until unrecognizable by the insatiable maw of the press. Politics were more inflammatory and more commanding than any sequence of photographs, however revelatory, however unique. Which was what Holly had been preaching since they met. Anger, impatience, disgust at his own foolish simplicity—on the night of his triumph—a brew of depressing feelings percolated through him.

He turned to Horatio Dirk, who was lifting a glass of French champagne from a passing waiter's tray. Muybridge helped himself too. "Newspapers," the photographer offered, his nostrils flaring in disdain, "not one article even mentions the damned months of trial and error. And I, a stumbling modern Diogenes without a lamp . . ."

Already slightly drunk, Dirk smiled as though from a great height. "Great expectations, Muybridge." The editor wagged a cautionary finger. "Inevitably the problem with great expectations."

Dirk wandered off, mutely smiling to himself. Muybridge knew that Mrs. Stanford was visiting her sister in Mountain View, so he wasn't surprised to see Denise Faveraux in the mansion surrounded by a clutch of admiring males. No one pushed or elbowed, but each suitor worked his hardest to snuggle closest to her, as though proximity might confer the ultimate reward.

Edward swung around a statue of a scantily draped Greek nymph titled "Morning" and crossed the room. Denise stood beside "Evening," the companion piece to the first sculpture, which was certainly her time.

She greeted him with a gesture of her stirring arms. "Hello, Mr. Muybridge. I'm sure you gentlemen are acquainted with our conquering hero. You know what they say, to the victor . . ."

Again, he thought.

She wore a chaste, white silk dress contradicted by its spectacular plunging neckline. With each breath her breasts filled the snugly fitted bodice to barely shy of overflowing. She smiled, recognizing the direction and intensity of the photographer's gaze.

"Miss Faveraux." He bowed slightly, his head moving closer to those rounded breasts. "Gentlemen." Muybridge wasn't anxious to suffer more well-intentioned amateur praise. "Has anyone seen Samuel Montague? I know he's leaving tomorrow morning."

Denise impatiently fanned her dance card in Muybridge's face. "Business, Edward, always business. You've just conquered us all, you've made Leland a pile. Tonight you're sworn to pleasure." Her sweet breath enveloped him.

Franklin Forster, a state senator, answered the photographer's question, "I believe Montague's gone back up to the site."

"Are there problems?"

"Aren't there always?"

Muybridge transferred his empty glass to a passing shoulder-level tray and picked off a full one. The tray floated away as Senator Forster offered congratulations. Others echoed the sentiment.

"I want to congratulate you, too, Edward." Denise's penetrating blue eyes feasted upon him, as though he were a tempting snack.

"Ahh, I have to see the governor," Muybridge lied. "I need a word with him. If you'll excuse me—"

"Since you're running off, I insist upon at least one dance, Mr. Muybridge. I've left two options open." She pointed to the empty spaces on her card after the numbers six and ten, ten being the evening's final number. Senator Franklin Forster and the others were not pleased at Denise's favoritism.

"Ten, thank you."

Denise wrote "Edward" in the space for number ten. Then she wrote "Edward" on line six. "First six, then ten. We have much to discuss about a certain courageous radical dancer and mutual friend." The Holly reference evoked slight discomfort from several gentlemen. Yes, her pluck was almost as attractive to Edward as her ice-melting smile and welcoming, opulent body. Directing his lingering gaze at her, Muybridge exited the Pompeian room.

He crossed the hall to the salon, which had plucked its decor out of the Austrian baroque. Cerulean blue enveloped the ceiling, a sky layered with fluffy white clouds and penetrated, here and there, by clusters of cupids and putti—plump, impossibly pink lads with precociously informed eyes. Gilt scrolls circled above, gilt edged the cottony clouds, turning the trompe l'oeil vault into a saccharine aerial paradise.

As well-wishers showered him with congratulations, Edward caught the effervescence of the moment. The gas chandeliers burned more brightly. The champagne lubricated him, fine oil in a stiff lock. His head seemed to float, balloonlike, several feet above his torso. The tension that had plagued him for months drifted beyond his arm's reach, until Luke Ransom approached with characteristic swagger. Muybridge presented his back to the reporter, but Ransom would not be deterred, "Why take matters personally?"

"You crucify a great artist and expect me to be civil? Ransom, you're a bastard."

Unperturbed, Ransom replied, "Controversy sells newspapers."

"Lies, distortion, mealymouthed preaching of idiotic conventions—that's how you flog your papers." Muybridge, barely straddling sobriety, liked the tickling sensation of the syllables as they welled up over his tongue.

"The community's standard of morality is at issue here."

"Oh, you're such a devoted servant of the public."

"Certainly."

"Ransom, you don't have a single original thought. You are a toady and a fawning slave."

"Who the hell do you work for?" The reporter stomped off, grumbling, "Hypocrite."

Edward circulated through the mansion, accepting kudos, chatting, and downing more champagne. Three, four, five glasses; he didn't count, then he couldn't count. His mind loped ahead in an easy, long-gaited way, like a racehorse halfway into its workout. At the same time, like a circus seal balancing a ball on its nose, Muybridge dedicated himself to maintaining the vertiginous balance between delightfully, loquaciously inebriated and staggering, falling-down drunk.

Back in the billiard room, as the financier Chester Croker racked up the balls, Luther Mansfield, a friend of Abbot Berkeley's, sidled over. "I wonder, Mr. Muybridge, do you resent the suggestion that Governor Stanford actually took all the photographs himself?"

Muybridge replied part factually, part facetiously, "Leland Stanford and I are collaborators in this process. He is the patron, I the inventor, technician, expeditor." Picking off another glass of champagne as it floated by, Muybridge excused himself.

A half hour later, moving by the Versailles room, he spotted Denise Faveraux with Mark Hopkins, secretary of the Central Pacific. She caught Edward's eye and held it, even as she continued conversing. As Muybridge was about to approach Denise, he noticed Mrs. Leland Stanford moving through the lavish room, having unexpectedly returned from her visit. A small, stocky woman, Caroline Stanford wore a canary silk evening gown. In her formfitting gown, everyone could see that the rumor was true—the childless couple was about to have a momentous change—she was pregnant.

It was also certain that, if she continued on her trajectory, Mrs. Stanford would intersect with her husband's mistress in the center of the room. Muybridge considered diverting his hostess by inquiring, say, about her greenhouse. He had already photographed the outbuildings and gardens along with her little "folly," a sumptuous cottage furnished in purples and gold and glossy satin that Marie Antoinette would have found congenial. Mrs. Stanford was not an unlikable woman, though emotionally high-strung. Muybridge thought about rescuing his hostess, but found himself too drunk and, meanly, too emotionally titillated to intervene.

As the guests became aware of the potential collision course, the room turned deathly still—until only a gangly, gap-toothed Union Army colonel was left nattering away at a bored matron with dingy, thinning red hair. Suddenly, the voluble colonel ceased. Except for the sound of Mrs. Leland Stanford's heels on the parquet, silence reigned.

As she drew alongside Denise Faveraux, Mrs. Stanford bestowed the hostess's customary smile. Then Mrs. Leland Stanford realized at whom she was smiling. The smile did not fade but became rigidly fixed, instantly glazed onto her face. Her body froze in midstride, her eyes brightened and seemed to enlarge, as though she'd been struck smartly on the bridge of the nose. Luminous tears filled up the irises and then a single tear detached itself and rolled down her powdered cheek.

Head back, chin up, avoiding Denise's seething, intrepid blue eyes, Mrs. Stanford directed a rigid nod at her husband's mistress. Denise Faveraux returned the chill politeness with an abbreviated curtsy. Mrs. Leland Stanford's shimmering yellow evening gown trembled like windblown leaves as she nodded a second time; Denise Faveraux again repeated her minimal curtsy—a barely discernible tuck of the head. They might have remained nodding and curtsying like two automatons if Collis Ward had not responded, grasping Caroline Stanford's arm and guiding her through the hushed crowd into the hall.

No one moved, no one seemed to breathe as Mrs. Stanford's retreating steps echoed on the polished parquet. The skittish silence continued for a long moment—the gilt-and-white room might have fallen under a spell—then came alive with a soft rush of voices.

An hour later the three hundred guests assembled in the ballroom. Mark Hopkins stood beside Denise Faveraux while, at the front, Governor Stanford towered over his wife. Mrs. Leland Stanford looked composed and foursquare, anchored by her inflating belly. But her eyes were puffy, and Muybridge wondered how many cold compresses she had applied to her face. Meanwhile, her husband expansively surveyed his distinguished guests then lifted a massive arm toward the assembled. "I needn't tell you, friends, that this has been a red-letter day, a day of delirious triumph. And I don't mean simply financially."

That drew vocal agreement.

"Oh, by the way, Abbot Berkeley sends regards to all." The crowd exhaled an explosive laugh. "He begs your leave, saying that he is indisposed and thus unable to attend."

More laughter and cheers.

"We've made great progress in the past months. Great progress into the heretofore impenetrable secrets of nature and the true and exact science of horse training. Mr. Edward Muybridge has done an incomparable job." The governor gestured toward the photographer who, in spite of himself, felt flattered to be commended before such a gathering. Holly had nothing but contempt for the governor and his compatriots, "smug, complacent, scheming men," as she put it. Still, part of Edward applauded their aspirations and accomplishments.

Suddenly everyone was chanting, "Speech! Speech!" The governor held out his palm, indicating that this was Muybridge's moment.

He found himself in the front of the ballroom, beginning: "With the help of Chief Engineer Montague and the governor's lavish beneficence"—Stanford beamed a lighthouse smile at Edward—"I've stopped time, actually broken it into discrete parts for the first time in human history. The units of movement that everyone saw today were only yesterday mistakenly conceived as an indivisible flow never to be stayed or interrupted." Muybridge examined his audience. "I—We"—he acknowledged his patron—"have captured and pictured time itself. If I do say so myself, not a bad day's work." The crowd erupted in applause, whistles, laughter, shouts, an unexpected gift.

Edward gazed into Denise Faveraux's wild blue eyes, and suddenly, absurdly, arose an unbidden vision of her at the croquet match, the moment when she slumped to the soft turf and exposed those slender, long legs. Muybridge saw the two of them picnicking in a lush meadow. He lay on his back looking up into a crystal blue sky—the color of her eyes.

He stopped as her importuning look fed on him. The eyes seemed to dance laterally, enticing him, removing him to that pastoral spot where they lay thigh to thigh. . . . Meanwhile, his audience waited. And waited. Looking out at those complacent, well-fed faces, he forgot where he was, forgot what he wanted to say. He turned numb, dumb, blank, enthralled by the azure-eyed vision before him. Before three hundred of the West Coast's most powerful individuals, Edward tried to pick up the thread he'd been weaving. Any thread. Nothing came. Then, as a form of grace, the image of his row of cameras snapped into mental focus.

"I employed twelve cameras, each of their shutters working at a speed of *one-thousandth* of a second. That enabled me to catch and freeze the gait of the nation's fleetest trotter moving at a speed of *thirty-six* feet per second.

"Partisan newspapers will continue to attack my work. There are individuals, perhaps a few in this very room"—he scanned the room melodramatically—"who contend that my results are a fraud. Governor Stanford and I will throw that lie back into their faces.

"And so every day for the next week or even two or however long it takes, if challenged, I'll make a photographic sequence of the trotter, and each time I'll guarantee, I'll *bet* any of you"—the remark drew a benign smile from Leland—"we'll obtain the same results. Come!" he offered, "Watch me make the photos! Come to our shed and stand outside the darkroom as I develop them! Invite the entire world! There's no magic or trickery here. And remember that from this time forward, at one point in the gait of the trotter, all four of its hooves defy gravity and do simultaneously fly off the ground!"

The applause broke over him. It came steadily, like a soaking rain. Edward stood in this welcome shower and inclined his head again and again, acknowledging their appreciation.

Stanford congratulated him again, and the triad of the Big Four—Hopkins, Huntington, and Crocker—paraded by with manly handshakes, capacious smiles, and an unstated promise of a shining, limitless future. Even Collis Ward commented how impressed he was with the recent deeds and the evening's remarks. More champagne flowed as Muybridge was toasted again and again.

After Mr. and Mrs. Stanford moved off, Denise Faveraux approached. "I never thought of you as a speech-making type." She was whisked off to dance as Edward was accosted by more admirers. *So very popular*, he thought, *the two of us*.

He shot an unsteady round of pool with Chester Crocker, then nibbled at hors d'oeuvres in the ballroom. By then the dancing had been in progress for an hour.

Edward was scheduled for the sixth dance on Denise Faveraux's card. When he stood by her, he babbled tipsily, "I've broken down time into discrete elements. Do you know what I intend to do next?"

Her bodice came alive with each breath.

"Someday, I want to wind the world up again like a giant clock. The idea is to put time back together again, to reintegrate it. I want to make life flow by in photographs."

She scrutinized him with head half-cocked, as if asking why he labored so hard when everything was so easy. "Edward Muybridge," she declared as the orchestra began a waltz, "For one minute shut the hell up and dance me around the floor." She added knowingly, with a barely audible chuckle, "You're one of those who has to talk. But I suspect you're passably fair when you get down to business."

He took her in his arms, and they moved together into the waltz. Her hand gripped his, her softly resilient weight leaned into him. Edward took control as they entered the long round, her perfume swirling up and around him like gossamer veils. They danced, and the intoxicating flesh-warmed feminine aroma enveloped Muybridge; her arms, hands, thighs, breasts moved with fluid intimacy, oh so very close to him.

"Isn't your friend away?" she asked. Everything about Denise seemed suggestive and bemused.

"She has a speaking engagement."

"Oh yes, the Great Cause. Where is Holly? San Raphael, San Jose?"

"Oakland, actually."

"You know, her lady friends were shocked to meet me. Because of my former profession. Not our friend Holly, who's splendid, but most of those dried up suffragettes and bloomer-ites, dress reformers, and gymnasts and free lovers—free love, now there's a hideous notion." The quip was funny, but it reminded him of the question of Holly's rooms, and the hulking, applauding Frenchman with the expanse of stocking. "They think that hookers are fallen and pathetic or too hot for 'it' to control themselves. They don't see the problem is money."

"Hmnn," was the only sound he could manage.

"Women don't have money. We're dumb about it. We don't understand money's power because you keep its secrets hidden from us, walled off in vaults controlled by—you. It's not a full-blown, thought-out conspiracy—men don't sit down and plot it out in their clubs, saying to each other, 'We gotta keep them dumb as dog dirt about the one thing that counts.' But it works like a conspiracy. Even if we marry rich, we don't control the purse strings. And if a girl's lucky enough to be born to money, men handle it for us, so it never really is ours. We're not trained to think about it, obsess about it, to make money get in bed with other money so it can increase and multiply. To spend it—that's our role, when it's dispensed by Papa or husband or lover. I see money—economics, to you—as the root of the problem. That's why you men think we're inferior."

Edward admitted to himself, *Never in a thousand years would I have thought of that. Yes, women are more interesting than men.* But he wondered if, for all Denise's insight and penetration, she owed her independence to Governor Stanford.

She answered as though she'd read his thoughts: "You see, when I was a working girl I spent years on my back—I once calculated all the hours: one thousand four hundred and twelve, not counting nonpaying mutual consent. That figure I can't give you because I never counted. For your information, Edward, most men are not interesting in the sack. There are more ways to pleasure each other than the missionary layout. Tell me, what do missionaries know? That's a joke, Mr. Photographer. Actually, two jokes." Her smile was worth waiting for. "And all that time, I preached to myself, 'Save, scrimp, keep disease-free, try to escape.' Now I'm free of financial need."

"I wish I could say the same."

Their waltz ended, Muybridge's admirers pressed again. Some called out his name, others nodded favorably at the evening's star attraction —him.

"Edward," Denise chastened, "at least look like you're enjoying dancing with me. This is your big night."

Then, pleading fatigue to a ponderous army colonel, Denise Faveraux excused herself from the seventh dance. Taking Muybridge's arm, they wandered from the ballroom into the painting gallery.

"Someday soon," Muybridge indicated the paintings, "I'll put them all out of business." But his heart wasn't in the boast.

"Why in the world would you want to do that?"

"It's a tired old joke. I used to have a debate with a painter friend—which was better, photography or painting?"

"I like both."

The east end of the room was dominated by a nude marble sculpture. The Greek youth stood half-upright, back rotated slightly, right leg bearing his full weight as he leaned forward—as though eager to sprint out of the stone block.

Denise took Edward's arm and led him toward the marble. She examined the muscular back, then circled to the front. She placed a hand on the nude's calf.

"Let me pose for you." She raised her head and one arm, which emphasized Denise's columnar neck and full breasts. "Why haven't you asked me to pose, Edward?"

Throat constricted, he replied huskily, "Lately I've been preoccupied with four-legged animals."

Absentmindedly, she stroked the marble leg then her fingers gradually gravitated up to the young man's thigh. Edward's eyes stayed with her hand. He turned away to examine a mammoth landscape by William Keith.

"You would make a very compelling picture," he said, unable to watch her practiced fingers, her taunting smile.

Keith's *The Upper Kern River* was an epic landscape. Beyond the first towering peak lay distant mountains, which opened onto misty blue valleys overshadowed by snowcapped peaks that dominated the background. The hazy depths were unreal to Muybridge, a sentimental gloss draped over the potent, wild landscape he knew intimately. Having walked, ridden, and clambered over the actual mountains, having spent months wandering through the actual counterpart of this rosy world, Edward hated the soft illusion. He also understood that the painter presented an image of America that tens of thousands found thrilling, even prophetic.

Denise nodded at the Keith. "That's a good-looking painting. Takes your breath away."

"It's also a lie and a sentimental delusion." Muybridge confronted her unsettling eyes. "I hate when so-called artists sugarcoat reality. These goddamn gilded 'epic' pictures—domesticating what isn't tamed. Or couldn't be tamed until the railroad started to lay tracks."

The big picture loomed over Denise and the photographer, unperturbed by his critique.

She moved closer and breathed in, looked down at her own swelling breasts. "Edward, aren't there frontiers closer to home you want to explore?"

Her mouth was tinder to his flame. "You're as beautiful as any woman I've ever met. You're more provocative than any woman I've ever met. But I'm in love with Holly."

Removing her hand from the cool, white marble, Denise condescendingly patted Edward's arm. He found it hard to keep his eyes off those curving red fingernails.

"Who isn't?" she asked.

He spotted Collis Ward standing on the threshold of the room watching them. Ward walked over, trying to look ingratiating. But his mouth would not stretch into a full smile. "Excuse me, Miss Faveraux. Governor Stanford would like a word with Mr. Muybridge in the library."

"I'll be back soon," Edward promised.

"Hurry back," she urged.

Each of the library's fifty-five hundred volumes was leather bound, the walls themselves draped in matching, flawless reddish steer hide, which spread a warm, evenly diffused light throughout the room. It was gentle light, designed to minimize eyestrain. Edward asked himself if indeed the former governor read all the books corralled on those walls. Then he posited: Stanford is a man who collects and devours information, who ferrets out details. A somewhat revised impression of the ex-governor fought its way into Edward's consciousness: dictatorial and inflexible certainly, but possibly Stanford was not as self-serving as Holly argued and Muybridge wanted to believe. Stanford's faith in progress, in science, these were quintessential American beliefs. Muybridge's boss was a villain, but a complex one.

Amid the burnished glow of the bound volumes, Edward counted a dozen men. The handsome room was stuffed with horse artifacts—racing prints, gold-rimmed plates painted with horses' heads, an entire wall given over to saddles, bridles, riding crops, and other tack. A silver horse reared on Stanford's desk, and next to the two-foot-high figure was an inkwell fashioned from a horse's hoof.

Governor Stanford stood in front of a handpicked audience, the select of the select. "Yes, it is a great and timely matter to carry a vision to fruition," he declaimed. "Even if the whole world opposes you, even if sightless conventional wisdom and misguided individuals mock you publicly." Stanford eyed the present company as though he knew each individual who had taken the odds against him, which occasioned subtle repositioning of certain bodies in certain seats.

"Magnificent work, Muybridge," Stanford opined. "Congratulations to you, to me, to the deity of progress itself." He lifted his tapered glass, and the company toasted the photographer. "We've had our disagreements, which is often the case with men of scale and character. You are unqualifiedly the best—you've proved that not only to me but to the entire world!" The champagne glass tilted toward Muybridge. Ward slipped a full glass into the photographer's hand. "I have a proposition to make. . . ." Stanford continued. Muybridge felt compelled to listen reservedly, knowing that ongoing contact with Stanford would further unsettle his life with Holly.

"I'm not afraid to tell you, we are having major problems laying rail over the sierras. Ten thousand–plus altitude is hard enough in summer, Muybridge. Already we're facing the worst winter on record. Meanwhile, our rival the Union Pacific is laying down six to eight miles of track per day. Their advantage is our disadvantage. We must speed up the work. How to do that is a multifaceted strategic and personnel problem. Which leads to you and your expertise. The directors and I would like to hire you to document the most ambitious construction project in U.S. history."

"Don't be modest, Stanford," Huntington called out. "In world history."

"Photography in the High Sierras, with ten, twelve, possibly fourteen feet of snow will be daunting work. But for a man as talented and inventive as you, the undertaking ought to produce a stunning, monumental photographic record. The enterprise will be fascinating—not, say, self-promoting. Though these days, I doubt you need our help.

"You should know, Muybridge, that the railroad has to document this winter's work not only for company records and contractually for the Congress of the United States, but also for posterity. There's a good chance that the right publicity—insider views of the process, visual records of the feats we're undertaking, telling images of the mad characters who people our mountains—all this will catalyze public and congressional opinion behind us."

Muybridge bridled at the phrase "the right publicity," which suggested he tailor his work to illustrate the benevolence of the Central Pacific Railroad Company. But this job offer was ideal. There was of course the paycheck. And the notion of returning to a world virtually as rugged and anarchic as the old frontier . . . *that* appealed deeply. Edward did not want to miss the opportunity to record the railroad as it scratched and bit and clawed its way inch by inch, foot by foot over the formidable mountains toward the climactic moment of the transcontinental linkup—if that event ever occurred. On the other side of the scale, he dropped the weighty personal anchor of Holly's hatred for Stanford and the railroad bigwigs. Here he was, volunteering for his own domestic civil war. He said, "An attractive offer, Governor. Of course I must have complete control over my work. Or—"

"Of course, of course, Muybridge," the governor graciously demurred.

If he were to become involved, the photographer explained, there were details to iron out—money, costly new equipment, the length of stay. "How long a commitment would you need?"

"I should think a month, five weeks at most, don't you, gentlemen?" Stanford turned to Hopkins, Huntington, and Crocker as though the quartet sat alone in the library.

"Five weeks tops," Hopkins assured Muybridge.

"But you must start immediately," Huntington asserted.

"I will give you my answer by tomorrow noon." It pleased Edward not to be rushed by these preening rich men. And he would have to discuss the matter with Holly, a prospect he dreaded.

"I've added a dollop of honey to sweeten this confection, Muybridge." Stanford beamed his magnetic smile. "In the sierras you'll be awarded 'hardship' pay. That will translate into an additional seventy-five dollars per week over your old salary." The ex-governor's largesse filled him with fellow feeling. "When you return, assuming your work's as successful as it always is, we'll raise the stipend to two hundred twenty dollars weekly." The well-briefed Stanford understood what an inducement such an amount would be to Muybridge. It amounted to a bribe.

"Here, at the stock farm, the next problem we'll tackle is the galloping equine. We'll build from our first brilliant step and develop a complete and accurate breakdown—'an anatomy,' as you like to say—of every gait of the animal. Imagine, Muybridge, the usefulness of such an encyclopedic review to trainers, jockeys, horse men. Imagine, gentlemen"—he turned to his guests—"its value to veterinarians, physiologists, artists, students."

Stanford pointed to an eighteenth-century engraving on the wall which depicted a roan's front legs rigidly outstretched forward, the rear legs rigidly thrust behind. "For years now I've been convinced that the conventional 'hobby horse' depiction of the gallop is as absurd as the recently discredited representation of trotting. I've never seen a horse move that awkwardly—and I've spent many, many years at many many rails. I'm also sure that if an animal moved in the manner depicted"—he pointed at the image—"it would break a leg every time it worked out."

He pivoted his bulk toward the photographer. "I've had a plan, Muybridge, that I've inwardly nurtured for years. I intend to set up my own zoological gardens. Here, in Palo Alto, a Leland Stanford Ark of the World's Creatures.

"At my zoological Eden, we'll create a scientific record of how All Extant Creatures move." Every sentence released concentrated bursts of energy, packets of power like flares radiating from the surface of the sun. "Cattle and sheep, lions and wolves, camels and rhinoceroses—or is it rhinoceri?" His audience smiled or chuckled, but he barely paused, "Dogs and cats, etcetera, etcetera—the myriad range of God's creatures in a temperate locale, here for study and wisdom as well as the world's delight. And I would like you, Distinguished Monsieur Herr Professor Photographer, to initiate the encyclopedic study of all forms of animal locomotion."

Edward's mind's eye galloped ahead: inside his current, state-of-the-art camera shed the mechanism for photographing the plethora of animals already existed. He would add more cameras: perhaps another dozen. He would upgrade his equipment. It was all crystal clear: one bank of lenses at a forty-five-degree angle to make photos from the side. He'd also shoot the creatures head on—another row of a dozen cameras. A third from the other side. The title of his next book materialized in bold gilt type before his eyes: *The Encyclopedia of Animal Locomotion*, Photos and Text by Edward Muybridge. After completing *Animal Locomotion*, he'd proceed to the study of human movement, starting with Holly herself. There would be dozens—no, hundreds—of photos of Holly, each expression of her mobile face, her dense forest of eyebrow, the rich hair, that maddeningly sensual mouth, the slightest movement of cheek and jaw muscles or alterations of mood in those changeable eyes, gestures of arm and sculpted leg and thigh down to the slightest uplift or downturn of her lips or twist of her torso or articulation of a sculpted foot and those practiced, unbelievably seductive toes that provided more interesting pleasures than any other toes he had ever met. His mind drifted: Holly in motion, Holly dancing, Holly Hughes immortalized. By him.

Fifteen minutes earlier, entering the diffused aura of the gubernatorial library, the photographer fervently believed that his affiliation with Stanford was over. Yes, a couple more photo sessions inside and outside the mansion and with his stellar pal Occident, a bit of dot-the-I's follow-up shooting, but Edward had expected the final firm, masculine handclasp and his good-bye stipend. Instead, the governor offered Muybridge the future he desired.

Muybridge exited the library with congratulations still booming in his ears, a two-hundred-fifty-dollar bonus tucked securely in his vest pocket and the prospect of unprecedented new work. So why did he feel such pricking anxiety?

Drunk, elated, and lust-filled, he revisited the feverish impulse that haunted him since the evening's flirtation with Denise Faveraux. (Holly was lecturing in Oakland. She would not return until the next afternoon.) He thought about Denise's blue eyes reflecting the color of the heavens as, side by side, they picnicked in that charged pastoral meadow. A hunter on stalk, Muybridge prowled Stanford's mansion, room after room threading through the crush of glittering women and thickset, self-satisfied men. In each space he entered—the Versailles room, the Pompeian chamber, the billiard room, and the picture gallery—he could sense Denise's presence, as though she were moving ahead of him, tantalizingly hurrying forward, managing to remain just out of sight. He could smell her sensual essence, feel the stir and charge in the air that she left in her wake. He pursued relentlessly, each time sensing that the elusive woman was in the next room, a few steps ahead. For an hour he shook hands and accepted half-heard praises, all the time scanning the surroundings and moving on in a riotously erect state, trying to gain on her.

In the entrance hall Edward thought he caught her reflection in a tall gilt mirror, but he missed her actual presence. In the ballroom he believed he glimpsed her long, golden hair, but the woman he accosted dissolved into a petite blonde with a drab, tired face. Oblivious to his well-wishers, Muybridge pursued Denise Faveraux's maddening absence until finally, exhausted and deflated, he took his leave and drove home to his desperately empty rooms.

"I do not want you to desert me, it's that simple!" Two mornings after his public triumph, Holly stood before him in his bedroom, her hip slung provocatively to one side. The loose white gown exposed taut throat muscles, the swellings of her breasts, her thighs pressing against the fabric. Lovely, irresistible, she was feverish, upset, in pain.

"Analyze what your Stanford wants, Edward. If you won't refuse him, which you should do after his behavior to me, do it for yourself."

"As you said, nothing's simple in our life. I'll only be there for a few weeks, barely in time for the final push over the sierras. Imagine, nine feet of snow already. The images will be superb." He paused climactically, then continued, "This will be the last chapter of my book, the final piece of the puzzle slipping into place, and they're paying me handsomely. I can't let the opportunity of a lifetime slip away."

His self-absorption, his blindness to her fears, maddened Holly. At the very moment she most craved his support, he was deserting her—to work for that despicable toad. Toadying to a toad.

"I'm about to do something I have never done before." She paused. He sensed something profoundly amiss here; she seemed too overwrought, too frantic. "Edward, I *beg* you to stay. Please, I can't—" Holly started to kneel.

"Don't," he ordered, reacting quickly—he dove down as she began to stoop and caught Holly before her knee could touch the intricate design of the Turkish carpet. Gently he raised her up. He could sense the resistance in her forearms, but grudgingly she let him lift her.

Holly felt hemmed in, unable to confess the true nature of the problem. "Stay an extra week with me. Just seven days. I need you, Edward."

She had never been abject before. "I'm flattered, darling."

"Don't 'darling' me, you . . . you deserter."

He settled the last shirt into his valise as she inwardly raged at his casual, throwaway charm. There was no way he could probe for the real reason she wanted him in San Francisco, yet his ignorance seemed his fault. How bitter her "joys and fruits of free love" tasted.

"I would love to stay. But they're predicting six more feet of snow this week," he went on blithely, as though eager to escape, "which will make it harder to get up to the peaks where the company's blasting the immense tunnel and laying track. If I leave tomorrow, I'll be back before you know I'm gone." His fingers, tapping the lock of his valise, made involuntary movements to close it and flee. "Three, four weeks at the most, I'll be home."

Holly felt as if her body were being drawn and quartered, pulled in opposing directions between the present and the past.

"The money won't hurt." He longed to touch the bare arm protruding from the sleeve of her dressing gown. Desire was unsuitable at the moment, but he could not reason desire away. If only they could resolve the tensions in bed. Lie down and fornicate the torrent of complications away.

"Money, money. An artist who thinks of nothing else. It's an oxymoron, Edward."

"Deep down, Holly, you've never understood what it is like to worry about money. How exhausting and humiliating that struggle is." Bile from years of scrimping, of counting single pennies and waiting for incoming dollars, the meanness of the repetitive calculations now rose dangerously. "How much do I owe? When can I repay a fraction of it to this one and not that one? Which bastard's about to call the police or send one of those charming bailiffs like the one who slunk up to my door and you so generously paid off? I say to myself: *When will that next check for $14.75 from the Menckens—I took three photos of their daughter—arrive?* Oh god, you say, it's two days late. You run to the post office to see if the check is there. When it finally arrives four days late, you sprint with the insubstantial slip of paper to the bank, asking the condescending teller as nicely as possible—it hurts the tongue to say this, 'How long will it take for this check to clear?' He sneers at you, knowing what's coming next: 'Is there any way to get it more quickly?' While all the time you think, *What in the world will I do in the meantime?*"

Muybridge felt throned in rectitude. "You have no idea how many hours I've spent balancing figures in my head, scribbling endless columns of numbers on slips of paper which I rip up and throw away as soon as I calculate how much more I owe because I didn't want you—or anyone in the entire world—to know the amount of red ink I perpetually drown in. All that time and anxiety juggling those ceaseless sums in this boring, soul-devouring round that has never stopped for a single instant since I left home at thirteen."

"*I'll* be your patron."

"You can't buy me the transcontinental railroad, dear."

"Stupid, bullheaded man!" she cried, recognizing that, romantic that he was, Edward found some corner of his poverty heroic. Knowing that she had lost this round, Holly feared that it might already be too late for them. How could she resist Jacques? Why should she?

He woke early and found her gone. Muybridge listlessly packed his equipment, wondering if she'd sneaked out to protest his desertion, hoping to see her one last time before he left. As he fitted the appropriate lenses into their padded cases, Edward reflected on love's inordinate power, how desperate it makes us all. For Holly and him, intensities alternated—like the potent electric current through his electromagnets, on, off, on and off. It was Holly's turn to be irrationally clinging. Till now, he had been more totally in love than she. Muybridge basked in Holly's current devotion. Deep inside he felt his departure was partial repayment for an old score—for insecurities thrust upon him by her amorous past and for the uncertainty he'd had to endure since Fauconier popped up in the theater, sitting an arm's length away. Yes, revenge indeed, most sweet because she wouldn't recognize his underhanded pettiness toward her.

At about 10:30 a.m., Holly entered Muybridge's bedroom carrying a suitcase. Her hair was up in a careless bun. She looked flushed and tired, her gray eyes clouded, as though she'd been crying. (Once or twice he had watched her eyes tear, but he'd never seen her cry.) "I'll make you a deal, Muybridge. One, I'll give up my rooms and move in."

After months of pleading with her to live with him . . . "Holly, darling," he said gently, trying to banish even vestigial triumph from his voice, "as soon as I return, we'll move in together. You'll throw away your keys; we'll take larger rooms."

"Two," she continued, not deviating from her text. "I'm offering you a partnership in my new firm, Hughes and Muybridge. You'll be a full voting partner, with all rights and privileges thereto, including capital, or dollars in crass terms." Futility tipped her wavering smile. "But I will not negotiate about the order of those names on the letterhead."

"It doesn't sound right—Hughes and Muybridge. Don't you think Muybridge and Hughes has a more enterprising ring?" Was her careless tone slightly forced, camouflage thrown over deeper distress? Certainly her drawn mouth did not relax.

"It's vital for women to own and use their own names. We don't want derelict maiden names cropping up only on school diplomas."

Charming, he thought, the hint about marriage. Charming and so unexpected from her, Miss "Marriage is a trap;" "Marriage is a prison;" "No. Never!"

Holly flung open the suitcase and whisked away a bone-colored scarf. Underneath the garment were stacks of fifty- and hundred-dollar bills. Wads and wads of money.

"Take my money," she urged.

"You're delightful, you're even rich, darling, but I can't."

"Don't 'darling' me," she replied harshly. Holly picked up a wad of fifties and flung them hard at the photographer. She began scooping the money out of the case and hurling the bills hand over hand at him, crying, "Take it! It's all yours, you bastard!" Her hysteria shocked and disturbed and touched him.

He moved around the room, picking up the money and piling it on his bed. "Holly, dearest, I would like to make you happy about this, but really I can't."

Her tear ducts gradually came under control. No, no breaking down in front of him. Or any other man. Unable to sort out her distress, Holly abruptly changed the subject, "I've made up my mind, Edward. I'm going to perform in this city—if I have to build myself a hall for a single night, if I have to dance in the damn mud streets or on a rooftop. I need to perform and they ought to have the chance to see me."

"I couldn't agree more." Muybridge was disingenuous here, certain that she would never perform again in Stanford's city.

"Whether you're here or buried in the sierra snows, you bastard, I'm going to dance." Defiance gone replaced by resolve. And anger at the injustice to her.

Something in her had suddenly changed, a seismic shift. Whatever it was, he needed to explore it further—when he got back. "I have a better idea," he said. "Wait for me. I'll be back in a month and then, with all my might, I'll help you. We'll build the theater together with our own hands."

He kissed her, and then he said, his voice husky, "All right now, lock that fortune away." He straightened the edges of each of the six piles of bills. "Wherever I am, whatever I'm doing up there, I'll be back in time to see you dance. I promise."

Leaning back, Holly pushed the case onto the floor, and they made love. A stolid, weighty sadness hovered over them like a dull sword; Holly's vulnerability outweighed her passion that morning. He was unusually gentle with her. Afterward, she clung to him for an hour, unwilling to let him go.

Chapter Eighteen

East of San Francisco, as though on cue, it began to snow—whirling white sheets draped over the mountains, erasing the ground, turning the sky a stark, endless gray-white. The locomotive clicked-clacked higher into the Sierra Nevadas. Stanford sat across from Muybridge; Ward lounged next to the photographer, one leg skittering up and down as though to the train's audible beat.

Staring at the solid wall of snow, Stanford grumbled, "In the survey, Montague assured me this route had the shortest snow line."

"Nature's as fickle as a woman." Ward, his fair eyebrows faint dashes in the high, balding, well-defined forehead, stole a glance at the photographer.

"The better you understand the ins and outs of the road, Muybridge, the more informed your work will be."

The train racked back and forth, the engine gasping and wheezing with troubled breaths. A sharp curve threw Muybridge too near Collis Ward. The man's cologne was overpowering.

"Whether we or the Union Pacific will lay the most track and control the largest quantities of land along the right of way, that's one major crux. We've fallen woefully behind, which means we're losing thousands of dollars each day. This cursed snow—the worst winter in history—grips us in its scenic stranglehold." He pointed out the window. "Meanwhile, our agents tell us the competition's charging across the prairie. So it's beer and skittles for them, and blasting and logistical nightmares and frozen extremities for us! You know from working with me, you know from the farm, I don't enjoy making men toil beyond their limits. But that's the only way we can compete with those blasted clodhoppers skipping hell-bent across the Great Plains."

As the ex-governor subsided into silence, Muybridge tallied up the tens of millions of dollars up for grabs in this cutthroat race. Meanwhile, the white landscape was drawn slowly by, as though on a parade float. Towering redwoods and giant ancient sequoias stood buried fifteen feet up their trunks in fantastically shaped drifts. Snow-piled branches were dragged down to the snow line. Outside the window the photographer viewed fairyland laceworks of branches, tree limbs festooned with silvered iridescence. Draped in crystal baubles, the world gleamed—huge stalactites from rocks, asymmetrical ice towers, white-on-white whirlpools shagged with glistening parapets, and wind-sculpted frozen whitecaps that held up twisted, tentacle-like fingers as though clutching at the air.

The train toiled blindly upward, into the evergreens, the trees growing shorter now as the tracks scaled higher. Stanford glowered out of the steamy window at the falling snow as though battling to hold back nature by force of will. "The Central Pacific's first locomotive, The Pioneer, arrived in October of 1863. Do you know how we got it to California?"

"Over the Guatemalan Isthmus?" The photographer was less interested in his employer's question than the stark finery outside the frigid, rattling window.

"Around the Horn, Muybridge, around the Cape itself—the very route that the transcontinental will render obsolete! Fine irony that, don't you think? When we finally got the monster assembled, the town of Sacramento gave us a sixteen-gun send off. They understood that their future was linked to our success." Like the engine now wheeling through a downhill curve, the governor gained momentum. "We waved good-bye to the crowd and moved it up to Cisco, then started toward Donner Lake."

"What is it, Collis, thirty-five or so miles overland?"

Ward, who obviously had heeled alongside his master through this tale a dozen times, sat up attentively. "Forty-one, to be precise."

"All went well until, as we were moving the engine across a minor tributary of the Truckee River . . ."

He paused. The ex-governor believed that, invariably, the halt at this moment in the narrative would prompt a question. Muybridge, gazing out at the graduated sizes of the snow-draped evergreens, volunteered nothing.

"What happened then, Muybridge?" He thrust his large battering ram of a head in the photographer's face. "A few ties on the track were not properly secured. Two or three spikes were not set well. Some incompetent worker and a negligent foreman failed to follow the correct procedures. Because of their criminal disregard, *the entire transcontinental dream was jeopardized*." Stanford underlined each word as he spoke.

Muybridge, insufficiently attentive, tracked the bouncing leg.

"The question—how to save that irreplaceable engine?"

Collis Ward took up his part, "Muybridge, you should have seen the governor, like a general under fire."

"The locomotive swayed—"

"Swayed?" Ward's eyebrows seemed vague accents hovering above pale, depthless eyes. "It actually started to tip over."

Muybridge sat as though in a theater, observing their performance.

"The governor had the courage and presence of mind to yell, 'Everyone, over to the high side!'"

Stanford picked up the thread: "It teetered. Fifty men inside, fifty grown men cantilevered out over the stream. Outside, thirty men plunged knee-deep into the icy stream and pushed against the shifting weight of that massive locomotive. Fighting for us, for our country, for what was then only a vague dream of a transcontinental link."

And for their paychecks, Governor, Muybridge thought.

"More men kept running to help. We must have had fifty then eighty or more Irish and Scots and Chinese all struggling like a single organism to right that tipping locomotive."

In spite of his initial resistance, Muybridge was with him now, leaning as though with a sled along the story's curves and banks. "Slowly, gradually, with screams and groans, with a devotion that surpassed belief, muscles straining and hearts about to burst, the men somehow—truly a miracle!—pushed The Pioneer—What's in a name?—upright. Then they dragged and rolled and shoved it backward onto the anchored track." He paused, physically spent. "Earsplitting cheers, congratulatory embraces followed by a moment of solemn appreciation. We handed out a ten-dollar cash bonus to every single man and topped that off with a triple ration of fairly potable Jamaican rum.

"Only afterward did I realize how close we came to disaster. I stood next to that huge panting engine and started to shake. I shivered and quivered and quaked as though I had ague, and all the time I keep replaying the scene over—that half-million dollar locomotive which came all the way around the Horn about to plunge into that wretched little stream. That was the closest I've ever come to despair."

The governor gave his auditors time to digest the saga. Then Stanford continued, "The groundwork for the railroad was laid back in the summer of sixty-four, at the start of the Nevada gold rush. To capitalize on that boom, we built a first-class wagon road from Dutch Flat up to Donner Lake. You know the area." Muybridge had photographed it four years before.

"A costly undertaking, but we had already begun negotiations with Washington for the railroad right of way. The wagon road gave us an opportunity to survey the terrain, begin engineering studies, explore possible alternate routes. Not to say, make a few dollars, which poured in over the trail. Our wagons might have been hauling the gold nuggets themselves."

Ward chimed in, his bouncing knee keeping time with the rickety beat. "Tell him about your opposition."

Around Muybridge, an achingly empty white. The blankness, that nothing that was out there beyond a meager pane of glass, chilled him.

"Of course the Central Pacific wasn't the only outfit interested in cashing in on the Nevada mining boom. The four of us had to battle the stage lines and toll road entrepreneurs, express companies, teamsters."

Stanford liberated his gold chain, whipping the watch in tight arcs. "Then there were the clipper ship owners, who wanted to control every item of cargo coming down from the mountains. At that point the only practical way to ship all that gold and silver east was by sea."

It had been snowing during the long climb till, unexpectedly, the sun broke through the cloud cover. Instantly, the sun's brilliance turned the mountain into a gleaming mirror, spreading light over the landscape.

"The four of us got rich then, Muybridge, richer than most men dream of. So we have a residue of success to draw on. Only"—he smiled tightly, baring large incisors—"our account is rapidly being drawn down."

Stanford spun toward Ward, grabbed his knee and commanded, "Stop that infernal tapping!" The junior vice president's face turned red. In front of Muybridge, he was utterly humiliated. Silence ensued for a long interval. Edward struggled not to smirk but wasn't entirely successful.

At six thousand feet above sea level, looking across at his employer, Muybridge toyed with the notion of making Stanford's portrait. The thick, dark face and massive head had authority, indisputable power. But how to capture the rapacious resourcefulness that lurked in those oddly undersized eyes? The danger that played like heat lightning around his brow? Muybridge thought of Gérôme, and Gérôme led him to Holly for a poignant instant, which made Muybridge visualize the sketches of a young Philadelphia painter named Thomas Eakins, Montague's friend. Montague had pointed out two stunning Eakins drawings in *The Philadelphia Photographer*. Maybe Eakins would be the one to capture the ways in which Stanford's unshakable self-confidence spilled over into imperial arrogance, a belief that he himself was a manifestation of a larger, unbridled fate.

The train coughed and wheezed and sputtered along a sheer rock wall to the summit of another ridge, then the white desolation outside the window was replaced by an endless tent city, sprawling up and over the next treeless ridge and onto one beyond that and on as far as Muybridge could see. After slow miles of switchbacks and vertical cliffs and emptiness, the Central Pacific base camp seemed like a preposterous legerdemain, a world conjured out of nothingness.

Edward's eyes surveyed the rows and rows of thin canvas shelters quaking and billowing like sails in the gale wind. Tent ropes blew erratically about, snapping taut then turning slack, which moved the shapes of the tents around like wild, shackled beasts. Not since the war had Edward seen two thousand men encamped. Off to his left, in a hollow, stood a cluster of crudely made wood cabins. These, it turned out, were reserved for the Central Pacific brass.

The engine inched tentatively forward to within yards of the end of the tracks, where it halted. Muybridge moved to the door, cradling a new camera body and lens under his arm. He stepped down from the train into a blast of arctic air. The wind caught a badly tooled edge of the lone passenger car: the metal gave off a hollow, plaintive wail. Muybridge realized the sound had been their accompaniment on and off all the way up the mountain.

Samuel Montague relieved Muybridge of the camera. "Dallmeyer, good old Dallmeyer," said the engineer, appreciatively viewing the lens. "And good old Edward. Welcome to Windy Hollow. Thanks for coming." Accompanied by the eerie whine of the wind-struck train, Edward smiled at the first agreeable words he'd heard in a day and a half.

Montague shook Stanford's hand. The engineer's eyes seemed to be set further back in his head. New, deep lines had dug into his brow; his shoulders bowed under an invisible weight. Edward's friend looked exhausted.

Glancing east, Edward watched scores of figures moving through the camp, bodies shrouded in furry pelts, gloves, and boots. With barely an inch of skin visible, the bulky forms were lumpy, misshapen, almost hard to recognize as human.

"We'll visit the site now," Stanford commanded.

"I'm afraid it's too late for today, Governor. By the time we got started, it would be so dark we'd have trouble keeping to the trail."

"I can't waste any more time!"

Samuel Montague replied with unhurried calm, "We've had quite a lot of snow, sir."

The camp was an arctic stick city draped in gray canvas. In the aisles between the tents, snow had been scraped away or trampled down to a thickness of six or even eight feet. Ice steps were cut into drifts and mammoth snow piles. Along the tamped tracks, men and animals moved unsteadily, all below tent level. Everything—the sprawling piles of ice-crusted snow at the end of the tent rows, the sheer, gray granite ridges—looked merciless and unyielding.

Montague led the visiting trio into a large, rough-hewn cabin where a fire blazed in the hearth and the fragrance of roast meats filled the room. They seated themselves around a plank table and sipped coffee laced with whiskey and stuffed themselves with venison and goose and duck. Stanford interrogated the chief engineer, "Start with the worst. Tell me the absolute worst."

"We've begun using the new blasting compound, but only inside the summit tunnel."

"That was in your last report," the governor replied dismissively. "Is it more effective?"

"Yes and no. Nitroglycerin's more powerful than the powder, but you can't control the charge. We're killing men wholesale."

"How many did you lose?"

The chief engineer's left eye skittered away to a far corner of its socket, as though ashamed to return his employer's gaze. "Six last week, the all-time record. Four the week before. The numbers keep climbing."

Muybridge thought grimly, *Almost one a day*.

Ward transcribed every word.

Shiny dabs of goose grease clung to Stanford's beard. "You know the coolies think that, when the vertical bore is finished, their relatives will climb right up into California."

Only Ward laughed.

"Tell Muybridge about our tunnel, Montague."

"Edward, the tunnel we're blasting is to be over a quarter of a mile long. If my drawings are accurate, 1659 feet. Through solid granite." Of course Edward had heard this before but he was tired, and listening to Montague's voice was music to the photographer's ears. Anyone, anything but the relentless dog-and-pony show of the Central Pacific tandem. "The longest tunnel ever cut in the world and, to make matters more excruciating, it sits at seven thousand feet, which makes it tough on the men to breathe, let alone work flat out. For months every day we've been banging and blasting away at all three faces simultaneously, the men on eight-hour shifts around the clock. We're not far away from breaking through on the vertical bore—if my calculations are on target."

"What happens if you're off?" Muybridge asked an innocent question.

"The end. Failure of the entire Central Pacific enterprise." Stanford growled this dirge as he targeted Montague's stable eye. Stanford changed the subject: "Why not ten-hour shifts?"

"That's too much at this altitude in frigid weather. They're already dropping like flies." Montague sucked in air, steeling himself for what was to follow. "Governor, the men need better grub. More of it, too. Scurvy's breaking out. They want more pay. The translators tell me there's a walk-out brewing."

Ward scribbled notes in his black book.

"Tell them I'll ship every last yellow devil back to China. No money, no relocation." Stanford canceled his anger with an opposing thought. It was like watching a rushing locomotive turn on a dime. "If they'll work ten hours, we'll up the rations. Bonus pay for every man whose work surpasses minimum output. I'll double the gin allotment. Take a note, Collis." Ward's pen was already accommodating the request. "Speed. We've got to speed up the work."

To his everlasting credit in Edward's eyes, Montague did not retreat. "In these conditions ten hours are way too much. The present setup is eight on, eight off. You can't squeeze them any harder."

"Hire new ones."

"We don't have enough trained men as is."

"This work does not demand skilled labor."

"Tell that to the blasters and the gandy dancers, Governor. You tell that to them."

"New ones," Stanford insisted as Ward kept up his infernal scribbling.

Montague took his last stand. "Training takes time and effort. New workers will only slow us down."

Stanford shook off the objection while he reached for another goose leg. "Send to the docks for more workers. We need fresh blood."

Montague took a long pull of brandy. The engineer had argued his case as forcefully as possible, and lost.

"Brief him." The governor nodded at Muybridge.

Montague began, "We couldn't engineer the railroad as a direct line over the mountains because the grades are much too steep. The steeper the grade, the higher the operating costs. So we're spending more money now—"

"Money we don't have . . ."

It wasn't the first time Muybridge had heard rumors of insolvency. Holly was certain the Central Pacific was in financial trouble. But Muybridge said nothing, filing away Ward's accidental revelation and instead asking, "Samuel, fill me in on the tunnels."

"The original survey laid out eighteen tunnels. But I've managed to cut back to fifteen. That'll save us time—"

"And nonexistent money." Ward grinned mirthlessly. Muybridge concluded, *He's drunk*.

The photographer settled himself in front of the fire, lapping his legs in a sheepskin robe. He had almost finished getting comfortable when Stanford spoke: "You look worn out, Muybridge. Time for you to turn in." So he was being dismissed—like a child. Edward was led off to an adjoining small cabin, where a slim Chinese servant showed him which bunk was his.

Shortly before dawn, Samuel Montague stood over the photographer's cot and stage-whispered, "Day's breaking, my good man. Time to ascend to the sierras' fabled snowcapped peaks." Muybridge rolled onto his side, trying to escape the inevitable, but the engineer would not be denied.

Edward's mule was perversely named Rosie. Every step the animal took flung Edward against one or another part of the frigid, rock-hard saddle, which bruised him fore and aft and pounded his upper thighs and rearranged his vertebrae all along his spine. The air was so sharp and dry it singed the nostrils, rasped the throat. Whenever the two men spoke, their breath crystallized so completely that an observer might have imagined their words came wrapped in frosted balloons.

They climbed a steep trail barely wide enough for the mule's mincing hooves. The day was blindingly clear, the wind whipped snow into fantastic whorls, and every now and then shifting white scrims flowed across a flawless blue sky. Under the blazing sun the snow became a silver mirror, collecting light and hurling it up into their faces. Muybridge pulled his scarf up over his burning eyes.

They rode in silence until the photographer asked, "Samuel, what's this talk about the Central Pacific being bankrupt?"

"All too damn true," Montague replied. "They're running barely ahead of the bailiff. They're only in business because the federal government keeps writing them blank checks."

"Why?"

"The government is in too deep to pull the plug. How do you say to taxpayers, 'Sorry, we've invested one hundred million dollars of your hard-earned money and we have nothing to show for it other than forty-six miles of non-contiguous steel track'? No"—Montague laughed bitterly—"Stanford and his diabolical crew has all of us, the entire country, over a barrel." His left eye took flight, as though checking behind to see if Ward was hovering nearby. "It gets reported as a 'matter of cash flow.' That's all I can say, Edward. And I shouldn't divulge even that."

As they rose higher, Montague cautioned Muybridge not to yell or sneeze or even snicker aloud since it might trigger an avalanche and "wipe out the two of us."

"What about Rosie?" Muybridge asked.

Samuel Montague fought back a laugh. "I told you, Edward, do not make me laugh. It's goddamn dangerous." They moved silently ever upward. The engineer stage-whispered: "Did I ever tell you about my original survey of the sierras?"

"No."

"Stanford and Crocker hired me for a deservedly princely sum to determine where the mountains began, geologically that is. I trotted out on a fine palomino, not a cursed mule, and surveyed the fall line that indicated the spot—precisely 22.3 miles east of Sacramento."

"How did you determine that?"

"Simple," Montague replied. "That's where the granite outcroppings start." He pointed to a vertical gray wall of stone. "Among geologists that's the agreed upon definition of what a mountain range is. The Big Four took one look at my map, fired me on the spot, and hired Newton Crawford to resurvey my survey."

"Who's Crawford?"

"California State surveyor. A Stanford political appointee but not incompetent as a geologist. But this time Stanford and Crocker went along to chaperone Professor Crawford. Can you guess what miracle occurred? The state surveyor found that the sierras began at Arcade

Creek. I quote the document: 'The true base of the mountains is the river, but for the purpose of the legislation, Arcade Creek is to be considered the start of the range.'"

"So what's the difference?"

"Fifteen miles."

"Wait, how much money is involved?"

"Well, Congress forks over sixteen thousand dollars per mile for track laid on the level, thirty-two thousand for desert, and forty-eight thousand for mountain. Those fifteen miles provided almost three-quarters of a million in government bonds, which helped finance the first stage of construction. I have no strong objection to the state surveyor picking up the sierras and plunking them down fifteen miles closer to the Central Pacific railhead. But I'm sure as hell not going to be the engineer in charge of moving them."

The sure-footed animals cautiously ascended the icy, twisty track, climbing into airy nothingness. Ahead, Muybridge heard the *whoosh* and heavy, rhythmic breathing of explosives. Under the animals the ground fluttered lightly as though a giant were jiggling pocket change.

As they topped the rise, the cliff face pressed itself on Muybridge—an enormous, vertical anthill swarming with laborers. Multitudinous Chinese crews clambered everywhere over the gray rocks, with the graders working out in front like an ant column's advance guard, and a team of gandy dancers—a team of highly skilled Irish workers who laid the rails—bringing up the rear, shifting their eight bodies in unison as they readied to lay down a twenty-foot section of steel rail on the precipitous mountain side.

The long climbing cut in the rock made a crude exterior staircase. Up near the summit, the photographer glimpsed the gaping black hole of Montague's tunnel.

"My Celestials." Montague pointed appreciatively to the Chinese workers.

"Celestials?"

"They have few of white man's vices—except for gambling and whoring, of course, which are not vices in my book. But Celestials, my friend, because they appear to live exclusively on air."

The photograph would be one of the most spectacular he'd ever made. Hundreds of men hand-chiseling the railroad right-of-way out of grudging granite. The steep diagonal climb of the roadbed would organize the shot. To top it off, the majestic monolith rose jaggedly a half mile above the icy thread of a river.

"To make the undertaking altogether impossible, locomotives can't handle an angle that exceeds eighteen degrees. We have to be scrupulous about the rate of both ascent and descent. Up till now we've been using thirty barrels of black powder on a good day. I've started training a handful of skilled blasters to work with the nitro. But I can only use it inside the tunnel because of avalanches outside."

On cue, it seemed, the air thinned, oxygen sucked into a void. Edward heard the explosion an instant later, as he watched massive gray columns sheer away from the wall, a vertical stone sheet blasted out of its eternal resting place.

The instant the air cleared, thirty or so ropes were draped over the cliff edge. On each one a Chinese worker in a deep wicker basket was lowered from the summit by hand-cranked winches. Dangling and swaying like sentient tassels, men and baskets inched down the wall.

When the worker in his frail basket reached the desired spot, he signaled to the winch man to stop, then cautiously stood up. Heart in his mouth, Muybridge watched a man brace himself, swaying in the downdraft like a flower in a perilous headwind, five hundred feet above the river. The man produced a drill and, like a silent woodpecker, began to hand gouge a minute hole in the rock.

A blast of wind caught one basket. It blew away from the wall, and the occupant, whose body had been braced against the rock, almost slipped over the side. Muybridge shut his eyes, but an instant later he saw the man was still suspended over the canyon. With an aerialist's calm, the young man clutched the sides of the basket then tipped his wispy body back toward the great stone column. Muybridge watched the baskets with their human cargo tossed and blown about the rock face. Unfazed, the workers hammered away while they twisted and danced and jerked up and down at the end of dangling ropes.

"How do they get the poor devils to do it?"

"No options," Montague replied grimly. "How do you get men to sail into the ocean on a rickety whaling vessel for two or three years in the hopes of coming home with a few hundred bucks and a flagon of sperm oil? How do you get men to charge gun emplacements, like Pickett's boys? You tell me, you were there." Montague was fierce, impatient. "How do you induce Ma and Pa to drag themselves and their five squalling brats thirty-five hundred miles across an entire blasted continent behind footsore oxen in a flimsy canvas-covered wagon? You've seen them, Muybridge. You even goddamn photographed them. Never overestimate the comforts of home. There's little keeping folks back where they hail from, or else they'd never leave in the first place." He changed the subject: "Watch. Now comes the tricky part—the blasting powder." Clearly, this was not his favorite moment.

In the skimpy willow gondolas the men readied the charges and began to delicately insinuate volatile black powder into the holes they had hand-bored into the rock face.

"Samuel, this is madness. Absolute madness."

The wind swallowed most of the engineer's words, "Don't be squeamish, my friend. It's merely our most up-to-date form of human sacrifice. And they have the gall to call Indians primitive. I hate this, but I've got a job to do."

Muybridge observed sharp flashes of light, like sparks from miniature fireworks, as men lit fuses all along the cliff. Scintillating flares glittered, faltered, then caught as the blasters wildly jerked on their ropes to signal to the winch men above to haul them the hell out of there.

Simultaneously, each basket-man began to shinny up his rope, a fraught and desperate race to escape the onrushing concussion. Meanwhile, the haulers strained at their winches as they frantically cranked their handles. Frail bodies scrambled up dozens of dangling lines, scrawny forms snapping their thighs and legs together as they fought to hoist up and away from the danger. The entire cliff seemed covered with elongated spiders all scurrying vertically.

Thhuumpp! Boom! Thhhumpp! First the mountain seemed to exhale, then the crystalline air went oddly milky from the explosions. The roaring mountain pitched and trembled and bucked underneath their mules. Rosie jerked back.

All clear, Muybridge reckoned, unleashing a deep, long-held sigh.

His body calmed; then, his eyes scanning the cliff, Edward picked out a man—hardly more than a boy—who was tipping out of the wicker basket. Then both arms jerked forward in what looked like a grotesque attempt to fly. The outstretched arms remained stiffly locked over the man's head. As one thousand men watched in silence, the body seemed to hang miraculously for an instant then drop. The young man flung a forearm down then up in a gesture of despair, which caused his body to spin out of control. Muybridge watched as the man cartwheeled over and over. Faster and faster he plummeted downward while every eye on the mountain tracked his accelerating fall.

The form smashed against a huge boulder, bounced absurdly high, flipped over, and was instantly gobbled by the icy river. It was over so quickly—if Edward had not witnessed it himself, he would not have believed it had happened. For a full minute not a man moved, not a sound was uttered, until the foreman blew a doleful work whistle.

Men resumed their tasks. Muybridge read suppressed fury in those bent backs, in the stiff stab of picks and the staccato thrusts of spades and shovels. Here and there on the rock face a laborer stood frozen in place, neck angled down, unable to lift his eyes from the obliterating river. For the second time that morning, Montague muttered, "One more. Like clockwork every day, every other day, one, two, three more." Neither man could look at the other.

Rosie was nosing in the snow, rooting for an imagined, buried delicacy below her reach. A furious Muybridge kicked the mule, and, when she didn't budge, whacked her persuasively in her tender ribs. They climbed higher. Ahead, Edward heard shouts and dull *thunk*s—too thin to be explosions.

Montague spurred his docile mount, which moved forward at a singsong trot. They topped the ridge and Muybridge found himself under another granite cliff that soared, almost unbelievably, eight hundred feet straight up. Leland Stanford was there, looming over the diminutive Chinese laborers. Only yards away, notebook at the ready, stood Collis Ward.

Stanford addressed his chief engineer. "Double-time, triple-time, all the time around the clock, whatever you have to do! Push them, drive them, Montague. We must pick up the pace."

Montague calmly replied, "Ten minutes ago, we lost another blaster.

We have been losing *my* people at an excruciating rate—three, four, five, six per week. Unacceptable, and not only morally. Functionally. I can't train men to be productive unless they're alive for a month or two. You yourself said that quality was essential when laying rail in these mountains."

"You're quoting me at a goddamn congressional hearing."

"You were correct." Stanford held up his hand demanding the engineer cease, like a traffic cop on Market Street in the afternoon rush. Montague went on, "We can't have rails bending or sliding under the weight of the rolling stock unless you want a repeat of Truckee Creek." Stanford shot Montague a blistering look. "Unless you want to lose a carload of passengers when a rail gives way. Imagine the lawsuits, the congressional investigation, the publicity. You can't afford that. We must have time and resources to do it correctly."

It was as though Stanford had not heard a single word uttered by his chief engineer: "I want speed! No time to waste! Bonuses, more booze, whatever you can come up with to bribe them to keep them on the job. Finesse the bastard government inspectors. Or buy them! I've been through this charade before. There is always a way." Muybridge thought of Denise: What did that luscious, witty woman get from Stanford—other than gobs of cash? What was he not understanding about the governor?

"The inspectors are human, too, remember that, Chief Engineer." Stanford gestured to an Irish foreman, who helped the big man mount a large white horse. The governor started down the mountain with Ward following behind as though attached by an invisible wire. In spite of himself, Muybridge couldn't help being impressed by the governor's physical and mental stamina. Fifty-five if he was a day, his wife expecting, and by sheer force of will Stanford seemed to be hoisting the steel rails himself, up and over the eight-thousand-foot range.

At first the photographer had wanted the incessant ringing to stop. Now the harsh, implacable music of the sledgehammers as they burrowed into the rock face became an urgent carillon, bells reaching down into the earth's core and resonating out from the monolith's measureless sounding board. The entire earth seemed keyed to this grating, steely music. As the raucous concert continued, Muybridge watched tempered steel bits shudder and twang like bass strings on a cello as they insinuated themselves centimeter by bitter centimeter into the wall.

Edward knew the cost of each bit. He knew that the nitro itself and the new tempering process that was supposed to turn the steel bits into a substance harder than that stone were the Central Pacific's last hope. To a layman's surprise, the Rockies would prove relatively simple for the Union Pacific to cross. The right of way of the rival railroad moving east to west would follow the old buffalo trail, for buffalo invariably moved along the easiest, though not necessarily the straightest, route. Over the decades, the buffalo had been followed in turn by tens of thousands of migrating wagon trains, all of which sought the most comfortable track. The Union Pacific planned to lay rails along the proven Overland Trail, up over the gentle slope of South Pass, then simply glide downhill out of the Rockies. Their mountain crossing would be completed without blasting a single tunnel. Not so the Central Pacific. Against his will, Muybridge smiled, catching himself thinking that this was indeed an heroic undertaking. Too soft on Stanford, she would have insisted. The vision of Holly invoked a jagged pang of uncertainty. Her absurd begging, the huge cash bribe, her pleas for him to stay seemed antithetical to her independence. The panic spread—should he abandon the High Sierras and rush straight back to San Francisco? That thought was gobbled up by what he saw.

"The Chinese call this face 'Killing Mountain.' It wears out steel, they say." Montague paused.

Muybridge completed the thought, "And men."

Montague stared venomously at the granite face. "On a good day we manage to cut seven, eight inches at most. That's a good day."

Meanwhile, Muybridge watched a whippet-thin Irish foreman measuring his workers' progress with a yardstick while yelling, through an interpreter, to make them drill faster. The interpreter rephrased the orders in Cantonese, and the workers responded. The process of translation seemed as painstaking and snaillike as the pace of the endeavor.

Edward surveyed the panorama, looking for his shot. A crew of fifty Chinese cleared away rock debris, another clutch of men attempted to clear out massive snowdrifts with long-handled shovels. Other clusters labored at leveling the roadbed, while still others—two groups of eight Irish gandy dancers—prepared to lay the next six-hundred-pound rail section in place. Ahead of them, dozens of workers clambered over a high retaining wall, a Montague design that attempted to keep falling snow and rocks off the track.

Montague said, "Hands freeze; we have wholesale amputation of fingers. I have a recurring dream: I enter a chapel, in front of me there's a grotesque side altar stacked with frozen fingers and toes, a skewered eye or two, arms cut off at the biceps, legs amputated up to the thigh. Up here, every bit of exposed flesh is vulnerable to frostbite. The wind makes it worse, as bad as twenty or thirty below. And every goddamn night the snow storms down and covers up the day's work."

Eyeing the wind-whisked thirty-foot drifts ranged into peaks like heavy cream, Muybridge wanted to cry out to his ally, *Stop! You won't succeed. This can't be worth it.* But the photographer held his tongue.

Chapter Nineteen

A weedy, tobacco-chomping foreman shambled up to Montague. "Sorry, sir, I shuh know yer not lookin' fo' mo' trouble, but we got a problem in that tunnel of your'n."

The temperate chief engineer could barely control himself. "What now?"

"They won't deal with nobody but you, sir. I been tryin', we been tryin' . . ."

"All right, all right," Montague muttered as the foreman led them into the tunnel. The three men—engineer, Muybridge, and foreman—maneuvered past clearing crews. As the trio edged into the heart of the granite mountain, the tunnel resounded with a horrendous cacophony—shovels clanking, men yelling, iron cartwheels shrieking on steel rails.

As they moved away from the opening at Mile 104, each man proceeded slowly, using a high, cautious step, trying to land on the ties as eyes adjusted to the oily, aqueous light. Erratic torches dyed the walls a shifting inklike blue. To Muybridge, the men on scaffolds and the bent forms who scurried by lugging heavy tools and steel replacement bits, the gangs of straining workers who scrambled and pushed and hurled their shoulders into overloaded handcarts brimming with rails and ties, the "sweepers" whose shovels banged and clanked and squealed in protest as they cleared the tracks of newly blasted stone, the laborers who toiled to lift and dump shovelful after shovelful of crushed rock ballast onto the right of way, even the mules and draught horses, all were slaves trapped in a clamorous circle of hell.

The three men high-stepped deeper, away from the thinning light. Muybridge repeated the Montague-induced litany: "Two thousand and fifty ties per mile. Forty railroad flat cars to haul the materials for a single mile of track." He couldn't help being awed seeing a thousand workers shoveling and sweating and lifting and hauling while entombed alive inside the belly of a mountain. More Montague statistics tolled in his mind: *Forty-five hundred men to shovel the snow. Ten thousand tons of equipment required per month! Thirteen thousand men at work over the entire line, seventy percent of whom do not speak even subsistence English.* Fifty thousand *mules and horses and oxen.*

Edward calculated they had walked one hundred yards into the proposed four-hundred-yard tunnel. After months of backbreaking, nonstop, round-the-clock labor the blasting had progressed only that far. Yet Montague, characteristically not an optimist, vowed that the pace would now accelerate. Another two months, the engineer claimed, and they'd break through. There they'd stand in the sunlight and raise champagne toasts at the eastern end of the longest tunnel ever constructed. Break through in the spring—if Montague's compulsively detailed calculations proved accurate. If his three separate borings actually joined—one inching east, one crawling west, and the third, the trickiest, a vertical, right-angled bore down through the mountain that was conceived to interconnect to the other two in the tunnel's absolute center. If wrong, if his calculations were off by a foot, a mere ruler's length, the multimillion-dollar gamble was lost. It would take too long, cost too much to recalculate, reblast, and redrill. Muybridge half-believed Stanford would have Montague murdered if he failed.

The gelid chill seeped in and under and through Muybridge's sheepskin as he tiptoed after the others into the shadowy tunnel where, with each breath, a metallic pall drove needlelike ice shavings into his lungs while, simultaneously, frigid sweat and the charred essences of black powder and nitro crammed itself up his nose and down his throat. He spat and blew his nostrils, but nothing wiped out the infernal metallic taste.

Meanwhile, on the tunnel floor, an army of men and animals labored to haul away tons of debris. Clusters of stooped coolies hand-dragged large granite boulders over to mule- or horse-drawn carts. Every single scrap of refuse chipped or blasted from the tunnel's innards had to be pushed or rolled or carted back to the entrance, which each day got a foot or two farther away. A vast two-way traffic arose, a seesawing motion that shuttled supplies in and ferried out the loosened guts of the cave.

A "tea boy," younger and more frail than his emaciated countrymen, hovered at the edge of the group with a five-gallon keg slung on his back. A laborer with a long, dangling braid stepped up to the tea server, flipped open the keg's valve, and released the amber-colored liquid into a small wooden bowl. Bowl in hand, he took a consoling sip then folded back into the ranks.

Montague commented, "Tepid tea seems to be their staple. They love their tea, and, as I said, Oriental women, and gambling. They're inveterate gamblers, and will bet on anything—which cockroach crossing the floor of the barracks will reach the wall first, or who's the next poor devil to tumble off the edge of the mountain." Montague's mood shifted with his left eye. "They claim Lincoln freed the slaves? Mule shit! Here is the slave trade resurrected. The coolies are shipped over on ever-renewable contracts that the California high court held are legally unbreakable, even if one of these lads understood enough to hire a lawyer.

"Their 'ladies' are in a worse bind, at the mercy of a mercenary group called Chinese Six Companies. This corporation is a giant, corporate pimp. It's also China's largest exporter, with a direct line to the Emperor himself. I'm sure His Exalted Highness makes out like a bandit, and that he and Leland have cut any number of deals. None of the girls speaks a word of English. They have to service literally battalions of men. Up to thirty customers a day, I'm told. Two hundred–plus men per week." Montague's contempt for these abuses strained his voice as though he'd been shouting too long.

"To safeguard our men—the work force—I've ordered weekly inspections by the doctor. Thursday's quite an active day. You can imagine the, uh, emotional complications our translators have to suffer weekly, isn't that right, Lin?"

The translator, a pale, slender young man named Lin Son, offered a shy, boyish grin. All the Chinese looked like children to Muybridge.

"But today's snafu's a novel one. Unlike the Irish, who'll go jaw to jaw with you about wages or the liquor ration or will argue that there's too much fat in the bacon, the Celestials have been docile—till now. The timing couldn't be more hazardous to the enterprise. We've got to close the Cold Stream gap in two weeks or we'll lose three quarters of a million in government bonds for the delay—the rails have to be contiguous or we won't be handed a cent."

They reached the granite face. There Montague, Muybridge, and the foreman halted in front of a team of thirty Chinese laborers. The coolies were draped in sweat-stiffened gray jackets and bulky leather gloves. Even enveloped in their hoods, all appeared undernourished, rows of skeletal faces with fuming almond-shaped eyes.

"Lin"—Montague gestured to his translator—"ask the foreman what's the problem?" Montague's eyes, the left included, never left the Chinese foreman, Min Yee.

Min Yee was rail-thin, with an unmanageable, wispy gray beard that shot off in all directions; a tattered rattan hat was jauntily slung on his back. He had sad, evasive eyes. Muybridge couldn't help noticing the foreman's hands—braided with wiry veins the color of annealed metal. The top two joints of the right index finger were gone, leaving shiny, snakeskin-like scar tissue on the stump.

Min Yee spoke, the translator relayed the message to the white men. "Three good men killed last week in tunnel. One man fall and dead now. We no use new bombs."

Min Yee had positioned himself a step in front of the coolies, with the others pressed together behind him, barely an inch separating man from man.

"Tell them this clearly: Go back to work!" Montague's rasping voice bounced off the granite, boomed back down the tunnel, making the air itself quaver.

The silence and immobility of the Chinese caught the attention of others at their headlong labor—men swinging ringing hammers, men dragging top-heavy handcarts along the rails, men hefting rock ballast between the rails onto the right of way. They, too, halted. The entire work force stood idle, hanging on the outcome of the debate.

Samuel Montague's eyes did not leave Min Yee. "I'll say it one final time: Back to work."

No one stirred. Muybridge noticed that the tunnel workers—Irish, Chinese, all of them—were a uniform gray, as though they'd all been dipped whole into granite dust.

Samuel Montague gingerly produced a small vial from his waistcoat. In it, an oily, yellow liquid—the nitro itself. Terrified, the Chinese workers drew back as one body. Min Yee stood his ground.

The new procedure dictated that no one but the designated "explosives expert" handle the nitroglycerin, which had been introduced only weeks before. Orders commanded every single worker to vacate the tunnel whenever the explosive was to be used. After all, nitro was five times more powerful than the deadly black powder. And much more unstable. So unstable that they cushioned it in transport, swathing it in blankets. And brought the substance into the tunnel only when they were ready to blast.

With each man watching as though his life depended on it, slowly, with great patience, Samuel Montague placed his index finger up against the vial's opening and tenderly poured the explosive substance toward the lip. Steadying himself, the engineer pulled his finger back from the lip, holding it up like a cautionary note. It was coated with the yellow liquid.

The laborers squeezed together more tightly, as though hoping, as a group, to survive whatever terror the Tunnel Man proposed for them. The chief engineer took two rapid steps at the coolies, then sharply flicked his finger at the granite wall. The explosion startled everyone. Rocks shifted, a few loose, smaller pebbles rattled down as the wall, the floor—the entire cave—rumbled and trembled crazily then gradually settled back.

"If any men—any single one of you—refuse to work, I'll bring the entire goddamn mountain down on your heads." Shaking his explosive index finger, Samuel Montague threateningly jabbed at the rock ceiling. "Say that in Chinese."

The translator broke into a fierce, lilting singsong, the words falling back over Muybridge like a drumming rain. Min Yee grimaced, gritted his teeth, and shrugged his shoulders, then reset his feet as though trying to find firmer purchase. Engineer and foreman stared at one another for a long time before Min Yee muttered a syllable or two in his tongue. The translator let out a sigh then exclaimed with relief, "They're ready."

"They need to be careful, tell them I understand that." Montague didn't look triumphant at all, which may have strengthened his point with his workers. "But it can be done. In fact, it has to be done."

Instantly the entire tunnel reanimated. Shovels, picks, sledge hammers struck up their earsplitting cacophony as the crews pecked away at the lowering rock face. Meanwhile, yardsticks at the ready, foremen strode about or scaled scaffolds to measure the depths of the borings. Once again the cave sprang to work, but now all the men's movements were tinged with fear and a grudging respect.

Montague tersely suggested that Muybridge swing south to observe one of the Central Pacific's sawmills in operation, where he might take a photograph or two. (It was too dark to shoot in the tunnel.) Then Montague moved off with another of his Irish foremen to confront a problem with the footings of the half-mile-long bridge at Mile 109. Yesterday's avalanches had swept away eighty yards—two weeks' round-the-clock work—of the laboriously constructed wood trestles.

To Muybridge's surprise, Rosie the mule seemed to enjoy moving down the snow-covered ridge. Her mincing gait threw Edward against the pommel, so he braced his legs in the stirrups and fought to lean back in the saddle. Muybridge stopped to make a photo of yet another expansive, white-on-snow-white panorama, then lower on the slope he tried unsuccessfully to squeeze a shot into his camera's frame of the long bridge at Mile 107. The bridge reminded him of the photo he was preparing before the stagecoach robbery, the brilliant afternoon when he met Miss Holly Hughes. Edward swore to write his love a long, impassioned letter that evening. He'd been too busy and exhausted to write as yet.

Edward stationed himself at the base of the half-mile chute, which was a rough-hewn, twelve-foot-wide wooden trough that ran steeply from the crest of the ridge down to the sawmill. At the top, lumberjacks winched a denuded forty-foot redwood trunk into position at the slide's welcoming upper lip. Each logger looked on with childlike glee as the wooden behemoth was arduously balanced then tipped over the edge and crashed and rolled, slithered and thundered the half-mile down.

Laughter, shouts of "Go, go, go!" and "Timber, watch out below!" rang through the forest. Close to the bottom, the heavily reenforced flume angled up fifteen or twenty yards, and as it started uphill, the monster tree banged and heaved and spun, then slowed until it finally stopped near the lip of the slide at the stream's edge.

Muybridge readied his fastest camera. The new dry plates, coated and at the ready, would help him here. He didn't have enough cameras to photograph the entire thundering slide of the huge logs. But now he could catch a part of this drama. Cascading timbers and trotting horses and all else that moved and ran and crawled and danced under the sun—particularly one lovely dancer—they were gradually becoming reproducible. He had indeed stopped time and now felt able to literally grasp it in his hands.

He photo-documented smaller trees being cut down and slashed up and stripped of bark and scaled down into rough-squared beams and tunnel supports or further divided and subdivided into numberless railroad ties. Through most of the afternoon Muybridge, hemmed in by snowdrifts and the large, accreting mounds of sawdust, shot and repositioned the camera. As he worked he recalled what Ward had said the night before: The railroad operated twenty sawmills to produce the needed wood. Twenty! Twenty sawmills, fifteen tunnels to blast, hundreds of gallons of nitro, thousands of animals, thirteen thousand workers—Edward Muybridge felt like the dwarfed Lemuel Gulliver, awed at the scale and logistics of the enterprise.

It was already late afternoon when Rosie four-footed her way down to Crescent Lake, not far from base camp. Muybridge observed teams of men working on the ice. Dozens of men thrust long handsaws down into the lake's frozen surface. Meanwhile, a team of horses pulled an ungainly, plow-like apparatus back and forth across the lake, scraping drifts from the surface to prepare it for scoring.

Muybridge approached a friendly-looking man with a T-square dangling from his belt, introduced himself as the company photographer, and asked the fellow to explain the ice-cutting process. Sim Smith politely answered that he was the "marker" who measured the ice into 22-by-32-

inch blocks. Muybridge looked on as Smith measured then scored the ice to a two-inch depth with a handsaw, each jagged, rusting tooth set at an opposing angle and looking as ominous and decayed as a shark's mouth. Muybridge photographed him as he inched his crowbar into the ice while his assistant split it with a long-tined metal pitchfork. Smith then picked up a sharp, slender spade and began to lever the bluish block away from the larger mass. As it moved, the ice threw off silvery highlights like an unearthly flat fish. Once the block came free, the water below was flawless cerulean, as if the sky had dived down and reappeared under their feet.

Master and apprentice hefted the oversized ice cube onto a stack of other cubes arranged on a skid.

"Looks heavy."

Breathing deeply, Smith replied, "Depends how thick she is."

His freckle-faced, leprechaun-like assistant, a fifteen-year-old named Rusty, grinned, as he said, "Don't believe him, mate. It's heavy. And it gets heavier every lift."

Toward sundown, Edward approached a heavyset man in a cumbersome coat who was deftly bandaging a draft horse's legs. A black bag rested next to him on the ice.

Muybridge asked sympathetically, "What's the problem?"

The man looked up. "You Muybridge?" he asked without waiting for an answer. "I'm the vet; name's Asa Bushnell. Problem, you ask? Oh, no problem, my friend, except that this mountain ain't fit for man or beast. Beasts mostly manage better than men. But when the snow's this deep, once it ices over, the crust cuts like a scalpel, Mr. Muybridge. Slices up their legs. This poor bastard's hock slashed almost to the bone. I patch them; they go back to their work, a thaw and a freeze, and it starts all over."

"Sorry to hear that, Mr. Bushnell."

"All in the day's work."

"What do you do with all the tons of ice?" Muybridge later questioned Sim Smith as they stood in the failing light and studied draft horses hauling skids of thick ice blocks up an inclined plane to the storage shed at the lake's edge.

"They sell most of it in San Fran and around the Bay. You can imagine how much money they make off hotels and saloons. That's just a start. We got ships in the Bay crammed with sawdust from our mills waiting to pack the cubes in and sail it down to them hot as hell places—all the way to the West Indies even. Then there are fish sellers, butchers, dairies. Hospitals chew tons and tons. Oh"—Smith smiled— "and beer. The firms making lager, they brew at low temperatures."

"But most of it melts away, doesn't it? There must be an enormous amount of loss, yes?"

"In winter, just about nothing, friend. Even in summer now, them new double-lined icehouses like that one here"—he pointed to the nearby cabin—"and insulated wagons to haul it, it's only eight percent loss."

Impressive, Muybridge thought. He himself paid one dollar per month for delivery every third day of eight pounds to his rooms. Squirreling away this information made him feel virtuous for, with his help, Holly would soon be almost as thoroughly informed about the fiscal workings of the Central Pacific as Ward himself. Holly . . . his mind filled his body with a mixture of love and lust and a vague disquiet. Yes, he would write her tonight. Or, if not tonight, the next time he could steal a moment for reflection.

"Who owns the Sitka Ice Company? The Central Pacific?"

Sim Smith looked at Muybridge as though he were a rube. "Who else?"

As night threatened to wipe out the light, Edward stood at the lake's edge trying to get a final panoramic shot of the ice cutting. As his timer ticked, Edward skimmed a flat stone out across the frozen surface. The queer, hollow skittering echoed out and up the snow-draped ridges toward the brooding white peak. It seemed to Muybridge that the entire lake had become a sounding board for his distracted play. Near him, men sweated and sawed and hauled away, while all around him, silent, deadly snow began its ritual descent.

Chapter Twenty

The next morning he stepped into a foreign land—the camp's Chinese quarter. Here four thousand of the ten thousand coolies employed by the Central Pacific were gathered in paper-thin tents, and together they had cobbled together a roughhewn China Town. Muybridge paused to gaze at the hand-lettered characters on boards tacked on poles beside the tents. The impenetrable, asymmetrical characters looked often like hieroglyphs set on stilts. Men in shabby greatcoats muttered singsong rhythms as they kowtowed before odd, colorful shrines to Confucius or Buddha, while joss sticks poured sweet, overripe vapors into the frigid air. In one tent, four men played what looked like a complex game of checkers with shiny black and white marbles. Next to them, dominoes clicked like castanets in front of workers whose braids trailed down to their waists. A few enterprising men eschewed the flimsy tents and had dug down, creating igloos ventilated by slender airshafts and heated by wood-burning stoves topped by gerrymandered iron chimneys. In all of his travels Muybridge had never seen anything like this high-altitude world.

He wanted to photograph them, to catch the startling conjunction of physical delicacy and open-eyed clarity, these foreigners. *Calm stoics,* he thought, their eyes offering a record of fate's caprices. But no one would pose. Whenever he set up his camera, men backed away; they rushed by, zigzagged around, or quietly yet adamantly refused to pause. Always they were deferential to the white man with the "eye-box," but no one would oblige him. Finally, Hop Kee, his translator, explained that most of his countrymen believed that Muybridge's apparatus entrapped the soul. His photographs might separate the men forever from what they valued most, allowing them no future and, worse, no way home. They would not take the gamble. Years before, Muybridge had confronted the same attitude on the Plains among the Sioux and the Cheyenne, the Arapaho and the Crow, and he knew only one prescription, which was to allow enough time for them to get to know him and his work—a commodity he had precious little of. All he wanted was to make his pictures and get home to Holly as fast as possible. Muybridge had not yet heard from her, which worried him.

Hop Kee fronted him as they toured a wooden bunkhouse reserved for the Chinese foremen and skilled workers. Here the photographer observed a collection of pasty, skeletal bodies in exhausted, motionless poses as each man tried to cram in as much rest as possible between the newly instituted ten-hour shifts. Muybridge was shocked by the pale faces—not yellow as expected but a sickly, fish-belly color. A few wakeful men chatted or gambled or clicked the spotted dominos. Most workers favored a short chin beard, and almost all wore grubby long johns topped by the traditional buttonless blouses. The bunkhouse was saturated with a stale but inoffensive smell, as though a brew had been allowed to steep too long. When Muybridge mentioned the odor, Hop Kee couldn't suppress a brief laugh—his countrymen, he explained, would think the comment hilarious. The translator did his best to be diplomatic, but his message was that the coolies found Occidental body odors nauseating. This was a new notion for Muybridge, and, as he moved around the cramped, orderly bunkhouse, he wondered if some of the averted heads and the occasional wrinkled nose had as much to do with the terrors of his stench as with their fear of the camera. Like everyone in the camp, Muybridge was limited to a single hot bath a week.

By Edward's unscientific estimate, 25 percent of the Chinese were missing a finger joint or two. They had lost them setting fuses or blasting or getting a hand pinched while moving rails. In warmer weather the slightest cut or scratch without immediate medical attention led to a festering wound, and, if things got bad, the doctor would simply amputate the offending digit. Later, when Muybridge asked him, Doctor Isaiah Greene assured the photographer that toes were worse than fingers—they got bashed or cut or crushed and were prime candidates for frostbite since the feet sweat in boots. If frostbite went unattended, it could lead to lethal gangrene unless the surgeon "chopped." The veteran coolies had organized a thriving pool that posted odds on how long it would take for each newcomer to lose his first joint.

Late that afternoon Muybridge and Hop Kee strolled into the Chinese whorehouse. Some soul had dutifully attempted to outfit the place with several accoutrements of the trade. A moth-eaten scarlet drape; a chandelier with erratically placed crystal teardrops; a pair of rickety, questionably stained love seats; and a floor-length, fissured mirror completed the decor of the "parlor," where half-naked young women—girls really—lounged on display. Two or three had lovely features and glowing, flawless skin. One young beauty, newly arrived as he later learned, looked Edward in the eye and lifted a small, perfectly shaped breast out of her chemise. Her eyes on Edward's flushed face, she fingered her nipple until it stood red and erect. Muybridge stared at the stunning creature as she approached and backed the photographer into a corner then pulled up her skirt, revealing taut, slender thighs and an astonishingly rich black bush. As the other women laughed and chided, Muybridge managed to break away, but he was breathing heavily, and not simply from his escape effort. Outside, he drew long, slow heaves of air, trying to eradicate her torrid image.

That evening, Muybridge wrote his first letter to Holly. Certainly he was fascinated by what he had seen, that was one reason for writing. Also, something about Montague's "Celestials"—this transplanted alien community—who supported each other in the midst of subhuman conditions—moved him. He wrote:

Dearest,

I miss you more than I can say. I adore you. Your image haunts me. (I'll get back to that soon.)

The work is exhausting, frustrating, fascinating, epic, all that I hoped it would be. I wish you were able see these high mountain sites.

You'd be both fascinated and outraged. On the one hand, I watch thousands of men employed in tireless attempts to scratch their way through a granite mountain at 7,000 or 8,000 feet above sea level in the midst of the worst winter ever recorded in the Sierras. No one on this continent has ever undertaken such a gargantuan task. Yet the undertaking reduces men to abject slavery, treats them like brutes while the work itself causes two or three or more deaths per week as men are accidentally blasted to kingdom come by the most potent explosives on earth. I watch this creation and destruction in two minds. On the one hand, the building of this transcontinental dream inspires; on the other, the costs are inhumanely high.

I've made photographs of horses and mules, donkeys and oxen with legs and hooves and hocks cut to ribbons by the crusted ice. The railroad works more than 1,000 teams of beasts at this site alone. The noise from blasting and the toil and the swirling crowds of men and animals is enough to drive any sane being to distraction—and beyond. I've been in hostile environments, but nothing was as dangerous or disturbing as what I witness here every day, every hour. Yet the work forges on.

I'm assured by the powers that be that three woodblocks derived from my photos will appear in the *Clarion* this week. Write me your opinion of the work. Please explain the formatting, placement on the page, the captions the photos carry and whatever else occurs to you. If possible, beloved, please forward the newspapers and any relevant journals to me.

I feel like a combination of reporter and spy. In my diary I jot stray bits of information picked up from a brandy-soaked foreman or an unguarded comment that Montague or Ward lets slip late at night after too much brandy. (Stanford has gone back to S.F. to deal with his pregnant wife and other issues.) I'm certain that Ward and his surrogates watch me closely, so I never make a notebook entry in public. It may sound ridiculous, but I even secret the diary in my clothing, and I've been forced to hide my most revealing photos under my mattress. I am the photographer spy who is constantly being spied upon. I gather facts that will shore up your case against the Big Four. Still you must remember that, even if we come up with evidence to embarrass them, or less likely, bring them to trial, the country devoutly believes in the transcontinental railroad. The nation has already invested too much to halt its progress, even if we can prove that the Central Pacific has committed dire crimes, which they surely have. To make our case even more difficult to prove, three-quarters of these workers are Chinese, and Caucasians are not concerned about these men or the handful of Chinese prostitutes who are encamped here. With no political constituency, voices go unheard.

I have to tell you a state secret I witnessed three days ago: ten yokes of oxen inch a huge steam engine—they dub it "The Black Goose"—over a quarter mile of twisting and ascending then steeply descending mountain trail. Crews of Celestials (Montague's term for the Chinese laborers) scramble ahead to shovel and fell then lay down tree trunks which are rough-fashioned over the worst of the frosty ground into a "corduroy" road. Swearing, grunting teams of men line up on three sides of the engine then, together with the oxen, men and beast bump and drag "The Black Goose" forward one or two feet. Moving uphill is Herculean labor, men/oxen sweating, slipping as they fight to inch the engine forward. Believe it or not, downhill is even worse—workers jam tree-sized timbers under the train's wheels as foot-thick logging chains are secured to the tallest, sturdiest trees around. Everyone stands aside as the blocking trunks are knocked out from under the wheels and, with the ancient trees swaying and threatening to buckle, the precious engine slides a yard or two or three down the slope.

I learned from Montague that the railroad does this exercise to fool the government. Why? The Federal money for each mile is paid *only* if the rail line is contiguous. The C. Pac. has vouched to Congress that it already has 135 miles of uninterrupted rail in place. But the Congressional investigators aren't scheduled to arrive until late April or early May. When they find "The Black Goose" waiting for them at the 135th mile, they'll believe that the track has been completed as reported. For how else could a fifteen-ton locomotive engine climb over a mountain? If explanation is required, the missing sections of rail links will be conveniently "wiped out by avalanche." Thus Stanford and his cohorts will be able to keep the loan monies and receive further government payments.

I think of you constantly. I love and adore and I miss you more than I can possibly express. Let me know if and when you are performing, and I'll race down from these frigid peaks to watch your warm, living body in motion. Now you've made me crazy.

I love to hear you think, love to feel you feel, adore to see you move. I even love to see you pee, love the long fine line of your naked legs and thighs, the sight of your breasts as you sit—I see you in profile, the curve of brow, your mouth. And then you turn and smile, not coy, unaware of how beautiful you are and open, playful, receptive. I love that crooked tooth. I long to lick it. I adore when a fragment of that dark eye stuff you use migrates out of perfect placement, a passion-induced "flaw" outdoing perfection. Your forehead, eyes, mouth, each lovely portion offers its own tastes. When I kiss your brow, I feel different temperatures, a range of climates—like swimming in a lake and passing over unknown hot spots, cool zones—so you bathe me in invisible but distinct eddies of feeling. I adore your gray-green eyes, a light-filled sky in a matchless frame. Your calves, your legs, your thighs . . .

I must stop, my love. I just came.

Yours eternally,
Edward

Hands trembling, Holly folded the letter, slipped the sheets back into the envelope, and scrutinized her face in the mirror. How happy she was to hear from him, to feel his lust descend from on high. But what timing. Holly recognized the import of the letter being hand-delivered by Montague's trusted assistant, since it contained potentially explosive revelations about Stanford and his cronies. The terrible irony was that the letter had arrived an hour before her evening's appointment. Edward's sentiments and her own tempestuous thoughts and sense memories accompanied Holly to Cleary Street and the Maison Dorée, San Francisco's idea of elegance.

The restaurant, mirrored from floor to ceiling, swarmed with fashionably dressed couples as brisk waiters flowed about. Gentlemen wore full-length black Prince Albert coats; women adorned themselves with bright, extravagant hats or suggestive veils.

She spotted Jacques Fauconier erectly seated at a corner table, a bottle of champagne at the ready. As Holly entered the room he rose, all eyes.

She moved toward her old lover through the predictable field of hostility and feigned indifference. Several men acknowledged her with a glance or discreet nod, but few women looked her way, at least not until her back was turned. Fortunately for Holly, she still was invited to speak to women's groups in the area. Occasionally she did see Denise, but since that afternoon at Augusta Hannibal's, Denise and she were not in frequent contact. Whose fault it was—hers or Denise's—Holly did not pursue.

Smiling regally, Holly swept past Mark Hopkins, secretary of the Central Pacific, sitting at his large table. Hopkins inclined his head, ambiguously acknowledging her presence. Once she passed, his eyes furtively followed her, admiring her figure, the quietly captivating pearl necklace, the vivid, cream-colored camellia in her hair.

Holly and Jacques Fauconier kissed on both cheeks, like old campaigners greeting one another after years of separation. "They'll think I'm awarding you a Croix de Guerre."

"I could use one. Along with a glass of that Moët." As Holly relaxed, she realized with relief that, whatever sexual parrying lay ahead, she was at home here. "It's always a marvel to see you, Holly."

"I'm pleased you weren't devoured by a grizzly bear. Or scalped by an Eskimo."

"Eskimos don't value scalps, darling. Furs, yes." Looking around the room, Jacques asked protectively, "Is it as chilly as it appears for you in this provincial outpost?" A muscular male shoulder to cry on—she sensed concern and also opportunism in his offer. Fauconier mistakenly believed that, because she was tired and sore, he could have her. Holly changed the subject, quoting his last letter. "Well then, tell me about this 'vast land of opportunity' to the north."

Jacques flashed a preemptory signal to the waiter, ordered the second bottle of champagne to be iced, and, as he poured for her, explained that Alaska offered unlimited potential for mineral development, mining, and timber. "The country's fascinating. Huge beyond comprehension. Sublime, really." He spoke quickly in English, then slipped into more rapid-fire French. "Untouched mountains, untallied resources—there are fortunes to be made up there. Unfortunately, winters are unimaginably severe. The ground stays unworkable eight, nine months of the year."

He launched into diverting tales of dog sleds and seals and polar bears, glaciers and the exotic natives, ending with free-loving, wife-swapping Eskimos—"who apparently savor the exercise, among other incentives, to keep the blood circulating." He told Holly that Secretary Bill Seward's recently purchased "folly" was in fact an extraordinary boon for the United States that would underwrite the next century's economic development. "But I do not want to bore you."

"Not at all. Go on."

"Everything is frozen. Shoot a deer and it's stiff by the time you reach it; six months a year you must heat the water to make it—how do you say—liquefy, and you must thaw what passes for victuals. The people, too, they're frozen solid from October through April." A faint smile graced her features as she thought of both of her men in icy lands. "Summer, they tell you wistfully, 'Ah, it's marvelous, you ought to be here then,' though the mosquitoes are larger than our European sparrows."

Cloaked by the tablecloth, he took Holly's hand and stroked her fingers, trying to coax her back into their shared sensual realm. It was like thawing, she thought. She would have liked to abandon herself to him. But she was aware of eyes on her—Hopkins and his crowd as well as others. Defiance reared its head—What did she care about their opinions? The verdict was already in. The weeks of not dancing, of making variants of the same now tedious speech to sparse crowds of women, San Francisco's rigid disregard of her manifested in averted eyes, muttered imprecations, intercepted head-shakings, Edward's prolonged absence. . . . And here was the eager, exceptional pleasure-giver ready and willing to volunteer. Yet Edward's letter still glowed in her mind and body like an intimate kiss. Betrayal. His leaving her. She took their clasped hands out from under the table and laid them on the cloth for all to see.

Sipping champagne in the candlelight's flickering aura, their fingers entwined, she couldn't help responding. Together they struck showering sparks. *Like Paris,* she thought.

"Philippe sends his regards." Jacques explained that Philippe had recently sold a celebrated Gérôme at auction for a notable price, the highest yet paid for the master's work. The news had arrived in Seattle, where he'd stayed attending to his shipping business for a fortnight. She'd remember the canvas, *The Corsaire*.

In the studio, north light spreading over the three of them, Gérôme had said, "Too bad there were no female conquistadors."

"She can't be in every painting," Fauconier had responded. "She is," the painter had contradicted. "She is." And there was that final painting. . . .

Fauconier claimed he had left his cigar in his overcoat. Would she mind if he excused himself for a moment? Holly suppressed a smile, knowing that when he was nervous, he had to urinate frequently. Meanwhile, the champagne inscribed tantalizing inroads into her reserve, calling up memories—she laughed quietly to evade those thoughts. Such a strange position, she considered, fending off a man she loved.

Holly rose and walked to Hopkins's table. At his left, Mrs. Marie Hopkins, to his right, three business associates. Holly's boldness surprised Hopkins and his entourage, but he made a snap decision to be civil. After introductions, Holly said, "I'm sorry to interrupt you, but I wanted to ask how things are progressing in the sierras?"

"Thank you for inquiring," Hopkins replied, his chin tucked stiffly on his starched shirtfront. "Epic, challenging work yet, in spite of the difficulties, we progress." To deliver such a canned response to an arch-enemy—after all, he wasn't addressing congress. Holly felt sorely tempted to sandblast the pretensions that lurked under his pseudo-grandiose facade, to rail at Hopkins about the theft and exploitation she was uncovering, but she stilled her tongue. "My friend, Edward Muybridge . . . I trust he's safe and well?"

"Well, and in excellent spirits. He's taken impressive photographs I'm told." All the while Hopkins's wife stared haughtily at the empty chair where Fauconier had sat.

"I look forward to seeing the prints." Holly had already seen a half dozen of the photos that Muybridge had surreptitiously sent in that long-delayed first letter via Montague's assistant.

"Yes, we all do. I believe *The Clarion* will feature woodcuts based on them any day now."

Hopkins's smile bared small, pointy wolflike teeth. His beard was dyed, she realized. She nodded her leave to the company, then returned to her own table.

Seated again, Holly watched Jacques stalk back across the room with long, confident strides. She liked to see him in motion. Edward, too, she reminded herself.

As they dined, Jacques described crystalline lakes and towering mountains—"Higher than the Rockies. All of it is, how do you say, bigger than life, outsized. Alaska has far greater riches than Nevada, say. Billions, I think, if I could count that high. If I threw in my lot in Alaska, we would require huge amounts of capital. I tell you, if Stanford and Hopkins hadn't insulted you so profoundly"—Fauconier glanced over at Hopkins, who was rising to leave—"I'd approach them right now about participation up North."

"At the moment I'm told they have their hands full."

They supped, talked. Jacques picked up her cues, appreciated Holly's jokes. He displayed a delicately attuned responsiveness that she had forgotten. Touched by his sensitivity, she told herself, *There's no one like an old friend.* Over her objection, he paid for their dinner.

Leaving, they ran a gauntlet of stares, but now Holly floated at arm's length above the burghers' self-serving disdain. "I don't want to go home yet, Jacques."

He responded with a familiar reply. "I know a place . . . ."

So typical of him, Holly thought, to know more about San Francisco in a few days than she had discovered in six months.

As they approached the infamous Barbary Coast, plank streets gave way to mud and dust. Here wary policemen patrolled in pairs, nodding to flamboyant local madames and raucous barkers. Sharply dressed touts and pimps roamed up and down like voracious mastiffs; lounging, hard-bitten men eyed passersby like raptors their prey. The quarter teemed with foreign sailors in stiff white or navy blue pinafores. There were Mexicans with striped serapes rakishly angled off their shoulders, dark-eyed Spanish women in flaring, multicolored skirts. A sign announcing PRETTY WAITRESS GIRLS hung over the door of a grubby saloon. The women of the night, some improbably young, were decked out in silks, taffetas, lace, and cut velvets, even a Little Bo Peep outfit, each costume intended to incite a customer's wildest or most perverse fantasy. A number of prostitutes favored the short "rainy day" skirt, designed to keep hems out of the mud and, more to the point, show off their legs. A forward young whore sported a plunging batiste corset and a pair of black lace stockings, nothing else.

Jacques Fauconier led Holly to a dance hall called "The Red Lion," though the sign above its door depicted a cocksure red rooster. They took three rickety steps down into a basement, where the air was layered with cigar smoke and cheap whiskey smells. Holly caught the unmistakable odor of urine, mixing with the other scents. She whispered to Fauconier, "It's like walking too close to a pissoir."

He laughed aloud, and every eye in the place swung toward them—hostile, bored, bemused at the presence of the wealthy slumming couple, or too drunk to care.

They stood at the bar and ordered beer, which Fauconier assured her was the safest thing to drink. Casually he examined the Red Lion's clientele, gauging each for potential trouble. She studied Fauconier's almost brutish face—the dark caverns under his eyes, the thick, potent nose. She had to look away from him, realizing she was approaching a point of sexual no return. The place seemed to Holly well chosen, with an aura of danger but not, she felt, too threatening. Holly exclaimed that the Barbary Coast reminded her of Pigalle, only dirtier, if that was possible. Just then the band struck up a sprightly, out-of-tune waltz.

They danced, they whirled around the floor, the dinner champagne rising to her head as she spun. As they glided in rhythm, Holly's body literally ached for her lover. Edward's letter, his heat; she remembered his tongue on her body; his light, agile fingers. She remembered Jacques lifting her up, wrapping her thighs around his, and riding her around the floor pinned on his cock. Perhaps something in her breathing or the pressure of her hand suggested her mood, for at that moment she noticed the bulge in his trousers. She could see the shape, remember the full, curving outline of its head, imagine it thrusting into her. In Paris, when they were together, they didn't make love, Holly thought, they fucked. Hard, dirty, as close to bestial as the last clinging scrap of consciousness would permit. With Edward, they talked filthy talk, trading fantasies, memories, gloriously hot unexpurgated lies and truths. In her riotous mind, Edward replaced Jacques replaced Edward replaced Jacques.

As they moved together in this dubious public place, Jacques pressed against her hungrily. Meanwhile, her mind in concert with his presented him slowly, painstakingly fucking her feverishly in midair against her unyielding blue-gray Parisian wall.

Fauconier waited for that telltale moment when her eyes would pool, would melt for him. He always knew when she was ready. She was almost there when, suddenly, two men at the bar started arguing. Without appearing to hurry, Jacques firmly guided Holly past the men and out into the lively, blighted street.

"Both had pistols, Holly. The tall one had a hidden dirk. I didn't want to take the chance."

Back in her rooms Holly asked herself, *Why struggle against the inevitable?* Aloud she said, "Jacques, before you ask, the answer is no. Yes, yes, it started on the floor, I agree, but the answer's no. It's not a rational decision entirely, I grant you. . . ."

He groaned, his body twisting in pain. For three months Holly had preoccupied him obsessively. As he roamed over frozen wastes, searching for likely mineral deposits out among the elk and moose and grizzly, in those godforsaken hamlets populated by wild men mummified in animal skins, sensual thoughts of her kept him alert, kept him going. "You received my letter?"

"I was very moved by it."

"Not moved enough," he responded bitterly. He towered over her now, looking as though he'd devour Holly.

"I was flattered that the memories are so strong and lasting for you. I'm not so sure that's true for women."

"Bah!" he spat out. He didn't want words, discussion, evasion to camouflage the issue.

"Our . . . my mind controls my feelings, up to a certain point. Later, yes, the body takes over."

"I know all about your body. I've been thinking about it, remembering your body for over a year now."

"I need time, dear friend."

He flared, fury blazing along his trunklike form. "There's very little time, Holly. I have business in France."

He stopped, then said, "I could feel you on the dance floor." Making his final bid that evening, it was as though he touched her, placed his leverlike, prying fingers on the core of her response. "This all feels so arbitrary, provincial." He wanted his words to wound, to burn, to rip a gap in her resistance. "Aren't you the same woman who insisted you could love both Gérôme and me?"

"Love making must be voluntary, Jacques. If it's not . . ."

He moved a half step, furious, threatening, sexually overwrought. Fauconier was rarely balked. Even the lowlife thugs in The Red Lion had sensed the danger in the man. Jacques Fauconier could be a bully. But not with her, which made Holly feel prized. And even more disposed toward him. *Why not?* she demanded of herself. The phrase, more like a tune than a thought, kept insinuating its wild, inviting, gratifying melody. *Why not? Why not?* Yet some new, unknown obstacle impeded her, a virtue—sexually an alien term to her—or failure of nerve or declaration of loyalty stopped her. Was this love? Could it be that love was an impediment even when her body wanted it, too?

As he rose to leave, kissing her on both cheeks, she could almost hear Fauconier making an oath to himself, *This is the last time I'll endure this from you.*

Chapter Twenty-one

Outside the tunnels, railroad construction had stalled. Snow had fallen steadily for four days. Six more feet of snow and howling winds had dropped temperatures to fifteen below zero.

That evening the leaders of the construction team sat down to a huge meal, as usual, brought in the day before along with tons of road-building materials and forty miserable, braying mules, all of them seemingly Rosie's offspring. Supper consisted of a half side of beef, two whole pigs, a deer, a baker's dozen of chickens, and ten ducks. Everyone gorged himself, including the usually moderate Muybridge and the birdlike Montague. Between courses, the chief engineer paced up and down on the board floor, restlessly monitoring the storm. They could sometimes hear faint, muffled sounds of blasting. Whenever the wind gusted, Montague moved to the door to listen more intently, checking to be certain the tunneling work continued.

All the upper-echelon employees—Ward, Montague, two explosives experts, an octet of crew chiefs—drank heavily, brandy being the spirit of choice. They drank to ward off the chill; they drank to keep themselves from thinking about the impossible schedule they were commanded to fulfill; drank to forget about a woman or to prep themselves for a pilgrimage to the Chinese professionals. Again that evening the shopworn joke made the rounds: Dr. Greene insisted that each man push his alcohol intake as high as possible so he wouldn't freeze to death when working outside.

Later, in Montague's private cabin, the chief engineer explained to Muybridge that the toe-tapping Ward had relayed an ultimatum: Rail construction had to resume in the next two days—or else.

The older man leaned across the table. "You know, before Stanford left, I asked him if the railroad could apportion a minuscule percentage of the profits from selling ice or granite or timber or the Nevada freight contracts or whatever else they're hiding from the congressional auditors. Just one percent set aside to hire another nitro expert, a brace of blacksmiths, and another three lathe operators. You know what he replied?"

"He'd be overjoyed to oblige."

Montague didn't manage a smile. "He said, 'You keep your end up, Samuel, we'll cover ours.' My end, my ass."

"Shortsighted bastards." Muybridge was also suffering the brandy's effects.

"Shortsighted, cheap bastards," his friend emended.

Samuel Montague avoided the photographer's gaze. The cramped, smoky cabin suffered another shift in mood. He could barely mutter, "They told me to watch you. . . ." His voice trailed off. "Keep an eye on . . ."

Muybridge set his glass down hard, spilling liquid. "What? What are you saying exactly?"

"Stanford and Ward, they're afraid your photos might not invariably serve the sacred cause. That you might catch a man who looks a little peaked, shall we say. Or a blaster after he's blasted to bits. Or a guy falling two hundred feet." Montague paused, then continued in a doleful voice, "They're watching you." Now the engineer examined his friend, right eye glued to its subject, left eye wandering off. "It's not as though you're a trusted employee—like some folks we know."

Muybridge had no illusions about Stanford or lickspittle Ward, but he wanted to believe that Montague was above that. Weakly, he asked, "Did you agree to watch me?"

Samuel Montague laughed the mirthless laugh of a cornered man. "If I had not agreed, Muybridge, would I be telling you?"

For a moment neither spoke. Montague mutely passed the bottle to the photographer. Muybridge poured, drank.

"Good thing there's an endless supply."

"Bottomless. That's one thing this railroad's good for. Samuel," the words poured out. "This is hard."

The engineer concurred, "Goddamn hard."

They sipped in silence.

Even when plastered, Montague had a drawing pad on the table in front of him. "Progress happens, but it doesn't proceed in a straight line." He scrawled a hopelessly crooked line. "No, better way to look at the philosophical problem of progress is to remember that evolution occurs at variable speeds." Muybridge did not understand a word his friend uttered.

The engineer sketched rapidly. Next the hand slowed as Montague drew with painstaking precision. "But Darwin knows. Sir Charles knows. That's what Stanford and Ward and the others can't fathom." Montague was drunk enough to slur, yet the pen now moved in precise, informed arcs. "Why? Because it doesn't fit their tidy little picture of how things have to be.

"They got the wrong metaphor by the tail. You see, Darwin understands the process of growth and differentiation is *dis-con-tin-u-ous.* Stops and starts, my man, stops and starts, not one continuous flowing line of development that the uninformed believe in because it doesn't tax their tidy, simplistic portrait of reality. Stops and goddamn disruptive starts, that's how it works—great leaps, unlikely conjunctions, mixed metaphors that work themselves out over time." Montague measured his friend, convinced that his formulation was crystal clear to the photographer. "Like motion, Edward, like your precious, bloody motion mania, man, don't you see? Motion itself can only be comprehended through a series of disconnected, apparently separate still frames. *You,* you alone showed us that, with a timely technical shove from yours truly." The chief engineer smiled sweetly, a child's smile, then his head pitched forward and hit the table—out cold.

Edward Muybridge sat in his chair, head spinning, the log room revolving at immeasurable speed. He resisted the nagging impulse to pour another drink. *No drink,* he thought fuzzily, not until he understood what Stanford's next move would be. Edward didn't know how long he sat puzzling his deep question while an unsteady stomach threw vile tastes up at him like residue from a clogged drain.

Montague's head bobbed up. "Think I got it." Samuel Montague doodled on his pad, chuckling softly, "No problem with manpower now. Thirty percent of them been idle, snowed in—or is it out?—for the last four days. Lumber, we have endless supply. So, Montague, why not?" He directed a moronic smile at the ceiling and concluded, "Why not, Capulet?"

"What are you raving about? Speak English, Samuel."

Montague pushed a sketch of what looked like a shed toward the photographer—only, this three-sided wooden shed was perched over what Edward deciphered to be railroad tracks. Two primitive, parallel lines indicating rails, and the rails were crossed at right angles by what might pass for ties. "All right, it's a shed," Edward conjectured, "over what appear to be railroad tracks."

"Muybridge, you are an exceedingly insightful young man. Answer my first question: What is stopping us from laying rail? Tell me that in a single four-letter word starting with S."

"Snow."

"Bingo! And how can we protect the right of way from tons of that cursed white impediment? Hmmn? How do we do that, genius with a lens?"

Edward didn't object to being catechized. "You mean, build a shed over it?"

"Not shed singular, Photographer, miles and miles and miles of sheds. Stretching off to the vanishing point." Samuel sketched rapidly now. "In the cuts where we have to build retaining walls, we'll only need a one-sided shed to keep that blasted snow off the tracks. Which will speed construction. You see?" He pointed to his cross-section drawing of a shed leaning against the said mountain, and penciled in lines extending from the edges to create the three-dimensional illusion of an elongated building.

"They'll have to be reenforced to withstand all the weight."

"We'll make it strong enough to survive anything but avalanche. Which nothing survives in any case. Muybridge, don't forget we'll be building these sheds out of the thickest trees in the world." The chief engineer had not looked so buoyant since Muybridge arrived.

* * *

The next morning Samuel Montague began work on the wooden "snowsheds" and the simpler, two-sided lean-to forms that he called "galleries," both of which were to be poised over the entire outdoor right-of-way through the High Sierra.

Muybridge watched and, when he thought appropriate, made photographs as teams of workers shoveled away drifts and cleared and leveled and graded the roadbed. Surveyors surveyed the view through their transits, waved their assistants into line at the far end of a measurement, and made their notations, then Montague's Celestials heaved stalwart timbers into place. Carpenters pegged the posts and lintels then men swarmed all over the skeletal frames, thunderously nailing in place the planks that formed the roofs and sides of the snow barriers.

Over the next week the giant saws sputtered and whined and coughed and turned out thousands of posts and beams and planks and bracing struts while, outdoors, the right of way bristled with carpenters measuring each angle of each foot with their spirit levels. As they toiled, workers dropped from exertion. The men sweated so profusely that skin froze—hands adhered to subzero shovels, coat sleeves to cheeks—and noses were perpetually runny. Frigid feet accidentally struck by hammers or rocks or shovelfuls of ballast were too chilled to feel the insults. Not until later, when the men limped or crawled or were carried back to their cabins, did the workers realize how grievously they were injured. A steady flow of laborers hobbled or were dragged or carried on stretchers to the infirmary, where Dr. Isaiah Greene and his overworked round-the-clock male nurses tried to patch them up so that they could get back to work as soon as possible.

On clear days, workers ineffectually shielded their eyes from the glaring sun, and dozens of men spent agonized, disoriented days and nights, their faces swathed in bandages, praying to regain their sight. Fevers and ague rampaged through camp. Frostbite, hypothermia, and the sheer difficulty of breathing at the mile-plus high altitude while toiling away at these laborious tasks crippled then decimated the work force. Meanwhile, the tunnel blasting continued to exact its weekly toll of two, three, or, twice, four lives. Yet, in spite of the daily setbacks, as Montague's sheds snaked down the right of way, the pace of construction surged.

Under the engineer's covers, rails were laid. The line inched tortuously forward.

Ward pumped up the stakes in the sierras by announcing one morning at the chow line that the dread and hated rival, the Union Pacific, was plunking down rail at the unprecedented rate of *ten miles per day* across the Great American Desert. The fever of the race spread to everyone, from the lowliest snow-shoveler to the chief engineer himself.

A letter arrived from Holly, pleasant and affectionate, yet the tone unsettled Muybridge. She had delivered a speech to a minuscule group of women in San Raphael and another one, almost identical but with a few improvements, in San Jose, the town that had rejected Edward's sensible bid to photograph its records. She had written two articles for *The Suffragette*, one on the question of the vote that she could have penned in her sleep, the other on dress reform, which likewise "felt stale, over-rehearsed." She asked him, How can a person maintain spontaneity, evoke the indispensable fire necessary to move others, when forced to rhetorically retread the same ground? Wasn't the ability to create enthusiasm in the audience each time she stepped on stage the sign of the true professional? If so, as a feminist rabble-rouser she was a rank amateur. (Ah, but when she danced, Muybridge thought, that was different: Then, Holly felt she reinvented the world at every step of every performance.)

She closed by saying that she missed him sorely. She added a brief postscript:

> I've decided to mount another evening of dance in late February or early March. To date, no one, no institution, has agreed to let me hire a hall.

Edward perused the letter like a cleric with a Biblical text, poring over each word and phrase for clues to Holly's feelings for him. He reserved the most intense exegesis for the issue of the second dance performance. Odd, he considered, that she should consign an event of such importance to a postscript. Holly's performing without him nearby to protect and comfort, that disturbed him. For, with January now ending, Muybridge feared that he would have to break his vow to be back home in three or four weeks. Once the snows lessened, there would be unique opportunities for photos. March was the time to be in the High Sierras.

After three grueling weeks, Edward knew enough to avoid Collis Ward whenever possible. Several times the junior vice president had warned Muybridge that he was being paid to record the progress of the Central Pacific, not to appeal to bleeding hearts—or one particular female bleeding heart—in San Francisco. One morning when Ward was out of the way trying to pacify an experienced crew of Irish gandy-dancers about an overtime dispute, Muybridge stole into the camp infirmary and made photos of blast victims who were missing arms, legs, and hands. He photographed a sleeping young Chinese whose face had been ripped off by an explosion—features so rearranged they seemed like a grotesque jigsaw puzzle lacking key pieces. The nose puffed up so bulbously it touched the upper lip, while the raw blood pancake of his lower lip appeared hinged from the chin. Behind the freakishly gerrymandered face lay a pair of skittish, deranged black eyes. Other patients begged to have the Chinese boy put out of his misery since he whimpered and moaned and screamed, keeping them awake day and night. Nearby, Dr. Greene was amputating an arm that clung to an Irishman's body by a few attenuated, bloody strands of muscle tissue; the former Confederate surgeon announced that this was the hundred and sixth amputation of his medical career.

The next morning, mail call provided Muybridge with this welcome surprise.

Dear Mr. Muybridge,
After weeks of fretful delay, my copy of *Scientific American* arrived. At last I have your commentary on the trotting horse photographs in front of my eyes. As you know, our mutual friend Samuel Montague had

already sent me your astounding photos of the trotter. I studied them as a translator studies his original tongue and, as magnificent and informative as they were, they are ever more enlightening when glossed by your informed notes.

Sir, thank you. Thank you for peering with such inspired clarity into the mysteries of the universe. I regard both these pictures and your work as a key not only to the future of painting but also to ways in which we will perceive our world henceforth. I acknowledge you as a modern Cortez or Balboa, another Linnaeus or Darwin who extended the range of our vision and also of human possibility.

As Montague related, I am a painter. I teach at the Pennsylvania Academy of Fine Arts, although for how much longer I would not venture to guess. To oversimplify for brevity's sake, one of the focuses of my work is an attempt to create what I call a "*photographic* stillness." This stylistic approach is not dissimilar from what you in your article called "the stopped eye of the camera." To achieve the feeling of both arrested action and dynamic poise I place figures or objects that embody action—say, a rower or a galloping horse drawing a carriage—into the picture plane. I employ mathematical perspectives to determine the location of these figures as they pass through space. I want to create individuals or objects (the single scull enclosed, for instance) with abundant energy and largeness of form, figures that fill up a canvas with latent, potential life. When this "works," the painting will have presence as well as sculptural roundness. I try to render every *telling* detail of figures, objects, and landscape. (The adjective is significant, because the painter's eye must be selective, not encyclopedic.) Excuse me for running on unbidden, but from your work I sense that you possess a surpassingly informed interest in these issues.

In the enclosed drawing, I create a day of utmost clarity, a universe flooded with light. Part of my process involves articulating reflections from Philadelphia's Schuylkyll River and interrelating the linear shapes of the figure, the rowing shell and its oars on the perspective grid. In preliminary sketches, I plotted relations between the forms on this grid to construct a spatial network sufficiently complex to imply or imitate reality itself. To nudge the process forward, I make sketches and,

> frequently, clay sculptures as well to help capture volume and roundness. Most recently, I have used the camera, though I am still a stumbling, humble amateur in your emerging technology. Yet, even with my ineptitude, the camera is increasingly helpful in my studies.

The artist's words half-intrigued the photographer, but they seemed overly intellectual until he extricated the drawing from its meticulous wrappings: an oarsman leaned back in a single scull, head cocked to the right, shoulder partly turned as he looked toward but not directly at the viewer who was positioned beyond the frame. The man had stopped rowing the instant before, and he held both oars, positioned athwart, in his left hand. The reflection of the rower in the water, the calmness of the river, the burnished sunlight around him was rendered in precise optical detail. The signature in the corner of the drawing: Thomas Eakins.

Below the oarsman, in the river, lay a rippling reflection—a kind of distorted portrait—of the upside-down figure and the scull and oars. This was ingenious, but what most intrigued Muybridge was the single dark line in the water amidships to the scull's right. Edward realized that he had seen the same faint but recognizable line each time he worked out on a river. Only Edward had never elevated this half recognition of the oar's track, its narrative path, to consciousness before. Brilliant, he judged, to re-create that barely discernible, evanescent yet clearly sequential line which marked the spot where the oar broke the water's surface. Thus the painter Eakins unveiled the actual progress of the shell, the mini-history of a distinct moment on that bright, singular afternoon. As Muybridge's eyes drifted into the painting, he further recognized a trail of paired, parallel feathery lines following in the boat's wake: evidence of the scull's progress along its liquid path. *Drawing on water,* Edward mused, temporal progress made concrete—Eakins's rendering of this solitary rower incorporated a narrative of effort, accomplishment, fatigue. More, as the scull sped on, its diagonal thrust led the eye out beyond the frame, into a dimension that the sketch did not encompass but unambiguously implied. Eakins's drawing, a distillate of time and space, led the eye into the future.

Muybridge turned the letter over, and found this post script.

> Since I received your photographs, I have been considering a new painting. It will offer modest homage to your trotter photos—my current conception involves four galloping horses pulling a coach. I'm spending hours on Broad Street, a main thoroughfare of our City that passes in front of the Academy where I teach. Not to appear to be a sycophant, but none of this could have occurred without your groundbreaking (excuse the pun) work. Again, thank you heartily.

A colleague, Muybridge thought. Except for Montague, for years Muybridge hadn't exchanged ideas about his technique and craft with one that he considered a peer.

Samuel Montague strolled in and broke Muybridge's reverie. "What have we here?" Montague leaned over the sketch. "Ah, our dear friend Eakins—I applaud artists who won't duck difficult assignments. And Thomas is a strange and lonely man, also as ambitious and talented as anyone I've ever met, including you and me. Be warned, a great talent, but without an iota of humor."

He took a half step back, presumably to rein in his roving left eye and force the image into stereoscopic focus. "Look at the Girard Avenue Bridge here—the intricacy of all those cross-angled steel struts. A metaphor," Montague playfully pontificated, "of the *engineers'* conquest of space and time, the bridging of—"

"Samuel," Muybridge retorted, "spare me."

Chapter Twenty-two

Holly Hughes would have made a credible historian. Or a detective. During the six weeks Edward had spent in the sierras, she combed the local libraries, reading every newspaper and magazine item she could find about the Central Pacific and its quartet of owners. She filled two notebooks with facts and hearsay, deluged U.S. congressmen with letters inquiring about the particulars of the legislative acts that established and financed the transcontinental railroad. She noted where "the Associates" laid rails that ran up and down on maximum grades instead of providing the legislated deep cuts and fills, where they substituted inexpensive wood for culverts instead of more costly and durable stone. She read the incorporation papers of the Central Valley Irrigation Company, which bought riparian rights for a song, built a reservoir with state funds while Leland Stanford was governor, then irrigated ten thousand acres of the Central Valley, reaping millions in profits. Holly concentrated on the lobbying activities of the Big Four, opening her analysis with Huntington's published quotation, "There are more hungry men in Congress than I have ever known before." She noted the five thousand dollars paid annually to California Congressman Bryan Axtell for unspecified "services rendered" and tracked down dozens of other questionable "gifts." She located the 1863 amendments to the original Pacific Railroad Act that excused the directors from paying even minimal stockholder dividends and unearthed how Stanford had pressured the

Sacramento and Placer County legislatures to trade valuable bonds for questionable railroad stock and thus hand the Central Pacific a sixteen-million-dollar subsidy before a single pebble of railway ballast was tamped in place. In return for this, as she wrote indignantly in her draft letter, "In return for millions, the State of California was granted *free transportation* for its militia in times of emergency. What an absurdity." At the time the crookedness of the deal had ignited a barrage of outraged anti–Central Pacific newspaper editorials from Stanford detractors back East. She reproduced several of these articles for state and federal legislators. Holly schooled herself in bonds and stock certificates and interest payments, she compiled statistical charts detailing what had allegedly been spent and what so far returned. Her conclusion: "The Directors were skimming massive profits from timber and ice sales and revenue-producing enterprises while basic railroad building was starving for funds, unable to meet their repayment schedule and crying to Washington for yet more subsidies." She incorporated Edward's information as well, unleashing a torrent of signed letters to the editor while deluging her representative and the state's two senators with lengthy, intricately detailed reports.

She wrote and lectured about women's issues with declining energy; she attended scores of committee meetings, which she detested. And she danced. The muscle tear in her calf had knit slowly and now, almost healed, she practiced with tenacious vehemence, driving her body as hard as she could to try to ease the seesawing uncertainties. Daily she expected a second letter from Edward. Since Montague's courier had handed her the first letter, she had heard nothing. Why no other note for almost a month? Holly had no definitive answer, though she suspected that Edward had written and that Collis Ward or another flunky had intercepted his letter or letters. The absence of contact made her feel deprived, frustrated, and testy. Four letters to him, only one in return—another blot on his account.

Fauconier remained intent, an undeterred hawk poised to stoop. One evening, a few hours after delivering a lecture on dress reform before seven women, she almost broke down in front of her former lover. "You must stop importuning me." Fauconier, who had never seen her cry—not even after the furor about the insulting painting, not even after

Gérôme's death—was chastened. And also encouraged. He understood that Holly was nearing the breaking point.

Meanwhile, she plotted her return to the stage. She considered buying a building. Then she could perform at will. (Fauconier offered to share the expense of the venture. When she asked him what he'd do with the property when she finished dancing, he replied, "Sell it. Burn it. I don't care as long as you dance at least once more for these cretins.") Finally, Holly located a hall in a place called Berkeley, across the San Francisco Bay, that the Women's Christian Temperance Union was willing to rent her at an exorbitant price for a single evening.

When Holly Hughes arrived at the hall, a crowd of young women was marching up and down, loudly protesting. They hissed, they booed, they shouted, "Strumpet!" "Hussy!" They formed a barrier near the entrance to dissuade potential patrons from entering. These women—girls, really, most barely seventeen or eighteen—carried signs:

INDECENT PERFORMANCE. STAY AWAY!
CITIZENS ALERT: BOYCOT THIS SHOW!
"GOOD" FOLKS, DO NOT ATTEND!
ATTACK ON MORALITY ON STAGE HERE TONIGHT

Miles Drummond, a local corset maker, had chivvied his employees into picketing the performance. He stood at the edge of the group, directing a superior half sneer at Holly who impatiently pushed through the jeering women to reach the entrance. One burly female stepped into Holly's path. Holly said under her breath: "Please, you are blocking my way."

The woman did not budge.

"Out of my way."

The picketer leveled her sign at Holly. It read: DIRTY LEG SHOW INSIDE. Holly smiled inwardly, thinking that might draw in a few customers. The woman twirled the sign around in her hands then stabbed at Holly with the stick end. Holly Hughes dodged, pulled the wood stick past her body, leaped, and aimed a two-footed kick at the attacker's sternum. The big woman went down with an exhaled "Oof!" The others obligingly parted and Holly proceeded into the hall.

She was loosening up in her dressing room when Fauconier knocked. He entered laughing. "They say you put a corpulent young Frau on her rump."

They laughed together. "It was such a pleasure, Jacques."

He looked her up and down, then asked, "Are you hurt?"

"I'm fine." He waited for the story. "A little kung fu movement for that pork chop of mademoiselle. How can they turn on me? Do you think that reason's a vestigial tool for them?"

"All too often." He went on, "I tried to reason with the picketers. But they're—how do you say?—thick skulls."

"Jacques, go count the audience for me."

"I already did." His eyes were full of solicitude.

"How many?"

"Not many."

He did not have the heart to tell her that only eight people occupied the hall, among them a grubby, if not deranged, derelict who had slipped in to escape the chill evening and three or four men who had probably come to see Holly Hughes's legs and breasts.

"Should I go on?" she said, trying to be brave, tears threatening to well up. "I'm becoming a weepy old dishrag."

He seemed extremely close to her, closer than the few feet that separated them.

"Should I go on?" she asked again.

"Of course. I've been waiting months to see you perform again."

She danced brilliantly, the Frenchman judged, with even more verve and delicacy than that night months before in San Francisco. Less than two dozen people witnessed her genius and that total included the piano accompanist, two stagehands, and the aforementioned derelict who snored fitfully throughout the performance.

Afterward, Jacques was there.

"You were brilliant, my darling." His fervid eyes made him look younger, still more dashing.

"I must say, I wasn't bad." She loosened her vivid hair. "But it's not enough."

He nodded agreement before he said, "You know, I considered hiring people for the hall."

"Why didn't you?" she asked, unlacing a slipper.

"I knew you'd disapprove."

He was by her side, inches away. Bending over her discreetly, Jacques was, somehow, neither protective nor condescending, both of which she would've despised. He was there, as a dear old friend and lover should be. Holly thought of Edward's desertion, his absence. An involuntary sigh shook her body. She was in Jacques's arms before she knew it. They made love there, in her cramped dressing room. Jacques was so strong he held her midair, bodies interlocked in rhythm, Holly's back against the wall. Then they lay on the floor, bathed in each other's juices and sweat. He felt enveloped in her hot, pearly smell—opulent, moist sweetness. Again, they coupled. Again she climaxed, a run, a trill, a glissando of shifting sensations that carried her off to a place beyond thought or guilt.

Later in her rooms, they made love for hours. He sucked and nibbled and tongued at her core; she writhed and moaned and bucked on top of him as he stabbed up and up, lifting her up off the bed until she felt airborne; with Holly draped over the edge of the bed, he took her from behind. He slammed into her feverishly, then teased her with his big cock, slowly drawing it out until it teetered at the edge and she gasped for more: "More! More! Harder, Jacques, harder!" When he wasn't stiff, his fingers prodded, explored, worked like brutal, loving pistons. Feeling engulfed by the moist heat, surging in or over or through her body. Holly could not tell where it began and where it ended.

Later, Jacques commanded, "Touch yourself." Holly complied, and, opened and spread, she stroked herself as he looked on. She stood above him, she dripped on him, his eyes riveted on that juncture between her thighs until, his tongue lolling out, he licked his lips then kissed her. Her mouth on his, he got hard again. He moved up above her now, riding high on the pubic bone, a finger working itself in and out of her gaping, wet asshole. Centers of pleasure spread to her toes, her hair, raced through like hot, liquid tongues until, when the next climax approached, the tension grew so great Holly felt she would dissolve. Her entire body—thighs, legs, breasts, torso—reached greedily for climax, a shuddering, rich suffusion. Lovely patterns of color rose before her shuttered eyes, colors shifting and merging as though spread out on a vast moving warp and woof.

"Profound," she said softly, lying back.

"You're extraordinary. Your body's a magnificent instrument, darling. It plays, it gives, it sings."

"Moans and screams and gasps, that's more accurate."

He kissed her. "This coming and coming. The dew that covers your chest, breasts, forehead—it's the most—how do you say it English?—the most gratifying gift a woman gives a man."

"Why?"

"Because it makes a man feel like a man, powerful, potent."

"So it's about power."

"Naturally. Everything is about power, no?" She nodded agreement, but something was missing from the formulation. He paused, the blue eyes exploring hers. "But it's more than that also. You know."

"I do know." It was curious, she thought, to be lapped in pleasure with a single unquiet thought snaking into her consciousness. The snake in Eden? She vividly remembered Edward saying, "You're a gift." When she asked what he meant, he replied, "The more pleasure you take, the more I take. It's that simple."

Jacques was soon asleep, his thick, hairy thigh draped over hers. Looking at the contrast between her skin and his dark thigh, she smiled affectionately. *He's worn out as much from waiting as from lovemaking.*

She settled back, trying to dwell in that drifting-body-induced state of pleasure. Only her mind stayed unquietly alert: the vessel of her being, filled to overflowing a moment before, had sprung an imperceptible leak. One drop at a time—no, less than a drop because she only vaguely sensed the loss—pleasure emptied out of her. Was this guilt's onset, the sneaky undeniable worm of the soul, an orphan incubus that snuck under and over and into her being's chambers to lodge in the space right under the heart? Was she insulted that Jacques reduced sex to physical manipulation? She watched him, as he wore the contented half smile of conquest and pleasure. Edward's emotional antennae were almost always extended, on the qui vive. Paradoxically, he was at his most alert when he didn't fathom her mood.

Lying beside him, Holly examined that rugged oversized face—of course she loved Jacques. Yet, suddenly, it wasn't the same as before. Edward had dived deeper inside her, into more emotionally complex depths. Because he knew her better, understood her temperature and pulse in a way that Jacques could not. Holly felt it was pointless and unfair to compare her two men. To escape, she wet her palm thoroughly then took Jacques's penis and stroked it gently. As it rose, thoughts of betrayal surged through her. Edward had betrayed her with her sworn enemy, his "governor." Hers was a different order of betrayal. Holding Jacques's large, admirable penis, she felt anger rise at both men, that they always found women secondary to their sacred pursuits. "Free love?" Muybridge's infuriating replay of her phrase coursed through her mind like a persistently nagging off-key melody. He'd asked her, "Free of what?"

Two days later, a pamphlet signed by Holly Hughes attacking the Sitka Ice Company circulated throughout San Francisco. In it, the author revealed that the Central Pacific had "stolen" money from the bond issue of the U.S. congress to finance the ice enterprise. In the opinion of one Chicago lawyer this was a crime, but more heinous was the fact that the Central Pacific returned none of its sizeable ice profits back to the railroad and thus to the government, which by law was owed 20 percent of all revenue until the tens of millions in loans were repaid. In spite of impressive fiscal gains on its various ancillary undertakings, the Central Pacific itself admitted in internal memoranda that it was bankrupt. Indeed, the railroad was broke while its subsidiary companies were "raking in money hand over fist." Although the author confused a few fiscal details, her basic charge was accurate.

Each time Edward Muybridge visited the Chinese camp, the prostitutes ritually taunted him for not joining in. Edward learned that Li Chang, the slim beauty he found so stirring, was called Frisky by her customers, which made her still more seductive. Whenever Li Chang spotted the photographer, she rolled her suggestive tongue around her blatant lips or opened her blouse to reveal a piquant nipple or lifted her skirt and spread her slender, supple legs to display all. Abashed, he resisted politely, backing away from Frisky while unable to pry his eyes away from her beckoning, sinewy body.

One night he had an erotic dream: his sleep flooded with riotous sexual fantasies, featuring Frisky's breasts, thighs, pussy all eager and ready for him. She humped his thigh, her eyes rolled back into her head, they came together. Edward woke up with a wet blanket stuck to his groin. He smiled, feeling like a boy again. The next morning, an embarrassed Edward Muybridge asked the doctor how safe it would be to have contact with a whore, and Dr. Isaiah Greene replied candidly, "This inspection business doesn't do a fuckin' bit of good unless I just gave the girl the all-clear, and you're the lucky bastard who's next in line. I do have a whole barrelful of sheep gut condoms, which will do the job just dandy, stud. Great believer in them myself." Edward did not approach Li Chang's tantalizing flesh—pure in deed, though not in thought. He was sure that she thought him impotent.

At six a.m. the water began to trickle. The gurgling liquid, like light, sibilant syllables whispered over and over, insinuated itself into his sleep. The sun's glare woke him to a world glazed with ice frosting. All morning the frozen landscape thawed and dripped and trickled away. By noon, thunderous bass rumblings began, formless, chaotic noises that sounded, perhaps, like the onset of time. The melting sent avalanches down the mountain, crashing booms outstripping the nitroglycerin explosions, echoing over the granite slopes and on across untracked snowfields. To Edward it seemed as if the landscape wept.

Muybridge was watching a Chinese crew as they prepared a stretch of track. The first group shoveled in a two-foot layer of gravel and crushed stone. When the surveyors finished the choreography of leveling the ground, the next group pounded in the sleepers or transverse timbers that served as ties. Meanwhile, the gandy dancers stood at the ready, one group on each side of the right of way. Then—with such dexterity and speed that they seemed like a synchronized chorus line—all together they strained to lift and coordinate the unstable weight on its way up, took two measured steps back as they hefted and shifted, then gently settled the backbreaking, recalcitrant six-hundred-pound twenty-foot-long rail down at a right angle to the ties. Men wielding sledges swarmed in, hammering oak wedges and iron plates and the final finishing touch, the steel "fish plate," which was spaced a precise inch from the spike to allow for the necessary expansion and contraction of the alloy in changing temperatures.

One hundred yards ahead of the rail layers, a six-man team of Chinese shovelers attacked a thirty-foot drift. The men were delicately tunneling into the snow when, above the retaining wall to their right, there came a low warning sound. A mere split second later, with a deepening growl and rumble—like magic, the volume thunderously amplified—a blurred white wall plummeted down toward the toiling figures.

The avalanche drove white upon swirling white without edge or limit. Like a swift, sensate beast sounding a roar, the indistinct swirling snow leaped down upon the men. Muybridge and scores of others watched as the terrified figures reacted. Tossing away their shovels, three managed to scramble out of danger. The other three took a panicked step or two before they were seized and tossed and whirled away by the roaring white cliff, while picturesque, rippling traceries danced at the edges of the onrushing cloud.

The three escapees huddled together, shivering fearfully. An Irish foreman sprinted over and hugged them as though they were his sons. Others crowded up. A Chinese lad offered mugs of tea while hundreds of eyes anxiously scanned the slope below for signs of life.

Suddenly Muybridge flung himself down the mountain, skidding on the unstable snow. He slid and tumbled and belly-flopped headlong down the precipice, moving with odd, floundering motions, like a fish struggling on a line.

Out of control, careening down, for some absurd, unfathomable reason, Muybridge wanted to save one life. In the past month and a half he'd witnessed too many men die—die because a fuse had been snipped a half inch short; die because the charge had a few extra grains of black powder; die because of flying rock shards or a frayed strand of rope; or because a foot slipped or arms were too fatigued to haul up fast enough. He was sick and tired of seeing men die before his eyes, bone-tired and heartsore of his surreptitious photos of the unmoving dead.

As Central Pacific workers looked on, Edward slid and finally stopped where he thought he'd seen one man go under. He dug frantically with gloved hands in the loose top snow. Above him the mountain rumbled and hacked and threateningly cleared its throat. Mere yards away on the far side of him tons of snow cascaded down. But Muybridge was oblivious.

They watched the photographer dig with fiery, tingling hands, scraping at the white powder until his fingers burst through the leather gloves. His hands were stiff and raw and bloody when he hit something—flesh. More frantic scrapings with his freezing fingers and he scratched at the beginnings of a leg. The coolie's pants had been ripped away from the calf, which felt warm and cold simultaneously, the pale skin fishlike clammy on this springlike afternoon. Edward dug anxiously, hoping the man was still alive, his torn hands leaking red traces on the snow. The avalanche had flipped the worker upside down, so that Muybridge thought if he dug fast enough, the poor bastard might still have a chance.

He could sense the crowd above staring at him, a madman. He couldn't yell for help because the least noise might set off another slide, and, besides, he wasn't sure that anyone would come to his aid. He scratched and dug and tore at the snow with mindless frenzy until two Chinese workers slid down the hill on their backs and gently pulled Muybridge away. He never understood what one of the Chinese men said to him, but the pain and fear in his voice penetrated. Together the men slowly freed the dead worker from the snow.

Meanwhile, high above Muybridge and the buried Chinese, Collis Ward shook his head with triumphant dismay as he studied the photographer through binoculars. "Stark-raving mad," he concluded with finality. For once, his leg did not shake.

Late that evening, after downing a bottle of brandy, an exhausted Muybridge lay on his cot, too disturbed to sleep. His hands ached and burned, and he kept visualizing that upside-down human calf. The man he'd touched had not been alive. Dr. Isaiah Greene pronounced that the fall or the weight of the snow had first snapped the man's neck, then crammed enough snow into his mouth and nose that "the poor devil suffocated if he wasn't dead in the first place." The foreman's words played in his mind, "Maybe we find the other poor buggers, but those guys, they buried real deep. Won't come up until spring, like daffodils—if ever."

It was one a.m. when Muybridge reached under his horsehair mattress for the flat box that contained his "unofficial" photographs—a decapitated figure, almost symmetrically halved by the nitro; a head-on shot of a man seared by powder on one side of his face, and smooth-faced on the other side; other grisly casualties of "progress," men who had lost feet or hands or arms or, perhaps worse, their eyes. Muybridge sent his tentative, burning fingers in search of that familiar tin box. Only it was not there. He jumped up and flipped over the mattress. The box was gone. He crossed the tent and pulled out his painstakingly arranged file of original dry plates: Not a single one of the damning plates was there. Gone, all gone.

Without his greatcoat, Edward rushed outside. Two sentries, alerted by noise and movement in the still night, raised their weapons. Muybridge shouted, "It's me, Muybridge. Don't shoot." Then he half-staggered, half-sprinted across the filthy, tramped-down snow to Collis Ward's cabin.

"Ward!" he yelled as he charged inside. "Ward, you bastard!" With bandaged, shredded hands, Muybridge yanked Collis Ward upright in bed by his nightshirt. "Where are my photographs?"

"Are you crazy? Take your hands off me now!"

"Crazy enough to strangle you."

"What is the problem?" Ward was all innocence.

"My photos, my dry plates, everything's gone." As he spoke, Muybridge felt despair burying him like the obscuring, crushing avalanche. Only a simpleton could have been so naively trusting. *How easy*, he thought, *to destroy the photos*. All over the mountain, thirty-foot drifts waited to hide and obliterate his fragile images. Some day next summer, after the snows melted, a casual hiker might unearth the "evidence," what little was left by then—like the perfectly preserved corpses they'd perhaps uncover next spring.

"I know you don't want anyone to know what actually goes on up here, but to stoop to this!"

"I haven't the foggiest notion what you are raving about, you lunatic." The smile betrayed him—for the first time since Muybridge had met Ward, the junior vice president offered a full smile.

The shouting alerted the sentries, who came sprinting toward the cabin. Muybridge knew all was lost.

As the sentries neared, Ward became bolder, taunting the photographer, "You mean those photos you snuck behind my back? The unauthorized shots of the cripples, the dead?"

As the sentries reached the door of the cabin, Muybridge grabbed him by the throat. "Ward, I'd kill you if it didn't mean jail time." He flung his nemesis back against the bed frame, then banged his slender head hard against the metal once, twice. "You're loathsome, contemptible. Someday everybody will know the truth."

The sentries stormed in, rifles leveled. "Mr. Muybridge," one said, "better calm down."

Ward chuckled. Muybridge grabbed the junior vice president's windpipe. The guards caught Muybridge before he could do serious damage. After a brief coughing fit, Ward began to laugh. He laughed and laughed until tears trickled down his pallid cheeks. He laughed more loudly as the two men dragged the photographer to the door, kicking, beyond fury.

"Muybridge, you're an irrelevant fool, an idiot idealist. By the time anybody knows what you term 'the truth,' whatever that is, we'll have finished the railroad. Without one more dollar's worth of photographic help from you."

Late the next morning, Montague interrupted Muybridge's packing. The photographer explained to the engineer that his best work, his most revealing shots had been destroyed or stolen. "In any case, I overstayed my welcome."

"They say you ran amok. You had provocation, Edward, but you could have been killed, you know. Hell of a way to take on an avalanche, single-handed, man. You need a break. Badly."

Montague knew Muybridge's departure would make his life easier. At the same time, the engineer felt a part of himself was leaving.

"I was trying to save a life."

"Whose life?" Montague asked. "Understand, I never did sell you out, though I certainly had inducements." He cracked the thinnest of smiles.

Edward looked hard at his friend. "Thanks. I can guess how difficult it was."

Montague looked embarrassed, a rare phenomenon. "Oh, there's one thing I wanted to tell you before you go. You remember my request, the business about the highly heralded bonus pay?" Muybridge nodded. "Stanford did raise the pay—an extra quarter per hour. He also increased the booze ration of these poor devils. But he changed the size of the glasses. They're smaller; they hold less than before. Good luck the rest of the way."

Montague reached down and handed Muybridge a Smith & Wesson revolver. Muybridge pushed it back but the engineer insisted, "Take it. You don't know who's out there."

Odd to be handed a weapon, he thought, since he was in a murderous mood. He realized he'd left his own pistol in San Francisco. Edward asked, "Meet violence with violence, is that it?"

"Protect yourself if you have to. Purely selfish motivation. Who the hell else can I talk to when I get back to the city?"

They clutched each other for an instant, aware that each had their loyalties, and their betrayals.

Chapter Twenty-three

As he goaded Rosie the mule downhill, Muybridge knew that he'd lost. He'd been outmaneuvered. With all of his puffed up self-importance, he was a naive fool, a dupe—as Holly had predicted. Plus, his hands were killing him. Odd, he considered, how strange that snow made his fingers and palms burn.

Retracing his route on muleback along the endless railroad tracks, he knew, at last, that Holly had always understood who Stanford was. "He is not only dangerous and duplicitous and a crafty viper, he would do anything—spend thousands on what most men deem inessentials, dig up gutter gossip—to put you at a disadvantage in order to outwit you, control you." Why could she understand that and not he? Because he wanted to document the Building of the Nation? Because he wanted steady income? Because he was a rube and an optimistic self-deceiver, and Holly perceived things clearly? He catechized himself: *Accept her insight. Learn from her. She is wiser, fool.*

Thinking back to her performance and the corset diatribe, Edward considered, *How courageous of her to face the tyrant in his den.* He had underestimated her heroism then. She needed and wanted nothing from Stanford and his world—unlike her pathetic, prideful, defeated lover.

He owed it to her to rectify the long string of mistakes caused, largely, he admitted, by his own gullibility—and overreaching ambition. For the rest of his life, Muybridge vowed, his first priority would be to love her. That would be calling enough.

During the endless, exhausting, snow-blind ride, he whacked poor Rosie's touchy ribs but, for the first time in their unhappy relationship, he felt sympathy for the evil-tempered, foul-smelling mule.

His rooms were empty. Holly had obviously visited in the last few days, for the front pages from the *Clarion* were spread over the dining room table. He smiled, thinking of his compulsive tidiness versus her tendency to what now seemed like such sweet disorder. The sizable engravings on page one of March 3, 4, and 5 were all derived from Edward's photos, which should have pleased him. But the captions offered a radically different slant on the reality he had captured: of a heroic rescue attempt by fearless railroad employees, of humane treatment of workers, of solicitous medical care. His photos had been doctored, distorted, eradicated, his tumor of outrage surgically excised by a handful of subscripts. Holly was preparing a batch of clippings for mailing, complete with a large envelope addressed and stamped: EDWARD MUYBRIDGE, PHOTOGRAPHER EXTRAORDINAIRE. Another mailing that would not have reached him if he had remained in the sierras.

Crossing the late quiet of San Francisco toward Holly's apartment, he felt lower than he'd ever felt. The palms of his hands seared and burned; his fingers ached so much that he was tempted to chop them off. Meanwhile, some of his finest work—irreplaceable photographs that would have indicted the railroad and, moreover, documented the truth—were gone forever. He was broke, with no job or future. He felt too tired, too old and defeated to go back to photographing brides and babies, but he had no options. As the carriage carried him across town, he recognized that he was another casualty of the transcontinental railroad. For two months he'd had almost no contact with the woman he loved. His suitcase sat beside him. Among the few salvaged photographs, Edward had tossed in a fresh shirt and clean underwear. He hadn't even bothered to unpack his dirty clothes, nor the sidearm that Montague had forced upon him to protect himself on the uneventful trip down from the sierras. The weapon was wrapped in a ragged pair of work pants to keep the grease off his other clothes.

He was lost in thought when the carriage pulled up in front of Holly's apartment. Edward paid the driver, grabbed his suitcase, and stepped down. As he entered the building and trudged up the stairs, he had one impulse: to simply lay his head on her bosom, relinquish all effort for a time, and lie with his love until the wounds scarred over. *Back,* he thought, *to the one safe, consoling place in the universe.* Using his key, he softly entered Holly's apartment. He wanted to surprise her, so he moved silently through the space.

Light-headed and almost swooning with exhaustion, he carried the suitcase as far as the bedroom door, which was slightly ajar. He set the suitcase down and noiselessly pushed open the door. In the dawn light he saw her lying on the bed, one lovely breast provocatively exposed. Beside her, a naked man—Fauconier, Muybridge realized in shock, the Frenchman who had quieted the house the night she danced. The room seemed to move, to pick up speed. Like a locomotive, the room thrust itself at him, rushed fiercely at his eyes, dominated by that bed and those two nudes stretched upon it.

The man's body lay torqued to one side, leaving his thick, sinewy thigh exposed. The beige blanket had slipped off so that an end dangled on the floor. The penis was limp but large, elongated from pleasure.

Edward's fury lodged in the sides of his head, where his blood pulsed as loudly as a kettledrum. He felt nauseous, but calm. Silently, deliberately, he stepped back, reached down into the suitcase, pulled out and unwrapped the Smith & Wesson. The gun felt cool to his anguished fingers, lighter than the Colt he'd carried through the war.

Too close together, he thought with supernatural clarity as he took a few paces across the room. *Must separate them.* Muybridge stood over the sleeping couple for a moment, trying to will the intruder away. Then he leaned over his love and whispered to her in a soft, even tone, "Holly, move over." His voice reached down into her sleep and stirred her, and she slipped slightly toward Edward, away from the naked male body. Then, as Edward raised the pistol and took aim, she sat up, terrified. What was Edward doing here? As Holly awoke, she saw the pistol and him leaning across the bed, his arm draped over her to restrain her in case she made a sudden move back toward Fauconier. Holly reached for the weapon a split second after it went off.

She had a moment of dazed incomprehension—the flash, the deafening explosion by her ear. She saw Muybridge from below, his thin face wilted, enraged, grotesquely twisted. She felt Jacques's body clench and spasm; he did not move again yet blood showered over her—warm, thick, clinging blood. Gouts and gouts of blood shooting like a geyser out of his chest as though it would never stop.

She screamed agonizingly, "No! No!" but it was too late. Holly looked up in horror and fear and hatred at Muybridge's ravaged face.

Chapter Twenty-four

The image came back to him countless times. The large, muscular body jerking, twitching, then laying back lifeless. That hulking slab of a body next to her, blood gushing from the useless exploded heart. Blood everywhere. The nauseous, sticky, overly sweet blood coating both of them as they partook of the finale of the soluble essence of a man's life. Muybridge's conscience offered no outlet for escape, no escape at all from his insane anger, his crazed, unforgivable presumption.

Encased in four-foot-thick stone walls in the dank cell, a small, barred window above his head, listening to steps approach and retreat down a long corridor, Muybridge waited—for death, for acquittal—he really did not care since he knew he had lost her. Forever. The only woman in the universe he loved. Did he welcome the simple finality of death? Why not, with nothing to live for? He did not wish to spend his life as a ghost, perpetually denied her presence, growing paler and less earthbound through time as the source of his being, his vitality, his life itself remained remote and inaccessible. Holly hating him, knowing him to be the source of her anguish, was not a fate he would choose. And yet he had chosen just that.

For the thousandth time he replayed the scene—the dim, hovering gray light; the hairy, powerful thigh; her beauty; the bedroom drenched with the smell of sex. *Move over.* He spoke to her so gently. At the moment of their greatest separation, he had played upon their intimacy, used it to protect her. That grim irony provided the only comfort Edward could offer himself.

She had lost the Frenchman; he had lost her. No one could ever right the imbalance.

He wrote to Matthew Brady, telling the old man how right he'd been when he said that anyone could turn lunatic under the right—or was it the wrong?—circumstances. He grimly joked with his former mentor that, given where he stood now—awaiting trial for first-degree murder—he just might beat Brady to the grave. He wrote to Montague, telling the engineer that he alone, Edward Muybridge, was to blame. Defeat had unhinged him, he realized that now. But that was no excuse. He wrote to Eakins, providing technical information about lenses and shutter speeds and tactics for photographing movement that barely interested him now, yet Muybridge felt it necessary to pass on whatever he knew to someone with the avidity he himself once possessed. And he wrote often to Holly, emotion-drenched letters, not begging forgiveness, which he could not in good conscience plead for and knew would not be forthcoming, but attempting to convey his understanding of his crime—not simply that he had killed her lover, horrible enough, but admitting the colossal, inexcusable arrogance of what he'd done, making such an ultimate decision for Fauconier, and for her. He felt angry and betrayed by Holly, too, but knew that she had always kept open the option of another lover—or lovers. He asked her if she could ever imagine seeing him again. He knew it was premature, but he had to know if there was the remotest possibility. If so, life would be worth living. If not . . . In his heart, Muybridge knew that there was no way back to her; that she would never forgive him. He wrote to her certain that his letters would not be read. He wrote endlessly, obsessively, hopelessly, spilling out guilt and sorrow and the torn, hopelessly scattered scraps of his love. He never received a syllable in reply.

The newspapers had a field day with the murder, and Edward read every word his jailers provided about "the love triangle" with a furious and shamed voyeurism, as though the three of them were tented together inside the vilest secrets. Reading the confused, erroneous, and false reports gave Edward a curious two-way vision of the event. The language itself—the terms *lover, paramour, mistress, disreputable woman*—were splashed across headlines and featured on each page, retroactively tainting his former blessed intimacy with her. Reporters made up the titillating scene as though they'd been flies on the wall—"caught in bed," "surprised in the act," "discovered in flagrante." One thing puzzled him, however. The *Clarion*, Stanford's mouthpiece, remained remarkably restrained, and Muybridge could not understand why.

The stone jail admitted only a thin gruel of light, which made him feel akin to a nocturnal creature. The cell was cold even for April in San Francisco. On the third day in the small, grimy hellhole, with its bucket, its acrid smells, and the surfeit of darting cockroaches and waterbugs and silverfish, Denise Faveraux burst in trailed by two rapt jailers. Her radiance lit up the dreariness, but Muybridge felt so removed from the world beyond his bars that he found it painful to look at her. *So,* he thought dispassionately, *I must be preparing for death*.

Denise understood his mood. She grew muted, as though self-consciously dimming her candlepower. They spoke like sister and brother. During their hour together he recalled, with a sense verging on disgust, the blistering red heat with which he'd pursued her only two months before through the halls of Stanford's mansion. Denise never mentioned the shooting, but offered to contact "a good lawyer" she knew to represent him at the trial. Edward, wallowing in his guilt, seemed oddly indifferent to his legal situation. Denise took this as approval to proceed.

Desperately trying to ingratiate himself with Holly, he fed Denise choice tidbits about the Central Pacific. Not having seen Holly's pamphlet on Sitka Ice, Muybridge explained in detail how they milked profits out of the subsidiary companies but never returned a cent more than was mandated to the almost bankrupt railroad corporation. He explained, though she already knew, how the laborers improvised a corduroy road to move the giant engine overland in order to give the appearance to congress of contiguous track. Edward related how the Central Pacific manipulated federal bonds and land guarantees, how they borrowed millions of dollars from undercapitalized reserve funds. He briefed Denise on how the Central Pacific bribed senators and representatives wholesale, and gave her several names of the implicated congressmen. Using his diary, which he had kept in his coat, he read aloud what Montague had revealed one drunken evening. "'Huntington wrote to

Stanford from Washington—Ward had showed the letter to my friend Montague, who quoted it to me: "I stayed in Washington two days to fix up the Senate Railroad committee. It is just as we wanted it." Another Huntington letter proclaimed, "It costs money to fix things here. I believe that with $200,000 I can pass our new bill."'"

Denise so much enjoyed playing intermediary that she took notes. Muybridge pondered her interest in the affair at length, the unbroken solitude giving him time to contemplate why this beautiful woman was willing to act as go-between. He unearthed no answer.

Mostly, Edward suffered in silence—even when reporters bribed their way in. This was not because he was a martyr, but because he saw no point in burdening anyone but himself with his guilt. Denise listened, she understood. But any form of consolation seemed to beg for the relief he did not deserve.

The trial opened in the courtroom where Wilson Lardue had stood trial. The first day's proceedings went smoothly and quickly. To the surprise of San Francisco's citizenry, Muybridge looked anything but depressed. Few observers, other than Denise, attributed it to the fact that for the first time since the shooting he had the chance to be in the same room with Holly, who, in the interests of mourning and to escape Edward's prying, importunate eyes, wore a thick, black veil.

Even after the prosecuting attorney demanded the death penalty for "this cold-blooded murderer," the photographer's mood did not alter. In fact, as Edward left the courthouse late that afternoon, he felt buoyant. He had spent the entire day gazing at her and trying to determine her expression through the veil. At the same time, his eyes had tried to tell her that though he could never make amends for the deadly deed, he was infinitely sorry and ashamed and, he tried to communicate, he loved her with all his life.

Outside the courtroom, being hustled back to jail that first day, Muybridge became aware of a round-faced man in a slouch hat, scowling at him with uncommon intensity. The face seemed vaguely familiar, but Muybridge couldn't quite place the fellow.

Back in his icy cell, Muybridge was handed a letter from Thomas

Eakins. With Montague's help, the painter had persuaded the University of Pennsylvania to offer Muybridge a professor's chair at the Veterinary College. The letter informed him that at the university, in Philadelphia, he would be able to study locomotion in both animals and humans. The irony of the offer arriving at such a moment kept Edward laughing until the guards thought that their infamous prisoner had gone stark-raving mad.

The second morning in court Muybridge's attorney, Harper Ross, called Leland Stanford as a surprise character witness. Muybridge leaped to his feet and shouted, "I will not allow that man to speak one word. Do not let him take the witness stand."

Stanford was shocked into silence, as the courtroom slowly filled with astonished murmurs and whisperings. Ross asked the bench if he could speak privately with his client. Leaning close to Edward, the lawyer said in a low but impassioned tone, "Are you mad? You know what it took me to get the governor here? Do you understand how much Stanford can help you?"

The entire court strained to hear what the two men were whispering so fiercely.

"I won't let him sully this, too. I don't care what it costs me."

"Only your life," Ross murmured under his breath, then turned and addressed the bench. "Clearly, Your Honor, my client is momentarily deranged. He refuses to allow Governor Stanford to testify in his behalf."

"So be it," the judge intoned, as though pleased to thus seal Muybridge's fate.

There was a short embarrassed pause while Stanford retired, sporting an ironic smirk and shaking his head with exaggerated sadness, as though aggrieved that his ex-employee had lost his mind.

Like a child, he has to win, Muybridge thought, remembering the croquet match and the trotting bet and the rackety train ride into the sierras. Yet the big man looked older. Edward had heard that the Stanfords' only child, Leland Junior, was a sickly infant.

The defense called Holly Hughes.

Watching her move across the courtroom—making the commonplace majestic—pleased Edward, but it also made him immeasurably sad. He loved to see her regal stride, the springy dancer's gait; and then despaired to have hurt her irreparably.

As she stepped onto the witness stand, Holly tripped. Edward lunged forward before Ross caught his sleeve. Holly quickly recovered, gained the dais, and stood uncertainly by the witness chair.

After the swearing in, Harper Ross addressed the witness. "Before I get to the night of the shooting, I have two questions: Miss Hughes, did you during the last few months attempt to rent a hall in the San Francisco area for a lecture and dance performance?"

"I did."

"Miss Hughes," the judge intervened, "the court would like you to remove the veil. I commiserate with your tragic loss, but the jury may find the witness's facial expressions useful in making their determination."

"If you insist."

Holly shed the veil but not her hat, which partially shielded her eyes from Muybridge. She looked tired, fragile, yet the pallor made her all the more exquisite to him. Greedily he studied her face, feasting like a starving man on those changeable gray-green eyes. He forgot that he was on trial for his life—he wanted to draw her, to shape the line of the cheekbone he'd once caressed, to lovingly detail the precious, subtle volume those bones enveloped. Nothing she did escaped his notice—from the smallest movement of a finger or a hand traveling to her hair or, once, the tapping of a boot heel, none of it escaped her devotee's regard. He would have been happy to brush her hair or wash her feet, to prostrate himself like a rug before her. Anything, to be in contact, to absorb her pain and drink in her loveliness again.

"Were you successful in these attempts?"

"Excuse me?" So much was happening each instant she sat there—his eyes, this room, a rush of old imagery—that Holly only half-heard the last question.

"In your attempts to rent a suitable hall for your performance."

"Oh, for months I could not find a hall."

"Were you in fact barred from renting these spaces because of the, ah, controversial nature of your first lecture and dance performance?"

"Barred?" Contempt tinged her voice. Muybridge thought, the entire world could change, the universe could go to hell, but Holly would be Holly. "It has been virtually impossible for me to rent a hall, yes. As to the reasons why I've been refused, you ought to have asked Mr. Stanford or, since he's left, his cabal of cronies." She glanced disdainfully at Mark Hopkins, not bothering to search out the others.

"Have you been unable to perform in the San Francisco area for the past five months?"

"As your question presumes, I performed last week."

A blow staggered Muybridge, as though a sledgehammer bashed into his ribcage. He had missed her performance. Too intent on his work, the "epic ending to his tale of the nation," he had broken his word. *No wonder,* he thought, *she took Fauconier.*

"Is it true, Miss Hughes, that you are an advocate of what is referred to as 'dress reform'?"

"Yes, I am." Muybridge willed his eyes to plead his case with her. She did not look his way.

"Are you also an advocate of 'free love'?"

Muybridge jumped up, not letting his eyes stray from her, though she would not so much as glance at him. "Counselor, I will not allow this line of questioning."

The court erupted. Quick-sketch artists, working on portraits for the newspapers, struggled to depict his face and her face as the judge ferociously slammed his gavel. "Mr. Muybridge, sit down right now. Sit down. There will be no more outbursts in this court."

Muybridge sat back in his seat.

"Miss Hughes," the defense attorney spoke softly now, "one more question: Have you or have you not used a word in public, to a mixed audience, to describe an article of female underattire?"

"You're referring to the *cor-set.*" She enunciated distinctly, broadcasting the syllables through the air. "Of course I did. Everyone in the courtroom—and probably all over the state—knows that." As many spectators snickered loudly, the judge predictably gaveled; the room quieted.

"And what are your views on physical relationships between the sexes?"

"I did believe in free love, if that's what you mean to insinuate, yes."

Edward rose again, this time heavily. He hated having turned her life into a tawdry public melodrama. "Please, Mr. Ross, cease this line of questioning. It's not relevant to my case. If I must, I'm prepared to be hanged, but I will not hear *one more word* denigrating Miss Hughes's character, which is virtuous and courageous and altogether impeccable." A few women mooned, others sighed.

The judge played his part. "Mr. Muybridge, one more outburst, and I'll hold you in contempt."

Muybridge thought about how barely a year earlier Wilson Lardue had shouted down a contempt citation in the same courtroom with the words: "What are you going to do, hang me twice?!"

"Sir," Muybridge said aloud. "May I confer with my counsel, please?"

Muybridge whispered in his lawyer's ear, "Not only will I fire you and deprive you of all the free publicity you are getting, you tinhorn shyster, but I won't pay a cent of your goddamn exorbitant fee—not a penny—if you impugn her in any way."

"I'm only trying to establish the nature of her character."

He whispered fiercely, "She's got more character than all of San Francisco. Drop the subject, Ross, you understand?"

"You're tying my hands, Edward," Ross whispered loud enough for the first few rows to hear.

"Damned right I am."

Excruciating questioning followed about what had happened that fateful night. Holly couldn't remember much. A voice—Muybridge's voice—softly urging her, commanding her, to move over. Edward's forearm holding her back for that split second before the shot rang out, then being drenched in blood that she was afraid would never cease.

The lawyer did his job: Did Miss Hughes actually see Muybridge fire? Or did she only see him holding the smoking pistol afterward? She was asleep; she did not see him fire the weapon. Or maybe she did, she couldn't be certain. Ross now reached the core of the defense. "On that night, on that fateful night, did the defendant, Edward Muybridge, appear insane to you?"

"Can a sane person kill another person?" Holly Hughes answered conscientiously. At that instant Holly looked at Edward for the first time. She held his gaze for three full seconds, her eyes declaring that she despised him, hated his arrogance and murdering cowardice. There was no forgiveness in those gray-green eyes. "Certainly he was furious," she offered aloud.

"How could you tell he was furious when you were dazed and half-asleep?"

"Because I knew him well enough to have insight into his moods."

The verb *knew* devastated Muybridge—it put everything in the past, behind him. That single word left him without promise.

"So you cannot tell the court that, in your opinion, Edward Muybridge was not insane at the moment when the shot rang out?"

"That is correct."

Muybridge felt no relief. Her eyes had swept him off the earth, dismissed him as a contemptible speck of dirt. He didn't believe he had enough interest or strength to drag through life without Holly. Eternal exile from her was a sentence he feared more than death.

Denise Faveraux came that evening wreathed in a smile and carrying a bottle of champagne along with a rich meal of veal chops and rice. Animated, almost pleased, she kept repeating, "Holly saved your shapely little ass today, Edward. Oops, I forgot, sisterly comments only. No talk about sex. And absolutely no sex in spite of the habits of a lifetime." The bemused smile flashed on. "If you think your life is over, you're wrong. Such heroism from her, the grieving one. I never met anyone, woman or man, with more courage."

"What's life without her?"

"Come on, Edward. She saved you. She must have feelings for you."

"Denise, I took more from her than any person should. A man she cared for, a man she loved"—he spat out the word—"I killed him. She'll never forgive me, and I won't forgive myself. She was so noble on the witness stand. . . ." He choked a little. To commit murder, to do the unthinkable, Edward Muybridge, who'd imagined himself a "civilized" being. Then the image of the man in the slouch hat assailed him. Something about that round face in the courthouse hall—those disturbingly thin lips, that venomous mouth—nagged Edward. . . . The link came to him as an image: the stage robbery—Lardue. The man was Lardue's brother, the younger one who shot the lock off the strongbox. Edward, who desired death, who never wanted to feel anything again, felt his interest involuntarily quicken. If the court didn't hang him, Edward would not give the younger Lardue the satisfaction of murdering Photo Man.

Denise noted the animated look, the brighter eyes. "What is it, Edward?"

"Nothing," he lied.

But she'd seen the glimmer—that intense flicker of interest—and, for the first time in jail, he'd experienced an emotion other than his coffinlike deadness and all-consuming self-pity.

What followed was reflex, not thought. Edward asked Denise to go to his studio and search in the top drawer of the left-hand cabinet for his stereoscopic photographs of the stagecoach robbery. There were five, no, six matched small photos. He wanted to examine them again. Edward felt like a sort of postal package, delivered back from the land of the dead. He was not particularly pleased about the change of state, for the transformation did not allow him to believe that Holly, the woman of his soul, would ever consent to see him again. At the same time, he felt life—messy, uncontrollable, anarchic life—flood back into him even as he tried to dam it off.

Chapter Twenty-five

District Attorney Laughton Hills elevated himself on his toes as though trying to enlarge his unimposing presence for the jury. He inclined his head toward the twelve men, spun theatrically on his heel, aimed a damning finger at the perpetrator, and declaimed, "This is a cold-blooded killer, a heartless, heinous murderer. He offers no excuse whatsoever for his crime. Your verdict, gentlemen, should be—in fact, must be by law—the full and ultimate penalty, death by hanging." Hills craned his scrawny, crosshatched seventy-year-old neck toward the jury, as though giving them a visual preview of what lay ahead for Muybridge. The old man then dragged himself slowly across the courtroom where he slumped into his seat.

Edward's collar tightened like a noose. Watching Harper Ross, his lawyer, make the same dramatic walk in reverse, Muybridge felt that all parties—the judge, the opposing lawyers, the twelve gentlemen of the jury, most significantly Holly—were morally correct. He was the lone guilty actor in the drama, and, whatever they decided, he'd abide by his fate without complaint. Having acceded his rights, all he had to do was sit and wait for those unknown men to pass sentence. This uncharacteristic passivity was frightening but also oddly relieving.

Edward's lawyer began the plea to save the photographer's life. "My client is a gifted man, a brilliant man, one of the great artistic and scientific innovators of our age."

Holly permitted herself a glance toward her ex-lover, employing the veil's cover. Yet she felt underhanded, indirectness not being her style. Why couldn't she look at him? Disgust. Yes, but not entirely. She found it difficult because she hated him, because, even now, he demanded so much from her—forgiveness, legitimization, and, worst and most insulting of all, love. She knew his strengths and weaknesses as a mother knows her child's, knew his fears, his demanding emotional needs. She saw him entire now, now that she no longer loved him.

"My client is, we all know, an artist. He is universally considered an eccentric, a man so intense and inventive, so driven and sui generis that he cannot be understood or judged in terms applicable to us ordinary citizens."

Opposing counsel rose to object while Ross continued, "Does that mean that he has special rights that we do not? Of course not. Legally and morally, such an argument is absurd." The prosecutor reseated himself. "But what his uniqueness does mean is that we, as a community that benefits from his talents, indeed, his genius, we must consider him not narrowly but in all of his dimensions. We must recognize his artistic propensities and his ultrasensitivity, which is, I'm afraid to say, never far removed from madness." Muybridge suppressed a smile. Christ, what a plea. Brady would be rolling on the floor; he'd be laughing so loud the judge would bang down that tyrannical gavel to shut him up. Bierstadt would jump up and scream, *No! No! This is utter poppycock!* Edward dared not look at the jurors lest he break out laughing.

Like a lasso thrown over the entire dozen, the lawyer scanned the jurymen. His sweeping gaze contacted each of them without hurry or lingering. Edward wondered how one learned the trick. "Why was this hypersensitive gentleman so distraught on the night of that terrible shooting? How could Muybridge—a household name throughout the Golden State, a man of such brilliance that he has controlled time and improbably isolated and rendered the precise gaits of a champion horse as it trotted; an artist so gifted that his camera has captured the epic sweep of the United States itself—how could his man be capable of such an evil, dastardly act? I'll tell you how, gentlemen." He nodded toward his client.

"This man was sorely troubled. In the Sierra Nevada mountains, working at the request of the mighty Pacific railroad, he had witnessed men dying daily under terrible, horrendous, soul-shattering circumstances. Only one day before he returned to San Francisco, he was mere inches away from being buried alive in an avalanche himself. Then, tempting fate itself—eyewitnesses told us they have never witnessed such a recklessly heroic and, frankly, insane act—Edward Muybridge leaped into the mountain snow to save three *Chinese* laborers buried in the snow slide." Jurors seemed stunned by the last assertion. A white man risking his life for Chinese workmen?

Edward considered the infinitude of ways in which reality can be distorted, amended, rewritten. The lawyer raised a question about motive, knowing nothing about Edward's instinctive dive to rescue one life—about the calculated indifference the railroad executives displayed to the deaths; about his working for a man he hated and a company he loathed; about the ghostlike spy with the seemingly surgically attached notebook who dogged him every day. That Edward's mad fury led to the futile attempt at rescue. Not insanity, certainly not virtue. His lawyer knew nothing about the facts of his blasted efforts, of having been tricked and trumped and defanged and declawed by Ward and Stanford. Meanwhile, the tedious legal charade went on: For a crime he committed in hot blood, boiling blood, reason was supposed to prevail. The lawyer's questions, the witnesses' replies, the tennis match of unreason while voyeurs watched and Holly suffered and a dozen men weighed their fateful decision. "I implore you to see this act—sliding down a mountain, trying to dig a dead *Chinaman* out of an avalanche—this was not the action of a sane person. If you can imagine Mr. Muybridge madly risking his life for unknown workers, men from a far-off continent, you can understand that he was deranged. To me it's clear that the heinous shooting, tragic and horrific as it was, was not the act of a man in his right mind."

Maybe he *was* mad, Muybridge considered. Why did he feel that this entire proceeding was of so little consequence to him? He killed a man, and there was nothing to be done about it. There was no defense for that. He could not give Fauconier life. And Holly, his world, was lost to him.

"Always eccentric, Edward Muybridge was driven temporarily insane by his shattering experiences in the High Sierras. He returned to Miss

Hughes's apartment exhausted, devastated in body and in mind. In his deranged state, seeing the naked lovers, Edward Muybridge went *mad* and shot his rival in a fit of *insane* jealousy. Overwhelmed by passion he took his rival's life, a sacred life. All this we readily admit. Now, as you prepare to make the ultimate judgment on this gifted yet volatile man, temper reason with mercy. Recall that Edward Muybridge has never, in his twenty-eight years, harmed another human being." *How absurd,* Muybridge thought, *that last statement*.

"Recognize that this aberrant, tragic act will never be repeated. And find Muybridge not guilty, not guilty by reason of temporary insanity." The lawyer took his first audible breath in that long speech. "All he asks is for a second chance, a chance to live his life and to continue to create his extraordinary, world-acclaimed, life-enhancing work."

Like everyone else seated in the courtroom, Holly Hughes appeared quietly immobile. Undetected, her hands stayed fiercely clenched as she wrestled with herself in precise, isometric equilibrium—muscle rigidly tensed against muscle. Behind the veil, tears streamed down her cheeks. She did not want them to take his life. It would provide no revenge or compensation or relief. The only thing she desired was a gift that no jury could deliver—to forget every man she had loved.

The judge roused himself, directing his attention to the jury box. "Gentlemen, you will now retire to deliberate."

In the crowded hall, Muybridge paused to catch a glimpse of Holly before she disappeared. He was struck by an irrational fear: Maybe she would not return to the court tomorrow. Just then someone bumped hard up against him from behind, and he spun around to find himself face-to-face with the younger Lardue. Johny Lardue glared and whispered fiercely, "Photo Man, you're dead as dirt. I'd blow a hole through you right here, but I'm gonna live a long life after I bash in your skull."

Muybridge shouted, "Get him! Get him!" But Johny Lardue quickly shoved his way through the crowd and was gone.

It was an odd feeling, Muybridge considered in his cell. Events were conspiring to recall him back to life, he who only hours before had been prepared to die.

* * *

Entombed with him in the dank stone shroud later that afternoon, Denise Faveraux was effervescent. A few steps away from the inescapable, odious slop bucket, in a tomb where despair collects in corners, her blue eyes were aglow. She poured tea for him, tea for herself, amid a stream of nonstop wishful thinking. "Don't give up. I watched the jurors, Edward, watched very closely. They looked sympathetic, except for that little ferrety guy first row, two from the left."

"Are you a mind reader, too?"

"Not to boast, and with no exaggeration, I do know something about the moods of your average john." He smiled at that. "Holly is leaving," she said abruptly.

"Where? Back to Paris?" His heart plummeted as he pronounced the sentence.

"If I were a betting woman, I'd say a year or two of traveling."

He thought, *You've always been a betting woman*. But he asked, "Where? Where will she go?" Muybridge had a consuming need to attach her to a specific locale, to be able to ponder his lost jewel in an actual setting.

Denise replied impatiently. "It doesn't matter where, Edward, don't you understand? She wants to forget, to lose herself."

Her sensual lips thinned, her mouth sharpened. Disdain threaded premature furrows across her brow. Again he remembered that he'd killed a man and deserved little consideration.

As requested, Denise produced the original stereo photos of the stagecoach robbery. The departed Lardue was immediately recognizable. For over half an hour Muybridge examined each centimeter of the six twin photos under his magnifying glass. Unfortunately, the younger brother, who had stalked him so nakedly in the courthouse corridor, had been too far away from the camera—and too blurred—to be recognizable. Muybridge recalled jabbing at the images as he bobbed and weaved his way down the line, snaking lead lefts at the shots while he tried to persuade Holly that the younger bandit was the elder's brother. But she never saw the similarity. Everything in his life now seemed not about the future but about the past.

Denise remained with him till nine that evening. While she knitted, he wrote Holly then Brady then Montague and obsessively examined the pointless photos. He'd decided that if he wasn't "hung by the neck until dead," to quote the district attorney's melodramatic turn, he would have to face off with the younger Lardue. Having lost the only thing that mattered, Muybridge had no desire to hand over what was left of his life to a surly bandit.

At 9:22 p.m., the jailer clinked and clanged his way through the various locks and doors. "You'll have to go, miss. They're back in." The man smirked, licked his badly chapped lower lip, cleared his throat portentously. "Time to go."

Go where? Muybridge wondered, feeling doomed. He weighed the jailer's expressions and those paltry syllables, trying to squeeze encoded meanings from the matter-of-fact phrases. Did that slight hesitation in the jailer's speech reflect pity for Edward's pathetic end, or some muted, perverse pleasure in his upcoming death? Or was he in a compulsive housekeeping mode, concerned about cleaning out a cell in the endless round of turnovers?

Muybridge felt absurdly talkative: How many had the jailer seen go to their deaths? How had the worst behaved? How had the best? The cowards, the courageous, the religious, the babbling, or the puking idiots fouling their prison grays, what did the jailer recall of the departed just before departure, he the repository of men's (and perhaps a few women's) last minutes on this earth? And what could he remember of that robber and murderer Wilson Lardue, later murdered by the state? The jailer seemed about to formulate an answer when they reached the courtroom entrance.

At the door, Denise glided into Edward's path and kissed him with sisterly devotion. He could feel her saying good-bye—bracing for the worst. He longed for an erotic charge and she offered friendship instead. A chill ran through him; he felt icy cold and void, as though the plug had been ripped out of his being. He thought clearly, *I'm dead*. Yet Denise's fragrance lingered—a faint, sensual benediction—as he was led in hurtful ankle irons into the mobbed courtroom. Almost all had waited to hear his fate.

A command performance, he thought, as everyone's eyes, even those luminous ones obscured by Holly's veil, turned toward him. He read pity, fear, hostility, execration in the looks—a barrage of human emotion discharged at him. Yes, death—one's own, that is—certainly did concentrate the mind.

The silence was compromised only by his shuffling forward step, the clank of the leg irons ringing like dulled chimes. He sat and an instant later the judge indicated that Muybridge should rise. The jury's foreman rose at the same cue.

The air around Muybridge turned sodden, like that supersaturated air before a thunderstorm; it stuffed his nose, his throat. Fearing that he might suffocate before they pronounced ultimate judgment, he gasped loudly. All eyes examined him mercilessly, searching for vulnerability, contrition, tears, a telltale wet stain, any and all marks of a coward. And, still, Holly's head remained tilted in his direction.

At this very last moment—*Too late,* he thought—Edward realized that he did not want to die. He felt a stirring, chordlike anguish—an organ at full throttle, stops open and every key sounded simultaneously—for all the pain he had caused her. She loved them both, he realized. She had always, bravely and candidly, explained that the other lover was a possibility—if not a fact. The insistence upon her own rooms; his cursed, overlong stay in the mountains because of his ambition; his working for the man she hated most; the presence of her old friend—and lover—as a temptation she had every right to. Fauconier had been as close to Holly as he himself had been: He had tasted her, loved her, brought her to climax, sat with her quietly, talked, shared. How dare he murder Holly's lover! Muybridge, who'd been able to improvise his way out of countless moral tangles, had no excuse for this crime. On his feet awaiting judgment before the black-robed arbiter, Edward Muybridge acknowledged to himself that he deserved to be hanged. He had been pathetically weak and blind and inexcusably, tragically selfish.

"Gentleman of the jury, have you reached a verdict?" the judge asked. Muybridge squared his shoulders, trying to playact a self-image worthy of respect.

The foreman, a short, balding man with a strawberry-colored birthmark on his forehead, intoned, "Yes, we have, Your Honor."

Muybridge's future gone, swallowed up by nothingness, he weighed the full-lipped intensity of each instant. Time ticked by in ungainly stop-motion, instants spaced themselves as they wished, moments stretched—a pregnant women's legs yawned obscenely wide to deliver blankness, nothing. His entire existence swallowed up by dread.

"What say you?"

Breathe, Edward counseled himself. *Breathe.* But the autonomic function would not kick in; air did not flow, again he knew he'd suffocate before the foreman spoke. Too much time, no air.

"We find the defendant not guilty." The courtroom shook silently, as though a massive, noiseless earthquake shifted the earth under everyone's feet. For weeks Edward had stared down into the gaping, black chasm poised to swallow him forever; now as he teetered on the brink, suddenly the all-consuming earth snapped shut beneath his feet. Edward wanted the strawberry-crowned foreman to repeat the words a second time so that he could be absolutely certain. Even that wish was granted. "Not guilty by reason of temporary insanity."

Edward saw himself standing at Manassas next to a Civil War surgeon, Anson Briggs, as the doctor bent down over a panicked soldier and answered his pathetic pleas about a shattered thigh. "No," Briggs had offered, "we won't have to amputate, Corporal Powers. The leg can be saved." And now Edward was "saved."

As onlookers erupted in wild cheers, he rushed across the courtroom, his eyes never deserting Holly's veiled face. Reaching her, he pleaded, "Holly, what I did was inexcusable. I know that. But I love you more than I can say. Tell me what I can do to—"

She cut him off in a frigid, unrecognizable voice, an utterance imposing planetary distances between them. "Edward, you killed our wonderful love." The veil moved as she spoke. "You killed my choice."

"Holly . . ."

As she turned to go, a messenger, a boy of about fourteen, shoved a crumpled envelope into Muybridge's hand. With Denise at her side, Holly moved away.

Edward tried to follow, but the jubilant, unthinking crowd surged up around him. A sea of familiar and unfamiliar faces cut him off from her: Luke Ransom, Horatio Dirk, Chester Crocker, even Collis Ward was there (Ward had wisely remained out of Muybridge's reach). Prominent men of San Francisco and their wives and unknown persons congratulated him for his acquittal, chorusing, “Splendid.” “Marvelous, Muybridge.” “Well done.” “What a relief for all of us.” “Thank God.” Someone—Dirk, he thought vaguely—pounded him on the back. The bright sun of the world’s opinion had pivoted back in his direction. All the while, she continued receding, moving farther and farther away. All he wanted was to pursue her, stop her, prostrate himself. . . . Then Holly disappeared through the door, Denise beside her. Gone forever.

After the interviews and statements and congratulations subsided and the crowd dispersed, Muybridge opened the envelope. Scrawled almost illegibly, with fat, wavering lines, erratic curves, and indistinct loops was this curse: “Your dead Photo Man. Dead as dirt.”

For the second time since the shooting, Muybridge laughed. Having survived the legal attempt to execute him, this threat struck Edward as a lousy, ungrammatical joke.

Chapter Twenty-six

In mid-March, Denise Faveraux and Edward met for dinner at O'Connor's, a boisterous watering hole on the Bay. He explained that he'd requested a table in the back yet positioned so that if the younger Lardue was watching—as he did so often now—"Johny" could spot his target from the street. However, they weren't in a direct line of fire. Furthermore, Edward wished them to dine in a public place because Johny Lardue had provided one vital piece of information to his intended victim, which was that the would-be assassin did not wish to hang or do jail time.

They ate well, savoring the food and augmenting their pleasure by slowly sipping a rich Pomerol. Muybridge drank moderately, for he had to be alert. He glanced frequently out of the window, and two or three times thought he glimpsed a slouch hat draw back into the darkness on the far side of the street.

"Do you know the real reason why Holly left that French painter, Gérôme?" She garbled the French name almost as badly as he did.

"No."

"It was over a painting. She found it insulting."

So typical of her, Muybridge thought. "What is it called?"

"*The Slave Market*."

"Have you seen it?"

"No."

"Tell me more."

"That's all I know."

He knew that wasn't the case.

They started to leave the restaurant with utmost caution, taking pains to have a carriage standing outside. A select crowd accompanied them. Muybridge explained to Denise that this was their most vulnerable moment, since an outdoor night attack by Lardue would be difficult to fend off. Muyridge was betting that Denise and three waiters, the doorman, and the coachman would temporarily dissuade Johny Lardue from attempting to gun him down on that San Francisco street.

Muybridge was right. He did spot the slouch hat lurking in the shadows near the corner but, so far, Johny Lardue bided his time.

At the studio, Denise Faveraux burst into carillon-like peals of laughter. Standing behind the camera and cloaked by the fabric hood, were a pair of Edward's trousers, stuffed and upright and quite convincing. "I see, I see," she exclaimed, delighted by his hooded camera apparatus. "Edward, you are a sly dog."

He felt oddly relaxed. But there was no time for patting himself on the back. He lowered the gas jets to darken the room and, after fussing over last-minute preparations, turned to the lovely Denise, "You needn't continue with this. It would probably be better if you—"

"I wouldn't miss it for the world," she interrupted gamely.

"This is not a joke. It's risky for you."

"It will be a lot riskier for you if I don't use my, ah, natural talents."

He accepted the considerable gift of her help. "Tell me—you started this at dinner—how is she?" Edward compulsively straightened the black pant legs under the camera.

"She's genuinely glad you're alive. She wouldn't object to you being tossed into the slammer for years, but she doesn't want you dead." A new, more embracing intimacy emanated from their shared danger. The tone was conspiratorial, but underneath there was another ingredient which Muybridge found, even at this late date, a gift. Denise truly cared for him.

"Let me ask one question, Denise. Is there a chance for me, ever, with Holly?"

"You will never see her again, never." She pronounced this sentence with dread finality. "As solemnly as a nun takes a vow she told me."

He sank down, desolate.

"I'd better get started," she said, needing to rouse him from his stupor.

She smiled easily, comfortable in her skin. It was a lot to ask, he thought at first, but Denise was more than willing. She told him, "I always liked taking off my clothes. It's my natural state." She had also said, "Your bandit will never believe you've let your guard down unless we do it my way."

Denise slipped off her blouse, then her camisole. Her full breasts were striking, the brown-red nipples prominent and, whether from cold or fear, erect. He could not stop gaping at her. Speaking earnestly, she said, "This will sound like blasphemy now, Edward, but you will get over her. You enjoy women too much; we're too important to you."

With languorous movements, Denise Faveraux removed her skirt and the multilayers of her lower undergarments, all those intriguing underskirts and straps and buckles, and all tinged, he imaged, with her evocative scent. Edward did not know this, but she wore the unfamiliar garments to increase the drama of her disrobing.

He forgot his lifesaving preparations as his eyes surveyed yet more of her emerging body. Layer by layer, she eased off the rest and spoke in her rich voice, "Edward, you're too fickle." Their eyes locked. "And you're too much of an appreciator to play chaste monk and forego us poor women forever."

He started to object, peeling his eyes away from her gifts and focusing on the mundane wood-paneled door, uncertain whether he imagined or heard footsteps outside. His eyes strayed back to her, traveled down, over and up her chest, dwelling on her soft skin and large, firm, suckable nipples and, most of all, her come-hither-and-even-further smile. He was in two places at once—aroused by her loveliness yet absorbed in the impending task.

She returned his gaze with interest, further igniting him. Now his eyes roamed freely over her breasts and arms, trying to drink in her every curve and fold. He wanted to memorize her form, for Denise was as beautiful as—no, more beautiful than—he had imagined. Her nipped waist and swelling thighs and startlingly lush breasts . . . she was magnificent, utterly delectable, almost irresistible. Yet Denise's know-it-all attitude irritated Edward, her natural presumption that women, and women alone, understood the complex ins and outs of emotions and sex, that men had no standing on this mysterious, ineffable, slippery turf. Tonight he didn't have the leisure to contend with Denise. A more pressing problem—his life—was on his plate. Yes, he knew that she correctly stated the facts about who he had been. After all, he'd pursued her all around Stanford's mansion. If he'd found her that night when he went looking for her, they would've made love. But what she could not understand was that that was before his twin murder of Jacques and of Holly's love. He was no longer the old Edward Muybridge. He wanted Holly and her alone. His jealousy, the crime, months of living with his crushing guilt, this had reshaped his lustful, errant, ordinary clay. For Muybridge there would be no substitutes.

"Do you want me lying here?" Denise asked, both nervous and bemused by her upcoming role.

Muybridge nodded. She stretched out full length on the red-and-beige-striped chaise longue, Holly's gift to him ages ago. Her thighs were full without excess and there, at their source, was a forest of burnished gold. Velazquez, Titian could not have begged for more. Muybridge moved to the back of his camera, looked in at this woman, aware of the stunning photograph she would have been. He fussily readjusted the pant legs again, asking, "Why help me?"

"I don't want your career cut short. You should have a long life so that you can work." Impatience tightened her voice. "And I want you alive because I want to find out about this vow of celibacy. Will you break it? When? Who will be the fortunate lady? Will you love her as much as Holly? Reason enough?"

"Yes, thank you."

She gave him a full smile as rich as her body, her eyes comfortable—no, pleased—with his visual appraisal of her charms. She shifted to make herself more at ease. "Remember, I said you couldn't do this without me?"

"It certainly helps to have such a . . . such a beautiful distraction."

Denise mused, *I like a man who can smile when he's about to face death*. She felt no fear for herself, which pleased her. They had been over the plan a dozen times, and Denise Faveraux believed she was in capable hands.

With the first sound of footsteps charging up the stair, Muybridge retreated to his closet. He opened its door, stepped in, leaving the door open a crack. He saw Denise's stomach muscles tense, her breath involuntarily quicken, go shallow. Suddenly the door exploded into splintering fragments. Startled, Denise watched in open-mouthed terror as Johny Lardue burst in.

He took a step forward then halted. His gun hand dropped to his side, enchanted by the gorgeous nude apparition arrayed before him on the chaise. Then, remembering his mission, the younger bandit spun toward the camera and the pant legs beneath the cloth.

"You dirty bastard, Photo Man!" he yelled. "You got my brother killed." Lardue's Colt Peacemaker blasted away, firing into the dummy poised under the camera's hood. At the second shot, the black veil over the camera peeled away from Muybridge's decoy as the pants propped up by two sticks slumped to the floor. Frozen in place, the intruder got off one more round at the decoy before Muybridge leaped from the closet and slammed the butt of a pistol into his would-be assassin's skull.

Muybridge checked to see that Lardue was out cold, which he was, then deftly trussed his arms behind his back to his legs. Edward moved over to Denise, who lay trembling, too terrified to move. He held her head in his hands, then gently wrapped his houndstooth jacket around her. "Are you alright?" Denise Faveraux, who could not speak, nodded yes. "I have to ask my downstairs neighbor—I already set it up—to get the police. Is that all right?"

"Can you stay a moment?"

"Yes."

She lay beside him wrapped in his jacket for a full ten minutes, his hand gently stroking her hair, his weapon pointed at the recumbent Lardue. Finally she managed to say, "Mr. Muybridge, you sure lead an exciting life."

When Johny Lardue stirred, Muybridge handed Denise the pistol, loudly told her to shoot the dirty bastard dead if he moved a single inch, left the room for a moment, and asked his neighbor Todd Hundley to summon the police.

When the police arrived, Muybridge outlined the younger Lardue's blood grudge and explained how he had tricked Johny into firing off three rounds in his studio, then handed over the incriminating, ungrammatical note threatening his life. A fully clothed Denise verified Edward's account for the three policemen who then escorted Johny Lardue off to jail, but not before the sergeant turned to say, "Try to stay out of trouble for a while, will you, Mr. Muybridge?"

Alone in the quiet room, the two trembling, exhausted friends poured generous glasses of scotch and sat down side by side. A few drinks and a few hours later, Edward escorted Denise home.

To Muybridge's disappointment, Johny Lardue got only a seven-year jail sentence for attempted murder and other assorted crimes. (The D.A. could pin no murders on the younger brother.) But Muybridge figured the younger Lardue would not track him to the "civilized" East. Or if he did, Muybridge would confront the problem then. Besides, in seven years, who in the world knew where he would be? With no work in San Francisco, and no hope of contact with Holly, Edward took the one opportunity he'd been offered, the appointment to the University of Pennsylvania in Philadelphia. Before leaving, Edward made several attempts to visit Holly a final time. He wrote her, sending a score of notes declaring his undying eternal love. No reply. He lurked outside her rooms for hours, but never caught a glimpse of her. Finally, he stormed up to her door and stood trembling on her threshold. But, after what he had done, he could not force his way in. In any case, she wasn't there. Only Denise Faveraux knew Holly's hiding place, but Denise would not reveal the secret, saying only that Holly was traveling.

When Muybridge took leave of his friend Denise, he made a final attempt to find out.

"Holly said you must forget her." She looked almost demure in the full-skirted, blue satin dress. "Give her, give yourself a year or two or three. I know that sounds like forever, but by then who knows? Don't pity yourself, Edward," she said, laughing, and its tone seemed embedded with a raucous suggestion, as though throwing down a challenge to his theoretical renunciation of women, of sex, of love. Amazing to him that her laugh could be suggestive to him at this moment when existence had become a bottomless pit of despair. . . . The instant of relief passed, then universal bleakness rolled in like a mordant fog, obscuring all hope.

"I won't charge for the two-bit philosophy. Only promise one thing." He nodded; he could deny this woman nothing. "Stay alive and continue to do good work, so that you will be yourself—not a pathetic shadow of yourself—in case, in the odds-off, million-to-one shot, she ever changes her mind." There were tears in those sea-deep blue eyes.

"Am I to be hopeful then?"

"I can't encourage you on that one front, but of course be hopeful. How else can we live?"

Another good-bye took place that week—at the San Francisco harbor, as Holly was about to board the steamship that would take her around Cape Horn to New York, where she would board another ship that would carry her to Palestine and points East. (The irony, of course, was that if Stanford's railroad had been completed, she could've crossed the continent by train.)

The two women stood side by side. Denise was wrapped in elegant dark silks and Holly wore the maroon traveling cape she had brought from Paris, high kid boots, and a gray blouse with matching parasol. Her hair was pulled back, offering an unusual expanse of her handsome, sad face. She looked determined, her features set, reminding Denise of a woman who'd been walking into a headwind for weeks.

Denise feared that what she was about to say might destroy their friendship. Being brave, she gathered herself and plunged on. "I'm not here to play cupid, Holly, but he really loves you. I can swear to that."

"Not another word."

"He loves you. He's a stricken man."

"That's not enough!" she shouted, pulling scores of curious eyes their way.

Holly turned, imperious. Above them, the steamboat's horn blasted a throbbing, impatient note, filling the air with promise. Holly shook Denise's hand with chilly rigor, and was the first to break away. Denise looked searchingly at Holly then hugged her friend hard, as though reminding her of their past together. Holly wanted to deny Denise the intimacy, but instead her arms reached out and they clung together. They rocked back and forth in a deep embrace, as though trying to force their beings closer. Both women sensed they'd never see each other again.

"Oh, I'm about to liberate another Chinese prostitute. This is really going to drive them crazy. And I got a postcard from Sung Wan. She's working in a milliner's, about to be married. She said that she's working for the next generation."

Denise watched Holly board. They waved, and as the ship began to back out of its slip, attended by clouds of noxious, ill-favored smoke, Denise had one final thing to say. She ran alongside the slowly moving ship, her long hair streaming opulently in the late afternoon sun, shouting at the top of her lungs, "He loves you! Don't forget that!" Denise halted as the ship slowed to swing out into the harbor, and Holly came alongside the pier. high above her. "Edward loves you!" Every eye on land and on board fixed on Denise as she waved farewell to her departing friend.

Chapter Twenty-seven

Philadelphia was then the second largest city in the United States, with almost three times as many people as San Francisco. But to Muybridge, the City of Brotherly Love felt smaller than his former home—and also smug, complacent, stolidly set in outmoded ways. Philadelphia seemed as inflexible as its grid of streets, predictably punctuated with tree-lined squares, around which stood handsome centuries-old brick houses. Muybridge had rented rooms on Ludlow Street in a small, well-proportioned house. A fine Adams fan window quietly distinguished his front door. For Edward, the house was too orderly and neat, too low-ceilinged and diminutive, as though the architect had cut down the dimensions to convince the inhabitants that they were persons of scale and substance.

Though Thomas Eakins was temperamental, Muybridge liked the painter immediately. Eakins had tirelessly lobbied the trustees of the University of Pennsylvania to hire Muybridge for its School of Veterinary Studies. The painter had insisted that Muybridge's crime was a singular aberration that would never be repeated, and that the university needed his services to advance the standing of both its veterinary and medical schools. He, Eakins, would vouch for the photographer's sanity and conduct. Thomas Eakins was so persuasive that by the time Edward Muybridge arrived in Philadelphia in spring of 1869, the university had set aside two working areas for him—a sizable indoor space in the new gymnasium and, for temperate weather, a large, rubbish-strewn vacant lot behind the hospital. As per his instructions, the equipment he ordered was already in place, courtesy of the University of Pennsylvania.

Muybridge went to work as though in an enduring fog. The work nonetheless proceeded because Edward had imagined the three-angle photographic arrangement so often and thoroughly that he could have supervised construction in his sleep. He ordered a twenty-foot board runway built both inside and outside, and positioned a dozen cameras twelve inches away from one another, shooting at right angles to the path of the subject. He arranged a second bank of a dozen cameras at the far end of the runway with the third twelve aligned at a forty-five-degree angle to the subject's locomotion. This geometric triangulation would record all of the principal's movements, and the cameras could be relocated at will if the photographer desired different angles. As with the trotting horse, the camera shutters were operated by Montague's electromagnetic mechanisms. Thus Muybridge restarted his investigations into the physiology of human and animal motion.

In the beginning, he worked fourteen- to sixteen-hour days, laboring mightily to obliterate his past. His nights were troubled by visions of Holly and memories of his heinous crime. In odd leftover moments, Edward studied his photographs of Holly. Or he'd feebly draw her, trying to catch the pressure of the cheek, the fluidity of her calf, the maddening richness of her thighs, the fecund curvature of breast. He sketched her auburn hair, shading in the color as best he could, remembering the multicolored shifting highlights when she moved near or away from a lamp—as though each strand contained unlimited possibilities of color, texture, light gathering and diffusing. Or he'd try to capture the swelling of her lips, the comeliness of her eyes, never—with all his effort—getting them right. Not even close to right. Even with 412 photographs fanned out before him, Edward could not hold his vanished love entire.

On May 10, 1869, in a tiny hamlet named Ogden, in Utah, to the accompaniment of four bands and a rash of dignitaries, Leland Stanford lunged and missed his first stroke with the sledgehammer. On his second try the governor drove a golden spike into the final tie of the transcontinental railroad and, for the first time, the nation was truly joined. Muybridge avidly devoured the newspaper accounts, noting the rhetorical dreariness of the speakers who eulogized the triumph of the Union Pacific and Central Pacific's Big Four. He was not surprised that Theodore Lochlin provided the "official photographs," which were to be hawked around the nation as postcards at inflated prices.

When Edward reviewed the photos, he didn't need to comment about the execrable shot of Stanford brandishing his sledge next to T. C. Durant, president of the rival Union Pacific. Both faces were slightly blurred because of the tripod's movement. There was, however, a passable photo of a one-eyed Montague exchanging a manly handshake with the Union Pacific chief engineer, Grenville Dodge. Muybridge was puzzled by the absence of Collis Ward, a mystery cleared up months later when the photographer learned that Ward had died of influenza in the sierras at the age of thirty-two.

Over the next nine months and then for another year, Muybridge steadfastly photographed ponies, horses, an ox, a bull, a recalcitrant bear that had been retired from a traveling circus, two cows, three goats, and half a dozen dogs of various breeds. The animals walked, ambled, cantered, paced, trotted, ran, and leaped. Beasts of burden hauled. Birds, too, flew before his aligned three dozen indoor cameras. He felt himself a veritable Noah minus the ark, besieged like the roaring Biblical lush by a welter of noises and potent droppings as well as the vagaries of his beasts' temperaments.

In spite of the odds against success, Edward kept searching for a method to create a visual record of Holly's dancing. In Philadelphia he spent months researching all existing or proposed contrivances for recording motion, and he tinkered with his own primitive instruments, including a device for projecting a sequence of drawn images onto a screen. If the images followed one another quickly enough, they appeared to move, literally, to reconstitute motion.

At Eakins's suggestion, Edward began photographing male athletes in action: sprinting, jumping, fencing, tumbling, wrestling. He made twelve distinct sequential images of a gymnast in the act of performing a back somersault—the tension of the muscles, the takeoff, the gravity-defying airborne instants caught forever, and, to top it off, the man's balanced, symmetrical landing.

Work offered partial distraction but no balm. Holly occupied his thoughts to the exclusion of much else. But occasionally, watching an athlete storm down the runway with the pole raised in his hands and seeing the man deftly skewer the long metal bar into the chute, rise above the earth as he thrust his body vertically upward, then skim over the high metal bar, every once in several hundred exposures, a vaulter's precision or the fluid rhythms of a cantering horse or the elegant, articulated flight of a dove would bring Edward momentary relief from his guilt and gnawing emptiness. He would not allow himself to photograph women.

The university's board of trustees praised the photographs but, after two and a half years, they were becoming increasingly restive about the purpose and destiny of Muybridge's detailings of human and animal locomotion. What was to be learned, after all? Were these experiments not repetitive? And some board members vocally and frequently demanded to know why so many of his male models were naked or mostly naked. Muybridge replied, "Because that's the only way you can record and delineate anatomical structure." One disgruntled trustee questioned Fairman Rogers, board chairman and Thomas Eakins's patron, "Is this really science or just high class—and inordinately expensive—lasciviousness? If it's pornography, we should terminate this charade immediately and save the university thousands of dollars." Rogers defended Muybridge's experiments, "designed," the chairman quoted the photographer, to "scientifically document the entire range of human and animal locomotion." Still, an alarming number of board members were leaning toward pulling the plug on what had become, for them, an expensive indulgence.

Early in July 1872, three years after Muybridge trekked to Philadelphia, Leland Stanford's personal physician, Harold Stillman, published a volume of photographs featuring Occident and Mahomet and several other trotting and cantering and galloping thoroughbreds. Muybridge, who had perfected the mechanism, chosen the lenses, evolved the timing devices (with an indispensable technical nudge from Chief Engineer Montague), and taken every single one of the shots, was not mentioned on the title page. Edward did not locate his name until he thumbed through the large collection of his own photos leaf by leaf and found himself consigned to a solitary footnote on page 106 where he was denoted as, "Edward Muybridge, the technician who executed Governor Stanford's directives."

Muybridge stormed off to an expensive Philadelphia lawyer with a dramatically broken nose who counseled the photographer, "Sure, you might be able to win a lawsuit against him, but you must be prepared to spend six to eight thousand dollars, and probably more, in order to get me or any effective legal counsel to pursue the case. Stanford has unlimited resources, so it pays to be forewarned about what it will set you back." Muybridge decided to absorb this final injustice and hold on to his money—the paltry sum he had.

In spite of his anguish at the governor's self-serving lies, in spite of his struggle with the university, all these problems reached him as mere echoes of an immeasurably distant past. Edward lived as though submerged under fathoms of water. Looking up from below, he only dimly perceived life's passionate bombast and pain and maddening ambition. These echoes of the being he used to be filtered down to him through the transparent yet insulating substance.

Still, thoughts of Holly bled through—Where was she? Was she performing? Was she still restlessly roaming? Or had she alighted in a fortunate spot? Did the bright lights and fashionable soirees of Paris or Rome or London or wherever she landed evoke a new, gay, sparkling world for her? Was she modeling for a younger Gérôme? And, most torturous of all, did she love another, did another currently enjoy her incomparable favors?

Life did not stand still, but importuned in its cajoling ways. Eakins himself created a series of sculptures based on the anatomical positions of four horses pulling a stagecoach, and these clay sculptures, executed because he required a sense of the volumes he planned to paint, had to be critiqued by Muybridge before Tom could move on to the large, ambitious canvas of Fairman Rogers's matched four-horse team.

Rogers himself requested a photographic series anatomizing a boxer's movements as he punched and took a series of counterpunches, in an attempt to maximize one talented, young pugilist's future. The celebrated surgeon Dr. Samuel Gross respectfully approached Muybridge in order to better inform medical science about the nature and conduct of human musculature during various forms of intense physical exertion. These professional challenges helped poke time along through its tedious, slow-moving course. In this way, the year 1873 arrived.

Chapter Twenty-eight

In early April, Thomas Eakins invited Muybridge to be a guest at the painter's drawing class at the Pennsylvania Academy of Fine Arts. Muybridge walked north on the city's principal north-south avenue, aptly named Broad Street. On this fine spring day the sidewalks were thronged with fashionable strollers—colorful parasols twirled, setting off the multicolored outfits of the women; well-dressed and well-heeled gentlemen postured and smoked; lavish carriages rolled by. In spite of the festive atmosphere, Muybridge felt disembodied and unreachable, more ghost than man.

He halted in front of the Academy, impressed by the multicolored facade, the chunky brownstone blocks suggesting Renaissance rustication crossbred with the architect Frank Furness's whimsical gothic figurations. The exuberant stone and brick, the arches and pilasters and pointy medieval-style cutouts worked together to fashion a striking exterior. The bricks were laid as though to visually boast of the range of the bricklayer's craft—flat, diagonally, arrayed in diamond patterns, and also with their corners jutting out underneath a series of raised sculptural panels. Such eclectic, unabashed energy and unlikely grace—*America,* Muybridge thought, what extraordinary combinatory powers, an ode to native inventiveness and restlessness.

Holly appeared in his imagination—what clarity she possessed on that single night he'd watched her perform, the single-minded courage and unstinting devotion to her craft. Pampered by birth and wealth, yes, inflexible at times, but an unabashed American original. Unwittingly, he had teamed up with the enemy Stanford to diminish her possibilities. His was the ugliest crime, he judged—to taint that woman with a headline-spawning, tawdry tragedy, to reduce rather than elevate her. Through his hallucinations, guilt's whiplash rose and fell, rose and fell within his tender mind; the wounds were both suppurating and boring. Equilibrium resulted only when fatigue balanced pain.

He entered the Academy through a dimly lit foyer that flared from semidarkness into a three-story light-flooded courtyard. He paused in homage to the soaring space, weighing the thought—how little we initially perceive of the best creations. Even when one tries to open one's soul and be receptive, so much eludes the first glance. All truly interesting work—Holly would call it art—makes demands on us, confusing and stretching us. "And a good thing, too," he grumbled, the worst of his mood lightening a shade or two because of the eclectic setting and the pleasures of reflection.

Muybridge took the left fork of a regal double staircase up toward the airy, high-ceilinged hall. Above, a riot of color—thickly impastoed red and gold walls; paired columns of rose, black, and gray stone; a star-studded evening sky on a scintillating blue ceiling.

He entered a studio that presented a maze of sculpture—classical, Renaissance, and Baroque—displayed in no apparent order. The cool marble forms displayed the human anatomy in a variety of idealized, dramatic, or intimate poses. A dense congregation of students' plaster casts also stood in place, copied from Eakins's controversial animal dissections—a throng of skeletal depictions of horses, dogs, cats, even what must've been a lion festooned the space.

Students of all ages and, as Muybridge observed, a range of talents, industriously chipped away at their marble slabs, filling the air with a fine, diffused dust. Two or three students copied ingeniously, the remainder with stolid pedestrian hands. Yet Edward felt welcomed in the cathedral-like space, at home in the room where his pedagogue friend struggled to mold the next generation of American artists.

He heard his friend's high-pitched, slightly adenoidal voice. In a corner, the rail-thin Eakins lectured while gesturing at a large, run-of-the-mill copy of the Laocoön. His students seemed attentive, some even adoring, except for a pair of dapper young men hovering at the group's edge, backs angled away from their instructor.

Edward moved closer and heard Thomas Eakins declaim, "A big artist does not sit down monkeylike and copy a coal scuttle or an aged crone or a dung pile or a blooming young nude—if in our benighted country he is actually permitted to draw a nude. He keeps a sharp eye on Nature and steals her tools. He—and I mean 'she,' too—observes what Nature does with light—the big tool. Then the artist moves on to the rigorous study of color and form. Once you appropriate these tools for your tool bag, you can build a canoe strong and capacious enough for most artistic endeavors. In our canoes we can pick up a breeze and sail according to Nature's navigational rules. So everyone, please construct your own well-made canoe."

Eakins pointed to a copy of Velázquez's *The Weaver*, a painting he'd greatly admired in Madrid. "In a *big* picture like this, the alert observer can tell what o'clock it is, if it is hot or cold or windy or calm, if it's winter or summer, all because the artist has bothered to do the work that the casual onlooker—and the mediocre artist—misses. Your work should convey what kind of people are there, what they are doing and why. So why should we fuss and strain and grapple remorselessly with all these questions? To obtain accuracy and clarity and in order to reflect your vision of reality. *Your* vision, not your instructor's."

While students scribbled away in their notebooks, neither of the sleek, well-dressed youths jotted a note.

Eakins waved Muybridge over to join the group. "Our heroic guest." The two shook hands. "Edward Muybridge," Eakins introduced his friend to his pupils, "pioneer photographer, inspired innovator—a *big* artist."

Muybridge nodded modestly and looked beyond Eakins through colorful Moorish arches into the studio off the main gallery. There he acknowledged Albert Pinckney, a young athlete who often modeled for his photographs and who now posed for a life drawing class, prudishly draped below the waist with the loincloth so often ridiculed by Eakins. Of course Holly had posed undraped when modeling for Gérôme. Her body had been bared to the students' and the Master's eyes in unpuritan Paris. Emptiness dropped on him like a stone.

"After years of devoted work, Mr. Muybridge exposed Nature's capacious charms, presented a vision to us as magnificent and varied as Phidias's art itself. Muybridge has demonstrated that Nature possesses infinite moods and postures. Remember, 'the big artist' cannot be too rigorous a thinker or too scrupulous an observer. The world is literally his—or her—oyster or lobster or beefsteak, according to your taste." Scattered smiles, soft, slightly bewildered laughter.

Eakins indicated a copy of a celebrated discus thrower attributed to the Athenian master Phidias. "As I explained to all of you, even Messrs. Tyrone and Gustaf . . ."

Tyrone, the older of the two disaffected pupils, was employing a calipers to measure the toe of the discus thrower. He thrust the instrument into the air like a dagger, then guided the instrument into its sleeve as though sheathing a sword.

The painter continued, "Muybridge has analyzed movement more precisely than any artist or anatomist or philosopher ever. He is now attempting what was thought impossible—to project motion. Here is our national pioneer, a man devoted to stripping art of its straitjacket, allowing us room to expand our vision."

"Thank you, Mr. Eakins," Muybridge began, "for your kind, if overstated, introduction." He addressed the students. "Greetings." Turning away from the acolytes, Edward directed his remark to the pair of insouciant young men. "You are fortunate to have a gifted and devoted artist for a teacher."

Muybridge thumped down a thick volume of twelve-by-fourteen-inch stop-time trotting-horse photos on a table littered with wax models. The students surveyed Occident's musculature and the hinged motions of his lifting hooves and legs. "I'm wrestling with trying to create movement out of discrete images. The ultimate question is: Can I or can anyone synthesize action from still photographs?"

The eager upturned faces waited for an answer, a dramatic resolution of matters beyond their knowledge, like a constellation not yet spied. Internally, Edward turned contemptuous: None of these hopeful whelps could see the life-curdling disappointments that each would confront. Meanwhile, they impatiently anticipated wisdom, truth, beauty from him as casually as they would stroll around the block or light a cigarette.

"When I began shooting photos before the Southern Rebellion, I could only make immobile images. Why? Because exposures took minutes. Back then I could only photograph landscapes—or corpses. The slightest motion caused a blur." He held up two early shots—one an attempt to catch a bird in flight, the other a Modoc warrior's stringy hands straightening an arrow. Both presented badly smeared, barely discernible images.

"Today, because lenses are faster and take in more light in a shorter interval, exposures are sharper. I'm able to take photos of a galloping horse or an athlete sprinting or a tree falling. Recently Mr. Eakins asked me for images of men jumping, running, even throwing the discus."

"And he hands them to me just like that," Eakins snapped his fingers.

"Now I can provide visual prompts for Mr. Eakins's paintings. Now almost every few months my equipment—dry plates, shutters, lenses—gets faster. But making these photographs is only the start of exploring movement. The two *big* questions for me are: one, how to anatomize movement—how to break it down and depict how the subject moves"—he pointed to his celebrated photos of the trotting horse—"and two—and this has been driving me mad for years—how to *capture* and then also *project* the variety of ways in which creatures locomote." He produced his flip book of an athlete and demonstrated the art of pole-vaulting for his audience, then another flip book displayed the celebrated photos of Occident trotting. "The flip book is a lovely toy, but I face the final giant step to which I have no answer—I'm trying to put movement, or time, really, for they're interchangeable—back together again."

"Like dear old Humpty Dumpty," Nelly Pinto, a handsome, slender, black-haired student with dramatic hazel eyes, ironically chimed in.

"Exactly so, young lady." Something in her look—wistfulness, perhaps—caught Edward's attention. Just then Tyrone let loose a loud yawn.

"Muybridge has liberated art from its eternal stillness. That's an epic breakthrough. But don't be seduced, young friends. Photos are not literal descriptions of reality. Actually, they're brief, artificial interruptions of an indivisible flow. Muybridge and I have this argument often.

"Remember, painting from nature demands precision precisely because nothing anywhere ever remains the same. Light changes, a cloud slips its form and as it blows on turns into variegated shapes; that perfect, bucolic configuration of sheep on the hill always drifts toward sweeter grass—and alters location, form, light, and shadow. Everything metamorphoses forever, my lambs, because our world won't and can't stand still. Since time marches on, art, to be art, must suggest the flux; it should use this evanescence to be memorable."

He pointed to Muybridge's trotter. "In spite of my friend's stirring breakthrough, you cannot rely on photographs literally. Employ these wonderful counterfeits of reality to help nudge the eye and mind back to what you've seen outside, in Nature." Eakins pointed his tapered fingers toward raucous Broad Street and the world beyond the Academy. "Photos are limited, two-dimensional and black-and-white. Which isn't their fault. I'm not blaming the poor second-class citizens." Edward found this too cute. "What they can do is: one, jog memory; two, bring the past into the present; three, transport the outdoors indoors, which is invaluable; four, assist in providing the artist with observable detail; and five, help give the painter or sculptor a sense of a whole. Using these aids you can begin the arduous process of reshaping your vision of the world. Now that I've diminished the genre, don't forget that thanks to the man who's standing here, we can begin to make paintings *move* or *incorporate* or *imply* movement. Which, on some level, the entire nineteenth century has been about. That's no mean accomplishment."

Eakins signaled the students to follow and led them past copies of antique kouroi and the baroquely writhing Laocoön group and into the adjoining skylit studio where they halted to observe a small, elegant drawing on a worktable. The male figure was nude, but his genitals were blank. All the force, all the sight lines of the sketch converged on the white space—the man's missing parts. "Who made this drawing?" Eakins inquired appreciatively.

"Nelly did," a student replied.

"Miss Pinto, this is a skillful sketch, remarkably provocative. . . ."

Tyrone, who had lingered in Eakins's lecture room, snickered; a half beat behind, Gustaf chimed in with an overstated guffaw. Nelly Pinto looked wounded. Edward felt an impulse to horsewhip the young cynics, then checked it—no physical violence ever again.

Eakins responded more vehemently than Muybridge had ever heard him: "Before your interruption, Mr. Tyrone, I was about to say provocative *intellectually*. There's nothing lascivious here, anything but—except for those whose minds lie in the gutter. Miss Pinto's piece suggests that we ask the question that the Pennsylvania Academy won't sanction: What is missing from our pathetic, puritanical Philadelphia art? But Miss Pinto doesn't lecture; she lets us decide about the nature of the loss, the failure of candor and, yes, beauty. Nelly leads us to the brink, leaving the eye and the mind to puzzle out the answer. Outstanding work, Miss Pinto. Profound thanks."

"Thank you, Professor." A blind man could see that this young woman was smitten with Eakins.

Following their instructor, the class trooped over to the dais where Albert Pinckney, resting between poses, had slipped on a white cotton smock. The men shook hands then, at a signal from the drawing instructor, Pinckney stood, shrugged off the garment, and took up a standing pose. As before, a short drape—like a diaper—hid his groin.

"Here's a demonstration of the problem addressed by Miss Pinto." Tyrone groaned audibly. Eakins continued in a tense, sober voice. "The nude human body—male or female—is the architecture, the baseline, the ground on which Western art is based. Ignoring the body limits your training and growth as an artist and person. After all, we are all housed in these frames." Eakins talked to the class, but he specifically targeted his comments to Tyrone and his companion, offering the insouciant pair a chance to learn.

"You've seen Muybridge's photos of athletes moving, including this gentleman, Albert Pinckney. There is no false modesty, no turning aside in those shots."

"Nudity in antique statuary is one thing, Mr. Eakins," Mr. Tyrone broke in. "Remember, *sir*, the Greeks were pagans, not *Christians*. And, don't forget, these pagans glorified relations between men." Total silence in the room. "Requiring your students to pose without a stitch on is unseemly, not to say immoral. We all know that, as of Tuesday, the Academy board insists the practice must stop!"

"You know and I know that the students who *voluntarily* pose for one another are not wealthy enough to hire their own model, Mr. Tyrone. Do you realize that in the last two decades, two thousand American painters have studied at the Paris Academy of the Beaux Arts?" The sweep of his hand pointed to the Pennsylvania Academy's selectively harvested crop of nude marbles. "In Paris, every single day from dawn to dusk, students are required to draw from the most meaningful and transcendent of forms, the naked human body.

"As long as I am here, we will study *art* in this Academy, not prudery. Western art originates in Greece with the male nude, and it develops through numberless treatments the nude female. If a student is not mature enough to absorb this basic fact, there is still time to pursue another discipline."

"Is that a threat?" Tyrone asked, imitating the painter in a piping, high-pitched voice. He angled his head coyly to the side, giving his amateurish impression of a homosexual.

"Certainly not. I'm describing my pedagogy." A slight tremor vitiated Eakins's voice. "In a moment, I want everyone in the class to sketch this *seminude* male. But first let's thank Mr. Muybridge for his fine, informative visit."

Edward gathered up the photo books as students politely thanked him. He shook Eakins's hand and took leave of his embattled friend. One lovely young woman requested an appointment to watch him work. Edward lied, explaining that the Veterinary School would not permit visitors.

The photographer concluded his tour of the Academy by strolling among the statuary, examining antique, Roman, and Renaissance notions of human perfection. He walked under stone and marble copies of timeless grace—the bold, columnar kouroi as well as poised discus throwers and javelin hurlers and sprinters and a handsome stone lad sitting cross-legged and reaching down to pluck a bothersome thorn out of his high arching instep. Edward paused to admire Michelangelo's David and the surpassingly noble, horned Moses. The arrangement of the copies was not, as he first believed, without order. In fact, Eakins had organized evocative juxtapositions, Greek beside the Roman revisionists as well as figures paired and contrasted with Renaissance reinvention of human nobility in marble and stone. An encapsulated history of Western art, all present for students or the strolling visitor.

Yet, in spite of all that Thomas Eakins had provided—inspired instruction, exhaustive critiques of the student work itself, an informed survey of Western art—the Academy's Board had stated its displeasure with Eakins's "morbid insistence on dissection." And one powerful board member repeatedly complained about the painter's "obvious obsession with the male nude." An academic guillotine blade trembled over the head of Edward's only true friend in the City of Brotherly Love.

All through the tardy Pennsylvania spring Eakins created scores of sketches for "a big work," and by late summer Muybridge was spending a few hours every second or third evening with the artist, going over the day's output and occasionally advising on how to plot out and piece together a large, ambitious painting.

One evening the sketches of *The Gross Clinic*, on which Eakins had been working on and off for two years, were arranged on the dining table. Behind the painter stood a blackboard—the largest Muybridge had ever seen—where Eakins plotted the figures in chalk and rearranged them as he saw fit. The painting itself was based on Rembrandt's daring *Anatomy Lesson of Dr. Tulp*, which focused on the irresolvable tensions between "objective" science and inherently subjective human emotion. Eakins claimed he wanted to "update and Americanize" the classic scene. His painting was to represent the latest advance in surgical procedure as developed by the noted Philadelphia physician Dr. Samuel David Gross.

To Muybridge, the painter's process was like a jigsaw puzzle: the relationships of all the figures—surgeon, patient, patient's mother, surgical assistants, and the audience of shadowy heads observing the procedure in the amphitheater in the upper background—were painstakingly plotted and linked together on a perspective grid.

In his latest study the mother sat upright in an unyielding, straight-backed chair, her left arm flung instinctively in front of her eyes to ward off the sight of what was being done to her child. Her right hand was clenched, clawlike. The mother wore shabby, genteel black clothing and was, by implication, neither well off nor well educated, thus prey to exaggerated fears as she confronted the incomprehensibility of medical science. "She could've been a Hottentot in the operating theater," Eakins explained. "That's how little she could fathom of the procedure. Except for the irreducible gut feeling that her own flesh and blood is being ravaged."

Eakins indicated one pencil sketch of the central figure, Sam Gross. Still holding the bloody scalpel in his fingers, the surgeon looks up to the gallery at his colleagues and students to illustrate a point about the operation. The portrait had an accuracy that Muybridge himself had helped Eakins create by asking Doctor Gross to sit for a dozen headshots; those images of the doctor lay next to the drawing.

Edward leaned over and compared the drawing to his photos. What wasn't right? Eakins had captured the alert mouth, those weighty eyelids, the intriguing depression on the doctor's left forehead that seemed to telegraph the very process of thought; the latest drawing also caught the bushy gray curls that formed a wiry halo around his fine head. The figure had solidity, presence, gravitas—like the man himself. But something else—

"Painters like to say, 'A portrait is a painting with something wrong with the mouth.'" Eakins said.

"Don't be too abstract with him, Tom. I hate huge, pompous abstractions. Make him real, catch his spirit. He's your friend."

"Isn't he there?"

Muybridge said, "Down to the curls. But something isn't right." The light, that was it. Eakins's lighting was melodramatic—a plunging spray of light struck Gross as he delivered his medical opinion, spotlighting the confident, reflective face. It was too much, bordering on the sentimental. But that wasn't the entire problem.

"What? What?" Eakins asked, frustrated by Edward's critique.

"I know what's bothering me. Where is the light coming from?"

The way Eakins's lips compressed and looped, Edward knew he had fingered a sore spot. The painter knew that he'd fudged the light.

"Okay, tell me, where is the light source?"

"A skylight."

"We both know there is no skylight in the operating theater at Jefferson Medical College in central Philadelphia. Besides, no skylight I've ever stood under could throw that precise a stream of light."

"I put one in." Eakins temporized to protect his vision. All those hours of work, all that effort and retouching, and now, yet again, another major revision loomed.

Muybridge pitched Eakins's own dictum back at him: " 'Big paintings have to be credible.' " Doctor Gross stood in that blaring column of light like a latter-day saint. "Tone it down. No cheating. There's too much at stake." He realized after he'd spoken that Holly had charged him with a similar crime on the first day they'd met—the manipulated "night" photo of Woodward's Gardens with his "tricky" double-shutter apparatus.

Eakins riffled through the sketches. "I told you, the light is from the heavens."

"Indoors?"

"Art needn't be a slave to verisimilitude. Our friend Gross *is* a modern secular saint. He's as much a savior to our generation as Christ was to his."

"Talk about overstatement."

"He is," Eakins insisted petulantly, though the photographer could see the painter was acceding the point. "The good doctor relieves pain, he gives hope. He literally saves people's lives; he's brought more than a few back from the dead."

"How big do you think he should be?" Eakins's eyes scoured the drawing of Doctor Gross for other flaws.

"Three, four feet high?"

"Not bigger?"

"I don't think so."

"Life-size, he has to be life-size."

"Now, I need a favor from you," Edward said.

"Name it. Anything."

"I want to see reproductions of every painting Jean-Léon Gérôme ever painted."

"Done."

Days later, Muybridge viewed reproductions of most of Gérôme's paintings. And when he first saw *The Slave Market,* he began to understand why Holly had left the painter.

Gradually, day after day, week after week, the painting of Doctor Gross began to emerge from its tenebrous background. Sketches were refined, rejected, reconceived, re-revised, and each figure was painstakingly placed, fitted, adjusted to the grid. The grid on the blackboard that determined relationships of the forms reshifted as though rearranged by earth tremors, then, at last, stabilized. Muybridge watched the figures inflate from cartoons and small sketches to two-third life-size. Toward the end, a bodiless sea of spectators' heads seemed to float in the steeply raked operating theater. Just before completion, in the deep background, Thomas Eakins painted himself in the theater, sitting with lowered head at a desk, taking notes on the medical procedure. Like his idol Rembrandt Harmenszoon van Rijn, Thomas Eakins grabbed a ringside seat at his "big" work.

In June 1875, Eakins finished the massive painting, in time for the oil to be entered in the nation's Centennial Exposition art competition. By then his friend Muybridge believed *The Gross Clinic* was the finest painting ever painted in America.

Chapter Twenty-nine

Muybridge titled his first public demonstration of the device "Moving Pictures." A pantheon of colleagues, sponsors, and friends waited expectantly for the photographer: Thomas Alva Edison was there and Dr. Samuel Gross, the publisher J. B. Lippincott, Fairman Rogers, and, of course, Thomas Eakins. The editors of *The Philadelphia Photographer* and *Scientific American* were both present, as were a number of journalists and writers, including the white-suited, leonine Walt Whitman, whom Muybridge had first met in a Washington D.C., army hospital, looking on while the poet tenderly held the hand of a dying eighteen-year-old Union soldier. Whitman, irrepressible though partially paralyzed, was living in Camden, New Jersey, a ferry ride across the Delaware River from Philadelphia. The sixth edition of his storied volume, *Leaves of Grass*, had recently been published in a special edition to mark the first century of the American republic.

Since Muybridge's upcoming demonstration had been heralded in two elite scientific journals, physicians, anatomists, track touts, academicians jammed the large hall along with artists and writers and the curious. Whitman, looking around, quipped, "Not since the Continental Congress has Philadelphia assembled so much raw brain power." Whitman laughed raucously at his own joke as Edward Muybridge stepped on stage. Since arriving in Philadelphia, Edward had grown a full beard. Always thin, his face was lank, making the shelf of cheekbones still more prominent. As he leaned over the podium, those who had not seen the photographer before might have taken his patriarchal appearance for age. Indeed, though only thirty-five, Muybridge looked old because he felt old.

The expectant buzz of voices quieted as the photographer began, "The puzzling problem of projecting pictures in motion—what I've called 'moving pictures'—is solvable, *theoretically.*" Ah, the same word that had exasperated his coworkers during the struggle in Palo Alto.

"All one needs is a lens to focus images and a light source to project pictures onto a surface, and of course the images or pictures themselves." Muybridge produced an oversized flip book with drawings of a trotting horse and, resting it on the podium's edge, turned the first page toward his audience. Onlookers watched as Muybridge manipulated Eakins's sequential drawings and, as the pages streamed past, the horse trotted before the eyes of his public. "We've all enjoyed flip books since childhood."

Muybridge's assistant, Hubert Fell, handed him a familiar "visual toy," the bird and the cage. The bird was drawn on one side of a large cardboard circle; the opposite side held a drawing of a birdcage. Using an attached string, Muybridge rotated the cardboard back and forth. As the photographer twirled the card, the bird appeared to fly into the cage. "Doctor Gross," Muybridge asked, "will you please explain this phenomenon? Why does the bird appear to hop into then stay in its cage?"

The surgeon rose. In the gaslight, he appeared to be an underlit, slightly diminished version of Eakins's richly pigmented protagonist. "What Mr. Muybridge demonstrates here is what physiologists term *persistence of vision*. Briefly, when the retina is stimulated by images moving faster than about one-tenth of a second, the illusion of continuity results. As you can see, the still image appears to move."

"Thank you, Doctor Gross." He went on, "Ladies and gentlemen, I ask you to retain this concept of continuity of vision—the way the *mind* and the *eye* team up to create continuous motion—for a moment, please."

Muybridge produced a disk on which he had pasted drawings of his recent photographs of a solar eclipse. "Because the photographs themselves were so small, I've enlarged them for tonight's viewing. The actual shots were made during our recent eclipse at intervals of three, three, and two minutes and so on during its duration—at 3:46 P.M., 3:49 P.M., and 3:51 P.M., etc.—until I made twenty-one photographs. Now, please observe a most singular phenomenon: rapid changes in the shape of the crescent of light as the moon passes over the sun. In the first phase of the solar eclipse"—Muybridge pointed to his first drawing—"the horns of the crescent point south. In the course of the half minute during which this extreme occultation—ah, blockage—of the sun occurs, the horns of the crescent reverse position until they point north to the zenith." He paused, then declared, "Here for your delectation, ladies and gentlemen, is a complete eclipse of the sun." Holly had always considered him too much of a huckster. *What,* he wondered, *would her reaction be tonight? If only she were here to see this event. What a pleasure, what an inspiration, relief, salvation she would be.* Then he spun his disk.

By rotating the wheel, Muybridge made the crescent horns reverse from south to north: Before the audience's enchanted eyes the sun disappeared and then reappeared.

"Enough of child's games. Now I'll unveil the device which is the reason for tonight's gathering."

The photographer rolled his apparatus onto the stage apron. "I call this slovenly looking contraption 'the zoopraxiscope' or 'the animal motion machine.'" Muybridge's creation appeared to be part sewing machine, part wood cabinet anointed with two horizontal rods cantilevered in front like horns. The projecting lens, which stood detached from the larger mechanism, resembled an elongated metallic eye. "The zoopraxiscope combines a projecting lantern, which is fueled by the oxyhydrogen light contained in these gas cylinders." Edward indicated the horned lamp and the two cylinders at its base. "And here is the rotating glass disk on which the images are placed sequentially. My friend Tom Eakins kindly consented to produce eleven hand-painted silhouettes for this demonstration, and the silhouettes themselves were adapted from my photos of Occident trotting, which some of you already know."

Muybridge found his presentation dull, plodding. Unable to discover the flow, frustration blocked his speech. He felt an irresistible impulse to scream belligerent words at his auditors' ignorance of how arduous this cursed process was, how the days of his life had ebbed out into the photos, the daily ego-shriveling sequence of failure after failure that marked the quest which, shortly after his great triumph in Palo Alto, had ended in self-created catastrophe. Afraid he was going mad, Muybridge gestured to Eakins, who, seeing something amiss, took over.

"Each painted image had to be attenuated ever so slightly because, we learned from sad experience, as the glass disk turns, the shapes elongate. I had to correct for that attenuation or these images would appear squashed. That's why they look a bit peculiar when they're at rest."

Eakins turned back to the photographer, uncertain if he should continue buying time for his friend. Meanwhile, Muybridge struggled to control himself. Then he noticed Edison scribbling in a slim leather diary, and that brief notation saved Muybridge.

Still tense, Muybridge picked up the thread. "I designed two disks, one covered with precisely spaced images; the second, a counter-rotating, slotted disk. The latter disk acts as a shutter, cutting off all light for an instant, which is necessary to create the perception of intermittent motion and also to eliminate blurring." He did not mention that the slotted disk revolved at eight times the speed of the other. Too much detail, he thought. Edison scribbled feverishly now.

Relieved to be finished with the preliminaries, Edward ended by saying, "Hubert, please turn down the lights."

The room gradually dimmed as the gas lamps were lowered. The audience sat in blackness listening to the projector cough and sputter and whir as Hubert ignited the gas cylinder. Then, miraculously it seemed, a stream of light flashed before the assembled: an intense expanding funnel leaped across the darkness and drew a white circle on the blank wall behind the photographer. Immediately, a horse, almost life-sized, appeared —really, a drawn silhouette of a horse—and began to pace across the screen.

The onlookers sucked in an audible exultant breath. Awed murmurs shuttled around the packed room. "Impossible!" "Marvelous!" "It's magic." "Black magic." "No, light magic," one wag responded. "Have you ever seen anything like . . . ?" An instantly minted reverence spread through the audience—the distinguished, intelligent, worldly-wise men and women knew they were in the presence of a technological breakthrough, yet another earth-changing modern advance as great, perhaps, as the steam engine or the harnessing of electricity. Each individual viewing the images cast by Muybridge's projector would never forget this evening. They'd buzz and brag about it for years, like veterans after a decisive battle, conscious that they'd been self-selected as participants in the epochal event.

Edward tried to mute his triumph to keep it to himself, but he felt as he had that afternoon at the Palo Alto stock farm: in tune with the universe. Of course the feeling would pass. For the moment he rolled it delectably around in his mouth. As the pictures played, he couldn't help commenting, "You'll see God's own creation walk and trot, gallop and fly. Men will wrestle and run and leap before your eyes." Glib showmanship, but so what? For the moment, Muybridge was not at war with himself.

As the demonstration continued, to all eyes it seemed as if actual living creatures traversed the screen—a horse pranced with syncopated strides then, with the swift insertion of a new disk, stretched its legs into a rolling canter. A deer bounded across their fields of vision with undulating, airborne grace, each stretch and gather of its muscles and limbs outlined with startling clarity. Then a lovely dove winged gracefully over the gray, measured background grid.

Standing at the edge of the projector's light, with Edward's shadow occasionally cast like an omnipotent genie onto the screen, he literally became a part of the first motion pictures ever seen. Thomas Edison avidly watched as the enchanting ark of animals paraded by. Edward pointedly thought, if Edison were interested in helping him perfect the zoopraxiscope, his financial future would be assured. For Edison, clever as he was, had even greater genius as promoter and businessman.

Edward studied Edison closely as silhouettes of gravity-defying athletes soared through space—a runner sprinted; an acrobat executed a backflip; a solid, muscular figure (Albert Pinckney himself) hurled a twenty-pound stone as effortlessly as if it were a baseball.

Afterward, the room erupted in thunderous, sustained applause. Men and women rushed to shake his hand; several dubbed him "brilliant," "a genius," "a great benefiter of humankind." One labeled him "our national treasure." In the midst of his greatest triumph, Muybridge felt strangely numb. Acknowledging the nonstop fulsome praise, Muybridge reviewed the status of his once acclaimed, breakthrough photos of Occident the pacer. Today they were not legally his own but belonged half to Stanford and half to Stanford's private physician, who had never drawn focus or mixed touchy collodion on a wet plate or squeezed the release on a shutter. Authorship? Who remembered? And who in the world gave a good goddamn? A name in a gazette, a day or two, if lucky, in the newspaper, then . . .

Edison was one of the last to reach Muybridge, but others deferentially cleared a path for him. Clean-shaven and of middle height, Edison was square-faced, with a splayed nose and penetrating brown eyes. The mouth turned down, which made him look dour until he smiled his carefree farm-boy smile. As they shook hands, Muybridge noted that the Wizard of Menlo Park possessed an iron grip.

"Mr. Muybridge, sir," Edison opened buoyantly; others crowded in, anticipating that each word would be of historic import. "I have rarely been so impressed. I'd like us to meet as soon as possible—say, Thursday—to discuss your brilliant, timely invention and, among other potential applications, explore the possibility of mating my new phonograph with your pictures in motion." Newspapermen jotted fervently, people exchanged weighty looks as they vicariously basked in the aura of the paired geniuses.

Edison turned to the reverent crowd. "In a sense, the entire century has been an attempt to synthesize movement and exhibit it. Tonight we all witnessed an event that in a less-enlightened era would have been described as Satan's magic. Who knows, in the Middle Ages they might have burned Muybridge at the stake." That drew hearty laughter. "But the only magic here tonight is the great and true magic of scientific invention leavened with an abundance of determination and the indispensable teaspoon of inspiration."

The banquet provided relief for the photographer. The wine and acclaim, the smiles and congratulations pushed his personal anguish into the wings for a good portion of the evening.

He awoke to banner headlines: "EDISON AND MUYBRIDGE TO JOIN FORCES—AMERICA'S SCIENTIFIC GENIUSES LOOK AHEAD TO 'PICTURES OF MOTION.'" He rushed out into the street and bought up multiple copies of every newspaper he could get his hands on—there were ten dailies in Philadelphia. Every front page carried headlines and artist's renderings of the historic meeting. Edison and Muybridge, Muybridge and Edison. That had a seductive ring to it.

Edison's extensive Menlo Park facility was crammed with equipment —workbenches topped with delicate glass retorts and test tubes and slim beakers, metal rods and vises and lathes and cams along with improbably thin filaments and heavy welding apparatus, all the moving machinery powered by overhead leather belts that ran the length of the cavernous 400-by-100-foot space. Edward was given the "grand tour" by Robert Dugan, a lively Irishman who was a chief Edison aide. As they passed men at workbenches and inside curtained cubicles, Dugan discoursed about his mentor's revolutionary stock ticker and the electric pen that made multiple copies of documents "Right on the spot, Mr. Muybridge," as well as the latest developments in electricity and the new phonograph. The idea of multiple copies was so like Edward's attempt to photograph San Jose's documents that he mentioned the failure to the irrepressible Dugan, who growled, "Politicians, what do they know?"

Edison's private office was reminiscent of the Flying Studio—an enormous amount of material systematically stowed and densely packed into minimal space. The orderly bookshelf bristling with reference books, the latest scientific journals stacked in aligned piles, the spotless laboratory apparatus arrayed by the wet sink next to the window, all spoke of compulsive mental order. On the large desk lay a notepad, three sharpened pencils, and a fat, odd-looking fountain pen, perhaps the electric pen Dugan had lauded. Behind the desk sat the inventor himself.

Edison's acute brown eyes rapidly surveyed the photographer. The eyes were not dismissive, but they were not warm. "Your device is brilliant, Muybridge," the great man began, indicating a low, straight-backed chair to the right of the desk (Edison always sat higher than the chair's occupant). "You've solved virtually all of the vital questions: how to project the images with the illumined throw of that clever gas cylinder, the lenses, and the shutter mechanism, how to capitalize on the intermittent nature of vision with that one lens geared to rotate at one-eighth the speed of the other." Mr. Edison had done his homework, Edward thought.

"We're very impressed, Muybridge, very impressed. You've made a great contribution." Edison let Muybridge bask briefly in the warmth of his spotlight, then the tone altered—as though the light beam had dimmed. "The single remaining problem is the limited number of images your disk can contain. We think that the zoopraxiscope won't be commercially practical unless you can radically increase the number of images. The viewing experience must last longer."

Muybridge felt bludgeoned. "Too brief," he echoed, recognizing the truth of the inventor's statement, his heart leaping into a void. While the heart plunged downward, downward into bottomless space, Muybridge offered a feeble self-defense, "We've begun to enlarge the disk to hold two dozen frames."

"A dozen, two dozen frames repeating in a closed circle is dazzling for this moment, but the entire performance can only last—what?—a minute, minute and half at most. Then what?" He paused as though readying to execute the coup de grâce. "As I explained, I intend to combine the phonograph with a mechanism that projects pictures in motion. Two, three, even five minutes will not be enough for tomorrow's audiences." Edison declaimed this with Old Testament certitude.

Muybridge's body was coated in sweat. He felt the chill of a flu victim. In the three-day interlude between Edward's widely acclaimed presentation and this wildly disorienting interview, Thomas Edison had reviewed the pluses and minuses of the zoopraxiscope and detected its singular flaw. Muybridge understood that he could not compete with Edison, with these satellite armies of chemists and engineers and tool- and die-makers the inventor had clustered around him. For Edison was right—this disk with its childlike cylindrical format locked Edward into a dozen or two dozen images forever, and, in the long run, that would not do.

Muybridge could actually hear the Menlo Park facility humming like a turbine, its industry pulsing around him as he sat frozen in the low chair. Somewhere a stylus dropped onto a surface and encoded patterns of sound vibrations played back with uncanny fidelity. Somewhere in the vast warehouse of ideas a slender filament trapped inside a glass-cased vacuum glowed as a hand-cranked generator turned. A magic pen scribbled. Here was a promised land where Edison and his team shaped the future, a factory to transmit comfort and pleasure and entertainment into people's lives while making ever larger mountains of money.

Edison, the analytic entrepreneur, had looked ahead, betting that this projector of images had enormous potential. What the commercial applications were he had not yet divined. All that the Muybridge format lacked was a method of projecting more images, a sequence of visuals that could continue, *theoretically,* forever. His mistake was to rush ahead heedlessly and make his device public before the ultimate problem was solved, a problem, he had to admit, he didn't really know existed until Edison revealed it to him. But Edward had mindlessly, enthusiastically, characteristically handed the New Jersey Wizard the key he needed.

For form's sake, Muybridge asked, "I've been working on this for five years now, but I still don't have a practicable system for expanding the number of images. Perhaps together . . ."

Edison's mind was already careering ahead, working on that problem along with a host of others. "We'll contact you, Muybridge, if we need your participation. Right now we need to clarify some of our own ideas. Mr. Muybridge, it's been an absolute pleasure."

The powerful hand was icy, the smile as indifferent and as firmly affixed as a postage stamp.

Back in his bachelor cell, sitting before an ill-drafting, smoky fire, Muybridge knew that as long as one lives, one can never utter with finality, "This is the worst." Failure can conquer all, and all the momentary, hard-won triumphs are as nothing—less than nothing—since, by their perverse and innocent optimism, they only mock one's current despair.

Muybridge felt positive about one thing: He hadn't revealed to Edison the existence of the photographer's new "motion camera," as he called it, which took thirty views of moving objects on a single photographic plate. He was also working on a new disk that would project thirty images. Though, of course, in his Delphic mode, Edison had already declared thirty or forty or even fifty insufficient. But Edison might be wrong. Why, thirty or forty images certainly could convey a sense of the subject in motion. Why would anyone be interested in sitting in the dark watching pictures move for twenty or thirty minutes, even an hour?

Muybridge took up sculling again. He did so to get back into decent physical shape and to accompany his friend Eakins, who was an accomplished oarsman. But mostly Muybridge tortured his body on that insistent sliding rack to exhaust himself, a state he devoutly desired. Edward remembered, all too clearly, Holly's firm hand on his stomach when she declared he needed "tensile" strength. He frequently recalled with hot sorrow the liberated lovemaking that followed their impassioned wrestling match. Against his better judgment, the photographer laid out his several flip books of Holly—Holly walking, Holly dancing, most stirringly, Holly taking off a long white dress. He masturbated to them compulsively, wildly, hopelessly. But the difference between their lovemaking and his erotic self-communings became too much for Edward to bear. So he stashed the moving photos of his love on a high shelf in a closet for what he assumed would be forever.

Eakins painted two portraits of the photographer and often sketched him. A sculling Muybridge appeared in the backgrounds of Eakins's muscularly elegant paintings of oarsmen on the Schuylkill River.

In the spring Eakins finished another big work, *The Swimming Hole*, which went on display at an avant-garde Walnut Street gallery a half block from fashionable Rittenhouse Square. It was an outrageous painting, one that presented five linked nude males, each based on an idealized Greek form. (Muybridge could have led a tour through the Pennsylvania Academy sculpture gallery and pointed out four of the corresponding classical marble sculptures. The figures owed a portion of their verisimilitude to Muybridge's photos as well.) The young men stood or languorously stretched on granite boulders or plunged into the water, each nude body tightly related to the others in homage to the classical frieze. One boy stood waist-deep in water that barely covered his groin. Another young man, the tour de force figure, remained suspended in air, caught in the act of diving—from the textured background of a vernal forest into the inviting aqua water. And there, in the middle of the large canvas, the cramped fingers of one fellow's left hand are raised and reaching for, almost touching, the dimpled buttock of the youth to his right. This standing figure's back is turned, weight shifting forward, hips cocked, the fissure of the butt clearly visible—and available. The eye dwells on the hand reaching up to the bare ass crack running down. (The reference to God's omnipotent finger in the Sistine Chapel further compounds the painter's blasphemous irreverence.) *No loin-hiding draperies here,* Muybridge reflected with glee. But also with profound concern, because his friend was about to call down the wrathful local powers upon himself. And just whose behavior did that recall?

As Eakins had devotedly slaved over the painting, Muybridge played devil's advocate—Wasn't the outstretched hand too overt, too suggestive? And self-incriminating? Daringly, outrageously, Thomas Eakins had painted himself swimming out of the lower right-hand corner toward his handsome group of nude lads.

"You know, Tom, you're handing in your resignation. As soon as Philadelphia sees this, the directors will want your head."

Eakins responded flatly, "That's the idea, fool—a sense of beauty leads us astray."

The suggestiveness wasn't lost on the art critic for the *Daily Ledger*, who declared *The Swimming Hole* "disgustingly salacious. The painting overtly celebrates the sins of sodomy. It is without question the most ignoble and immoral painting of our nineteenth century." Most of the public was outraged, too. Muybridge had been right all along—Holly and Eakins would've enjoyed each other.

Late one night Eakins and Muybridge stood in the painter's dining room in front of the heavily used blackboard examining a sketch by Nelly Pinto.

"Well, she's a beauty, that's undeniable," Eakins said.

"She's intelligent, she has a unique sensibility." Muybridge braced himself for the painter's reaction as he continued, "She's gifted and very much in love with her mentor. What more could a man ask for?"

Eakins coolly replied, "I'm not certain about her talent." His gaze slithered away from the photographer.

"Oh, you're right about that, Tom, unlike someone I know, she probably isn't the contemporary Rembrandt." It seemed odd to Muybridge to advocate this match, but he felt Miss Pinto's need, and he understood Eakins's loneliness better than the painter himself. "But she can draw like an angel, as we see here." He indicated her self-portrait, a blooming yet unsentimental representation. "And, more importantly, she can think and feel. She has commitment and the desire to learn—the attributes you stress that are indispensable for an artist."

"I suppose it's selfish of me—"

"It is."

"I can't marry. It's absurd."

"She loves you." Muybridge wanted to say, *Maybe love will come for you, too.* Eakins sighed, his eyes still skirting Muybridge's. "I imagine you can keep a portion of your freedom. She wants to be with you, to share time with you, to grow old with you. What's wrong with that impulse?"

"Nothing," Eakins demurred, casting his eyes along the delicate lines of the self-portrait as if searching for an answer there. "It's deeply flattering."

"She will help you, you know. She'll pad the isolation, make it more bearable."

"Sometimes it's lonelier to be with another person."

"I'm not ignorant about that question." Muybridge hesitated, feeling the weight of his presumption. He understood what his friend meant. Yet solitude was no safe haven either. Muybridge trusted and believed in Nelly Pinto's devotion to Eakins. "Don't throw away such a fine person's devotion, Tom. And don't, for Christ's sake, hide behind that huge, overwrought abstraction you like to call art. I hate the goddamn term. Whatever rewards *art* offers, I'm convinced life holds more—more diverse, more surprising, more human, funnier too. And you're incredibly lucky, deserving, too, yes, but you do not have to choose between them."

Sorely pained, Eakins broke out, "How can I marry any woman, especially one as fine as Nelly? Isn't it unfair to her?"

Muybridge did not respond immediately. He carefully examined his heart before he spoke. "No, it's not unfair, Tom. The question is only about two people's closeness and compatibility. They are the telling issues."

They left it at that.

* * *

Edward had his minor pleasures and a moderate triumph or two. One afternoon he visited the racetrack and witnessed a race in which two horses crossed the finish line in a dead heat. For over an hour, he waited along with hundreds of others for the judges to decide the winner. They could not. That left the purse frozen, which led to a mini-riot, with track officials running about with megaphones trying to calm the belligerent crowd. While the yelling and the destruction continued—rowdy fans tore down the inner track's railing and recklessly threw the wood around while several thrust and parried at one another with improvised swords—Edward strode into management's lair and presented them with a plan. They accepted eagerly. Two weeks later, he'd perfected a camera to take instantaneous photographs at the final pole. The innovation was widely applauded and publicized, earning him royalty payments as well. In an earlier incarnation, Edward would've been ambitious enough to patent the invention and sell the device to multiple racetracks. But not now. He had his university stipend and the work, and that was enough.

Often his mind felt like a balloon cut from its tether: He'd created the apparatus to capture the trotting horse but, because of Stanford and the arriviste Dr. Stillwell, the published photos did not bear Edward's name. He was the first in the world to create a motion picture camera and projector, yet fate condemned him to remain an afterthought, if anyone bothered to give him any thought at all.

He worked steadily at the studies of human and animal locomotion. Through 1875 he noted with escalating interest the extreme oddity of certain individual poses he caught in a single frame. He became a connoisseur of awkwardness, of the disturbing, the grotesque. Sometimes Muybridge would transfer his most bizarre photos onto a disk of the zoopraxiscope, synthesizing the inept, isolated gesture into surprisingly graceful movements. But he alone viewed these transformations.

He negotiated an arrangement with the Philadelphia Home for Incurables and spent two months photographing the malformed and the diseased. He produced nine hundred startling images, a vision of a physiological and mental dark side of life that, until his exhibition, remained unglimpsed by the American public. He peopled the gallery with long, bloodless faces, bulbous noses, curiously unfinished features united with undersized eyes oddly situated in the cheekbones. The photographs created a sensation in the small Chestnut Street gallery where they appeared, reviving Muybridge's penchant for controversy. One angry article labeled him "Philadelphia's Perverse Photographic Voyeur."

When pressed for explanations about human locomotion by university trustees or outraged citizens or eager newsmen, Edward earnestly replied that he shot all his specimens for "scientific investigation." In fact, a number of his younger male subjects reminded him of what it was like to move buoyantly and unscarred through life.

Edward's open wound healed, leaving the scar which, in certain mental weathers, he fingered obsessively. Over time, the self-lacerating bouts of anguished memory occurred less frequently. At his best, Edward kept faith with Denise's insistence that he retain his work and his pride. So, miserable as he was, he clung to some faint vestige of who he once had been—just in case.

Chapter Thirty

Holly Hughes spent the better part of five years traveling—first to the Ottoman Empire, which she'd visited with Gérôme eight years earlier. In Istanbul, where she paid patient homage to the treasures of the Topkapi Palace, Holly particularly admired the tile work, relieved by the nonrepresentational beauty of the art. Gazing at the abstract floral patterns on the walls and in splendid, sun-drenched courtyards, she would lose herself for hours following the intricate weave of hauntingly vibrant colors and flowing lines that, mazelike, went on forever. She considered choreographing a dance using the intertwined motifs, but no inspiration came. With Clarence Godwin, a sprightly septuagenarian uncle on her father's side and an English diplomat who had been posted to Athens years before, she traveled on to Palestine and select parts of North Africa. Denise's letters reached her sporadically, and it was after spending a month with a Bedouin tribe that Holly read about the completion of the transcontinental railroad. Months later in the Himalayas, she scaled mountains higher than she had ever dreamed of, trekked through passes on the top of the world where the gelid air bit into the lungs as sharply as a scimitar. Here the news of Muybridge's triumph with the zoopraxiscope arrived, and, six months later, in Peking, she read Denise's report of his crushing disappointment with Edison. All through her sojourn, Holly was haunted by her inability to make permanent her fleeting impressions of the strange and changing worlds she encountered. Then she went back to North Africa to face herself.

In Tangiers, where she'd stayed for a month with Gérôme eight years earlier, she bought a camera fitted with a Dallmeyer lens. The irony tore her in two. She stayed there a fortnight photographing the Arab quarter with mixed results. She made pictures of the site of her humiliation, the courtyard in the souk where in the painting she had stood naked. Gérôme had depicted the Arab trader prying open her mouth to inspect her teeth while three fully robed men looked on lasciviously or indifferently and a sleeping dog splayed in the dust nearby. The buyer had obscene, overlarge hands, his fingers probing her palate, violating her mouth in the act of vetting her two front teeth. Of course she hadn't posed naked outside in front of three men. No, all her sessions were indoors, in a rented studio. He had surreptitiously introduced the slave buyer and the seller and that third young man later, after she'd finished posing. Gérôme was occasionally secretive about his big paintings—Holly had seen only a few preliminary sketches of *The Arab Market,* which was what he'd called it originally, but she'd had no idea it was she who was for sale; and that iron collar around her neck, with three men invited to partake of her disgrace, he must've used another model to pose for those details.

So she hadn't fathomed the extent of her exploitation until he unveiled the painting in Paris for that gross hog of a German collector with the lank, dirty hair whose eyes leaped back and forth from the painting to her, delving for the naked flesh under her thin dress.

In the painting, Gérôme shrunk her down, leaving Holly shorter than the men. Her head tilted toward the slave buyer—she hated that abject tilt. The viewer's eyes were led down from Holly's forcibly opened mouth to the full breasts—the fleshlike nipples, *her* nipples, were composed of fifteen or more paint layers—to the pussy, which was thrust forward, bare. She had shaved for him, the one and only time she'd submitted to that. The angle of her naked thighs, the all-too-suggestive curving forward advertised her availability to any and all comers. Most obscene was her skin's creamy whiteness—an oversweet confection, all too white against the exotic olive and brown skins of the men.

A younger man (the buyer's son?) stands just behind the older man's shoulder, not even bothering to look at her. His posture suggests that he is in no hurry; once his father has finished, he'll toy with her for as long as he cares to.

Even now, seeing the painting in her mind, she relived the overt display of her sexual need, the blatant, boastful statement that Gérôme could hand her on to whomever had an interest. So had the master defiled her, subjecting her to violence without raising a finger. It went sour after that. She went to stay with Jacques partly to punish the older man. In doing so she trumped the old man's visual prostitution of her. So this was her bold, revolutionary credo of free love?

Stalking through the sprawling, secretive market and narrow, winding alleyways, camera in hand, she could not evade Edward's influence. It was as though he were leaning over her that first time in the red-rimmed valley, laying the camera's squeeze bulb in her palm. Each time she shot in the souk—the spots where she chose to stand, the angles that appealed to her, the disposition of light, the framing—she couldn't escape his eye.

Holly Hughes arrived in Paris in June 1874, three years after the Commune had been overthrown and merciless repression destroyed France's latest revolution. The conservative government of Adolphe Thiers ruled as though it had been in place for decades. To her surprise, Holly discovered that most of her old friends, even the radicals and the former avant-garde, were pleased to accept the stability and prosperity of the Third Republic.

The beautiful city's formality seemed alien. Paris was undeniably stately and handsome, with its elegantly proportioned plazas, manicured public gardens, and multitextured cobblestones. But the City of Lights felt oddly cramped and overdefined. Everyone wore his or her appointed costume—the gentlemen in frock coats and monocles crowned by top hats or bowlers, the women in long dresses and those abhorrent waist-pinching corsets, still. The street cleaners were decked out in blue denim, gendarmes sported short navy capes, butchers were apportioned leather aprons. A glance told the observer volumes about occupation and class and caste. Mystery and wildness were banished here. Holly looked in vain for a ten-gallon Stetson or the trapper's raccoon cap with its dangling striped tail, but none ever hove into sight along the wide, tree-lined boulevards.

One afternoon in the winter of 1874 she lunched at Café Guerbois with Philippe Lavoix, Fauconier's former partner and one of Paris's leading art connoisseurs. They spoke of Jacques, but he was also curious about Muybridge, and Holly found herself telling him about their courtship, their life together, and their affection for each other—before the murder. When coffee arrived, Lavoix asked, "How was Jacques the last time you saw him?"

Hard question to answer. "He couldn't have been more himself."

"And Gérôme, tell me, how was he the last time you saw him?"

She saw where his interrogation was heading, but Holly would not duck the inevitable. "Gérôme was himself, too, as you know. But he was outraged that I was leaving him, that I wanted Jacques, too, that the demeaning painting—"

"Oh, I remember," he interrupted. "There was a fight."

"Just short of a duel," Holly said, her throat constricting.

"Yes, I intervened with the old man. Don't *you* remember?" Philippe's eyes never left hers. Holly felt trapped, skewered.

Philippe pressed, "Later Jacques asked you to marry him, yes?"

"I couldn't." She almost pleaded with Philippe now. "He was too jealous, too overbearing."

She knew what her old friend Philippe was thinking: *You broke the old man's heart and for an encore killed Jacques. And you have the nerve to pretend that you are not responsible.* That was what Holly read in his unforgiving eyes.

She stood and abruptly walked out of the restaurant, took a carriage home, sobbing all the way, all the time regurgitating Philippe's justified rage, the scalding look that cursed her for the death of his life-loving friend, partner, alter ego. She could not fault Philippe. For his reaction was more tolerable than the response of others—Madeleine du Guy, for one. Du Guy and other old friends treated Holly with a cool, velvet-gloved condescension, as though she had been recently released from a mental asylum.

She visited several of her favorite places—the Louvre, where she had listened so attentively to Gérôme as they admired the da Vincis and Bellinis and Titians. She dined at restaurants where she and the painter had dined. But nearby was always one of Jacques's places—the Bistro de Compagne, La Madrigale for late supper. Paris was haunted by two uncongenial ghosts.

With Hilaire Haas, an old painter friend, and his young mistress, Yvette, Holly spent an evening at the celebrated music hall, Moulin de la Galette, where she watched the cocottes stagger through their routines in cloddish disarray. They moved on to the Moulin Rouge, where the management passed off similar ineptitude as the latest in dance. After too many glasses of champagne, Holly hatched a plan to train the dancers, and a month later she opened a school. But only a handful of the young women attended with any regularity, and, after spending too many francs to outfit the studio, Holly was left a good many hours of the day with a large, mostly empty space. The investment in the lease and the renovation had one advantage—it coerced her into dancing again. For the next two months she practiced, working herself back into condition and slowly preparing for the arduous solo roles she had invented. Two months stretched to six months and on into a year, and still Holly told herself she was not yet ready for a public performance.

Meanwhile, she lectured on women's issues—dress reform; the necessity for exercise, particularly dance; the perils of the corset. The response was polite, a trifle bored; with so little resistance or interest, it felt as though she punched at air. For some, she, not her message, was the chief attraction—the scandalous free-love advocate and dancer whose French paramour had been murdered in California by her American lover. To Holly, her public pronouncements came back like faded echoes of earlier, more passionate enthusiasms, not because she lacked fervor and commitment but because her words had less resonance here. Few Parisian women would risk their social position by speaking out about equality for their sex.

One incident seemed to her to typify how little Paris cared about her cause. Around eleven one evening Holly left her studio and took a carriage to the Nouvelle Athenes, a fashionable café on the Left Bank, a few doors away from the restaurant where she had regularly dined with Gérôme. Stepping down from the carriage, she noticed Hilaire Haas and a group of artist friends entering the place. As she swept through the door a few steps behind them, the maître d' halted Holly. "But, Madame," he said, "you cannot enter without a companion."

"I don't understand."

"All women must be escorted."

"You are telling me that I must have a male escort to enter this establishment?"

The man offered an oily grimace in reply. "That is correct."

"You're joking."

"I'm afraid I am not."

Annoyed, Holly drew herself up to her full height. She had four inches on him. "Please call the patron immediately."

The owner, a thick, balding Parisian named Maurice La Brea, bustled over. First he apologized profusely, then he said, "Madame, you are of course not the problem, but I cannot allow unescorted women into the Nouvelle. You must understand that I can make no exception or—"

"You mean to say that your café will attract throngs of prostitutes if you allow me to walk in the door and over to that table"—she pointed—"to sit with my friends?"

The patron stayed planted in her path, reminding her of that threadbare San Francisco bailiff who had camped on the doorstep to collect Edward's arrears. She was tempted to dodge back and forth as that fool did. Instead, she shouted across the room, "Hilaire, please rescue me from the local mores. Or is it morons?" This caught the artist's—and everyone else's—attention. Haas bustled over and, taking Holly's arm, said, "She is my guest, Maurice." He led her the scant twenty-five feet from the doorway to his table.

Furious, Holly remarked to the assembled, "And I thought America was backward."

Haas tried to placate her, saying, "They are stupid rules, but rules nonetheless."

Charles Normande, a burly sculptor who was half-drunk, broke in, "You can't let women run around by themselves."

"Why not, Mr. Normande?"

"Because they'll either be taken advantage of, or they'll take advantage."

"That is the stupidest remark I've ever heard—on either side of the Atlantic."

Seeing him tense, Holly knew that if she were a man, he would have struck her. She would've delighted in a physical contest. The image of her match with Edward barged into her consciousness. She waved it away, instead picturing a fight with Normande—she'd grab his tie and jerk the jerk all over the café, from wall to wall. But rather than inviting hand-to-hand combat, she rose and shouted to the room, "I've been insulted twice this evening. First by these ridiculous, archaic rules directed against women. Then by a half-witted, pretentious, drunken buffoon, M. Normande, *sculptor manque*. Have a pleasant evening, ladies, and those of you who pass for gentlemen." She spun on both heels as gracefully as though at a command performance and swept out of the café, startled or bemused eyes following in her wake.

Back at her apartment, all the limits of the glittering Parisian world flooded in. Most of the women she knew did little but shop in fashionable boutiques and pay social calls or drive in the Bois de Boulogne during the afternoon—with or without their lovers, depending on the day—then bustle off to the theater or opera or the cabaret in the evening. Empty, meaningless existences. In the opera houses and the city's theaters, fashionable Parisians were so concerned with being seen and flirting and talking that theater managers had adopted the stratagem of flicking the lights on and off in the middle of the first act so that the audience would pay at least minimal attention to the goings-on behind the proscenium.

For all of the Parisians' heralded sophistication, for all the rhetoric about the Third Republic's "new democracy," French society was decadent and hopelessly class-bound. This was not, as she had remembered, a challenging, roiling world that asked hard questions about existence. Or art. Or love. No, Paris now seemed to be an inviolate bourgeois orbit where the most depraved led curiously settled lives. For almost two years, Holly realized, she had been oppressed by the constraints of this magnificent city.

She thought of Edward and their journey across the rugged, vast, ever-changing landscape, the rude characters in those adobe way stations, the thickset husband with the birdlike wife who ate little but appeared to feed vicariously off his plate; Sung Wan and Denise, her magnificent partner in the nascent antislavery movement for Asian hookers; that scurvy vermin Ward, the newspaper lackeys, even the unregenerate, elephantine bastard of an ex-governor himself. . . . That country was huge, multiple, infinitely complex, and it was still growing, still occurring. Here everything—social custom, trysting, art itself—was settled and decided. That unstated agreement made life urbane and civilized, yet the social pact came with a set of rules that turned existence too tepid and predictable. She realized how much she missed the raucous energy, the scale, the frenetic, improvised air of the United States. Holly also admitted to herself, battling doggedly against the feeling, that somewhere, against all of her resistances, she missed him.

After blackmailing Lavoix by offering him a fine Gérôme sketch of a lion at a rock-bottom price, he grudgingly handed over the key to the painter's old studio. Finally, she made her long-delayed pilgrimage. She walked through the skylit space, feeling Gérôme was there, perhaps napping in the bedroom. She could almost smell his pungent, biting tobacco, the hint of the cologne he used after shaving around his wispy beard. Holly felt choked up as she examined the two remaining canvases—Lavoix had negotiated an arrangement to sell *Allegory of the Fall* to the Louvre for a princely sum. Alone in the eerily resonant space, she scrutinized the big painting, searching for the genius she had loved, admired, and, at one point, worshipped enough to debase herself. The painterly brilliance and intensity were there. As Gérôme would have said, the colors, a multicourse feast; the light, a shaping deity. He had genius, she solemnly confirmed to herself. Yet after a half hour, Holly reluctantly found the *Allegory* a touch dated, and even, in one or two passages—there, where Adam exits the garden; and closer to her, where Eve (a hideously mocking image of herself) is tempted by the serpent—the emotion seemed grandiose.

The final painting was called *Working in Marble* or *The Artist Sculpting Tanagra.* In it two Hollys—"The original and the echo," in

Gérôme's words—sat side by side. She is there in duplicate, the "live" model and the marble sculpture of her that the artist, Gérôme himself, is carving. (He rarely carved—that was a slight misrepresentation.) Posed in profile, nude of course, the live model's calf is too thick, her hair too slack, her mouth too unyielding. The model Holly's breasts are smaller while the cool, white marble figure has bigger, more shapely breasts with honed points of nipples—as though the sculptor imagined a more erotic version of his model. Fully clothed and wearing his smock, Gérôme bends over her as he chisels away at the marble upper thigh. Again, the painting speaks of his absolute control over her. Here he commanded not subjugation to other men's measuring eyes and probing fingers but total immobility—as though movement, animation, existence itself were dependent on his will. Holly choked on emotion in the old sanctuary, for the first time acknowledging Gérôme's brutality and his artistic limitations. For the first time, too, she cursed America. And she cursed Edward, though not for the first time, for having changed her eyes and sensibility so profoundly that she could no longer comfortably commune with her past.

Three days later she began a week of performances at a small theater in the Marais. Holly danced, and several critics gushed, calling her "brilliant," "incomparable," "the most magnificent woman who ever graced the Parisian dance stage." Yes, she had danced well and the praise was not without its pleasures, but since she had not addressed a feminist issue—no dragging a chalkboard onto the stage this time, no limned image of the corset for her audience—she fretted that she had not given her all.

Her innocence had vaporized: Holly would never recapture that rapturous extended moment of pure, mindless devotion when dance was universe enough. Too many other realities had elbowed in. She told herself that she was tired; that, being older, it was difficult to work with the same passion as before. She insisted she needed more rehearsing, having rehearsed daily without a break for the better part of a year. Yet she knew that dance alone could no longer exalt and redeem her life.

In her last letter to Denise, Holly had finally inquired about Edward.

Denise's reply—in which she had enclosed a blurred, amateurish photograph (both of them were trying to master the camera!) of Sung Wan and her four-year-old daughter, Eleanor—informed Holly that, "Edward's surviving. He's doing his work, though he complains it's not up to his old standards." This struck an odd chord in Holly. Her friend closed by saying, "I know you may hate hearing this, but Edward loves you still. His heart is broken forever."

Holly folded the note and cried to the empty room, "Denise, darling, so is mine."

Chapter Thirty-one

Late in the fall of 1875, Thomas Eakins was fired from his teaching position at the academy. The term had just begun, and he and Nelly Pinto had gotten married in a small civil ceremony. Eakins's model, a twenty-year-old man, sat before the class with a cloth draped across his groin. A young female student burst into tears. Eakins politely asked what was wrong, and she replied that she had been raised in a respectable family and had never seen a man without his clothes. Two male students broke into mocking laughter. Infuriated, Eakins shouted, "You still have not seen a nude male!" then he yanked away the drapery. Three female students exited. The next day the painter was summarily dismissed.

Muybridge helped him clean out his supplies and sketches and sculptural studies from the arched, high-ceilinged studio, with its shimmering gold stars emblazoned on a background of celestial blue. "Along with all the other rats, Fairman—Fairman, what's in a name, aye?—has deserted the sinking ship. Like Judas, my former patron voted me out. All that work on that painting of his coach, all those studies, hours, days of watching those overstuffed carriage horses. What can one do when a friend betrays . . . ?" He broke off.

"Tom, I understand this is difficult. But don't forget, your best work is ahead of you. Look at your Whitman painting." Edward nodded at the rough-looking, loosely painted head of Walt Whitman leaning against the wall. "Whitman told me it's the only 'true portrait' of him he's had the privilege of seeing. I call that definitive praise."

"Yes, the painting's tolerably good," the painter replied, "but I still think it's too rough, too much of a cartoon."

"That's one of its virtues for me—for Whitman, too, I think. It's so lively and free—like the subject."

Eakins waved at an early watercolor study of Whitman's crisping, halo-like hair. "It's odd," he offered philosophically, "but one of us is always out of a job."

"Are you suggesting that it's my turn next?"

"Don't be in a hurry. Someone has to pay for our dinner."

Preparations for the nation's Centennial Exhibition, scheduled a mere three months away in May 1876, transformed the sedate city into a swarming, bustling construction site. Buildings began sprouting up everywhere; dust coated everything; the clamor of construction rattled throughout the city around the clock like multiple drums raucously pounded to variegated rhythms. The Pennsylvania Railroad was adding a spur to carry tens of thousands of visitors to the edge of Fairmount Park, where they would clamber aboard the narrow gauge train that was laid out to circle the entire exhibition site. The locomotives would arrive and depart from Memorial Hall, lauded as one of the age's great miracles, for the huge central building was constructed entirely out of glass supported only by slender frames of wrought iron. From Memorial Hall curious pilgrims would be taken to any of the two hundred structures that were frantically being thrown up for the opening-day ceremonies on the Fourth of July.

Muybridge felt the weight of his mission as he stood in the paneled boardroom of the Century Association. Eakins had pretended illness—actually he was too nervous, as Edward had explained sotto voce to Fairman Rogers. Now Rogers sat twenty feet away, at the head of the ponderous table, waiting for members of the Fine Arts Commission, which he chaired, to seat themselves. Collectively, this group of gentlemen was to decide which American paintings would be shown in the Centennial Exhibition's Hall of Art, a neoclassical limestone structure that was rising on a bluff overlooking the broad section of the Schuykyll River where Muybridge and Eakins rowed every few days.

As Muybrige scanned the well-appointed boardroom, with its well-fed members, Persian carpets, and leather volumes, he nodded to his acquaintances. "This, gentlemen," he began, pointing to the eight-by-six-foot canvas set up on a easel, "is the most important—and finest—American painting of the nineteenth century."

One of the board members coughed uncomfortably. Men shifted in their seats. Fairman Rogers responded, "It's a fine work, we all agree, but some members feel that it's too, ah, pointed for the women and children in our audience."

J. P. Lippincott chimed in, "Damn it, Muybridge, you know Eakins's penchant for outraging everyone. Let's talk seriously here. People are offended by it."

"So much blood."

"Altogether too graphic."

"The painting should not be seen by our women."

"Women are changing," Muybridge replied as politely as he could. Constraint dominated every syllable he uttered. How Holly would've scowled at that "our women."

Smoke from Lippincott's cigar wound itself into the air in the form of a pudgy question mark. The assembled had resonant names in Philadelphia—Rogers and Franklin, Gerard and Lippincott, Dilworth and Strawbridge. The wall was festooned with severe-looking men—from bewigged colonial elders to today's magisterial merchants. Several of those paintings were excellent, insightful revelations of their subjects; most were stiff, pompous, lacking character. Not one of them approached the dramatic choreography and sweep and nobility of Eakins's oil.

Muybridge spoke, "This painting is a culmination of the enlightened impulses of our century. It melds the stunning progress we've made in medical science with that discipline's primary—indeed, its only true subject—the individual. Both science and human concerns are presented here in the most engaging drama I've ever had the privilege to witness—besides Rembrandt's *Anatomy Lesson*, to which it pays reverent and resonant homage.

"I won't praise its ingenious construction and the painting's remarkably deep space. I won't point out the impressive likenesses among those gentlemen who make up Doctor Gross's audience to several of our city's prominent leaders, whom I see before me now." Lippincott exhaled, then smiled at his colleagues. Dilworth nodded sagaciously. Traces of laughter lightened the mood of this august group.

"I ask you to simply step forward, my friends. Look at the light that ennobles the doctor's head." Lippincott Senior rose and approached the canvas. So Eakins had an ally or two among the arbiters. "He's created heroic light, transforming light, not inferior to the illumination that surrounds the head of, say, Aristotle as he contemplates the bust of Homer in a Rembrandt masterpiece."

Now Fairman Rogers rose and crossed the room, followed by several others. Edward's voice rolled on, "The fervor, the clarity, the commitment of Doctor Gross encapsulates his legendary career, a career of which we Philadelphians are justly proud. The gentleman doctor physician before our eyes is destined to take his place as one of the few exemplary individuals in the history of painting, as noble as personages painted by Delacroix or da Vinci, Michelangelo or"—he almost said *Gérôme*—"Raphael. But our doctor is no allegorical figure out of a pagan epoch. He is not a sentimental phantom. He is distinctly a man of our era. Gentlemen, I offer Eakins's Dr. Samuel Gross, a genuine American hero."

Not a single member of the commission remained seated, except for the gouty William Richardson, whose bloated foot was propped up on a scarlet cushion.

"As to the blood—as Rogers commented so aptly—indeed, Eakins paints blood. He does not gratuitously rub our noses in blood but does so because he must, for that is how contemporary medicine strives to keep us healthy and alive, delving into the physical realities it must confront to improve the human condition.

"The genius of this work is not just the intricately plotted perspective or the absorbing color and glowing light and inspired hues, though each hard-won effect contributes to its overall power. The tension, the balance between science and human emotion—between the doctor and the ether-soaked gauze and bloody scalpel and the agonized young patient's mother—that is what makes Eakins's masterwork so believable, so palpable, so *real* and of our time. Gentlemen," Muybridge concluded, "if you value your century, if you value all that we have accomplished collectively in science and art, you will select this brilliant, this revolutionary, this inspired oil to be exhibited in the Hall of Art, for no other painting of our time will dignify the exhibition by so fully embodying American Progress."

The room was still. Then Dilworth clapped slowly and loudly, and after him Lippincott Junior, then Gerard, then the assembled joined together in homage with their palms.

"Thank you for your eloquent plea, Mr. Muybridge," Fairman Rogers said when the applause had ceased. "Mr. Eakins will have our decision by Wednesday."

Muybridge bustled into the dining room and sat down before the figures on Eakins's changing blackboard, waiting for Tom's questions. Nelly eyed Muybridge as though her life depended on his answers.

"No sugarcoating, Edward. Was the presentation a catastrophe?"

Muybridge briefly explained his pitch to the commission. He thought that he had made a convincing argument though, in retrospect, he might have added one or two more telling points.

"Like what?"

"I didn't say that you had invented a new American visual language. I didn't fully explain the Rembrandt link. I should've presented them with an illustration of *Dr. Tulp*."

Eakins poured brandy, toasting Muybridge. "Edward, no friend could do more. I thank you from the bottom of my frigid heart."

Nelly cut in, "It's not quite that cold, Tom."

"Ah, a positive gloss. Thanks, dear."

The three of them clinked, then Eakins returned to the blackboard, where he'd been describing his portrait of Nelly in a rocking chair, "Looking as though," Eakins said, "she had married the wrong man."

"That's not funny, Tom," Muybridge said.

"I'm not in a comical mood."

"Please eliminate all self-pity. I've generated enough to last several lifetimes. I'm too competitive to enjoy having you for company in the misery department."

Eakins studied his friend, then the painter smiled boyishly, as Muybridge added, "You're going to take the pledge and swear off the debilitating self-pity stuff?"

"If you can do it, I can."

Rhetorically at least, the agreement was sealed.

On May 7, three days before the exhibition was to open, Eakins received the commission's reply. They were pleased to offer Eakins's painting "a prominent place" in the Hall of Medicine. Fairman Rogers explained that for reasons previously discussed—its gore, its inappropriateness for women and children—*The Gross Clinic* could not be exhibited with the other paintings chosen for the Hall of Fine Art.

"Gutless bastards," spat Edward.

"So much for 'Progress,'" quipped Tom.

"It's a brilliant painting," Nelly said fiercely. "Time will tell."

"If so, let's hope I have one hell of a lot of it."

Chapter Thirty-two

In April 1876, a congressional investigation determined that the Central Pacific Railroad owed the United States twenty million dollars in principal and interest on its unpaid loans. Muybridge was elated, certain that Holly had helped nab "the Associates." He carefully ripped the story from the newspaper, bought himself a bottle of four-star brandy, and got mightily drunk. The next morning, suffering a splitting headache, he climbed out of bed and bought copies of every newspaper covering the scandal. He mailed seven articles to Denise Faveraux, asking her to forward them to Holly in Paris or Rome or wherever she was.

A few days later Edward picked up the *Philadelphia Inquirer* and was shocked by a headline announcing that Leland Stanford Jr., seven years old, had died of brain fever. For days, Muybridge mulled over the tragedy. Stanford's life revolved around controlling all variables—the railroad, the politics of the State, the labor of a once reasonably talented photographer, the performance of an incomparable dancer. Here was a tragedy over which Stanford had no control—no amount of money or influence or the world's most talented medical specialists could save his only child.

Two months later the Philadelphia newspapers carried this item: Leland Stanford had bequeathed six million dollars for an institution of higher learning to be named for Leland Stanford Jr. The university was to be constructed on the grounds of the stock farm in Palo Alto. Muybridge considered: Had the death of that boy, Stanford's heir, and the humiliation of being fined and publicly chastised by congress tempered the man? Muybridge doubted he would ever have the opportunity to find out.

On May 10, 1876, the opening day of the three-month-long Centennial celebration, tens of thousands of Americans took trains, sailed boats, rode in carriages, and walked to Philadelphia to celebrate the nation's one-hundredth birthday. At 10:15 a.m., Muybridge and Eakins stood above the crowd on the reviewing platform along with dozens of other dignitaries, including Dr. Samuel Gross and Thomas Edison. They looked down at thousands of people, more than any of them had ever seen in one place at one time.

"Extraordinary, isn't it?"

"Awe inspiring. I'm pleased that we're not down there."

"We will be soon."

The orchestra struck up a medley of national tunes—including a hideously sentimental hymn by John Greenleaf Whittier that made Muybridge and Eakins, who ducked behind the men fronting them on the platform, chortle like naughty schoolboys—then, after the opening prayer, a series of interminable odes and speeches began. President Grant's address was mercifully short, but not so William Lanier's who, as president of the exhibition, formally presented the buildings ("All two hundred of them, one by one," Muybridge groaned) to the country. A rousing "Hallelujah Chorus" sung by four hundred voices followed, then the salute of artillery guns, incongruously accompanied by the ringing of chimes—a cacophonous oxymoron. A benediction was pronounced, and with that final Amen the International Exhibition of Arts, Manufacturers, and Products of the Soil and Mine—known to one and all as the Centennial Exhibition—was opened.

Muybridge joined Eakins and his wife, and the trio paraded in lockstep with the throng into Memorial Hall. Visitors' mouths gaped as they gazed up at the backlit, transparent tower soaring two hundred feet above their heads. The mammoth glass-and-wrought-iron Hall covered an astonishing 21.5 acres, Eakins quoted from the official exhibition guide, larger than the Crystal Palace Exposition of 1851, which was formerly the largest enclosed space in the world. The Main Hall featured products from the United States, the most popular of which they managed to catch a glimpse of through the crush—Louis Tiffany's eighty-thousand-dollar necklace, composed of sixteen matched diamonds amid a dazzling array of precious jewels. Nelly asked Tom if he'd give it to her—"once the exhibition's over." He bowed gallantly and kissed her ear.

As they shuffled on the heels of others through the mesmerizing space, Muybridge and Nelly and Eakins eyed beer halls from around the world where, given sufficient stomach and stamina, an individual could sample over a thousand brands of brew. The restaurants featured cuisines they never suspected existed. And along with these wonders was Philadelphia's own contribution, the soda fountain, where they waited in line along with scores of others to taste a new concoction—sweet fizzy water. "Delicious," Nelly judged.

Passing out of the Main Hall, they inched ahead with the crowd, Eakins obligingly carrying a misplaced four-year-old girl a hundred yards, holding her up above the crush until they reached the comparative quiet in the foyer of the Egyptian Hall, where he set the sniffling girl down and waited, along with his friends, for the distressed mother to catch up.

Edward and Thomas and Nelly headed toward one of the exhibition's most anticipated novelties, a giant bronze monument of an arm raising an unlit torch high into the air. The arm itself belonged to a 151-foot-high sculpture titled, Liberty Enlightening the World, designed for a site in New York harbor to honor the thousands of new immigrants flooding into the country. A few days before, Eakins had talked at length with the sculptor Frédéric Bartholdi about his unusual method of casting. Eakins learned that Bartholdi had cast the giant, hollow bronze in sections, assembled it to check the fit, then dismantled it for shipment to the United States. The plan was to reassemble it on site if the Americans ever raised enough money to pay for the statue's base. Unfortunately, the campaign to finance the base was languishing, and no one knew if "Lady Liberty" would ever lift her torch toward the sky. Privately, Eakins had declared the design, "Distinctly odd. Why Bartholdi insists the statue is female is beyond me."

"What's your objection—it's not realistic enough?"

"No, Muybridge," replied a smiling Eakins. "It's just that the figure is not even vaguely feminine. Look at the scale, look at her musculature. Nelly and I are certain that it's a male posing under a cheap wig."

The friends parted at Machinery Hall. Eakins and Nelly wanted to inspect the installation of his painting one more time, while the photographer had to man his own booth.

Like most visitors, Edward entered Machinery Hall looking up. High above, the glass enclosure spread spidery wrought iron traceries like modern-age wings over hundreds of machines that whirred and buzzed and hummed like a hive of stationary bees. In the center of the space was the monster Corliss engine, the star of the entire exhibition and the largest piece of machinery ever constructed. The dynamo stood forty feet high and supplied its fifteen hundred horsepower to every single piece of working machinery in the hall, the energy conveyed by a system of bevel gears connected to underground shafting and converted into working power by literally miles of leather belts. Plows, stamping machines, a McCormick reaper, spindles turning out a rainbow array of fabrics, the wallpaper machine, which produced varied patterns and colors at the turn of a few dials, and the quarter-mile of rival sewing machines, all these and many more were powered by the Corliss.

Dwarfed spectators standing under the Corliss's flywheel looked on as the wheel drove three mighty iron "walking beams," which plunged the pistons down and up, down and up without cease. Meanwhile, the lone engineer who serviced the Corliss lounged in an armchair reading a newspaper. Occasionally he would detect an odd noise and, after listening intently, would lay aside his paper and climb one of the three ladders that led up to the platform under the chugging pistons. The engineer would paternally oil a bearing, adjust a setting, or half-open a valve.

Having worshipped sufficiently before the celebrated engine, Muybridge approached the booth that housed Alexander Graham Bell's telephone. Bell was looking up admiringly at the crystal ceiling. Edward shook his hand, saying, "Magnificent, isn't it?"

"Transcendent," Bell replied. His device looked anything but transcendent with its wires, hand microphone, and round, black earpiece—more like a disjointed, outsized insect. Muybridge, who had met the inventor a few days before at Eakins's home, liked the man and had been intrigued to learn that Bell's father taught deaf-mutes, the family's interest in deafness being a principle reason Bell had developed the instrument.

Muybridge glanced over at Edison's booth and asked, "Where is the great Wizard?"

"Oh, he'll be along. You can count on that." Bell and Edison were involved in a heated lawsuit attempting to sort out just who had invented the telephone, and thus who owned the patent and the lion's share of potential profits.

A young man approached, preemptively waving for Bell's attention. "He interviewed me this morning," Bell informed Muybridge. "*Harper's*. His name's Seth Buck."

"Can you help me out with a few more details, Mr. Bell? Your instrument uses electricity to transmit sound, is that right?"

"Yes," said Bell graciously.

The reporter dutifully scribbled in a notebook. "What does the thing do?"

"It transmits spoken messages instantaneously. In fact, my telephone will allow a person to speak with a person he can't see in another part of a building or even across the street in another building."

The young man looked quizzical. "It's like something out of the *Arabian Nights*, isn't it, Mr. Bell? The genie in the telephone?"

"It's more practical than the genie in that romantic saga, young man. But if you insist on writing that the invention is a magical device from the *Arabian Nights*, please proceed. As long as you say it works well. You could even editorialize a little—as in: 'It's far superior to any other talking machine.'"

Seeing Edison and a crowd of followers approaching, the young reporter spun around. "Oh, thank you," said Buck, as he scurried off to try to interrogate the great man.

"Who knows how the damn things will be used, Muybridge. That isn't the point exactly, is it?"

"I agree, Bell. A man invents a device, and its applications are up to its users."

"Certain machines—the machine for washing dirty clothes in the Women's Pavillion, now that has an obvious application. Labor-saving, you could call it."

Edward, who admired Bell's lively mind, replied, "Your work is impressive. And practical. I don't mean to be critical, since I greatly admire what you've done, but the telephone lacks one of the great advantages of writing—a letter, book, even a scurrilous rag of a newspaper, they can be read and reread. There are no records of an exchange on your telephone."

"Many actually find the absence of records advantageous." Bell smiled benevolently. "Muybridge, you are a hopeless romantic. You're infused with highfalutin notions because you're an artist. Understand, most communications are rudimentary at best. Few should be kept for eternity. Besides, you can have both." Bell laughed. "Just write the letter *after* you use my telephone."

As Edison approached, Bell excused himself. "I'd enjoy continuing our conversation, but my lawyer insists I not utter a word to Edison while our case is pending. Let's have a drink tomorrow, Muybridge." Bell headed toward his booth, which was mobbed by the curious who giggled or shouted to one another other over his telephonic praying mantis.

Edison separated himself from his admirers and moved toward Muybridge, indifferent to the neighboring Bell. Edison greeted Muybridge cordially, his eyes exploring the revised version of the zoopraxiscope. "I'm told you've improved the device, Muybridge, along the lines I suggested. What's the duration now, ten, fifteen seconds and two dozen images?"

"Forty, actually. It now runs eighteen seconds."

"As I said, if you can appreciably increase the number of images, we should talk again." He skipped on. "Have you seen my lightbulb?"

Edward's booth had no visitors at present so he followed Edison up Inventors' Row. A crowd had already congealed around Edison's installation and, as the inventor approached, still more people adhered.

At the booth, Thomas Edison pointed to a bell-shaped glass with slender filaments visible inside. He flipped a contact and the filaments flickered uncertainly for a moment, then gradually began to glow. The light grew brighter as they watched.

"Daylight at midnight," Muybridge commented. He saw Woodward's Gardens, then Holly's face flared before his eyes; next to her, the now dead Ward looking sunken, ashen. *How uncontrollable these unbidden images,* Edward considered.

An elderly man stepped up. "May I please shake your hand, Mr. Edison?"

As Edison stepped toward the admirer, he flung a comment over his shoulder, "Well, Muybridge, a pleasure, as always."

Over the next two months, Philadelphia's Centennial Exhibition attracted more than 1.5 million visitors. Muybridge exhibited his improved zoopraxiscope, now able to project forty sequential images; the presentation lasting eighteen seconds. He had wangled a job as the Expo's official photographer, so he shot the grounds as well as each of the two hundred buildings. Uncharacteristically, Muybridge managed to make a tidy profit. Many of his older photos were featured in the Photography Exhibition, described as "the largest collection of photos ever gathered—2,882 prints by 700-plus photographers."

Muybridge frequented the Medical Pavilion. Relatively few tourists penetrated that technical precinct. But each time he visited, Muybridge observed an undiminished stream of artists and students setting up easels or with their sketchpads—copying *The Gross Clinic*.

Muybridge also haunted the Women's Pavilion. The women of the United States had raised a queenly thirty thousand dollars to set up their own exhibition. Edward wondered if Holly had chipped in. The space was filled with dishwashing apparatuses and devices for cleaning blankets and bottle washing and innumerable gadgets, each advertised as saving time and labor for the woman of the house. There were peelers and corers, knives and oddly angled brushes along with pots and pans and casseroles of all sizes and shapes. For twelve hours each day, a cooking school offered below-cost treats to hungry crowds. A revolving team of women (and the occasional male) lectured nonstop about education, nutrition, domestic science, and practical approaches to household work. There were even suffragists and proponents of exercise. Edward wandered through this pavilion in slack hours, feeling vague comfort in being close to so many of Holly's like-minded compatriots.

* * *

At the end of June, almost two months after the opening of the Centennial Exhibition, Edward asked his assistant, Hubert, to run the zoopraxiscope and hired a talented young photographer to make the pro forma portraits of visitors for him. He himself returned to his studio at the university where, after all the lapsed time, he began to photograph women—dozens of them.

Every single day Muybridge watched women parade before him. He viewed their every gesture; he talked with them; professionally, he befriended a number—painters, erstwhile photographers, students, housewives, two actresses, a ballet dancer. He photographed women riding, walking, dancing, playing tennis, practicing gymnastics. Often, all day, Edward Muybridge had young and not so young women moving before his cameras dressed in finery or semiclothed or naked. "Like a pasha in his visual harem," he confided to Eakins. "But only visual." He photographed Eakins's wife, the lovely Nelly Pinto, in the process of taking off her floor-length white dress. He photographed her leaping over a low stool, paying particular attention to her curvaceous legs and surprisingly mature breasts. He made comic images of a naked Nelly throwing a pail of water into the air, the arching, silver, fishlike sheen caught as it defied gravity for one miraculous instant, then, in seven subsequent instants, his stop-time images depicted each stage of the liquid's fall earthward. He made pictures of gorgeous women undressing and bathing and stooping down (angles from directly in front, directly behind, and from the side) to pick up a strategically placed bottle or canister. He photographed women getting in and out of bed. He studied their toes, their feet, pored over Achilles tendons and ankles. He spent immoderate time on calves and thighs and miraculously lovely angles of hips, the fullness of buttocks, the sweet rise of backs, desirable midriffs, and the flair of the waist on up to the rib cages and breasts. He made an encyclopedic catalogue of their necks, lips, noses, ears. He surveyed varieties of hair. Images of women smiling, laughing, speaking as they strode forward into eternity, images of mature and youthful, fat and thin, long and short bodies. When pressed by the university's trustees, he clung to the claim that his work was scientific. Purity and geometric proportion informed his thoughts, he insisted. He was "observing and detailing the fascinating, infinite process of human and animal locomotion." Edward insisted that he had only begun to catalogue the infinitude of possibilities provided by the "gentler sex," a term that had always perplexed him. But, naturally, the photos provided a privileged voyeurism.

Through all his twelve thousand photographs he seldom felt other than a professional distance or calm disinterest. Heavy, tall, emaciated, willowy, buxom, taut, slack, or thin, each moving in her distinctive manner, Edward watched them all, he photographed them all, and, every once in a long while, he would catch a hint of something profoundly familiar—a gesture of the hand; the suggestion of an incipient smile; a generous, spontaneous laugh; a unique thrust of a hip; the long, full flare of a thigh; the miraculous symmetry of a tapered ankle; the tender twist of an instep—something, anything, that reminded him of his departed love.

In the fall of 1876, high on the wall of his studio at the university, above all the women who moved through daily paces for him, Muybridge had mounted a large composite photograph of her face. It had taken him months of unflagging endeavor to complete what he called "the blow-up." He'd chosen one of his favorite photos—Holly's hair was down, a slight smile lifted her generous lips, the forthright, intelligent eyes questioned the photographer as she gazed out of the frame. Muybridge had painstakingly enlarged each square-inch section of the shot with his new magnifying lens. Having exploded the scale of the photograph until the entire composition measured three feet across by five feet high, Muybridge pieced together each component and glued them as seamlessly as possible onto a backing. He mounted his photograph on the north wall of the studio. And there Holly Hughes reigned, flawless and commanding and unreachable, larger than life, over all the inferior approximations of her character and beauty. It was an unprecedented composition, and Muybridge, half-proudly, half-miserably, ranked it among his finest work.

Her image was there, looking down at his studio that day in early October 1876, when Holly Hughes herself walked back into Muybrige's life. He was concentrating on head-on views of a tall, elegant black woman who had been a servant for most of her sixty-three years when he heard the familiar footsteps. He spun around so quickly his head ached, aware of a massive pounding in his ears. He thought his heart would explode into a thousand fragments. The apparition grew larger, more substantial, as she approached, her eyes locked on his until they drifted up to the large portrait that dominated the high north wall. He still could not believe that it was Holly walking toward him, the vision that he had devoutly hoped for but not believed would materialize during the eternity of six empty years. He felt abject fear, he felt crushing guilt. He felt terrified of this woman who had been everything and who, he devoutly believed, would never entertain a fleeting thought of him.

She crossed the room slowly, with purpose. Each step revealed a history of anguish, fury, grief. She halted in front of him. "I hate you for killing Jacques. I'll always despise what you did. . . ." Her voice sounded deadly to him, thickened by six years of mourning.

Words would not come. He thought she might spring at his throat and tear him apart. Of course he would have offered no resistance. He was certain that she carried a hidden weapon—that she would pull it out and destroy him on the spot. It was her right to do so. But, oh, how he wanted to look at her, to drink in her self, body, being, before death came at her hands.

"I had no intention of ever coming back. Six years later, I don't know how to forget your crime."

There was nothing for him to say.

"Yet I have to explain it to myself." In her voice he heard desperation, while her eyes were leveled at him like weapons. "I thought that smug collection of men who proclaimed 'Not guilty!' were criminals themselves. Every night I struggled to comprehend their verdict. But the jury was right—you were insane. That's the only way I can explain what you did without hating you forever."

He broke in: "Hate me, hate me! I just want to be with you, to look at you." His eyes flicked up to the wall above them, to the giant portrait of Holly—as though his eyes were a conveyance, a sled to carry her away from their past.

The impulse to win her over was so like him. The instinctive seduction carried both sting and comfort. Still, there was a weightier issue beyond the little flicker—Holly's accountability for her part in the tragedy. The only way to forgive him was, as Philippe had so brutally etched into her brain, to recognize her own complicity, and to give in to her overwhelming bond to Edward. The vital, unstoppable, irreplaceable Jacques, his death resulted from her appetites, character, cherished beliefs. In a secret, internal dialogue with herself, Holly's hope was that if someday she could learn to forgive Edward, then maybe she could begin to forgive herself.

"Could we live with Jacques, our dead man, lying between us every night? I do not know." Her sigh seemed to him seismic, shaking everything inside her, shattering everything they'd ever shared. Until she said, "But I've tried without you. And I can't live. I'm not sure I can go on without you, Edward."

He realized how much finer, more generous, and giving she was than he was.

"Maybe I want us to cower together in our guilt until a ray of sunshine breaks through."

It took Edward Muybridge a long moment to comprehend what she was saying. She had come back to find him. He stood, stunned. She still loved him, he realized, loved his miserable, petty, jealous, unhappy being as he did hers, only that much more. They would begin again though not at the beginning; they would have another life together.

She did not ask if he found her terms acceptable, knowing that he would welcome whatever she felt necessary. Then Holly reached toward his trembling body with love and ardor and even hope but without forgetting.

Author photo: Larry Ash

ROBERT J. SEIDMAN's first novel, *One Smart Indian*, was published to acclaim in 1979. He is co-author of *Ulysses Annotated*. Seidman's film credits include *Lush Life: Billy Strayhorn*, a documentary that won the Writers' Guild Award for Best Documentary Script, a George Foster Peabody Award, and an Emmy. He lives in New York City.